THE
SUBSTITUTE

Also by Nicole Lundrigan

The Widow Tree
Glass Boys
The Seary Line
Thaw
Unraveling Arva

THE
SUBSTITUTE

NICOLE LUNDRIGAN

SPIDERLINE

Published in Canada in 2017 and the USA in 2017 by House of Anansi Press Inc.
www.houseofanansi.com

21 20 19 18 17 1 2 3 4 5

Library and Archives Canada Cataloguing in Publication
Lundrigan, Nicole, author
The substitute / Nicole Lundrigan.
ISBN 978-1-4870-0235-0 (paperback)
I. Title.
PS8573.U5436S93 2017   C813'.6   C2016-906677-0

Library of Congress Control Number: 2016962172

Book design: Alysia Shewchuk

Canada Council   Conseil des Arts
for the Arts   du Canada

ONTARIO ARTS COUNCIL
CONSEIL DES ARTS DE L'ONTARIO
an Ontario government agency
un organisme du gouvernement de l'Ontario

*We acknowledge for their financial support of our publishing program the Canada Council
for the Arts, the Ontario Arts Council, and the Government of Canada through the
Canada Book Fund.*

Printed and bound in Canada

MIX
Paper from
responsible sources
FSC
www.fsc.org   FSC® C016245

For my three

Sophia
Isabella
Robert

· "I sometimes think that I enjoy suffering.
But the truth is I would prefer something else."
— Fernando Pessoa, *The Book of Disquiet*

THOUGH I AM NOT AFFLICTED BY IT, I WONDER ABOUT GUILT. When I was a child, I would crouch on the cement floor of our basement, building elaborate contraptions, and thinking, *Which piece of this system is culpable?* Sometimes a slender knife would fly forward and mar the wallpaper, or a needle would lift and destroy a balloon. Once I even built a system where the sharpened legs of scissors closed on photographs of my father. Straight through his skinny neck. As the grainy image of his face drifted left, and his suited body drifted right, I questioned what part of my machine was responsible for that destruction. The systems were no more than a mess of inanimate objects: croquet balls, yardsticks, greasy springs, plastic bowls, and bent spoons. If each one followed the simple rules of cause and effect, could the steel bearing be accused if it never came in contact with the flying paint? Would the rubber band be guilty when it had no choice but to stretch and snap? I imagined the liability lay somewhere within them all. Guilt trapped inside the weighty potential of the machine. Never in the tip of my finger. Never in the bend of my wrist. Never cupped in the palm of my hand.

I started this hobby for Button. Not only was she my little sister, she belonged to me, and I took full responsibility for ownership. I had thought the contraptions would engage her creativity and help develop her mind. Whenever I was building, she was hovering nearby. A happy constant. I admit I did not mind the attention. As each machine was nearing completion, she would whimper, waiting to ignite the chain of events. Generally, I allowed her this privilege, and while she was certainly amused by the whirr of movement, that was not my primary goal. I thought it was important for her to recognize her contributions, her abilities. For her to understand that she, too, had the capacity to set things in motion.

But I was wrong. Dropping a stone in a bucket or rolling a ball down a tunnel made no difference to the outcome — of the system I had constructed, or my sister's life. I acknowledge, though, that watching her die certainly had an impact on mine. I learned an integral lesson. Never again would I hide my face and hesitate. Or allow things to spiral out of my control.

When a current situation took a particular turn, my first thought was of my failure with Button. This time would be different. I was determined to handle the issue quickly and efficiently. Though a blade or flat rock would have eliminated the problem, I decided to honour my sister's memory and build a contraption.

Day after day, I worked on a plan, but nothing suited me. My annoyance grew, and I found it increasingly difficult to temper my rage. And then, captured within the bonus question of a simple classroom science quiz, I found my inspiration. I sketched my scenes on white paper with red ink, and kept them hidden in a clever place.

As I organized everything, I could practically feel Button vibrating in the air around me, excited about this new game. I knew she would be with me. Of course she was. I knew she would understand I was doing what needed to be done. That this time, I was not going to stumble. A friend once said to me, "The only point to a mistake is if you don't repeat it." I heard him, and I also listened.

Preparations in the backyard were simple. My design was uncomplicated, and I saw no point in trying to be inventive. I completed everything within a two-hour window. First I shimmied up a tree, and with my back against the trunk, I managed to screw a large pulley deep into the flesh of the thickest branch. A little further out, a hefty O-ring. Back on the ground, I glanced up at the hardware. Nearly invisible among the dying leaves and autumn shadows, the items I had borrowed from the classroom cupboard were side by side.

Next I worked a thin rope. It was cold and stiff, but I formed it into a c-shape, then looped it into an s-shape, and pinched the middle. Eight twists around, a little poke here, a tightening tug there, and the length of dirty yellow rope was transformed into something beautiful and precise. I sighed, moved my hand in and out of the teardrop-shaped opening. Then I secured it to the metal ring on another pulley and hid that the bushes. Satisfied, I walked home to my empty house, lay in bed, listened for heavy rainfall washing away any traces left behind.

A few days later, I returned to the backyard and waited. I had no worries about being seen; the darkness was thick. I gathered my hidden supplies and climbed the tree. Slipping slightly on the way up, I bit the inside of my cheek. Blood pooled around my teeth, but I could not spit. I had to swallow and swallow, and though it made me feel sick, it did not slow me down. With some stretching, I threaded the rope through the pulleys (one fixed, one not), then tied one end to the O-ring. Secured the other end with a slipknot around my stomach. I gripped the snare in my hands, and marvelled at my handiwork. How I loved these simple machines.

In that moment, I realized I was also a moving part, an element in my own production. I imagined Button joining the line, perched behind me, her pudgy hands on my shoulders, ready to push. We would share this experience, but neither of us would accept a shred of guilt. I would not allow it, as we did not deserve it. In her perfect voice, Button would squeal, "Thwee-ah, two-ah, one-ah, go!" straight into my ear.

Button. My sister was the reason I was there. Everything changed when she was born, when she adhered herself to me. That bond came with intense responsibility, and when it actually mattered, I faltered. In the months since she died, I have blamed others, but I know Button is rotting away in a white box, deep underground, because of me. Acknowledgement is difficult, but it drives me forward. Makes me move when others stiffen.

So I waited. I watched the mouth of the path, rope gripped in my fist, and listened for the sound of unsuspicious footsteps. And to engage myself, I thought of my little sister. The story that we shared.

AFTER ONE HUNDRED AND TWENTY-THREE TAPS OF HIS FOOT, two things happened at the same time: Warren Botts heard the toaster pop, and he caught sight of something odd in his backyard. Butter knife in hand, he ignored his breakfast, took a step closer to the window, squinted. There was a small person, standing beneath a thick branch near the property line, waiting in the shadows. Even though the sun was just breaking through the naked trees, he recognized her rain jacket, her striped stocking hat.

Rolling back against the wall, he let the curtain fall over him. Surely she had seen him bustling about in his red flannel pajamas, hair like a porcupine's back. *Oh*, he thought, *oh. I will not be home. If she knocks on the door, I am not at home.*

He had not expected this. Thought he had straightened things out, and the two of them had resolved the issue.

Coming to his home, waiting outside his home, entering his home once when the door was unlocked. None of it was a good idea. Like anyone else, he deserved some privacy. Principal Fairley, after hearing his concerns, had advised Warren to be firm with the girl. "No wiggle room," she said, smiling. Her teeth were narrow and beige, the same colour as her belted dress, her flat shoes. "I know you're a substitute here, but still, we don't want any sense of impropriety between teachers and students." He had done his best, explained this was where he lived, even if it was only a rental. The girl shrugged, and Warren had felt good about that conversation. Confident in his handling of the issue. But here she was, early on a Sunday morning, trespassing on his property. Changing his weekend routine. Two pieces of toast. Half a banana. Hot tea. Then thirty minutes to read the news, touching only the edges of the paper.

As he stood there, the knife fell from his hand, struck his foot, clattered on the linoleum. His cat, Stephen, startled, scuttled off a chair, and disappeared into the living room. Glancing down, he saw a smear of butter across the felted toe of his slipper, a glob on the floor. His hand formed a fist, and his agitation transformed into a tiny spark of anger. Part of him wanted to rush out into the backyard and yell, while another part, the stronger part, wanted to pretend he had not noticed her. That she was not there. Warren worked hard at that. Pretending. Trying to convince himself that if he could not see something, his mind could make it disappear.

He lifted the curtain, peered through the window. She had not moved. On Friday afternoon, he had found her sitting on his front step, graded science test clutched in her hand. This time, she had failed. Failed miserably, in fact. "This is the third time you've been here, Amanda." He tried

6

to step past her, but she angled her head, and his leg brushed against her cheek. "We can discuss it Monday. In school."

"We can discuss it now, Mr. Botts," she had replied. Eyes swollen and pink, she looked up at him, said her mother was going to strangle her.

"Of course she won't strangle you," he replied softly. "She might be disappointed, but that's not the end of the world. It's grade eight. And one test." Then he felt the warmth of her hand on the inside of his knee, and he had no choice but to step backward, take a seat beside her.

"I couldn't focus, Mr. Botts." She shook her test. "You need to fix this."

He shifted on the steps, touched his glasses. Six steps. Eighteen oblong knots in the wood. Two holes. "Me?"

On the opposite side of the street, a garage door lifted, and he could see Mr. Wilkes, one of his neighbours, seated in a lawn chair squeezed in beside a red pickup truck. Plastic stretching, his backside was only inches from the cement floor. Warren lifted his hand and waved, but Mr. Wilkes sipped from a brown bottle and did not respond.

"They're not divorced, you know." She brought the test to her lap. "My mother refuses, even though my father stole everything from us. She's such a sucker."

"Amanda." He wanted her to stop talking, to leave his house.

"He just took off. No warning. Took everything we had and gave it all away."

"I'm sorry."

"Did you know the jerk is selling crap on a beach in Florida? Coconut freaking monkey things? With some sleaze he met? She's not a whole lot older than me, you know. Isn't that disgusting, Mr. Botts?"

"I don't know what to say."

"Say you think it's disgusting, that's all. That you would never ruin lives. That you'd never choose that over someone you love."

Warren stared across the street, at the cracked driveways, the matching bungalows with darkened windows, the overweight man, probably two hundred and ninety pounds, lifting another bottle from a box. Why he thought of his own father then, he could not say. Perhaps it was the mention of choosing. Choosing something useless and pointless and irreversible over a small person that so blatantly needed him. He lifted his hand to touch his cheek, and considered that he had once looked out at the world through the face of a child.

A crack came from the sky, and huge drops struck the wood, instantly absorbed. He counted forty-three of them, then said, "It's starting to rain, Amanda. Your test is getting wet. It's smearing."

Unsnapping her backpack, she jammed the paper inside, closed it.

"Smearing, yeah, cause you used a ton of red ink," she said, and stood up. "A serious ton."

"I was trying to help you. To understand your mistakes. So, well, you don't repeat them. That's the whole point."

"I don't even understand the questions, Mr. Botts. So how am I supposed to get the answers?" She began to walk away, then stopped on the bottom step and turned. "But you will help me."

"Yes, Amanda. I will."

"Mr. Botts?"

He stood up. "Yes?"

"No matter what, don't ever sell coconut freaking monkeys."

"I can't see myself doing that."

"Promise it."

"Sure. I can promise. With confidence. But only if you promise not to come to my home again."

"Maybe," she said, shrugging. Then she had hurried up the sidewalk to her own home, four bungalows separating them.

As he waited in his kitchen, listening for a tap at the back door, he watched the fish in his tanks. The lights, with automatic timers, had just clicked on. A cluster of eight neon tetras darted back and forth behind the glass. Without choice or space or opportunity, they had a special kind of freedom in their nothingness. Their only task was to exist. "I know you're hungry," he whispered. "One minute, my small friends. One minute." He strained to hear the girl's footsteps, but could hear nothing above the water filters. Taking a deep breath, he smelled his toast, still sitting in the toaster, and realized his breakfast was cold.

Warren was tempted to peek out again, but decided against it. She had not approached his door, and if she was not already gone, she would see the drapes shuffling. Like an invitation. It was better to slip out of the house for his Sunday morning routine. Something new, encouraged by his girlfriend, Nora, who claimed exercise would help him manage his nervous energy. "Ten thousand steps," she had said. "Every single day, and you'll soon see a difference." He liked having the goal. More specifically, he liked having the number. Knowing how high he had to count helped him focus, helped to quiet his mind.

Even though Warren was tall and thin, he was not a person who stretched his frame on purpose. He hated when

9

his glasses slid down his sweaty nose, or when his lungs tightened and his muscles burned. When his heart struck the inside of his rib cage with excessive force, all he could think about was dying. But Nora pushed him to be healthy, and in order to please her, he had adjusted his eating, started walking, and now was able to warm up in the living room, jog around the neighbourhood. Last Sunday morning he covered a total of twenty-two blocks. That was nearly three miles. Six thousand one hundred and forty-one steps, to be exact, and Warren did not rely on a mechanical counter.

Without breathing, he ducked down, edged along the floor toward his bedroom. He slipped out of his pajamas and got dressed. Back in the entryway, he pulled a head-band over his ears, laced his white sneakers, not too tightly. He paused before opening the door. His tanks, all eleven of them, were bubbling and gurgling on the floor of his kitchen, filters working hard for his tetras, his rasboras, a single Betta, his spotted loaches. That gentle sound centred him. "I'll be back soon. And then I'll feed you. I promise." Stepping out into the cold morning, he glanced up at the sky, edges shot through with pink and purple, a dusty grey waiting right above him. If she were not already, Amanda would be gone when he returned. Spitting rain and dipping temperatures would force her home. Everything was going to be fine.

▌UNDERSTOOD THE CONCEPT—A SMALL THING WAS GROWING IN
there. Obviously, though, I was unaware it was Button. All
I remember was my mother's distorted body, slowly bulging
into something grotesque. I saw her fully naked when I was
seven years old, and the unfortunate image is permanently
etched in my memory. It happened about an hour after my
father died. She was going to shower, as people were coming
to visit, and I caught her staring at herself in the bathroom
mirror. Pasty arms, rolls hanging from her chest, purple lines
across her stretched gut. Her fingers gripped her stomach
in a most disgusting way. "What luck. What bloody luck!"
she repeated. As I watched her cry, I was mildly nauseated,
but my heart remained steady, a calm drum inside my chest.

Moments later she caught me staring and slammed the
door. "Why you always got to be so weird?" she yelled above

splashing water. I rolled my eyes. *How can simple observation be misconstrued as weird?*

That evening, people shuffled in. My mother, smelling much cleaner, told the death story over and over again, though she omitted some of the more interesting parts. She spewed on about a meeting, influential clients, a car accident. *Who does she think she was kidding?* My father overshot our driveway, slammed head-on into the Mighty Oak in our neighbour's front yard. Earlier, when the police were there, they discussed velocity and angle of impact. They mentioned, of course, his suspected inebriation. He was the single operator, no passengers. Lack of a restraint and the force of the crash were joint causes of his death. My mother was confused; her expression started to collapse as they explained that with no pre-impact skid marks, he never saw it coming. A woman officer leaned toward me, said, "Which was a *blessing.*" She gnawed on gum that smelled like artificial watermelon.

My first thought was for the beautiful tree. I had climbed my leafy friend many times and whispered my plans to it. The sudden shock must have vibrated its innocent leaves and roots, and I feared for its welfare. Once the police left, my mother buckled, shrank into a chair, emitted a vexatious sound. I could tell from her posture and expression that she was experiencing the initial stages of grief. At the time, I thought she must be worried for the tree, too.

More and more curious people came to see my mother. I crept out the back door, made my way across the dewy grass. No one noticed me leave. For a moment, I remained hidden inside the hedge marking the property line. Cedar branches scratched my bare legs and arms. I could see the tree and the limp yellow tape wrapped around it. The sun had already sunk, and in the moonlight, the ground around the trunk glittered, neatly shaped crystals of broken glass strewn among the fallen leaves. I was disappointed my father had been removed from the scene. At the time, I had imagined him completely flattened, a flapjack of a person, and medical workers trying desperately to re-inflate him.

I walked up to the tree and touched the damage. Deep cuts scored the bark. Scrapes of grease and dirt and a stretch of weeping yellow flesh. My hands formed into fists, helplessness welled inside me, and then a timely hiss of anger ironed the sadness out.

I wormed my fingers into the damp cuts, inhaled the heady sweetness emanating from the exposed layers. "I'm sorry for what he has done to you." I despised my father. A drunken waste of carbon and oxygen, calcium and phosphorus. A useless human frame that took up space in my home, stole the air from my lungs. Of course I hated him. I thought of my mother's bulging stomach then. Thought how that tiny thing would never have to meet him, never have to watch his sweaty hand close into a fist while his lips were smiling. The unfairness of it made my mouth go dry.

Shining my penlight on the bark, I noticed streaks of reddish brown, what appeared to be curls of translucent paper. Metallic scent, but more organic. Upon closer inspection of the papery shreds, I saw tiny hairs, blond, almost white. My pulse raced, and I did not slow it. Pressure in my chest, then. A swell of satisfaction.

SHARP FLECKS OF RAIN BOUNCED OFF HIS SHOULDERS AND THE sidewalk, though Warren did not slow his pace. Each step took effort, but it gave him strength to think about Nora. He liked to imagine she was behind every window in every home, row after row of postwar bungalows, appraising him as he passed. This juvenile device helped him maintain a certain level of speed, a certain degree of form, and besides, it distracted him from all of the other noisy thoughts clamouring about inside his skull. Unspoken conversations with his father. The lingering spikes of anger toward his mother. Concern for his little sister, Beth, who was sometimes missing, though always lost. And now, his student, loitering in his backyard, acting as though her life was over because of a failed test.

Warren tried to maintain his lower-mind counting. Upper mind focused on Nora. But it was difficult. Numbers kept dropping, images and sounds kept sliding. Was it normal to have a head full to bursting like that? He started back at zero, remembered the pattern in Nora's eyes, hoping those things would nudge the swirling mess in his mind toward a rhythmic blankness.

As he jogged, he kept his arms bent sharply, lifted his knees. When he was a boy, he had been mocked for his limp-limbed movement in gym class. A gangly spider. "Run Loser Run," the boys had cried as he passed them on the floor. The coach would scream, "Pass to Botts," and the ball in play was hurtled at his head. Basketball, soccer ball, volleyball, football, pickle ball. His cranium had kissed them all. That was not his fault though. He blamed his poor co-ordination on sadness. In the weeks after his father had died, when Warren was eleven, the grief seeped through his pores, and eczema soon bloomed and crusted. Red and weeping in the creases of his elbows, behind his knees, his earlobes. It had hurt to move, to bend, and he developed a delicateness to his manner. Feminine, even.

Count. And think of Nora. Perfect Nora.

He reminded himself that his childhood days were far behind him. He was grown up now, a man, a developmental biologist, a PhD. In the future, a tenured professor, if that was what he decided to do. Right now he was taking a slight sidestep, a year-long break from his lab to become a substitute teacher in middle school. He had just guided his young students through the physics unit. An introduction to forces and simple machines. Though most of them barely scraped through, it did not stop Warren from wishing some of his students would fall in love with the orderliness of the subject, the predictability. Physics and biology were his favourite topics, and he approached them with enthusiasm. When his students dozed off, pulled gum from their mouths, or stuck pencils up their noses, he did not give up. He learned never to turn his back on them, though. Several weeks earlier, he had caught a boy named Adrian Byrd misusing lab equipment, his t-shirt hauled up, alligator clips attached to his nipples. The boy was panting, about to slide wires into an electrical outlet when Warren rushed toward him, knocked him to the ground. "Are you stupid?" he had yelled, and Adrian had grinned. His face was riddled with stitches, black threads criss-crossing recent injuries. "I like pain," he said. "Not much pain if you're dead," Warren had replied, though he instantly regretted his statement. It was inappropriate. "I should not have said that. But it was a very dangerous thing to do, Adrian. At your age, you shouldn't need a babysitter." Everyone was laughing, a complete uproar, as Warren locked the clips and wires in a cupboard, and Adrian craned to see what he did with the key.

Tomorrow they would begin an easier unit on genetics. A basic study of Mendel's pea plants. Chromosomes, genotypes, and phenotypes, smooth versus wrinkled. He was uncertain if his students would grasp the concepts, but he was excited to try. As he was preparing the material, he had remembered his father had also grown pea plants. The leafy vines had wound their tendrils along thin netting, and somehow adhered to the edge of an aluminum shed. Watching his father inspecting his plants through round rimless glasses, Warren had often believed his father looked more like a scientist than what he was—a simple gardener, a full-time salesperson at their local Feed 'n Seed. A quiet, thoughtful man.

Occasionally he considered telling Nora. Though how could he articulate how much he had adored his father, and how much his father had adored him? Telling her the man whispered to him nearly every day, "You are the only reason I stay, son." Blue eyes so pale, they were hardly there at all. His father's words echoed relentlessly inside Warren's adult mind, but his child self had scoffed, replied, "I know, Dad. I know! You said that already. Millions of times." Warren had always pictured his father driving away in his rusting truck, swallowed by a cloud of dust. The sort of trip from which a man could always return. "Oh sure," he would say then. "Come here, my darling. Let me teach you something useful. Something you won't learn inside brick walls." They would sneak off together with a book, and hide in the shed, under a tree, in the tall cool grass of the neighbour's field. His father made every interaction feel like a great secret. A secret from his mother. Even from Beth, who they would often hear searching for them. Calling out, "This isn't fair. You're not playing fair!" Pleading for them to reveal themselves. To let her join.

While his father would not have admired Warren's choice of profession, he would have liked Nora. Warren was certain of it. Nora worked at the supermarket sandwich counter, and the first time he faced her, he was caught off guard by her enormous lopsided smile. What did that mean, when someone smiled so widely? "You're new around here," she had said. "Good to see a different face." He pushed his glasses up, then stuttered when she asked him if he would like avocado in his sandwich. He had never tasted that fruit (vegetable?) before and was slightly embarrassed to admit it. "You'll love it," she said with quiet enthusiasm, "it's nature's butter," and began to slice through the pale greenness, revealing a large smooth ball. She held up the nut, whispered, "You can't eat that, though," and threw another smile at him. "Seems a waste," he managed to say, his cheerful voice sounding very foreign in his own ears.

When he saw the enormous seed, he thought of his father again. Kind thoughts. The man, tall and lanky like himself, kneeling beside a row, pushing his fingers into soil, dropping seeds, coaxing food from the earth. As a child, Warren had thought their garden was expansive, that it rippled down over the horizon, surely enough to feed the world. Only when he grew did he see it was nothing more than an extended plot, food to feed the family and manage a small vegetable stand at the end of the driveway. It did not matter. In his memories, his father still planted that land. Still provided for them. Warren, his mother, Beth. Together, they sat around the table, a thick slab of waxed wood, scratched with years of schoolwork. Dull pencils pushed through the page.

His father would have taken that seed.

"Could I grow that?" Warren had asked her, looking down at the avocado pit.

"I haven't the faintest clue how, but I don't see why not," she replied. She wrapped the damp stone in a serviette and slipped it into his hands, her white wrist grazing his thumb. "Let me know if it works out for you."

That very afternoon, he went to the library, scoured several books on planting, and found a reference to avocado pits. At home he followed the procedure for sprouting it, suspending the stone with toothpicks, ensuring the base was submerged in fresh water. He counted every day as he watched and waited, dark skin sloughing off, seed splitting, until a spindly, almost obscene root emerged from below. He was euphoric. Twenty-nine days later, he placed the sprouting pit in a terracotta pot, covered it in soil, and then, when the leaves opened up, he did the brashest thing he had ever done. He brought her back the plant.

By the time Warren reached Main Street, his lungs felt as though they would burst. What if they did? What if they popped like balloons, and he choked out bits of deflated lungs, spat the bloody mouthfuls onto the sidewalk? In his scientific mind, he understood this was impossible, but the images preoccupied his thoughts. His throat was so dry, each time he tried to swallow, he sensed acid rising. Acid that was probably burning some part of him. He stopped in front of Andy's Pets, placed his hand against the glass, and bent at the waist. With his other hand, he reached inside his thin jacket, and rubbed the flesh over his heart.

The door to the store opened, and the owner's son, Gordie Smit, stuck his head out. His eyes were bloodshot and his head greasy, making his overweight face look even puffier.

"Shit weather, hey?"

Warren gagged again.

"You managing there, friend?"

"Tr–trying," he replied, though the words stuck.

They had met over the summer when Warren wandered into the store. He had wanted to purchase cans of food for his cat, but ended up leaving with dozens of fish, as well as tanks, lights, water plants, sand, gravel, and whatever else he needed for eleven aquariums. Gordie's father had given up on the fish, sales were non-existent, and was threatening to flush the entire lot. Warren could not allow such a mindless loss of life.

"Can I get you a drink, buddy? Some water?"

"No, nope. I got it."

"Catching raindrops? I'm sure you do."

"Just want to get stronger." Warren counted the number of bricks that lined the bottom of the window frame. Thirty-two. Seven of them chipped. He straightened his back, removed his hand from the glass, wiped it with his sleeve. "I'm sorry, I left a smudge."

"Don't sweat it, for shit's sake. We had more stuff smeared on that glass. You wouldn't believe some of the crap I've scraped off."

He was about to start moving again, but paused for a moment, glanced sideways at Gordie. "Why are you here on a Sunday? At this hour, no less?"

"The wife," he replied. "This place got a small apartment on top of the store. It's quiet there. Sometimes a guy needs a breather."

"I understand." Though he did not.

"Oh, and buddy? If you want to expand, we got a load of ferrets in."

Warren chuckled. "No, no. I'm good."

"And guinea pigs. Or skinny pigs. They got no hair. Strange looking little freaks."

"I'll stick with Stephen, my cat. And the fish."

"Well, then." Gordie swiped his hands in his hair, then glanced at his wrist. "Oh, Jesus. I got to get showered and go back. Breakfast with the wife. And the wife's mother. Stab me now. Right between my eyes. Out of my misery."

Warren laughed, took two deep breaths, and continued jogging. The rain had turned to ice pellets. They were popping off the top of his head, and the sidewalk. He hoped he never viewed Nora that way. As a chore to be endured. Not that he judged Gordie, but he knew Nora deserved better.

Over the summer months, he had learned so much about her. She was not a blatherer by any means, but he could gently coax her to share. Nora had had her share of struggles, and Warren was impressed she was not bitter. Her husband, whom she had loved since they were childhood sweethearts, had died of kidney disease. Complications from lupus. They had not known a thing until strange fevers arrived and his legs puffed up. She spent years going back and forth to the hospital. It was slow and agonizing to watch him, she had said, and Warren's heart squeezed as she spoke. He understood the pain of losing someone you love. And of losing them long before they actually vanish from sight.

Once, after Gordie had seen them together, he said to Warren, "Yeah, she's had a terrible time. A real shame, having to go through all that." Warren had not invited the comment, but nodded. Said, "Well, she won't have a terrible time with me."

His feet continued to slap the sidewalk. One step after another. Slow and steady. Nine hundred and seventy-three steps. Though, unfortunately, he had to restart twice. The ice had turned to snowflakes, the first of the season, and they swept in around his neck, cooling him. He looked at the road ahead. Only the hill was left, and everything was covered in a thin clean blanket. He came around the curve, began winding slowly up the cul-de-sac toward his home. Once there, he could lie down on the floor if he wanted. Twenty-one more houses. He pictured Nora at the top of the hill, standing outside his bungalow, cheering him on. "I'm getting there," he whispered. "Wait for me."

He hobbled up the stairs to his home, and lurched onto the porch. Stumbling to his kitchen sink, he leaned his head underneath running water, and gulped what he could. He wiped his mouth with his palm, took several deep breaths, then he unzipped his jacket, slung it over a chair. His cotton t-shirt clung to his stomach and his spine. Running his hand through his thick hair, he pulled aside the curtain and looked out the back window onto his deck. Snow covered it now, but months earlier Nora had sat there in the summer sun, sipping her homemade lemonade, waiting for him to barbecue, and—

And. And. He had not anticipated this. She was still there. She was still there. Amanda Fuller was still standing in his backyard. She had not moved an inch.

MY FATHER LOOKED PEACEFUL IN THE CASKET AT THE FUNERAL home. They had his hair combed straight down to disguise the wreck of his forehead. Thick beige makeup was substantial, and while there was too much pink in the cheek, my swollen mother had insisted on extra. "He doesn't look well," she tearfully told the director. "His colour is off." *No joke.*

His hands were folded together across his chest. Nails trimmed, four fingers resting upon four fingers. When I stood near the box, I reached out, touched his cool skin. I could almost detect a hint of warmth still lingering there, and I entertained the thought he would wake up once weighted under the soil.

Glancing behind me, I noticed funeral-goers were granting me some time alone. A tender moment to say goodbye.

I ran my hand over his, then gripped his middle finger, his "swearing finger," as I had heard kids say at school, and I squeezed it. "Oh, Dad," I whispered, "Where are you now?" With another quick look over my shoulder, I cranked his finger backward, pressed down, felt dead ligaments tearing, a distinct and pleasant pop.

When I stepped aside, his finger remained displaced. My mother waddled up for a subsequent pass, and noticed. Cheeks flushing the same unnatural colour as her husband's, she tried to reposition it, tried to slip it underneath his index finger. Tried to bend it the other way. No luck. It rose up again. Telling the world what he thought of them. I noticed other mourners smirking, nodding. I hope the bastard stayed like that forever.

Later that day, after the last intruder had vanished from my house, my mother swallowed another flat pink pill, fell asleep under a thin blanket on the couch. I had told her not to consume pink pills, that the thing growing in her gut did not require sedatives, and she had glared at me. Said I was too pea-brained to understand (*wrong*), and it was not my concern (*quite possibly*). While she snored with her mouth open, I crouched on the coffee table, arms wrapped around my calves, like a sullen bird, watched her chest lifting and falling. Her blatant displays of selfishness made me despise her.

Even though I was only seven at the time, I was left to wander the house alone. I sat on a pillow in the corner of my room, reading. Non-fiction, of course. At that age, I was intrigued by any material about survival—fire-building, shelter construction, knot-tying, methods to purify fusty pond water. Not that I was planning to run away. I just enjoyed collecting useful information.

The house was silent except for the sound of a goldfish, rising to the top of its bowl, gasping at the air. I found that rhythmic glug-glug soothing, and I would study the orange fish as it fought to endure in the cloudy water. Its swim bladder was infected, or deflated, and even though it tried to swim upright, it was often sideways or upside down. I could not grasp that instinct. To keep fighting. In those conditions, I would force my fins to stop. Sink to the bottom and get on with it.

I was reading about the use of falcons as small-game hunters when I heard a noise from downstairs. A drawn-out creak from the screen door. The knob clicking, the squeak of an adult shoe on the rubber mat.

I closed the book and placed it on the floor. I slowed my breathing so that I would hear everything; slowed my heartbeat so I could think.

Sounds of careful footsteps next. Moving around. Glass clinking.

On all fours, I crawled across the floor, fingers in the navy shag, and slipped my head out of my bedroom door. Someone was rummaging through the kitchen. I could see no one, with the exception of my dead-to-the-world mother on the couch. I stayed calm. Tried not to allow the excitement to take hold, as though my insides were licking a 9-volt.

Crunching, then. Someone was eating from the bowls of food remaining on the kitchen counter. Then I heard an utterance, a girlish squeal. "Fffff-uh-uh-uck!"

I recognized the voice. What a letdown. My aunt. Mother's stupid sister. She stepped into the doorway, her hand to her mouth. When she drew it away, there was blood on her palm. "Fucking bitch whore," she mumbled. Her phrase was grammatically incorrect; two nouns butted against each other. She yanked out her bottom lip, stuck out her chin, and glared downwards in a most unflattering lizard-like expression. Trying to see the injury.

On wobbly heels, she crept past my mother, paused, then leaned toward her, tapped her on the forehead with a painted nail. My mother did not move. Then my aunt went to the side table. Her hair was thin, dyed black, but from my vantage point, her scalp had a purplish tint. She reached into the basket of sympathy cards, picked up the first one on the pile. I shook my head, impressed by the stealth of her movements. Only a second or two for each envelope, picking it up, slipping her two fingers into the torn opening, extracting the small amounts of money and stashing it down the front of her polyester blouse. Then she reorganized the empty cards neatly in the basket. She also straightened the telephone book, and plucked up several fallen petals, poked them down into the vase of dying flowers. She leaned her head, left, right, left, and made a self-satisfied clicking sound.

When she returned the next day, she brought me a small parcel wrapped in pale blue tissue paper. Perhaps she experienced some semblance of guilt, or perhaps she saw me spying on her, and it was a keep-your-gob-shut present. I opened it to find a rectangular prism made of glass, a chafer beetle in the centre. Bringing it to my eye, I noticed six segmented legs, a pair of tiny eyes, a perfect turquoise shell.

"Considerate of you."

"Thought you'd appreciate it," she said. "Something special for you before the baby arrives. It'll suck up the attention, you know." *What attention? And from whom?* "Besides," she continued, "you like weird shit."

A dead bug. "I do." I stared at my aunt. "Was it alive when they poured glass over it?"

"Alive?"

"Or did they euthanize it first?" Turning the prism over in my hand. "I see no damage to the specimen."

"Youth-eyes?"

"Kill it."

"Oh." My aunt's eyebrows danced. She found me entertaining, but did not laugh. "Well, it's dead now." She stared back at me. "They are methodical little buggers. Beetles are. Did you know that?"

"Yes. Of course I do."

"Well, Kiddle." She pinched my nose, a reek of cheap perfume on her fingers. I flicked my head away. "They are, they are. Just like you."

Though I did value the effort, there was no need for a gift. I would never have exposed her. Knowing she had stolen was reward enough. Any time it suited me, I could lock eyes with my aunt, even at inconvenient moments, and she would be forced to stop and engage. I would wait until her fragility fluttered up, and she could not sustain my gaze.

The iridescent beetle was the first of many insects. That memory makes me feel a swinging happiness.

[6]

WARREN TOOK TWO STEPS TOWARD THE WINDOW. TILTED HIS head. Squinted. Reached his fingers up, tapped his lips. One, two, three, four.

The backyard was brighter now. Even through the light snow, he recognized the unnaturalness of her position. Her head lolled forward, her arms straight, dangling in front of her body as though she were an abandoned puppet. He took a step to the side, tilted his head the other direction, changing his perspective, and that was when he saw the rope. It had been hidden by the darkness of the tree trunk, the morning shadows. The rope was wrapped around her neck. She was not standing there, as he had thought. Amanda Fuller was hanging.

He glanced at his feet. Sneakers still on, he hauled open the back door, ran across the yard toward her. Stopped halfway. He could barely look, her hat askew, face and hands deep purple, tips of her toes grazing the ground, mittens fallen near her feet. Something was jutting from her mouth. Paper or cloth, he could not tell.

Warren tried to move his legs, tried to edge closer, but his muscles refused. Closing his eyes, he imagined his father was there, and he reached out his hands, groping only air. "Come on," he said through grinding teeth. "Keep walking. You're not eleven years old anymore." But he could not. Was incapable of going toward the body, wrapping his hands around the legs, lifting, trying to find ways to bring the girl down. Instead he focused on the branch of the tree, his mind assessing the mechanics. Calculating the angles of the ropes, determining how the pulley system would divide her estimated weight. A reduction in the necessary force. It was all so familiar to him. And comforting. Why did his mind do that? Making calculations, focusing on the elements of the system. He was a coward. That was why. No less a coward than when he was a boy.

"It's going to be okay," he breathed, "I'll get help," and his feet scraped a path backward, seventeen steps, into his house.

"There's a girl," he whispered into the receiver.

"A girl, sir?"

"I think she's hurt. Injured."

"Are you with her now, sir?"

"No, no. She's in my backyard."

"Is she conscious, sir? Breathing?"

"I don't know." His voice cracked.

"Your name?"

"Warren Botts."

There was a pause on the line, then, "I've dispatched an ambulance. It should arrive in about seven minutes."

One, two, three, four, five, six, seven.

"Can you explain what's happened, sir?"

"There's been an accident." He spoke slowly, while the operator rolled through her questions.

"What sort of accident?"

Warren swallowed. His heart was slamming against his chest, threatening to stop. "Up. Tree." Words broken, garbled. "Sh-sh-she's ha-ha-ang-ing. Tangled. Up rope."

"Mr. Botts. I'm having difficulty understanding you. You need to calm down. Is she hanging? Mr. Botts?"

He could not respond. He tried to think of Nora. He tried to count, a flurry of numbers bolting about, but he was stuck at twelve.

"What's after twelve?"

"Mr. Botts?"

"I can't remember. I can't remember."

"Mr. Botts. You need to listen carefully. You must get her down and begin CPR. Immediately."

How could he tell the operator that she had been there for over an hour? That he saw her in his backyard, but ignored her presence. Pretended not to see her, pretended she was perfectly fine, and instead he went out jogging. Thinking about himself, his life, his girlfriend with the soft brown eyes. All while Amanda was dying. His delusions made him retch.

"I'm so sorry," he whispered, his voice high and tight. "I didn't mean it. I didn't mean to."

"Mr. Botts."

"I have to go. I can't. I'm sorry. I need to look after. My fish."

"Please stay on the li—" but Warren gently slid the receiver into its cradle.

In a shaky daze, he went toward his tanks. One after the other, he selected the correct type of food, lifted each lid, pinched flakes with his tweezers, stuck pellets to his fingertips. Let the food drift down in the current. Tiny fish darted up or sideways or down. Some nipped each other or stole the food straight from a tankmate's mouth. The plecos ignored the chaos, kept their flared lips suctioned to the glass walls.

Warren did not glance into his backyard.

Once his fish were fed, he went to the front of his rented home, and stood before the couch. Bay window behind it, he could see the road, lined with evenly spaced oak trees, silent. All of the garage doors were down, single eyes closed. Snow snaked along the pavement. Across the street, a white plastic bag had snagged in some branches. The wind cut through it, shredding it, but still not setting it free. At the sight, Warren sat down in the middle of the room and chewed his nails.

He tried to count everything he needed to do. His lesson plans were ready. He could not see Stephen, but there was water in his dish. And his fish were fed. He would not have to worry about them until that evening. Both hands moved through the shag, separating a square inch of carpeting. Moving twists of yarn between his fingers, he kept track of each one, estimated, and then closed his eyes as he tried to determine the total number of strands that covered the floor of his little bungalow.

MY MOTHER GAVE BIRTH TO A GIRL SIX WEEKS AFTER MY FATHER died. It arrived earlier than expected, and I tried to ignore its presence as much as possible. Not that difficult, as it rarely left its crib. All it did was sleep. And eat. And gag on a bottle. It was skinny and covered in weird blond fur and smelled completely disgusting. The neck of its sleeper was always damp, full of yellow creamy blotches. It scratched at its face with its sharp nails, making it look even worse than it already did.

"Shouldn't someone cut those things?" I asked. My aunt laughed, then appraised her own lengthy claws, said, "Just as well she get used to them."

Several weeks after it was born, we were in the school gymnasium for a Christmas concert. My mother, aunt, the thing, and me. My mother, in a moment of strangeness, thought it was a good idea to attend, even though I had refused to participate. *Who would want to sing and hold hands with those dirty kids?* I was crowded by adults, but could still see a trail of kindergartners gliding down the aisle. They were dressed in puckered white bedsheets, a trim of blood red ribbon around their necks. I could not see their feet, and they appeared be floating, moving like ghosts toward the front of the gym. They were singing in high-pitched voices, something festive and untroubled, and it seeped into my head. My mind was straining, either toward something or away, I did not know. I felt sick. *Why are they so happy? Why are they so free?* Most likely my agitation was not connected to the voices at all. It was the result of my damp pants, or my winter coat filled with matted feathers offering no warmth.

When my mother handed me the bundle, I began to sweat. It was evident the thing was sweating, too, wearing my old blue snowsuit, an emblem of an orange dog sewn on the arm. On top of that, it was swaddled in a nubby blanket, and its face was pink, greasy-looking, lips open and mewling.

The lights dimmed, all attention turned to the wooden steps at the front of the gym. In my arms, the creature squirmed and made annoying kitten sounds. I bounced the small body with some force, but the snuffling continued. It needed to stop. I glanced up at my mother, but her head appeared miles away from me. There was no way to reach her ears, to tell her I needed help. I turned to my aunt. She was fanning herself with bent fingers, then touching the edges of her low-cut dress.

It made me angry.

I do not know why it occurred to me. Why I chose to do what I did next. So smooth, so natural. My hand crept over the blanket and came to rest just on its mouth. Slightest shift, and my hand moved up over the nub of its nose. Puffs of warm air moved through my mittens, steam between my fingers. I held my hand there, just the weight of my arm, my shoulder relaxed, limp, nothing more. I did not push. No, I did not push. It knocked its head back and forth for only a moment, but I did not lift my hand. And then its queer blue eyes locked on mine. There was no sign of fear in its watery gaze. In the shadow of the pew, I glared and glared, excited, until those eyes rolled upwards, and the lids came down. For reasons unknown, it trusted me.

Part of me had wanted it to scream so we could leave the oven of the school. Leave the trail of odd floating children who were humming and swaying side to side, making me feel queasy inside my chest. Part of me wanted the thing in my arms to simply vanish, no longer exist. To pass the time, I played around with this notion in my head. What if it were gone? What if the weight of my hand had pushed it into a really, really long sleep? It lay still and heavy, a brick in my arms, and I left the question hanging in the air for the remainder of the concert. The thought numbed my mind, but the beat of my heart remained steady.

My mother took forever to leave the school. People kept stopping her, asking how she was managing with her undersized offspring and dead husband. I could see my aunt chittering non-stop, talking to friendly husbands, turning her back to the scowling wives.

We walked home in the darkness, snow drifting down, brushing against my ears. After some mild insistence, I was permitted to hold the thing the entire way. I had wanted to grip the feeling, and wait until we were home. In case. I remember the rubber boots I was wearing. No longer could I squeeze my feet into the winter boots I had worn last year, and the rubber would have to do. "You're lucky you got that," my mother had said, even though I had not complained. On the outside, they looked perfect. Shiny black, the lining intact, the red label still perfectly affixed to the upper front. But no one knew of the hidden slash near the heel after I tripped on a torn piece of metal in our backyard. No one understood how that cut opened wide whenever I stepped in slush.

My baby sister grew and changed, and in weeks had transformed from wrinkled fuzzy alien to tiny human. As my mother kept her sequestered in a sour crib most of the time, I felt compelled to touch her. To interact. While she was sleeping, I would often place both hands on the sides of her pink skull and squeeze. Within my palms, I could feel slight movement in her bones. I imagined how one thin plate was still able to slide over another. Baby plate tectonics. Sometimes I would lean over her crib and press on the soft spot on top of her head. Her pulsing *fontanelle*. What an asinine word. It sounds more like a mild cheese than an area not yet ossified. When I pushed, her eyes would pop open, and then she would drift away. Eyes pop. Drifting. It was a fun game to play. Not just controlling that super-surprise expression, but knowing if I pushed hard enough, I could damage her. I could puncture her skin, and my knuckles would drive into the fatty tissue of her brain. But I resisted the temptation. After lengthy contemplation, I decided I wanted to see what would happen when she grew up.

I acknowledge, though, that as the months passed, the little goblin grew on me. It was clear that ball of dimples and rolls adored me (as she should). Once she could focus, her eyes followed my every moment, and soon she made efforts to tumble in my direction. Throwing her body this way and that. In desperation. Who could blame her? She crawled late, at fifteen months, but then moved toward me with lightning speed. I liked to watch her. She wriggled so quickly on the filthy carpet, she appeared to bounce. Like a bug. The only time that baby ever cried was when I left the room. She was a loyal little creature, and for the first time in my life, I was truly revered. She saw me for who I was, and loved me anyway.

The thought made me calm and uneasy at the same time. Feelings are sickly, unreliable, and I cannot help but notice the smaller word hiding inside. E-E-L. A slithering petulance that eases into cracks, disguising its narrow body against mossy rocks. When I was two, my aunt took me for a picnic, and I swam in a place not much more than a mucky hole. Before I dipped my toes in the water, the bitch snickered, showed her wine-stained teeth, and said, "Watch out for eels, Kiddle. Those water snakes can wrap around your ankles. Pull. You. Down."

Emotions are like that. Ensnaring, submerging, cutting off the air to rational thought. Feelings are a reaction, a waste of precious neurochemicals. Dopamine, norepinephrine. Some other stuff. But even I cannot deny that so much of our existence circles around to them. When I looked at my sister and had that faintest sense of softness, of belonging, I knew I was not completely immune.

I called her Button. A stupid name, I admit, but it originated at a party. It is not important whose birthday it was, or why I was forced to attend, but the backyard was full of sunshine, shrill noise, and the reek of human frenzy. Clusters of over-inflated balloons hung from leafy branches, and I stabbed as many as I could.

I would never have encouraged my sister to play mindless garbage, but I had been trying to instill the concept of object permanence. She was four, and should have learned it already. She could not grasp that when she shut her eyes, people could still see her, or that when the fridge door closed, the oranges were still there. So when the game *Button, Button* started, I pushed the little hob forward, made her clamp her hands together, and stood behind her in the circle.

"Button, button, who got that button?" There was a tall white male with a mouse brown moustache, dancing around the circle like a total idiot. He slipped his germy mitts inside the cupped hands of every child. Including my sister's. Once the deposit ritual was performed, the birthday kid began the guessing, and as each name was called, the small loser opened his or her hands to display empty palms, then took a turn.

"See? The button isn't in his hands anymore. It's hidden now, inside someone else's. Do you understand?"

"Buddon," she squeaked. She was so excited I had to keep my hands pressed on her shoulders to keep her from spinning.

An imbecile guessed my sister was the special holder, pointed at her, and said, "You!"

Clenching my jaw, I had to respond to such asperity.

"Her name is—" But before I could actually say it, my sister screamed, "Buddon!"

Everyone jeered.

"Buddon! Buddon!"

The kid's face flushed with anticipation, thinking the

cheap prize was his. "Well, Button-head," he said, "Show it." But then my sister opened her hands, and wriggled her fingers, revealing nothing.

Two rounds, and I reached my limit. She had no idea what was happening, even when I found the discarded button, brought it to her, and held it right in front of her shiny face. Placed the thing between her fatty palms, closed my hands over them. "Where's the button?" I said. She grinned, glanced at the empty sky. "Id gond." I pried open her hands, "No, it's not gone. It's here, see? Hiding away." My sister stared at that plastic purple thing as though it had just appeared in thin air. Then she placed it on her tongue and tried to swallow it.

I could not coax this basic concept into her brain. If something was not in front of her, it did not exist. Nothing in her world was hidden from sight; everything was obvious, open, innocent. Some might say that is the way it should be for children. I would say it is a dangerous mindset with an unpredictable outcome.

I took Button-head by the wrist and led her home, even before the birthday cretin had hacked into his fancy supermarket cake.

[8]

WITH POLICE MILLING AROUND HIS BACKYARD, WARREN remained seated in a brown armchair with a towel pressed to his head. White cotton with one, no, two shots of fabric softener in the rinse cycle. It was like a lavender cloud, and he wanted to drape it over his face, disappear. He wished Stephen would jump onto his lap, or Nora was there to make him tea, fix him another slice of toast, tell him he was safe. Pathetic, he knew, but when he squeezed his eyes closed, he could not wipe the image of the girl from behind his lids. And then his mind sputtered, and shot up that final image of his father. He wanted both to go away.

He heard a knock, the front door opening.

"Hello?"

"Nora?" Relief washed through him.

"No, sorry, sir." Two people appeared in his porch, a

man in uniform, and a woman, small and slight, her frame overwhelmed by a dark overcoat. "I'm Detective Reed," she said. "Is it okay, Mr. Botts, if I just step on in?" As she spoke, she pushed the last of a sugar-coated donut into her mouth. "Sorry," she said, holding up powdery fingers. "I'm such a stereotype. Skipped breakfast."

"Oh."

"I know this is all a little overwhelming. I understand." She licked the white from the corners of her lips. "The officer will just stand in the porch here. His boots are in a terrible mess."

"Please. Please don't let Stephen out," he managed, though his voice was shaking. "He doesn't go outdoors."

"Stephen?"

"My cat."

"Mittens wouldn't do?" She took several steps toward him, and sat down on the very edge of the couch.

"I'm sorry?"

"The name. Usually people choose something a little less, um, bipedal?"

Warren cleared his throat. "I named him after Stephen Hawking. He's a physicist."

"A physicist? The man, you mean, and not the cat? Otherwise that's one very smart kitty."

Warren blinked, he did not understand what she was saying. His throat was dry, and his muscles ached. He had not removed his sneakers after his run, and his feet strained behind the laces.

"Don't worry, Mr. Botts. I was just joking. I get it." She stretched, and a bone popped. "Physics, hey? That's your thing?"

With the towel bunched in his hands, he dried sweat from his palms. "I teach. Science. At the school."

"That's something. I thought about teaching, but I don't have the patience. Not big on kids. Especially that age."

Unsure how he was supposed to respond, Warren said, "I'm not a teacher. I'm a substitute."

"A sub. We used to always give you guys such a tough time. You don't want the position?"

He clicked his nails. "I don't have a teaching certificate. I'm just taking a break. From university."

"Oh. Well, what sort of things do you teach—do you sub?"

"A lot of general science. A bit of everything."

"Like, say, um, pulleys and stuff?" She took out a notepad and pen, flipped open the paper. Smiling, she said, "Can't live without paper. I have a terrible memory."

"Yes. We completed a unit on forces. Earlier in the year. It's part of the curriculum."

"Forces. Wow. Can you tell me a little about that? Science was never my strong point. I was much better in gym."

Warren glanced at her, thought for a moment to tell her about the three types of muscle in the human body. Six hundred and forty different ones. Three hundred and twenty pairs. Plus millions that just lift the hair on a person's skin.

"Mr. Botts? The unit on forces?"

"Um, oh." He blinked, stared at the hairs on his arm. All flat. Disconnected to the feeling inside his stomach. "I'm sorry. I meant, simple machines. Levers, inclined planes. Wedges, screws. Wheels." He took a deep breath, spine sliding back onto a cushion. "Just an introduction, really. Lots of hands-on. It's good to touch on everything before high school. You can look at my lesson plans if you like."

"Mm-hmm." She wiped the back of her hand against her forehead. "Did you know a girl named," flipping through that notebook, "Amanda Fuller?"

The detective stared at him, and the skin tightened on the back of his neck. Hair at attention. Arrector pili working now. His spine came off the cushion.

Did he know Amanda Fuller? He closed his eyes for a moment, imagined her. Average height, thin, long brown hair. Her nose was narrow, sharp, and her skin was whiter than he thought was normal. When he looked at her, seated at a desk near the back of the room, he wondered if she had low hematocrit. Wondered about her blood count.

"Yes. She is, was my — a student. In my class."

"Beyond that?"

He looked up, the detective's eyes never wavered.

"Beyond?"

"Yes. I mean, did you see her outside of school? Did she come to your home? Before this morning, I mean."

Turning his head, Warren glanced at the couch. Remembered her sitting there and complaining. "I like your house better, Mr. Botts," she had said. "Even though we're living in the same crappy style. Weird, hey?"

Warren looked away. Had the investigator noticed?

"No." He reached up, touched his glasses. "Nothing outside of the classroom." In the back of his mind, he heard the quiet thump, thump of his counting. A rabbit's foot, drumming the earth. He had not even realized it, but he was tracking the seconds since Detective Reed had walked through the door.

"Are you certain?"

Silent for a moment, then Warren added, "Well, she did come and watch the soccer games occasionally. She sat on the bench. Didn't play, though." She would sit there and stare at another girl. *Evie*, he thought, though he could not be certain. Often Amanda appeared angry, miserable, her mouth twisted into a bitter scowl.

"Was she a good student?"

"For the most part." Twisting the towel in his fingers. "I think she found it difficult. Challenging. The course material."

"I suspect I would as well." Light laughter.

"But she tried. Some of them didn't. Some couldn't care less. Maybe a bit lazy." He cleared his throat. "Not that I want to sound unkind."

"No, Mr. Botts. Don't worry. We're just chatting."

Chatting. "Would you like a drink, then? Water? I might have some apple juice in the fridge."

"Water would be fantastic."

When he stood, his legs felt like rubber, and he wobbled slightly, caught himself. Perhaps he should tell her he had been jogging, and had not eaten since he came home. At the sink, he let the water run, saw the toast still peeking out of his toaster, the butter still smeared on the linoleum where he had dropped the knife. That would be slippery. Dangerous if someone stepped on it.

Turning his head ever so slightly, he could see the backyard in his peripheral vision. Cameras were flashing. Amanda had been freed, and now a man in a yellow helmet was yanking a cord on a chainsaw. Warren quickly poured a glass of water, twisted the tap, and returned to the living room, thrust the drink toward Detective Reed. Some spilled over the lip, wetting his hand.

"They're cutting the tree?"

"Just the branch, Mr. Botts."

He sat down again. "That's too bad."

"Does that bother you?"

Pushing his hands underneath his thighs. "Yes. A little. Of course it does. Would bother anyone. But better than the whole tree."

"The branch has things attached to it. I'm certain you saw."

"Yes."

"We saw footsteps in the snow."

"Those would be mine."

"But you did not try to bring her down?" She took a sip, stared at him over the rim of the glass. "Help her?"

"No. No. I didn't think." His words popped out in a sputter. "I didn't know what to do. I came inside, right away, and made the call."

"Can you tell me exactly what you did?"

"I—I saw her through my window. When I came back from, um, jogging. I went out, Detective Reed, but I couldn't get close. I'm sorry."

"Why not? Why couldn't you get close?"

"I just couldn't." Lowering his head. "My legs. I don't know how to explain it. They—they wouldn't move." Warren scratched the insides of his elbows. The same location where he had once had eczema. Inside his head, his mother yelled, "Stop picking at yourself, Warren. How do you think it'll ever heal?" And he stopped moving his fingers.

Part of him wanted to ask if Amanda was okay, but that would have sounded absurd. He knew she was dead. Just as he had known, that sunny afternoon, his father was dead. Even without looking. There was a spoiled smell that radiated out from his father. Even from a distance, in the cold November air, that same smell had clung to Amanda.

"Okay." She gulped the remainder of the water, unbuttoned her coat jacket. "Phew, it sure is warm in here."

"My fish." His face flushed, and he touched his glasses again.

"Quite the collection."

"My friend, you see. He owns a store. Gordie Smit? Andy's Pets?"

"Yeah, yeah. I know it."

"They were going to get rid of them. Dispose, I mean. Their stock. Too much trouble with their tanks." He was rambling, and he clenched his jaw. "I wanted to care for them."

She made a note in her book. "Did you, say, want to care for Amanda Fuller?"

"I—I. Yes, of course. I liked her." He pulled his upper lip into his mouth, pressed with his bottom teeth. Did he like her? Or did he find her spoiled, bossy, entitled? Rude? "Like I like all of my students."

He noticed her staring at his lap, and when he looked down he realized his hands were twisting the towel. He focused on his counting for a moment. Took another breath. She looked him straight in the eyes, and he squirmed, fixed instead on the curious print framed over the fireplace. All furnishings had been part of the rental, and while he did not care for most, he liked that image. A close-up of a woman's head, pale green skin, bright lips, but instead of eyes, there were two ears. Just the outer portion, the pinna, attached to the front of her face. It was much easier to gaze at her when she could not look back.

"Did you close your curtains last night, Mr. Botts? Specifically, in your kitchen?"

"I think I—I think I forgot."

"So you got up, curtains open, you had a coffee, read the paper, or whatever you do, and didn't look outside that entire time?"

Untangling his hands, he placed them on the armrests. Fabric hitched from Stephen's hooked claws. He suddenly realized, *I will lose my deposit*, then tried to push the callous thought away. A thread came loose, and he wrapped it around his finger, snapped it. "I don't know. I don't. Um. I was distracted." He swallowed. Saliva moved through his throat like a thick slug.

"So you noticed nothing?"

"I don't know."

"How could you miss that coat? It practically glows."

"It was dark when I got up. I'm an early riser." Pain behind the bridge of his nose, and his eyes began to water. "And I do not believe her jacket is phosphorescent."

Detective Reed frowned then, just the slightest dip at the corners of her mouth.

"I'm really sorry. I am." His voice cracked.

"Why do you feel sorry, Mr. Botts? You can tell me."

"I—I. I don't know. Would that have made a difference? If I had seen her before I went jogging?"

The officer in the porch cleared his throat. "A word, Detective Reed?" Warren had forgotten he was standing there.

"Yep." She went to him, their heads close together.

They were whispering, and when she returned to her seat, her expression had changed. The pleasantness was gone.

"Mr. Botts, can I share something with you?"

He nodded.

"We're having a bit of an issue. You see, we suspect Amanda Fuller did not put herself in that position on her own. We're fairly confident the rope was tied around the tree after part of it was placed around her neck. Someone lifted her off the ground."

"Oh," he breathed. "Oh. I don't believe. No."

"Why would you say that?"

"I don't think something like that can happen. It's—it's.

Just. Not. Well. No." He tapped the arm of his glasses. "I don't think it happened like that."

"While we're not ruling out any possibilities, someone else could have been involved here. Currently, we do not know who that someone was."

Warren swallowed again. It would take seven seconds for the saliva to glide down his esophagus and reach his stomach. Why was she looking at him?

"We are treating your backyard as a crime scene. Do you understand?"

"I do."

"And Mr. Botts?"

"Yes, Detective?"

"You may remain in the house, but stay away from the yellow tape perimeter out there. It's supposed to warm up tomorrow, and we're going to need a look at what's under that snow."

Both officers exited the front door, but left it ajar. Warren got up to close it, pushed his face through the crack, and said, "I'm just going to lock it up, okay? I don't want Stephen to get out."

"Mr. Botts." Surprised. "I thought we closed it. Yes, I know, the cat."

"Mm." He tried to smile, ease the door closed.

"Oh, and Mr. Botts? I will take a look at your lesson plans. As you offered. Just the physics unit, please. If you could bring them to me?"

When both the front and back yards were silent, the ambulance and police cars had retreated, Warren began to search for his friend. He checked under both beds, behind the box of magazines, on every chair at the kitchen table. He even opened the cupboards, as Stephen had a habit of sneaking in there and falling asleep inside a ceramic bowl. "Stephen," he called, shaking the food bag. "Treat?" But he was nowhere to be found.

The fear was choking him. What if Stephen was gone? What if Stephen never came back? Then he heard someone crying. A wavering meow, so uncertain and lost, coming from outside. Warren did not hesitate this time. He opened the back door, rushed out into the diminishing light, lifted the yellow tape, and stumbled toward the sound.

[9]

FOR A PASSING PRESENT, MY AUNT GAVE ME A SIXTH INSECT TO add to my collection. A spider. Legs splayed, abdomen round and perfect, barbed bristles like a fine coating of hair. Even though the spider was visually boring, a dull brown, it was my favourite. We had something in common. Spiders are born with instinct, the inner instructions on how to build. Filaments of awareness, sensations, that eventually spin into cords of knowledge. Though different styles, we both construct webs.

I introduced it to the others, and placed it on the painted shelf in my bedroom. Besides that shelf, the blue walls were empty, no pictures or posters or other distractions. I sat down on my bed, a single mattress without a proper frame, and stared up at the shelf. My family was expanding.

"Hurry," I yelled at Button.

"Huhdy," she repeated.

She plodded behind me, huffing and puffing. We paused at a stream and I cupped water in my hand, swiped it across her mouth. Rubbed. A stain of orange had formed around her lips from lunch, and my mother had not cleaned her. She had been too busy staring at a fuzzy screen outlining the drama of other people's lives. "Happier people," my mother said. "It's moronic," I told her. "To be more interested in those lives. They're not even real." She frowned, but never altered her gaze. And so I opened a can of tomato soup, warmed it, and scooped it into Button's mouth. I clanked the pot, bowl, and spoon into the chipped sink. My mother did not flinch. "To thrive, a child needs fresh air and vigorous exercise," I told the mindless lump that had birthed us. "There's the door," she muttered.

This did not surprise me in the least. Since Button was a baby, I had warmed her bottles and trained her on the toilet. I had trimmed her bangs and clipped her screwed-up toenails. I had layered extra blankets and offered her popsicles when she was sick. When the appointments arrived (and there were plenty), it was me who pulled her in the wagon toward the doctor's office. Me who heard the doctor say her developmental milestones were in the lowest percentile. Her growth and speech were considerably delayed. They suspected food and animal allergies. Problems with her vision. Impaired brain functioning. There were serious concerns, and he wanted her to see an internal specialist.

At the end of each appointment, the doctor always ended with the same sentiment. "Though, I must say, she is the most jubilant child I have ever encountered." *Jubilant!* Then, "Tell your mother what I've said. Have her call me, okay? It's important. We should get support in place." I never told my mother anything. Instead, I dragged jabbering Button through the streets in that shitty rusty wagon with the wiggling back wheel. I bought her vanilla soft serve in a cup using the change I stole from my sleazy aunt's plastic purse. "Come on, come on," I yelled at her. Button was breathing heavily. Her stumpy limbs were not built for hiking swiftly over wooded terrain. When I saw her retch from exertion, I paused, knelt, and she climbed onto my back. "Fine. We're almost there." My knees wobbled, but I was able to carry her heft the last stretch.

I had discovered this gem two days ago, when I was wandering through the woods on my own. Someone had abandoned a large canvas tent. It was big enough to house a family and I could easily stand up inside of it. There were small tears in the corner, and something dark coated the inside. When we came into the clearing, I could see my treasure was still there. Button slid off my back.

She began to move toward it, but I gripped her wrist, said, "Wait." I went to the front of the tent, flaps tied back, corners held securely with rope and pegs. I unzipped the door, then returned to Button.

"There are rules."

"Yub."

"You need to follow my instructions. Do you understand?" She nodded. "Shut your eyes and move slowly. Don't flail about." She tilted her head. "I mean, don't move your arms in a fast way. You have to be slow and steady."

"Oday."

"Just be quiet and keep your mouth closed."

She closed her eyes and squeezed her entire face. I guided her through the open door, and once we were inside, I re-zipped it. Then I had her lie down on the floor. The air was warm and stale and strangely sweet. For a moment I stood over her and stared at her white hair and swollen abdomen. Due to her oversized thighs, her legs stuck out from her body like drumsticks. She started to smile, perhaps aware I was watching her. "Keep your mouth closed up. Tight," I whispered, and lay down next to her.

There was a faint hum in the tent. "Can you hear it?" Button nodded. "Do you feel like it's alive in here?" I twisted my head, saw her nod a second time. "Okay. Are you ready?" She gripped my hand, pushed her warm body against mine. I could feel her shaking with excitement. "Now listen. And don't open your mouth."

"Oday."

"I said, don't open your mouth."

"Mmo-mmay," she said through sealed lips.

"Good job."

I reached my arm behind me, and struck the main tent pole with my fist. In an instant, the walls and ceiling appeared to explode. Every upper surface on the inside of the tent had been covered with a tight blanket of black flies, and with the sudden vibration, they all lifted off, flew in a cloud of dizzying circles, striking one another, striking walls and floors, our faces and arms. Catching in Button's white hair. The buzzing sound was nearly deafening. I do not know what it did inside Button's mind, but in my own, the sound and display drowned out every thought. For those moments, I was suspended in fluid. Floating in nothingness. Like a fish in a perfect tiny tank. Then, as quickly as they had burst forth, they settled again. Re-establishing their living blanket of black.

Button had opened her eyes, and I saw the wonder there. She clutched my hand, nodded and smiled. "Mouth closed,"

I said. She was not skilled with remembering instructions, and repetition was required to refocus her. I struck the tent pole again, and the tent teemed with its deafening display of insanity. My heart beat inside my chest. I liked sharing this experience with Button.

Just before I struck the pole for the third time, I heard someone yanking at the zipper, saw two white hands reaching through the door, jerking the canvas apart. It was our mother. I knew before I saw her oily face.

"Get out of there. Jesus. Jeeee-sussss. Get out, right bloody now."

The flies were quiet. I sat up. "How did you find us?"

"Does it matter? Some nosy lady came to my door. Actually came and knocked on my door. Got me up from my show. Said she saw you two idiots horsing around in an abandoned campground. God only knows what you could catch here. Last thing I need is to be hauling your backsides in for tetanus shots."

As though she would.

"Careful," I warned Button as we crawled out. "Don't injure any of them. They don't deserve it."

"What were you doing in there?"

"Learning."

"About what?"

"Order and chaos."

My mother rolled her eyes. "Well, it's disgusting."

"Yes," I replied, taking Button's hand in mine. *Most beautiful things are.*

10

"WAR?"
 The front door creaked open, and he felt a chill slither around his bare ankles.

"Warren, sweetheart, are you home?"

Nora. Finally. He sat up, felt his lungs reinflate. "Yes, yes. I'm here," he said, scraping the corners of his mouth. "I was. Um. Taking a short rest." Which was not really true. He had been taking a long rest. Once he had captured Stephen, he sank into the couch, and though the sun had slipped below the horizon, he had not gotten up.

"Why are you sitting here in the dark?"

"Dark?" Warren looked around him, realized he could only see the outlines of grey furniture, grey doorways, a grey rug. Her grey face. As a boy, he used to fear the dark, the unknown, but he always knew his father would arrive to banish it. That stopped when he was eleven, and he had no choice but to grow up. "Oh. I'm sorry. I hadn't realized."

"I should be the one apologizing, War. I wish I could have come earlier. I had to work. You would not believe how many people get their groceries on a Sunday! And then I rushed home and made sure Libby had found something to eat, and was doing her homework. You know, that daughter of mine'd do nothing if I left her. And then the afternoon just vanished. I tried to call, but couldn't reach you."

"I didn't hear the phone."

She placed a knotted plastic bag on the coffee table, then eased in beside him. "You okay?"

"I just feel really tired. Exhausted."

"Of course you do. What a day. To have something as terrible as that happen right in your own backyard. Would suck the good out of anyone."

"Yes."

"Everyone is talking about her. Her mother must be beside herself. I don't know what to say about that lout of a man she's married to, but I wouldn't wish this on anyone. What goes through your head to up and leave your family? He was a decent person, and they were doing well for themselves. Then to drain every cent from their house, their accounts? And take off?"

"Mmm-hmm."

"I heard he just gave it away to a group. Some charity. Had an *epiphany* of some sort. Can you believe it? Leaving your family in ruins, young girl still growing up, not two nickels to rub together. I think of Libby, and how much she needs me. I'm like her backbone, and the whole thing just boils my blood. I think they're renting, now. A few houses up. Though to be honest, I don't even know how she manages that. Subsidies, I guess. His family's well off, but they can only help her so much. She got nobody." Nora frowned, shook her head. "Can you imagine?"

Warren shrugged, shook his head in time with hers. Her voice was tinny. Shrill, even. But he ignored that, focused on the number of words that leapt out of her mouth.

"Have you eaten, War?"

"No."

"I brought a soup. Just something left over from last night. Nothing fancy, but it's decent. Lots of vegetables, so at least it's healthy. You need to eat."

As she tore open the bag, pulled out the Styrofoam container, Warren's eyes began to sting. He slid his hand underneath his thigh, and pinched the thin skin. How could she be so thoughtful? Sometimes when he lay beside her in her bed, he imagined her late husband, stricken with his digestive problems, his lung issues, his swollen joints and kidney disease. Trips back and forth to the hospital. Tubes and machines, and eventually, that never-ending beeping sound. How had she not lost her ability to nurture? So unlike his mother. After his father died, bitterness had bloated her.

"I heard someone say there's going to be an investigation."

"Investigation?"

"You know how women talk. It was never-ending chatter today, and of course I'm stuck slicing off ham. I can't help but listen."

Warren blinked, touched the corner of his glasses.

"It's not all cut and dry, the way she was hunged up, but I'm sure it was an accident. Or kids messing around. There's really no other possibility." She rubbed Warren's back, and as her warm hand moved up and down his bones, his muscles began to relax.

Maybe the nurturing was innate, and Warren's mother never had the capacity. Maybe Nora and her husband had been in love, while Warren's parents only existed side by side, circling but never touching. Maybe Warren's father was broken, and his mother never bothered to tape him to her, the way a doctor would tape a broken toe to its stable neighbour. Maybe she had tried, but the tape never stuck or the roll had simply run out. He could not think in those terms, though, that his mother had actually made an effort. After blaming his father's death on her for years, Warren was unable to step onto that slippery slope toward forgiveness.

"They asked me a lot of questions," he said.

"Who?"

"Someone. A woman detective. I don't know the other one's name."

"Why? For God's sake."

"I do live here. It was my backyard. And she was my student. Maybe they thought I could help them."

"Yes, but. Help them how? What sort of questions?"

He focused on the painting above the fireplace. The eye-ears. He shook his head, said, "I don't even remember."

"Well, never mind that now. Come. Eat something. I already re-warmed it, and even brought a plastic spoon."

Warren hated plastic cutlery, the weakness of it, how it reminded him of his mother's laziness, but he would not mention that to Nora. "Thank you," he said. "Thank you for thinking about me."

"It's terrible, you know, War, but you can't let it swallow you up. It wasn't your fault."

"I know." Though he did not know with absolute certainty. Perhaps he could have done more. He had recognized Amanda was depressed. Maybe he should have spent time with her when she appeared at his house. Like most her age, she only wanted someone to listen, to offer reassurance, but Warren's goal was to nudge her out. Gently, of course, but still. He had wanted her gone.

"Well, then."

"But it's not just that girl, it's —"

"What, darling? Just let it out."

He could not tell her that after seeing Amanda dangling from a tree, he had spent the entire afternoon thinking not just about her, but also about his father.

Insignificant things. The white hairs in the scruff on his father's chin. The way his shoulders slumped, as though gravity overwhelmed him. The way he rarely spoke to anyone besides Warren, unless it was to assist a customer or encourage his struggling seedlings. Even his sister, Beth, who followed their father relentlessly, was largely invisible. During dinner, mostly canned food, dry toast, milk, there was total silence. Warren grew to hate the sounds of a meal — slurping, chewing, pushing lumps down the throat. Sounds that were all about staying alive, but nothing about living. While he ate, he tried to keep his ears covered, one pressed to his shoulder, his free hand clamped over the other. Relief always came when the final crumb was crunched, and Warren could escape outside, to a place full of grass and insects and sweet clean air.

"There's so much left unanswered." He lowered his head, not meaning to say that out loud. About Amanda. About his father.

"Of course there is. Listen to me. It's going to take time, War, sweetheart. To figure this out. To get past it. Libby says everyone really liked her. She was really nice. Smart. And popular. Everyone's beyond upset about it."

"I should have asked. Is she okay? Libby?"

"Fine, War. She's fine. Undone, of course, but don't worry. Kids bounce back from anything, don't they?"

Warren shifted his body, and Stephen awoke, stretched to the point of shaking, then dropped off the couch, went to his bowl, and crunched kibble.

"I am starting to feel a little hungry," he said.

"Well, I arrived just in time, didn't I? I'm going to turn on a light. Is that okay?"

"Do you mind?" he said. "If we just sit here?"

"Not at all. I can see well enough." Nora stood, glanced out the window. "Will you look at that."

"Something wrong?"

"No, no. Nothing wrong. Just a few nosy neighbours. Having a bit of a gawk."

Warren knotted his fingers together, shook his head. "But why? There's nothing to see."

"Pay it no mind, War, darling. People got too much time on their hands." She yanked the curtains closed. "Obviously." Then she took the blanket off the arm of the couch, placed it over Warren's legs, and tucked it in around his hips.

"Time to take it easy," she said, as she peeled the plastic lid from the container, stirred the soup with that plastic spoon. "Misery's over for today."

His heart skipped a beat. When he was a boy, his father would say almost the exact same thing. Every evening at bedtime, Warren would pull the sheets up over his head for a smothering wait. When his father arrived to say good-night, he took the cotton corners in his soil-stained hands, and folded them across Warren's chest. "Time to rest, son. Drudgery is done for now." Though his father had always said this with a faint smile, Warren's child mind set to work.

His brain travelled back through those scattered hours in his childhood, plucking out every scrap of sadness, every worry, every fear, and lined them all up. Surely there was goodness there, hiding behind that impenetrable hedge, but he did not care. All Warren wanted was to lend truth to his father's words.

11

THOUGH I COULD NOT ARTICULATE IT, I KNEW FROM A VERY EARLY age that my aunt was a useless slut. Button and I were her attention props. Designed to make her appear maternal and family-oriented if a particular role required it. Every six or seven weeks, she would arrive at our home reeking of perfume, her swollen breasts busting out of a too-small top. Freckles on her neck and face masked by smears of shitty makeup.

"You must meet my friend, Harvey," she announced this time. It was always a name that ended in that annoying long *e* sound. Larry. Bobby. Tommy. Practically interchangeable. "My *very close* friend." And she flushed slightly, bent down. "Button, darling? This is Uncle Harv."

"Heddo, Mistah Ahv."

(*Score!* I had told Button over and over again not to address

61

these flea-riddled cat toys with the term *uncle*. Button had learned.)

"Kiddle?"

I, of course, would never reply to her prompts. Just gaze at Chump or Loser until he shuffled his feet, and dipped his grimy hands into the pockets of his jeans. My screw-up aunt could not grasp that these men did not want to see her props. They only wanted to see her naked.

The man blew air out through his mouth, and my aunt's voice climbed an octave. "This is for you, Button," she said. "From me and Uncle Harv."

It was a small stuffed pig with poseable limbs and bendy ears. Button squealed, snatched the pig, and pressed it to her throat. I could see a split in the seam, discoloured stuffing poking out. "Dah-ku, Lahvee."

Larvie. Singular: Larva. How appropriate.

"Dah-ku, dah-ku, dah-ku."

Button would not shut up. I sighed inwardly. We would have to discuss this issue. Such a shameless display of gratitude for dollar-store garbage.

"And for you." I winced, certain there were elements of her voice that only a canine could hear.

My gift was a stag beetle. Trapped in its glass case. Gently curved pincers lifted in a fearsome stance.

"Ugly little bastard, huh?" Larva bumped me with his hairy elbow. I glared at the spot where his skin had touched me, then glared at him.

"Uncle Harvey chose it all by himself. What do you say, Kiddle?"

I understood the request, the social requirement. The need to demonstrate appreciation. "An impressive sample," I replied after examining the insect.

Larva snorted then. "That one's a real piece of work," he said to my aunt. "You weren't kidding."

My aunt shrugged, threw up her hands, as though to demonstrate her exasperation. Then she over-smiled, announced, "Okay, kids, let's blow this popsicle stand!" What. A. Pair. Of. Fucking. Losers.

My mother never questioned us leaving. Her heavy breaths, nonchalant, "See you...see you later," suggested only relief to have us gone. Once I asked her why she pawned us off so frequently, or why my asshole aunt was willing to take us; she said, "I help your aunt and your aunt helps me." That meant a monetary exchange. Why was I not shocked?

In the driveway, when Larva fumbled with his keys, I mentioned to my aunt, "His car's better than the last one's."

"He's a—" and she cupped her hand over my ear, whispered his surname, like a secret she had to share. I detected a slight slur in her speech.

The name meant nothing to me, but I opened my eyes, said, "Really?"

She winked at me. "That's called trading up."

In the back seat, Button squeezed in next to me, her fleshy fingers knotted into mine, cheek against my shoulder. She was so different than I was as a child. She was robust, big boned, stunted, while I was like a stem in darkness, thin, pale, but reaching upwards. Her communication was rudimentary, and she talked like a toddler, knew nothing of words or nuance. Conversely, I trained myself to read when I was only two. By three, I could identify every tree, both common and scientific names. I could label and describe every dip or crevice on the surface of the moon at three and a half. I sketched accurate depictions of the digestive tract, understood the questionable ethics of oil companies.

While Button made people smirk with feigned understanding, in my presence, most were uncomfortably amused. My
comments made them shift in their seats. My silences made
them babble. But Button. So distinct from me. She was born
a baby, and practically remained so, whereas I was born a
functional adult.

"This one's a real dud," I whispered to Button. "Don't
you think?"

"No, no."

"Caveman. Oooga Booga. Prehistoric dork."

She giggled. "No, no."

"Say something mean about him, Button. Say he's an asshole. Do it."

"He nice."

I frowned. "Seriously? Is that as good as you got?
Larva-boy."

"Yub."

"He gave you a garbage pig. Probably picked it out of the
trash."

"No, no. Id oday if piggy eadded dash." She grinned,
hugged my arm.

I sighed. Button liked everyone she met. Literally everyone. Was she dense? I did not like to think in those terms.
No, she was simply so pure and clean, she could not recognize a shit stain even when one was smeared on the sidewalk
right before her. Almost as though she were blinded by her
own white light.

I had decided some time ago I would be her shadow.

We went for a tedious drive, and then the obligatory
ice cream. A place beside the river, where after the spring
melt, the water raged violently. I liked to sit on the railing
and listen to the current roaring with impatience, thinking

how each year, one curious child would ignore all the signs, wander away, and be consumed. *Good riddance*, I would say. If a kid was that dumb, just as well it was eliminated as soon as possible. Why waste further resources on its growth and development? Last year was a bonus, when two parents jumped in to save their sinking offspring. A "heroic bystander" tried to rescue the kid, too. Four morons gone in an instant. *Perfection!*

Larva pulled in among a sea of other Sunday drivers, sugared children racing among the vehicles with smudged faces, adults screaming behind them. I declined the offer of a cone, but the asshole purchased a large mocha swirl for Button. "That oughta perk ya right up." Watching her consume an oversized coffee product made me furious, but I clenched my jaw, said nothing. Balancing Button on the damaged guardrail, I swabbed her mouth, and took consolation in the knowledge that she would surely retch in Uncle Larva's fancy car as we made our way home. I estimated three minutes of driving before she bent at the waist. I would kick away the rubber mat so the curdled milk and bile would soak the carpet beneath.

12

WARREN COUNTED THEM. ELEVEN ADULTS. TWO CHILDREN. Three cars stopped, plus another creeping along the road. He could not understand why they were there. Staring at his bungalow, pointing at trees, talking amongst themselves. What did they expect to see?

When he went out the front door, a woman approached him. Her jacket was undone, no scarf, and he glanced at her pale neck. He considered she must be cold, and as though reading his thoughts, she lifted her hand, rubbed her throat. "Good morning, sir. You the homeowner?"

"No, no. Just renting." He tried to smile. To be polite.

"Just a couple of questions. I'm doing a piece for—"

"I'm sorry," he whispered, as he nudged past her.

He had not anticipated a reporter might want to talk to him, and his heart began to flutter. "I do want to help." He really did. "But I'm running late."

"This afternoon perhaps?"

He slid into his car, and slowly began to back out. People were standing on the sidewalk and no one moved. Rolling down his window, he called to them, "Please. Excuse me. I need to leave. I—I don't want to hurt anyone."

They parted then, and as he slowly rolled into the road, he saw his neighbour, Mr. Wilkes. The man who lived opposite him, who sat in a lawn chair inside his open garage, and drank beer pulled from a box. Wilkes pressed his bearded face toward the driver's window. Eyes so wide, Warren could see the bloodshot whites all around his irises. "You're not so smart," he said. "You're not so smart as you think."

Warren's heart did not stop clanging until he stepped inside his classroom. People were upset, confused, but there was nothing more he could do to help. He had told the detective everything. Mostly everything. He had omitted nothing he determined to be important. Like the fact that Amanda had come to his house several times. Or that he thought she was depressed over her father's abandonment. Or that he saw her outside moments after he had woken, and had done nothing. Warren had not known she was dead. The thought never entered his mind.

He glanced around his classroom. Something had changed. It only took him a moment to identify that her desk had been removed. Almost imperceptibly, thirty students had become twenty-nine. Four neat rows of six, one row of five.

Laying his leather bag on his desk, he slid out the chair. Nothing was there. No glue or puddle of ink, or long hygiene product with the adhesive side exposed. His chair was untouched, save the cartoon image someone had carved into the wooden seat—a penis, as thick as a man's arm, with tennis ball–sized testicles. In September, he had to switch chairs with a student, Evie, if he was remembering correctly, as she was too embarrassed to sit down. *Teenagers are idiots*, he thought at the time, as the class went wild, laughing and groaning, Adrian Byrd yelling, "Can you take it all, Mr. Botts? Yee-ouch!" Now, though, as Warren stared at the genital art, that level of stupidity seemed innocent. Welcome, almost. Maybe that was normal. Hanging from a rope was not.

Warren eased into his chair, and tucked his knees underneath his desk. This morning, his room seemed quiet and calm, and this made him uncomfortable. He reorganized his papers, his pencils, opened and closed his drawers, ran his hands over the scarred desktop. Then he picked up one of the glass-encased insects that decorated his desk, a centipede, and he began counting the legs. Each time his eyes lost focus, he started again. Thirty-seven, thirty-eight, thir—

"You're here."

He looked up, saw Principal Fairley leaning against the doorway, wearing another version of beige. There was an unsettling surprise in her voice.

"Yes. I am." Warren coughed, replaced the insect in the row between the dull brown spider and the stag beetle. Spacing as exact as his eye could manage.

"I wasn't sure. I wasn't—I didn't know if you would."

"Come to work?"

"I mean. We have never dealt with such a situation, Dr. Botts. I doubt many principals have." She entered the classroom, stood beside him, then pulled on the tongue of her belt. "You look exhausted."

"I'm okay." His stomach gurgled, popped. Since he had awoken, his insides had been unsettled, and even now, he could sense bubbles of air jetting along his tubes. The soup. Nora's homemade soup. It had not agreed with him.

"Right now we need to try to re-establish normalcy. If possible. The students need to see strength, and we need to keep a semblance of order."

He saw that her mouth was moving, but could not process what she was saying. How many legs did the centipede have?

"Dr. Botts?"

"Yes, Ms. Fairley?"

"We will see how the day progresses. What the administration says."

"I'm sorry?"

"But first, I'm going to address the class." Another tug on the tongue. "If that's okay with you."

He nodded. His stomach ached, and he wanted to leave the room. Instead, he gazed out the window as a noisy cluster of students piled in. A single overgrown branch pressed against the glass of the nearest window, and with each gust of wind, it emitted a scraping moan. He imagined Amanda. Had she made a similar sound? Or was that impossible? Was her last breath still trapped in her lungs? The clouds were low and grey, a black line on the horizon. Though he tried, he could detect no patterns there.

Last night, after Nora had left, his phone rang. He had picked it up, but said nothing.

"Warren? Are you there?" A voice as scratchy as cheap wool. "It's Sarie."

"Sarie?" His mother's only friend. While Warren had rarely spoken to his mother since leaving home at eighteen, he received calls from this woman at least four times a year.

"Do you have a minute? We need to talk."

The way she said *we need to talk*, he knew bad things were waiting in her mouth. About to emerge. Warren was not ready, not prepared. With Amanda, there was too much already pressing out against his bones.

In a panic, he said, "Um, Sarie? Something's burning. I have to go to the washroom. The doorbell. I'll—I'll call you right back." Slipping the phone into the cradle, he unclenched his fingers and watched it drop.

Though he stared at the phone for the next hour, he did not call her back. And when it rang again, he let his machine pick it up after four rings. "Goddammit, Warren. Call me back this instant. This is..."

Ms. Fairley waited until everyone was seated and lifted her palms toward the classroom. "We are all deeply saddened by the loss of Amanda. I'm sure I speak for everyone when I say we will miss her. She was a brilliant student, an engaging and creative person, and a well-loved leader among her peers. This was a tragic accident."

Someone snorted. Another said, "Is it true she hung herself up in Mr. Botts's backyard?"

Ms. Fairley raised her hands again. "We will have grief counsellors on hand this afternoon and all day tomorrow to answer any of your questions. We are here to support each and every one of you." A nod toward Warren. "In the meantime, your teacher will press on with your lessons. Thank you."

Then she leaned close to Warren, whispered, "As I said, we will see how the day progresses. I can't offer you more than that." Warren opened his mouth, but said nothing.

He nodded at Ms. Fairley as she closed the classroom door. Looking around the room, he noticed that seven students were missing. The empty desks made the shape of a crescent moon. "Yes. Let's get started."

"Mr. Botts?"

"Not now."

"But, Mr. Botts."

"I said let's get started."

"But, sir!"

"We need to do as Ms. Fairley instructed. Act like today is no different." He counted the hair colours, blond, brown, black. Identified a gradient. Maybe he would rearrange them according to tone. "Look at it this way. That one of your classmates is out sick. Pretend. Close your eyes, take a breath, and pretend."

"But she's not sick." Dennis Cleary. Overweight, perpetually shiny. Always interrupting. Warren bit his lip. *But it's a way, isn't it?* he wanted to tell them. *It is a way to cope.* No better or worse than any other way. "That's just dumb, Mr. Botts."

Libby, who sat in front of Dennis, turned in her seat, elbow balanced on his desk. "Just leave him alone, Cleary!"

Thank you, Libby. Standing up for him. Seems Nora had taught her well.

He took a small piece of green chalk from his shirt pocket, drew a tiny dot on the board. "Can you imagine dedicating a good portion of your life to *that*?"

"What is it?"

"A pea. A tiny green pea."

"Don't look like no green pea to me, Mr. Botts. Looks like a green spot on the board."

"I think he wants us to *pretend*."

"Yeah. That's one sick pea." Snickering.

"I hate peas. Poverty in a can." Dennis.

Libby turned again. "What did I say, Cleary?"

"Um. Frozen ones aren't so bad," he mumbled.

"Okay, okay." Warren wiped away the dot with his fist. "Let's move on. I wanted to talk to you about a man named Gregor Mendel. He was a friar, a botanist, and the father of modern genetics. Our genes. Little tiny bits inside nearly every cell in our body that determine your traits. Like a set of instructions from your parents. We all look like our parents, right?"

"Not Adrian Byrd," someone shouted out. "He looks like a hammerhead shark."

"Yeah, hammerhead that smashed through a windshield."

Laughter among the students, and Warren squeezed the chalk in his fist. It cracked into three pieces, and he rolled them around in his palm. He was amazed at how easily some of them could be distracted from the missing desk. And the other empty desks. Adrian's, and his flat stitched face, included.

"Does anyone know why? Why are we blessed, or cursed, with those looks, those traits?"

"Genetics."

"Yes."

"Genes."

"Exactly. Smart bunch, today. Can you tell me what a gene is?"

Staring.

"Evie?"

Her head was down, but she gradually lifted it.

"I know you know the answer, Evie."

She sighed, straightened her shoulders. "They are segments of DNA found in every cell in our bodies except mature red blood cells, and they tell the body how to make proteins, which are substances that build or regulate everything. Genes are always paired, and we have about twenty thousand of them."

Twenty thousand. If Warren could pause, skip-count to that number by fives, he would able to relax. To breathe.

"Thank you, Evie. Thank you. That was textbook. More than we need for right now, but excellent."

He turned back to the chalkboard, and drew an outline of a cell, and then a double helix. That was the first time since early October that Evie had spoken in class. At the beginning of the year her hand was constantly waving in the air, but within weeks, she shut down. Every morning, she slid into her seat, and did not look at anyone. With her skinny limbs, overly stuffed trunk, and strange gait, she reminded Warren of a small squirrel. When she walked, he imagined that her back end was weighed down with an impressively fluffy tail.

Out of all his students, Amanda Fuller included, Evie was the only one who had a gift. He recognized her talent, coupled with her vulnerability. With the right guidance, she had the potential to achieve something amazing, but Warren sensed secondary school would destroy her. Libby, Nora's daughter, was kind to her at least, and Warren was grateful for that.

Drawing completed, Warren took several steps toward the row of windows. "Does anyone know what this—" but he did not finish his statement. In the parking lot below, he noticed several cars that had not been there before. Two men and two women, all in navy overcoats, were bent against the wind, rushing into the school. He knew they were members of the school board. There to meet with Ms. Fairley, and talk about Amanda. Talk about him.

[13]

I SAT DOWN ON THE PLASTIC-COATED COUCH, STARED AT THE POST-
ers stuck to the plaster walls. A sharp orange bob or brown
baby ringlets. A mess of feathery hair in blown-out waves.
I could not see her, but I knew my sister was wiggling and
rocking on the foam riser placed on the barber's seat. It was
obvious from the hairdresser's complaints. "Stop moving.
Stop spinning the chair." "Do you ever keep still?" Then,
"Honestly, I wish I could just tape this one down!" Next,
"Dammit, did someone shove speed down your throat, kid?"
"Are you *that* incapable of listening?" "Don't touch! These are
scissors, you know! Dan. Ger. Ous!" Finally, "Jesus! Look
what you made me do!"

Hearing the lady's drivel, I was growing increasingly
aggravated. Obviously she had missed the beauty school
sessions covering the basic concept of client versus service

provider. I stood up, paced around the waiting area, slipped two bottles of styling products, a boar-bristle hairbrush, and a nail care kit into my backpack. After treating a customer that way, the woman deserved to lose some of her merchandise.

When Button skipped around the dividing wall, I scowled. The blond bimbo, following close behind, announced, "That's the best I could do." She punched the numbers on her cash register. Button's white-blond hair was uneven; her bangs cropped too close, one tuft sticking straight out like an angry horn. "Really?" I replied. "Yeah, really." A snarl. She was chewing gum, cracked it. "Just tell your mom to let the kid grow it out. I can't give her a style when she don't stay still. What's the point in wasting your money?" No point, but still, the lazy bitch had little difficulty scraping every bill and coin from my outstretched palm. Leaving my pockets empty.

Outside, I whispered to Button, "You just met a real witch."

She giggled, said, "No, no. She weyahed yeddow. Widches don weyah yeddow."

"Well then, a bitch."

"Oo, oo, bad woud, bad woud."

"Look what she did to your head."

"I knowd." Squealing, she swung around, arms out. "Buddon haiya lood so pweddy."

"Actually, it doesn't look pretty." I inner-sighed, took her plump hand in mine, squeezed her soft fingers. "Your hair looks like shit."

"No, no, id lood pweddy."

"It doesn't matter. What matters is you let that whore talk to you like that. You didn't have to listen, Button. You can get up and you can walk away. Do you understand that? If someone, even a full big person, is not treating you right, use your two legs and get the hell away from them. I mean it." I cleared what mucus I could from my nose and throat, glanced inside, found the front of the hairdresser's shop empty, then spat on the doorknob. "And then do that."

Grabbing her stomach then, as laughter rolled through her. "Oday, oday."

I walked, while Button skipped her hobbling overweight skip. We turned off Main Street, strode through the area with expensive brick homes. Older houses with verandas, and sloping roofs, and two shiny cars parked in each circular driveway. Some days I would pretend I lived in a particular one — dull red brick covered in glittery ivy, rippling glass in the windows, a tiny balcony jutting out over the front door. I deserved a home like that. A home without stained carpet, nicked linoleum, and countertops covered in cut marks because someone was too lazy to use a board. The toilets (and there would be more than one) would never grow a film so thick it sloughed off on its own. Self-cleaning, my ass.

I stopped in front of my future home. A blue bicycle with a white banana-style seat was thrown down near the steps. Probably belonging to the ungrateful dirtbag that lived there. "Do you like this one, Button? This house? Would you want to live here?"

Button shook her head, "Nope. Nevah. No-sih-wee."

"What?" I squeezed her flabby fingers tighter.

"Owh-as beddah."

"Don't be stupid," I said, annoyed at her loyalty to a dump. "How could ours be better?"

"You livahs deah."

I live there. I released my grip, glanced at Button. She

was smiling at me. Of course. Her lips spread so widely, her eyes were lost in the chubby pink folds of her face. My heart tipped inside my chest, and I will admit, it took a moment to realign it.

"Shit, Button," I said, trying not to sound too soft. "I could live anywhere."

I sometimes wondered what it was like to perceive the world through my sister's brain. So full of false sugary thoughts. How could she float around in such rosy space, day after day, oblivious to all the suffering, the never-ending stream of misery in the world? How was she unaware of the pointlessness of most human life? Her mind packed with rainbows and kittens, ice cream and cotton candy. Pure crap. Surely that was some sort of mental disorder. There had to be a way to cure her. To treat that illness. Seeing goodness everywhere was just an alternate form of deviance. The Lollipop Syndrome.

"Hey, dickwads! Get your hooves off my land."

I looked up. A girl who no doubt owned the discarded bike and lived in my future house was standing a couple of feet ahead of us. I recognized her. She went to my school, was in my grade, though I was certain she had never noticed me before. Her summery clothes were unstained, and I would even guess they had been ironed. Another person clearly cared about her. The thought of that made me sick. I hated her instantly, and our interaction had barely begun.

"Heddo!" Button said.

In her arms, the girl held an ugly mutt, its face reminiscent of a fox's. Burnt orange, and pointy. She ran her hand down over its back, along its curling tail.

"Did you know poor people stink?" The girl ignored Button's courteous greeting. "It's an honest fact. They stink cause of what they eat. Cheap junky food. Oozes out their skin."

Watching her small mouth, I noticed tiny brown crumbs on her lips. She had been consuming chocolate cake or a brownie or something. Then I turned my attention to Button, to see how she would respond. "Heddo heddo," she repeated, wriggling her fingers. My sister grinned, plumped her horrible hair.

"That's my polite way of saying, I don't want your shit-smell near my house. All trash goes in the garbage. So, why are you out?"

"Did you hear that Button? She says you're trash. She's telling you that you stink, and she does not want your particular odour near her fancy house. Though if you will note, Button, we are situated on the sidewalk, which is legally considered public property."

"Huh?"

"Do you understand, Button? We are permitted to stand here."

"I don't care if it's the shitty sidewalk. Leave. Now."

"Button?"

Her reaction was not what I had hoped it would be. She raced toward the girl, cooed, "I luvas puppahs. I do." Dove her fingers into the dog's orange fur. Made kissing faces. "Led me see id dayull. Id dayull."

Seriously? She loves its tail?

The girl twisted, shielding the dog, "Back off, you fat fucking white-haired troll. Get your sweaty mitts away from her. Trying to pinch her." Then to the dog, "It's okay, Noodle. No one's going to hurt you." Back to Button, "Now, get to fuck."

Button whined and pinched her crotch. Said, "Dayull so pweddy. Pleadz. You ma fwend."

Her friend?

"Yeah, I know. Her tail's the best part." She unrolled it, took her hand away, and it sprung back. Did it two more times. Lifting the dog just out of Button's reach.

My little sister was fucking mesmerized.

"Oh, pleadz? Pleadz?"

"Plead! Plead!" She mocked her. "What happened to you, anyway? Lawnmower run over your gross head?"

I continued to observe the exchange with total objectivity. "Button," I said. "Are you listening? Do you recall what we discussed earlier, Button? About spitting, or using your legs to —"

She was focused on the dog. "No, I don. I don. I wanna puppahs."

"Button. Think!" My fingers began to clench. "Use your brain."

"Button? Rabbit button, rabbit button!" the stupid bitch sang. "What does it feel like to be named after crap? Hear that, Noodle? Her name's Button. And her friends call her little lump of shit." She laughed. "Oh, that's right. Crap don't got no friends. Cause crap stinks."

I gripped my sister's wrist. While I would have loved to see her slam that eleven-year-old in the guts, it was clear Button had learned nothing from me. Nothing yet. That level of personality alteration would be more difficult than I had imagined.

"Shut your prissy gob," I said calmly.

She took a step toward us. "Oh yeah? And if I don't?"

"Then you'll be sorry." I smiled at her, very softly, very gently. I imagined my slit eyes were twinkling. While she was the same age as me, she was several inches taller, several inches thicker. Not that height or weight made a difference.

Tone and eye contact were so much more important.

"Oh yeah? Just what're you gonna do?"

"I don't know." I tapped my chin. "I have to think. You'll find out."

"Yeah?"

"Not today, though. No. Sometime soon." I stared at Noodle. "You'll need to wait."

Her expression shifted, and she gripped the dog to her chest. Voice no longer as forceful, "You think your shit's special? Freak."

I smiled again, blinked. A picture of calmness. Of geniality. "Nice to meet you, Noodle. See you soon."

Hoping Button might notice, I had just demonstrated two of my prized traits. Patience and Control.

[14]

"**O**RANGE CONES," WARREN YELLED AT THE GIRLS. "CHECK IN the storeroom. They're in the same place they were last week."

He had dragged himself through the entire day, and had heard nothing from Ms. Fairley. In the staffroom during lunch, no one had spoken to him, or even acknowledged him. Seated at the corner table, he ate his dry sandwich, alone, counting the clicks of the coffee maker that came in six-second intervals.

Libby arrived with an armload of cones, and Evie tugged a red mesh bag full of soccer balls.

"Now put them in a row for warm-up. Eight feet apart, as accurate as you can manage, please. Oh, and an actual line." It bothered him. Uneven spaces. Wonky lines that should be straight.

Her back stiffened, bony knees touching, feet slightly apart. "I know, Mr. Botts. I do this every practice."

"Sorry, Libby." Softer, then. "And you do a great job."

Warren looked around the gymnasium. Libby was rapidly clapping down the cones, and while Evie normally assisted, this time she wandered away. Went to one of the benches, folded her arms across her chest, and stared at the seat. It only took him a moment to realize that was the same place where Amanda often sat. Watching the practice. Watching the girls. But mostly watching Evie.

Warren went and stood beside her. Her arms and legs were thin and purple, though the skin on her face was pale.

"You okay?"

She nodded.

"That's good," he said. He was not certain what else to say. Consoling a stranger was not straightforward. He could not determine the social rules.

"Can I ask you a question, Mr. Botts?"

"Of course."

She scratched at bumps on the back of her arm. "Does it make someone a weirdo if they're not sad? I mean, about her. If they don't feel upset?"

"Well," he said, and cleared his throat. "I don't believe so. Everyone's reactions are different, right? Everyone's emotions are unique. Who's to say what's right or wrong or weird or normal?"

She nodded again, unfolded her arms, then refolded them.

"You can join us in a minute, if you want."

"Thanks, Mr. Botts. But I'm fine."

Warren went to the bag of soccer balls, and let them roll onto the floor. "Should we get started?" he yelled. No one responded. "Girls?" Some were sprinting around the edges, while a few clustered near the door, heads pressed together, talking. He wondered where the rest of the team was. So many were late.

"I heard she was pregnant."

"No, her mother drove her insane. Constant pressure."

"Apparently, she was in love with—"

"They're looking at him, you know. Think he was involved."

"That he hung her up? Him?"

"Yeah. And left her there. Swinging. Thought it was hilarious."

"Girls!" Warren said.

Swinging. They turned their glittering eyes toward him. "Yes, Mr. Botts?" Singsong chorus.

"Get moving. Now."

Surely he had misheard. His mind was forming words that were not in the air. He wanted to blow the whistle that dangled around his neck, but he could not tolerate the sound. Lifting his hand, pointing at them, he felt the sweat on his shirt, cold against his skin. Eye rolls, and they brushed past him, a lazy swagger to the opposite corner.

"Does anyone know where the others are?"

"Nope."

"Should we wait?"

"For what?" Quartet of laughter. "Doubt if they're coming."

"Why?"

"Not allowed."

He frowned, shook his head. "Um, why?"

One of them made a choking sound, and Warren said, "What was that?"

"Naaaah-thing, Mr. Botts."

When he had agreed to teach, he had not factored in

coaching. Ms. Fairley told him *afterwards* it was the responsibility of each teacher to contribute to extracurriculars. "In fact," she said, "some teachers say it is the best part of their day. A time to really connect. Make a difference." Even though he had suggested leading a robotics club, or after-school chess, he was assigned to the girls' soccer team. Grades six, seven, and eight, though it was mostly eights that showed up, a pack of surly girls.

Warren hated it. Hated team sports. Every time someone's sneaker struck the ball, he could not help but wince, lift his shoulders, and tuck in his head. But he need not have worried much. During the ninety-minute activity on Monday and Thursday afternoons, there was minimal ball-striking. While some of the girls attempted the drills, and listened to his instructions, most of them did not want to be there. Soccer practice served as a place to go, rather than home, or walking the streets, or hiding in the woods, or someone's basement, or wandering up and down the aisles at the grocery store.

In October, his team had played two games against schools in neighbouring towns. A handful of parents came and sat in the stands, mothers and fathers staring at their daughters. No one cheered. Especially when his team lost shamefully. Many of the girls just stood there, hands on hips, annoyed, as though they were offended by the wind coming off the opposing team. If the soccer ball did drift their way, approaching their feet, more often than not they would gape at it. It could have been a rolling head. A face they did not recognize. Could not even bother to boot away.

"The parents blame you," Ms. Fairley had said after the game. "They've had some choice things to say."

"Blame me? What have they said?"

"You need to inspire them, Dr. Botts. It costs a pretty

penny to bus girls in, bus girls out. To host these kinds of events. And I don't need to tell you, our district does not have money."

"I understand, but—"

"It's supposed to build community."

"Yes."

"I don't see community happening here." She snapped her fingers. "Inspire, Dr. Botts. Inspire!"

Inspire!

While he thought he was capable in the classroom, he did not know how to inspire in the gymnasium. In September he had wheeled a blackboard in, and outlined various plays copied from a library book. The girls could not keep up, or did not bother, even though he explained the reasoning behind each technique, each piece of instruction. He complimented nearly every movement, every single time one of the girls tapped the ball, and though she refused ("On principle, Mr. Botts"), he had even asked Libby to allow a few shots to sneak past her in goal. With his own money, he purchased bags of oranges, kept them sliced and chilled in a flat container on the wooden bench. He bought badges they could sew on their jackets in hopes of creating a sense of responsibility to other teammates. A sense of unity. "No, a safety pin looks terrible," he had said. "Take ten minutes with a needle and thread. Please." Only Evie had affixed hers to her coat with a neat white stitch.

"Maybe you're trying too hard, Mr. Botts." Libby had said to him after the last practice.

"I'm supposed to get them excited about it. I can't do that if I don't try. It certainly won't happen if I try less." He was frustrated, saying too much to a student.

"I don't know. Maybe they just don't care."

"But why?" Warren had asked. He wondered how many lines were on the floor of the gymnasium. Red, navy, green, white. Circles, semi-circles, rectangles, dotted, solid. "How can they not care?"

Libby had shrugged, "Most people don't care about important stuff. Don't take it personally."

"Okay," Warren yelled, and was forced to blow his whistle, the sound vibrating in his enamel. "We're going to try something new."

Groaning.

"If you manage to zigzag between the cones, with the ball of course, in under fifteen seconds, you get one of these." He held up a foil-covered chocolate between thumb and forefinger.

"Oh. My. Gawd," one girl squealed. "Mr. Botts is giving out kisses."

"Ooo, kisses. Mwahh!"

Warren looked at the bag of candy. They were indeed kisses. He had not realized when he dropped them into his cart at the convenience store, and it was too late now. He heard them puckering and popping their lips. Face flushing, he said, "Libby. Can you hand them out?" She shook her head.

"I just did it, Mr. Botts," a girl squealed. "Were you counting? That was under fifteen. I get a kiss."

She bolted over, and reluctantly, he handed her a chocolate.

Another girl moved the ball through the cones.

"Kissies, please!"

He lay the open package on the bench. "You may take your own," he said, and instead of continuing with the cone warm-up, the girls surrounded the bag, tore it apart. In that instant, as Warren watched the swarm of them reaching and ripping and shrieking and elbowing, he missed his lab. Missed working in the silence with the fluorescent lighting, the gentle sound of water running, and the steady ticking of the wall clock. He missed the platform he had constructed, covered in sand, the necessary warmth of his space, the effort his tiny subjects displayed as they tried to adapt to their new environment. The fatherly pride he felt at their success. He missed the clink of a glass slide, slipping into his microscope, and the promising sound as the printhead spilled ink across the page. Just last year all he could think about was getting away from the lab, from the university, from the constant drone of responsibility, but now, he craved the peace of that tiny room. He wanted the memory of Amanda to disappear from his brain. Sarie's scratchy voice to dissolve from his answering machine. But then he would never have met Nora, and that thought made his heart seize.

"Girls? Should we get—" he started, but was interrupted by a slamming door near the sidelines.

"Evie!" A woman was hovering just outside the painted green line. She wore old sneakers, a crocheted hat. "Evie! Come here now."

As Evie went to the woman, Warren followed.

"I'm sorry," he said. "This is soccer. We're in the middle of a practice."

"Yes, and this is my daughter, and I left word with the office. She was supposed to go straight home." Evie kicked the floor, leaving black streaks. "Not a very good listener, is she?"

The woman would not look at Warren. One layer of his mind began to count. "For what reason?"

"I had assumed the children would be protected." She

gripped Evie's elbow, and was shaking her head. "Is that such an outlandish thought?"

"I — I don't understand."

Inside of her jacket, she was wearing a fuzzy yellow scarf. Warren stared at the simple knot. As her arms moved, a small piece of fluff lifted up and floated through the air. He gazed at it moving away, looping and dipping. When most people thought about buoyancy, they only considered water, but he knew all those principles applied to air as well.

"I don't want to go." A whisper.

"It doesn't matter, Evie. What I say is all that counts here. You can't question me on every turn."

He was distracted by the fluff, shifting, playing with the upward force of the air, and he resisted the urge to reach out and grab it in his fist. Two hundred and nineteen. Two hundred and twenty. Two hundred and twen —

"Right, Mr. Botts?"

"I'm sorry?"

"I told my mom you're a really good teacher."

"Oh, I see. Thank you. And Evie is an excellent student." Lowered tone. "She is incredibly bright."

The woman turned toward Evie. "Let's go. I've had enough. Grab your things."

"But Ms —" he could not recall her last name. He tried to picture the class list, scanning his memory, but the only name that glowed on the page was Amanda Fuller's.

"I don't know if what people are saying is true, but I'm not taking a single chance. My daughter is all I've got left." He could see the muscles in her jaw tightening. She was clearly trying to control her emotions. "A girl is dead, sir. One of your students is dead. And in a most horrible way."

Warren glanced at Evie, who was once again beside her

mother. Coat and scarf and knapsack and boots all gathered in her bony arms. Her head was lowered and she was looking at the gymnasium floor, littered with bits of coloured tinfoil. "Amanda is dead," Evie repeated. Warren glanced at her mouth. Was that? Yes. A grin. Faint and nervous, but still a grin.

Warren pushed the handle to open the glass doors. Once outside, he dug around in the pocket of his coat to find a tissue. He had forgotten his gloves, and did not like touching the metal with his bare skin. No tissue, and as he walked down the incline toward the parking lot, he crumpled the fabric of his pocket inside his fist, imagining that he was obliterating any germs he had collected.

"Dr. Botts?"

He turned, saw Ms. Fairley scurrying toward him. Scarf dragging on the ground. Lifting his hand, he offered a friendly wave, but she did not return the gesture.

"I saw you leaving from my office. I thought to let you finish up practice, so as not to be too disruptive to the students. But you're early."

"Things weren't going well. I just—I don't know. Decided to wrap it up."

"I understand. Everyone is distracted."

"Yes."

"As you might guess, I've had some calls." Her tone was clipped. "I have to ask. Did you tell your students to pretend Amanda is sick? That's why she's not at school?"

Warren looked down.

"Oh. Oh dear. I don't think that's appropriate advice at all. Do you? Parents are upset."

Hand still tucked inside his pocket, Warren began to

snap his damp thumb over his fingers. Regular, calming intervals. "I was trying to help them get through the day."

"Your intentions may well have been genuine, but very ill-advised. We need to leave the guidance to the experts."

He nodded. He kept his counting slow and steady.

"I spoke with my brother, and he assures me your character is beyond reproach." She lifted her scarf from the walkway. "I trust his judgement, Dr. Botts, but you have to understand my word doesn't carry much weight. No one knows you here. You're a substitute. A replacement."

Snap. Ninety-seven. Snap. Ninety-eight. Snap. Ninety-nine.

"I met with the administration today. The superintendent." Inspecting the tail of her scarf, she shook gravel from the fringe. "You're being placed on immediate administrative leave."

"Leave?"

"With pay." She would not look at him. "For now."

He removed his hand from his pocket, touched his glasses, lifted them. "Don't worry. I understand." Though he did not fully understand. What were they thinking? Did they blame him? Was it because he did not help? Or could they possibly suspect he was the person who had slipped the noose over Amanda's neck, held her aloft until she died?

There was a smudge across the left lens, and when the street light clicked to life, light splintered into his eye. *No, he told himself. That is beyond absurd.*

"You're not to come back into the school. Or on the property. If there's anything important in your classroom, I can collect it. Bring it to you."

Ms. Fairley still would not look him in the eye.

"Just the insects. The ones on my desk. In glass. They're important to me. I wouldn't want them to be damaged."

"Not a problem, Dr. Botts. I'm sorry this is happening. Hopefully things will be sorted, and the police will get to the bottom of what happened."

Warren was about to turn away when he heard Ms. Fairley take a sudden breath, then the sound of rapid clicking on the cement. A small ball of orange fur flew between Warren's legs, like a rabbit with a cropped tail.

"What's—"

"Oh dear. Will you look at that." Ms. Fairley's voice was softer now, as a small dog, nose like a baby fox's, rushed to the front entrance of the school, began yapping.

Ms. Fairley took a few steps, reached down and scooped it up. "Amanda's dog."

The words startled Warren, and he glanced at the dog, its tiny ribs expanding and contracting. "Oh," he said. "I didn't know."

"How could you know? Second time today it's been here. Looking for her."

"Oh," Warren repeated. He could think of nothing else to say.

"It's sad, really." Ms. Fairley cradled it. "They don't know what goes on in our worlds. Where we go when we leave. When we'll be back." She scratched it under the chin. "C'mon, Noodle. I'll drop you to Mrs. Fuller."

"I could," Warren offered. "I'm headed home and she's only a few houses away."

Ms. Fairley sighed, and shook her head. "You need to take this seriously, Warren. They are investigating. Trying to understand what happened. With your student. In your backyard."

As though on cue, a car sputtered to life. A police cruiser. It slowly looped around, gravel crunching beneath its tires, and stopped right in front of Warren. Window lowered, Detective Reed smiling. "Mr. Botts. I'm glad we found you."

"I wasn't hiding."

"Just a joke," she said. "We could really use your help."

"Now?"

"Is there a better time?"

"No, no." He dipped his hand back into his pocket, started snapping again. One, two, three.

"Get in the back," she said. "And we can head down to the station. Have a friendly chat."

THOUGH I AM LOATH TO ADMIT IT, I WAS WRONG ABOUT LARVA. He lasted much, much longer than I had anticipated. Over several months, my aunt and her air-wasting fling kept showing up. Kept "relieving our mother" of her parental duties. When they pulled into the driveway in his waxed car, Button practically barked at the front door, scratched at the glass. It was deplorable, deplorable behaviour. During those moments, if I had owned a choke collar and leash, I would have struggled to resist tethering her.

Our dishwasher broke on a Sunday, and my mother called Larva instead of a repairman. Button was at her post, perched on the front stoop, obediently waiting for her male master to arrive. I told her to stop embarrassing herself. Said she was acting like a numbskull. "Saint Larva can't stand you, you know that? He thinks you're so dumb, you should live in a cage." Button laughed, shook her head, as though what I said was the funniest thing. "I heard him tell Mother you belong in the zoo. Like a stupid fat freak show. He told her not to let animals eat at the table. And darling Auntie told her to throw your food on the floor."

Not even the slightest flicker of doubt in her eyes. It was beyond frustrating. She laughed again, flipped on her back, clapped her hands and feet. "Aundie luvas Buddon. Un-cah Lahvee luvas Buddon. And you! You luvas Buddon doo."

Shit. "Uncle" had worked its way into her vocabulary.

While I was galled, I could also not help but marvel at my little sister. Though I had tried frequently, it was nearly impossible to plant a mean seed in her consciousness. She heard what I said, understood it, but the thought disintegrated immediately. I prided myself on understanding people and their pettiness, but I could not comprehend my sister's simple, complicated mind. Button was special in her goodness. Her unshakable innocence. And beyond that, she was the only person who could tell when I was lying.

"Heddo, Un-cah Lahvee," Button announced when Larva strode though the door in a baseball cap, red plastic toolbox swinging.

"Uh-huh." Even for an uneducated adult, he had an extremely limited vocabulary.

"Are you going to be Harv's assistant today?" My aunt. "Babe? Is that okay? If Button helps?"

Before he could answer, Button yelped, "Yub, yub, yub!" She pressed her hands into her crotch and pinched. "Yub. Buddon can."

I noticed Larva tightening his jaw. My aunt noticed it, too.

"You know what, sweetie-pop?" Leaning close to Button's face. "Maybe you can work with Uncle Harvey another time.

This is a big job. Big, big job. Boy oh boy. Besides, we'll need to get you a tiny tool belt before he'll hire you."

That bitch was too freaking friendly. No wonder Button was able to ignore my words, giggle, nip her freaking crotch, say, "Oday. Oday. Buddon waid."

My mother walked over, smacked Button's offending fingers. "If you're itchy, go to your room and scratch. Harvey doesn't need you underfoot." Then, to Loser-Larva, "I hate to be a trouble, I really do, but I don't know what's wrong with it. Just started leaking water everywhere. What a mess! I used every towel in the house. Dripping down into the basement, even. It's not that old, really, but stuff just isn't built to last, right?" False lightness. Puke rising in my throat.

"Not these days. Nope."

"Is there anything I can do to help, Harv? Do you want a drink? A quick sandwich?"

I hated the way she was gawking at him. Head tilted, her eyes a little wider than they should be, spread fingers pushed into her cheek. I could practically smell her neediness. Cheap and fake and powdery. Dollar-store perfume. That neediness irritated me, when I was certain any monkey could repair a leaking dishwasher. If she was not such a waste of space, she could have done it herself. I had even asked her if I could try, but she tittered at me, then pursed her lips into a condescending smile.

"You cut the power?"

"Yes, yes. Of course, I turned off the power. It's all set. You don't know how much I appreciate it."

"Such a doll, coming over here like this, isn't he?" my aunt said. "Don't want my baby getting electrocuted." She wrapped her arms around his waist, curled into him. If she had been four-legged, she would have lifted her tail, sprayed him from some skunky glands to further demonstrate her ownership. I bet she smelled my mother as well.

Larva went into the kitchen, placed his toolbox on the linoleum, took a step back, and sized up the dishwasher. I watched him scratching his stubble, sighing, lifting his ball cap straight up, off his head, then forcing it back on. Such a display of manly behaviours. He slid over the locking mechanism, and tugged open the door. Stuck his head inside, ran his fingers over the plastic.

"Do you see what the problem is?" I asked, as though riveted. "Is there a hole in there, Uncle Lar, Uncle, um? Harvey?"

"Nope. No holes."

"What about that?" I pointed to the floor of the machine. At the drainage area.

"Drainage. Water comes in, got to get out, don't it?"

"Oh, yeah. I get it."

Pinhead. He did not realize I was mocking him. That I thought he looked like such an ass, exploring the interior of the dishwasher. Even I knew there was no answer to be found there. The leak was most likely caused by a loose pipe. The connection under the machine. I bet the clamp had wiggled off.

After unscrewing and removing the bottom panel, he reached in, flicked his hand, and a tiny crocheted mouse, coated in grease and dust, sped across the floor. My mother yelped, then froze. The dirty toy had belonged to her cat. The scrubby thing had carried it from room to room in its jaws. That was, until the day it limped out the door and never returned. Not that I could blame the cat for abandoning us. It had good reasons.

My mother stuttered. "H-h-how did that manage to squeeze under there? I couldn't even reach in with the vacuum cleaner." She must have forgotten. Before Button was born, the dishwasher had no bottom panel. When I was small, I could see the metal legs, tubes, wires. *Live* wires. I would lie there on the floor, my hand slithering in, moving my fingers through the maze of pipes and coloured cords, wondering what I might feel if my sweaty palm touched something.

Button dove for the toy, but my mother scooped it up, said, "Jesus, Button. Don't touch! That's filthy." She slipped it in her pocket, kept her hand over the mound.

"Well," Larva said, acting exasperated. "Looks like I'm going to have to haul the machine out. Turn it over."

Duh. Whenever I watched grown men work, I was always appalled by the approach. Moaning over a screw. Hauling up trousers with the forearms, wiping their brows, scratching their foreheads with a thumbnail. Stretching backs before they climbed onto machinery. *How can I make this rudimentary process appear as complicated as possible? How can I let onlookers know I am exerting significant amounts of mental and physical energy?*

When he pulled the dishwasher from underneath the counter, I could already hear the scrape of glass. It was a nice sound. Shards crunching, sticking into the linoleum as the machine slid over.

"Shit," he said. "You got enough broken bits back there to make a whole set."

He was right. When I saw all the pieces of broken glass tucked under the dishwasher, I could not help but think of my dear, dear old dad. Glasses, and other items, were frequently hurtling about the kitchen. A flash of rage, and he would smash whatever was handy. Sprays of sticky liquid marking the walls, shattered fragments everywhere. For the first years of my life, I could run outside barefoot without comment, but always had to wear shoes in the house.

By the reddish welts rising on my mother's neck, I could tell she was embarrassed by her sloppiness. But I understood the mess. I understood that after fighting with my father, she had wanted to remove the visible evidence, but also did not want to be completely free of it. Some part of her liked knowing the history was still there. Knowing that the house had not been swept clean, the brokenness erased. While a shiny kitchen made it easier for my father to forgive himself, the hidden glass made it impossible for my mother to forget. Why else would she broom all that glass under there?

Her eyes looked as though she might cry. Then she glanced at me, scraped at her skin. "I — I guess I'm not a very good housekeeper."

"No, that was me," I said, stepping forward. "I did that. Before the panel was there. Easier than picking it up." It was a lie, and I do not understand why I spoke at that time, absolving my mother from this tiny shame. Other than the fact I found it annoying to watch her squirm.

"What kind of lazy kid?" The asshole crouched, examined the underside of the machine.

My mother glanced at me again. Said nothing.

"Look-it," Larva announced. "Clamp is loose on the drainpipe."

He was the worst example of what my aunt dragged over here. The very worst. Usually, her apes drank a beer or two, watched sports on the television, adjusted their sweaty parts with alarming frequency. But never did they try to interact with the family. Connect with Button. Earn points with my mother. My aunt must have plunged her claws in deeply this time.

He grunted continuously as he did next to nothing. Jamming the rubbery pipe back into place, opening the clamp, and sliding it back over the hose. Righting the dishwasher, he lifted his chin to my mother. "I expect you want to clean that glass, right? You can manage to slide it in? Reattach it? Screw on the plate?"

"Oh, yes, Harvey. You've done so much. You don't know how much you've saved me." I nearly regurgitated my digesting cereal. "Waiting around for the repairman. The cost of it to get them out here on a Sunday, no less. You can't imagine what they charge."

Her cheeks were rosy.

To distract myself, I got down on my knees and examined the exposed floor where the dishwasher had been. Amazing how much damage the sun caused. Even with the dust and the grease and the abundance of glass, the green of the linoleum was so much brighter in there. Nice, almost. I tried to remove a larger piece of glass, but it was fixed. Sugary soda or juice had cemented it. It would be a chore to sweep out the loose shards, scrape the remainder, wash everything. And for what? My incompetent mother would cut her palms. Button would have slivers stuck in her fleshy feet. The evidence of my father's temper would disappear from our home.

"We're not cleaning it," I announced. "We'll push the dishwasher back into place, leave the glass there."

Larva snorted, shrugged. "Yep. Well. You the boss around here, aren't you?"

Yes, yes I am.

He tossed a screwdriver into his cheap toolbox. "I need a smoke."

After he brushed past me, I started to shove the dishwasher into its hollow. I could hear my mother's gratitude, sewage continuing to ooze from her mouth. Not directed at me, of course, but at her sister's jerk boyfriend. I hated my mother's fragility. Her pathetic feminine ineptitude. How could she be unaware of his feeble performance? How could she not see that, beneath his helpful exterior, he was wet with aggravation? Soaking in it.

She may have been blind, but I had a firm grip on the personality of our generous Uncle Larva. A bitter dog, dripping, moping around. I crossed my fingers, wishing, wishing I would be there when he finally shook himself dry.

[16]

AS THEY WALKED THROUGH THE POLICE STATION, THERE WAS A sour smell of food in the air. Takeout, Warren guessed, or an open container of cold food. Detective Reed led him to a room, grey floors and walls, a single table bolted down. Two parallel navy lines circled the room at eye level, and Warren detected the slightest angle, only a few degrees, and then the subsequent correction in the paint. A woman brought him a warm soda, opened it, and snapped off the tab. "Saving these," she said, "for wheelchairs," before dropping it into a hip pocket and leaving through the steel door.

"Take a seat," Detective Reed said.

Warren nodded, slid into a metal chair. As he tried to pull the chair toward the table, he realized the legs, too, were fixed to the floor. He was an unnatural distance from the table. His fingernail moved across the silver seat, the sound sending an electric rush through his teeth, his body.

"I just want to pick your brain a little. To get a better feel for who this kid was. It will help."

Her words echoed off the cement walls, and sounded as though they were coming from somewhere behind Warren. He resisted the urge to turn around and look.

"I mean, I don't know," he said. Her shirt had nine buttons, though that was an estimate as he was unable to see whether there were one or two hidden inside her pants. "I don't really know her." Clearing his throat. "Didn't, I mean."

"Anything you can think of might help. Did she have friends in the class?"

"I don't think she had a lot of close friends. It's hard to tell. She worked hard, though."

"How do you mean?"

"I mean, she really wanted to get the best grade. The top mark. She would ask me who got the highest."

"And did you tell her?"

"No. I keep grades confidential. I don't post grades on the wall, like some of the others. I did at the start, but I changed my mind. I don't think it's good practice."

"Yes. Okay. You mentioned some difficult students."

"I mean, well, a lot of them are difficult. Maybe they don't belong."

"What do you mean by that, Mr. Botts?"

"I mean. I'm not sure." Quite often, when his father was not working at Feed 'n Seed, he kept Warren home from school. "Sometimes it's good," he would say, "not to be alone." They tinkered in the barn, weeded side by side, plucked apples from the old tree, and once even made a butter pastry and created a pie. In his nearly inaudible voice, his father taught him about black holes, aquatic plants, the clever innards of a light bulb. "Though sunlight is the perfect creation, my darling," he had said. "Nothing made in a factory will ever compare to what nature can produce."

Warren tugged at his ear. "Maybe some students should be out. Working."

"Quite the statement coming from an educator, Mr. Botts. Just what sort of employment would you offer a thirteen-year-old?"

"I mean, out working, learning. Learning in different ways. That's a child's work, isn't it? To learn? Not sitting for eight hours at a desk. I'm not—I'm not explaining myself properly." He looked at the metal table, the corners rounded, edges pinched up. No one would be able to cut themselves. He tried to estimate the square footage of the floor. The walls, minus the door and mirrored window. The ceiling, minus the caged light fixtures.

"Mr. Botts?"

"Yes."

"I said your name three times."

"I'm sorry. I was thinking."

"Thinking."

"I mean. Just." *Counting*.

"Mr. Botts, are there any of Amanda's classmates that cause you concern? Considerable, or otherwise?"

"One, maybe?"

"Name, please." She flipped open her notepad.

"Adrian." He closed his eyes, and pictured the attendance list. "Adrian Byrd."

"Did he have interactions with Amanda?"

"Well, I'm not sure, but I did see them talking. And you hear whispers among students, sometimes, right? When they sound off. But who knows if any of it is true."

"What sort of stuff did you hear?"

"That they were, I don't know the term they would use, but spending time together?"

"Boyfriend-girlfriend sort of thing?"

"Oh, I can't say." He wove his fingers together, clicked his nails. "Does that happen at this age?"

Detective Reed cleared her throat. "Did you ever see them together?"

"Not really."

"So, just whisperings." Gripping the pencil and pad in one hand, she lifted the other, notched the air with two fingers.

"I suppose."

"And how was his manner in class?"

"Manner?"

"How was he acting today? Did you notice anything different? Was he uptight? Irritable?"

Warren pinched his chin, looked to the left. Visualized his empty desk. "I—I don't think he was here today. Yes, he was absent."

"Absent." She scratched something on her pad. "Okay, Mr. Botts." A rapid glance over her shoulder at her partner. "We have determined time of death to be between midnight and three a.m. Can you tell us where you were then?"

"I was with my—my friend. At my house."

"Your friend's name?"

"Nora." He blinked. "Nora." At that precise moment, her last name escaped him.

"I know a Nora. She works at the supermarket. Makes the best sandwiches. Always gives me extra tomatoes."

"That's her," and Warren found himself grinning. "Yes. Extra tomatoes. That's exactly who she is."

"You were with her the entire time?"

"I don't think so."

"Can you give us an estimate, Mr. Botts?"

"We were watching a film. It got a little late. She fell asleep. I think she left after one."

"A movie-type thing? What one?"

"I can ask her. I don't remember."

"You watched an entire movie, but can't remember anything about it, Mr. Botts?" Detective Reed tilted her head backward, raised her eyebrows.

"I guess I found the story rather dull. There was a girl in it."

"Girl caught your eye?"

Warren flushed. "No, no. Nothing like that."

"Fine. Did you do anything after your friend left?"

"A drink of water? Around eighteen minutes before two."

"That's precise."

"I went to the kitchen. Stephen was sleeping on the stove, and I lifted him down, saw the clock."

"You don't remember the movie, with the exception of a young actress, but you remember the time, Mr. Botts?"

"Numbers stick. I don't know why."

"Anything else? Anything at all? No matter how small it might seem to you."

Warren paused, pulled his bottom lip in between his teeth, and pressed down. There was something else, though it was just beyond the film of his memory. He had placed Stephen on the floor of the kitchen. The cat had stretched, appeared annoyed. Warren had gotten himself the water. Used a mug that was beside the sink. It had the faint flavour of coffee. And then he went to the window. Looked out. And.

"Yes. I saw a light."

"A light?"

"Just a quick glow. I looked out the window, and I saw

a flicker of light. Almost like a firefly. But higher up. Near the tree."

"A firefly? In November?"

Warren took a breath. "Well, of course it wasn't a firefly. I don't know. Maybe it was a reflection of something. Maybe I was confused. It was probably nothing."

Detective Reed made a note.

"One last question, Mr. Botts. Would you take a look at this?" She handed him a photocopied paper. "Please take a look at the portion inside that highlighted square."

Bright yellow ring circling a force diagram, three pulleys, a winding rope, arrows, and a trapezoid to represent a one-hundred-pound weight.

"Did you draw that?"

"Yes," he mumbled. His knees shifted back and forth. "It was a challenge question. I put it on the test." Though three or four attempted it, Evie was the only student who completed it. Found the correct answer. A perfectly drawn solution, though he did not mention this to the detective.

"A challenge question."

"Yes."

"Well, that's really curious." She tapped her front tooth with the nail of her index finger. "Would it surprise you to know this exact set-up was used to suspend Amanda Fuller from a branch in your backyard?"

Warren folded his tall frame into the back of the police car, and the officer pulled out of the station parking lot. Instead of driving straight back to the school, they went in the opposite direction, onto a country road. He stared out through the glass, past the streaks and fingerprints. The sky was heavy grey, black clouds moving in, and now that the light snow had melted, the land was a blur of brown and beige, dirt and dying grass.

"Where are we going?"

"Just the roundabout way. Traffic gets thick at this hour." Detective Reed was in the passenger seat, and she flipped her visor down, flicked across the plastic slide covering the mirror. Warren could not shift out of her line of vision, and she watched him relentlessly. "Better to use a service road."

"Oh. Okay."

They reached a fork, and Warren knew if they turned left they would pass the pig farm, and if they turned right they would pass an ice creamery to the east. The community was supported by two industries, and depending on the direction of the wind, the whole place either smelled like sour blood or sweet vanilla. Or some cruel combination of both.

Detective Reed was still staring at him. He tried to angle his shoulders, raised the collar on his coat, but he could not avoid her eyes. His chest felt tight, as though a fat fist was nestled there, taking up room. He exhaled with some force, but he could not dislodge it. A permanent, solid weight. Even though he knew he had done nothing wrong, his lungs strained with panic.

"You good back there?"

Warren nodded, rubbed his hand over his ribs. Two years ago, he had driven twelve hours just to see his childhood doctor. It was near the home where his mother still lived, but he had not slowed as he passed her driveway, and instead went straight to the clinic. After he described this constant sensation to the doctor, the old man nodded, pushed a prescription into his palm. "Try it, Warren. What can it hurt?" A very light dose. Warren began swallowing the pills, but after eight days, became preoccupied with edges. Edges of arcs and lines. Edges of dice and countertops and sheets of paper. Edges of spoons and shiny knives. Edges of cliffs. After sixteen days, the anxiety reducer had left him paralyzed with fear, and he flushed the remainder down the toilet. Stayed inside his apartment, often soaking in warm salty water, until his system cleared. When he called the clinic, the doctor said they could try another. "Sometimes it's hit or miss. We need to figure out what works with your brain chemistry, or else you'll have to find a way to cope." "Counting helps," he had told the doctor, and the doctor replied, "If it improves the quality of your life, then why not count?"

They turned right, and soon passed the enormous ice cream statue, with its painted sneer and gloved hands bouncing on rusted springs. Some part of him found greater comfort in the dirty white buildings of the pig farm, the sheltered funnels leading in but not out, and if the air was still, the faintest squealing of nervous swine. As he looked out the window, trying to ignore Detective Reed's gaze, thoughts fired inside his head. Hounding him, too many images, words, his mother's broad face, Sarie's single angry eyebrow, Ms. Fairley's teeth and gums, Amanda's purple fingers, such a deep purple, his father's sopping feet, his peaceful black mollies coursing back and forth in their tank, Detective Reed's irritated stare, Nora, Nora, the musty stench of overcooked vegetables rising up from her soup when she peeled off the lid.

"Stop, just stop," he whispered. He pressed his fingers into his scalp.

"What was that, Mr. Botts? Do you want us to stop?"

Warren grimaced, flicked his head back and forth. He leaned his head against the glass, tried to find something to count, but on the open road, nothing was constant, or predictable. And Detective Reed's earlier statement, swirling around and around his mind. "Would it surprise you, Mr. Botts?" "Would it surprise you?" "Would it?"

He had shaken his head, but no, the page from his notes had not surprised him. He had recognized the real-life application of his challenge question as soon as he entered his backyard. The three pulleys, two fixed, the rope, the branch as the stable structure, Amanda Fuller instead of the cement weight. Someone had recreated it. Someone had been paying attention. Someone besides Evie, of course. She was not capable of hurting someone. He was certain of that.

Crack of thunder, and round drops knocked on the roof of the car. The officer flicked the wipers on full force, and Warren sighed, began counting the number of times they slapped side to side. As they drove over the potholed road, he tried to think of Nora. But even with the numbers ticking away in his lower mind, her happy face would not emerge through the snarl.

When they turned onto the dirt road behind the school, Warren saw a man standing on the edge of the ditch. Leaning against the wooden post of a stop sign. He held his breath as he recognized the plaid shirt, three buttons undone, sleeves rolled up, fabric clinging to his body. On his head, the man wore a faded ball cap, bright orange block letters: *Feed 'n Seed*. Warren was positive he could read those words. Absolutely positive.

Warren pressed his glasses up his nose, and a memory from his childhood fluttered into his mind. He had slept in a small room beside the kitchen. His parents and Beth slept upstairs, and many nights he awoke, alone and afraid. The house shifted, creaked. Finger shadows edged across his walls, and often he heard something enormous skittering and scratching behind the faded sailboat wallpaper. Directly below his head.

If he could not fall back to sleep, which was often the case, Warren would sob, just loudly enough so someone might hear him. Without exception, his father arrived in the doorway. Always his father, never his mother.

"Kinda dark in here, hey, my darling?" his father whispered one night, as he sat down on the edge of the mattress.

"Uh-huh."

"Another dream?"

"Not a dream. Just pictures in my head."

"Tell me your pictures, and I'll take them away."

"You can do that?"

"Yes. Yes, I can."

"Okay." Warren spoke softly into his father's chest. "A fist. I think a man's fist. Holding something. A big worm or a rope. His hand is all dirty."

"Good. I got that one."

"Then there's a box all taped up. He was standing on it. Oh, and a door that's painted really blue."

"Like our basement door?"

"Yes. The same one."

"That's easy. Got it."

"Then there's a picture of steps going down. I can't see the bottom. And spiderwebs up in a corner. A dirty window. I can't see out cause it's got grime on it. Nobody cleaned it."

"They're mine now. Is that all?"

"No. A pair of old socks."

"Old socks?"

"Yes," Warren replied. "Wet and smelly. Grey. A hole in the heel."

"So there are feet in those old socks?"

"Of course, Dad. How else could you see the hole?"

"Well. That's very specific."

"There's other pictures in my head, but I can't remember."

"I'm relieved. That's all I can hold. I have them here, tucked inside my palms."

"How many was it?"

"Seven, I think. Maybe eight."

"Are they heavy in there?" He touched his father's clasped hands.

"Nope. No heavier than a button."

When his father asked him to explain his boyhood fears, Warren said he did not understand them, but when he saw those pictures, he had the sense something was there. Something unpleasant, waiting, and at any moment, he was going to bump into it. Then he would know, and he did not want to know.

"Darkness," his father replied. "That's what those pictures have in common. Though I'm not sure about the woolly socks."

"Oh."

"You know, my darling, when I was your age, I used to be scared of the dark, too."

"Really?"

His father lifted the quilt and slid his body in beside Warren. "Someone once said, I can't remember who, that there's no shame in being afraid of the dark. The real sadness comes when someone fears the light."

Warren was not certain what that meant, but he pressed his body against his father's soft pajamas. Yawning, he inhaled the smell of smoke and spice and earth. He felt his father's hand patting his back, and listened as his deep voice slowly counted the stars.

Hours later, Warren awoke, and his father was still there, elbow bent, chin in his hand. Moonlight streaming through a curtainless window, he could just see his father's features, those pale eyes open, staring at him.

"You sleepy, Dad?"

"No, my darling. I'm not."

"Why aren't you not?"

His father did not reply, but looked away, eyes wet, as they often were. In his expression, Warren saw what he had never noticed before. A worry. Or a secret. As though his father understood something important that Warren had yet to discover.

"You should sleep, Dad. It's almost morning. Do you want me to count for you?"

His father sighed, and said, "No, no. I'm going to enjoy these last few minutes. Last few minutes before light comes."

Warren curled like a bug inside the cup of his father's frame, and watched him as the sun rose and filled the room. Finally, his father's head dropped to the pillow, and he began snoring softly. Warren stared at his father's curled fingers. Those images were in there, he knew, and at the time, he had wondered if he should have given them to his father, or if he should have been a braver boy, and hidden them away for himself.

"Something caught your eye, Mr. Botts?" Detective Reed twisted in her seat. "You were gone there for a bit."

"I'm sorry?"

"You know, spaced out?"

Inhaling, Warren could feel his father, so familiar, so warm, the smell of cotton and dry earth and sunshine, rough hands touching his small cheek, and he felt a sudden and painful pang of false hope. He shifted, peered out the rear window, found the sign in the distance. The place beneath it was empty, as though the person had vanished. Or was never there at all.

"Here we go, Mr. Botts. I'll get that." Detective Reed yanked open the door to the car so Warren could climb out. "Don't go too far," she said before slamming it.

It was dark, and Warren's car was the only one left in the parking lot. In the light of the street lamp, he saw the white line. A deep scratch through the paint. Too thick and irregular to be from a key, it looked as though someone had pulled a jagged piece of shale along the side panel. Perhaps he had driven alongside a wall, parked too tightly against something, and just could not remember. That would not be unusual. He might have been counting, not heard the noise. Though if he had parked, how would he have gotten out? Through the passenger's side? He could not make excuses. Someone had done this on purpose. Damaged his car.

Warren examined the shadows beyond the light, strained to see through the growing darkness. Detective Reed was already gone, and he was alone. He noticed no one, but for the second time that day, he felt unsafe.

17

MY FATHER WAS A WIFE-BEATER. PEOPLE WERE FAIRLY COM-fortable with that. I could tell when they saw my mother at the post office, scrambling for the mail, or at the grocery store, paying with her head down. Her bruised face, long clothes in summer, shaky skinny hands. They frowned, shook their heads. But they accepted. Believed, no doubt, that such an existence was unfortunate. *Shit happens.*

One afternoon, my father was also an almost-wife-killer. A label that might have garnered far more attention, if anyone had known about it.

I remember my father stomping into the house that summer afternoon. A human-sized battle tank, fully loaded. He appeared so out of place in our kitchen, with its rooster wallpaper, shrivelling apples in a bowl. Something had happened before lunch, something about a "lost deal," but I never learned what that was. When he returned home from work, he dropped his brown briefcase, slammed the door, and paced back and forth over the doormat. Rubbing his hand over his stubble, a lock of his greased hair fell over his forehead. I could sense his energy, his jack-in-the-box mood, tinny chords of music almost complete. *Surprise!*

Sitting across from me, his knee joggled, hands tapped. I was aware of his scent. I have always had an extraordinary sense of smell, and this moment I detected something earthy. Yeasty. Almost like mouldy bread. As usual, he didn't look at me. I have no memory of my father ever peering into my face, or speaking my name. Never a "Hallo, my little friend." Or, "Hey, buddy, do you want to toss the ball around? Watch a show?" Around him, I was only vapour. A wisp of exhaust. And a man could not interact with a wisp of exhaust.

Instead of looking at me, my father stared at my plate. Peanut butter and bread, stuck together and torn into consumable pieces. A plastic cup of juice, as milk gave me intestinal pangs. He stared at the string of bunnies chasing each other around the edge of the dish.

"You fed the kid first?"

"You weren't home yet. Child's got to eat." A shaving of force in her voice. Just a shaving.

"What? What did you say?"

My breathing slowed. The clock inside my chest ticked quietly, and evenly. The faintest current moved down my spine.

"I said, almost ready, dear. One sec. Just one sec." She slid the sandwich out of the pan, hacked it into two pieces, dug into a bag of potato chips, dropped them next to the sandwich. A glass of brown soda, sides slick with moisture. "All set. Here you go. It's new cheese. Did you know they made a new kind? I just bought it today. Thicker slices. Not that stuff you can practically read through. Do you want ketchup? The bottle's almost done, but I could add a bit of water?"

Two ways my mother gave away her fear: her voice adopted a canary quality, and she talked way too much.

She hovered over my father. And watched him eat. One forceful bite. A second. A calmer third. And then, boof, a small tuft of offending cat hair stuck inside the melted cheese. It tickled his throat. Made him hack. Snort. Spit onto his plate. (Sounding very much like the offending cat, by the way.) Poking through the chewed lump of goo, he dug out the clump, worked it between his fingers, held it up to his glassy blue eyes.

Snap. Lightbulb bursting.

"Oh my, oh my. I'm so, so, so sorry. I'll make another one. Right away. I've got a fridge full of those slices. Plenty of bread. Don't move. I won't be but a minute."

Rambling, again, but my father did not hear her, and floated up from his chair. Slow motion. Calm. Collected. An onlooker might imagine he was about to kiss her gently on the cheek, refill his glass of soda, admire the shine on his shoes. I watched his fluid movements, understanding that this was when he was most dangerous. A drop of poison snaking through a pitcher of still water.

The hair obviously belonged to my mother's cat. A lanky stray she had adopted before I was born. At that moment, the geriatric tom was lounging on the window ledge, enjoying the lunchtime sun, unaware it had caught someone's focused attention. It extended a thin tabby leg, raked its pink tongue over the inside of its thigh. Dander and dust billowing in the rays of light.

Several long steady strides toward the window, and my father reached the cat. His expression was purposeful, heavy with glee. Scooping the culprit underneath its belly, he stroked its head, said softly, "Now, puss." Then, arm poised, full force, he catapulted it across the room. The cat flew, legs spread, tail straightened. Thunk. It struck the wall. Sound like a hammer hitting a rotten tree. Yellow-brown liquid squirted across the wallpaper, and the sour stench of feline diarrhea filled the room.

I saw my father wipe his hand on his trousers, and when I glanced back, the cat was gone. I never noticed it drop to the ground or skitter away. It vanished the same instant it hit the wall. A cartoon poof into air. It became like me, I considered at the time. Another wisp of exhaust.

My mother cried out, covered her open mouth with spread fingers, a jail over her teeth. She retched, though nothing came out of her.

"Shut it!" The kitchen floor shook as he marched toward her. With each of his steps, I saw concentric circles moving on the surface of my juice. His eyes were so wet, so focused, he appeared almost holy. Sharp religious rage, his fists about to perform a miracle. "Don't you make a sound." A strike to her forehead. "You." Another strike. "Bloody." Knee to her hip. "Bitch."

I lined up my sandwich parts along the edge of my plate. Covering the bunnies. I remember wondering if they might be hungry, and how the bread was so close, yet the bunnies could not touch it. How torturous to be fused to a plate. To have nowhere to run but round and round, face practically pressed into the dirty tail of a brother who would always be ahead. Why would anyone ever design that for a child? A juvenile image of Hell.

He continued assaulting my mother, and not once did I move from my chair, defend her, intervene. I never tried to worm myself between them, my sharp elbows swinging left and right. When she collapsed, and he showered her with kicks, I still never budged from my seat. His fighting leg weakened, face sweating, and eventually he stopped. I realize now he was not in great physical shape. Such a burst of activity had led to exertion.

As he was leaving, he offered his explanation to her. "Is a decent lunch too much to expect? I don't ask for shit from you. Just a fucking lunch. How do you expect me to do anything? No wonder I fucking lost my deal."

Whenever I remembered this, I always pressed pause at that moment. Closed my eyes, and moved through the memory slowly, purposefully. I watched her weep, body shaking, curled like a frightened pill bug on the linoleum floor. There was a smear of blood coming from somewhere. Her mouth? Her nose? Her ear? *Am I afraid? Excited? A marbled swirl of both?* Once I heard the car screech away, I took two steps forward, said, "Mom?" She did not adjust her crying, meet my gaze, or reach out her fingers, letting them waggle in the air between us. Her waving hand saying, *Come here, my good baby.*

She is ignoring me. I understand that now, but at the time of that incident, I did not. I admit, I experienced many childish and embarrassing thoughts. Even wondered if I was invisible to her as well. As I was with my father, I had become that way with her. Was I imagining my heart pumping, my lungs breathing air? Was I a ghost?

I do not exist. I am incapable of offering her comfort or assistance. Because I do not exist.

That realization made me angry. I edged closer, placed the heel of my shoe on her bare foot and pressed down, nipping the very edge of her skin. She squeaked, pulled her knee closer to her chest. "Don't touch me," I heard her mumble, even though her arms covered her face and hands. "Don't touch me." I liked the sound of her desperation. I liked that she acknowledged me.

"Mom."

"I said go."

"Um. Do you want a wet cloth? For your head."

"Just stop, will you? I'll get it myself." Now she was the one sounding irritated, indignant. How quickly roles morph and bend.

"Oh," I replied. "I understand." Though actually I did not.

I stayed beside her and thought about the many times my father injured my mother. The sight of it did not make me sad or anxious or confused. It was simply noise in the afternoon. Noise in the evening. Noise in the middle of the night. No matter the experience, as I have learned, a plastic brain will shift it, squeeze it, shape it, until it eventually becomes natural. Normal. A humdrum form of amusement, even. It was not shocking to witness my father launching the cat across the room, punching holes through the drywall, lifting and slamming chairs. Stabbing a knife so deeply into the countertop, it stood upright and twanged. For him, this was his way to exist, to cope, to manage with the everyday doldrums. Hardly different than those cookie-cutter families who sat side by side, a table without corners, fried chicken and coleslaw neatly arranged on mottled blue plates. Except they kept themselves hidden, their anger locked inside their jaws, while my father held nothing back. Not a word, not an act. He was a container, its bottom full of holes. Everything spiralling in a cloudy eddy, draining down and out. Liquid rage or liquid love. A sloppy sort of mess that always left the man empty.

I did not leave right away. I stood beside my mother until my interest waned. Once my mother was silent, I grew practically numb with boredom. She had brought me into this world, yes, but she was a stranger to me. An unwanted shadow wavering in the doorframe. And by the time I turned my back to her, I felt very little. Perhaps even nothing at all.

18

"JUST BREADCRUMBS," NORA SAID, AS SHE REHEATED SOME chicken pieces in the oven. "Add some herbs, a bit of grated parmesan. Everyone makes such a big deal about cooking, but it's not hard."

"Smells just like, like — what's the name of that place?"

"I know what you mean, War. It does. But it's so much healthier to do it yourself."

Warren was relieved to be inside his own home. Listening to Nora's pleasant banter about recipes. When he had pulled up outside, there were neighbours still gathered in his driveway. And two white vans parked near the curb. One had *Local4* on the side, but he could not make out the text on the other. The same woman as that morning rushed toward him. "Just a few questions about Amanda," she called, as Warren tripped up the front steps. "I have nothing to say," he mumbled. "I told the police everything." As he closed his front door, she called, "Who killed Amanda?"

He had twisted the deadbolt. *Killed Amanda?* Someone might have killed Amanda. Or she could have rigged the whole thing herself. Or it could have been a few of his students, trying to play a prank on him. A prank that went terribly, terribly wrong.

"You look completely worn to bits, War, darling."

"I'll be okay." He kissed her lightly on the cheek.

Over her shoulder, she snapped at Libby, "Can you stop wandering around the kitchen? Haven't you got no homework?"

"Nope to no homework."

"What does that even mean? You got none, or yes, you got some?"

Warren coughed, said, "I think she just meant to say no."

"I know what she meant, War, doll. But it was a simple question, and she replies with attitude. I mean, did you give your mother attitude?"

Warren's heart started to beat. De-dun-de-dun-de-dun. No, he had not given his mother attitude. He gave her nothing. Barely spoke to her, walked around her as though she did not exist. And she had accepted this behaviour. She never tried to change anything, was content for him to mow the lawn, replace the rotten boards on the fence, press seedlings into the turned soil. While she washed the laundry, peeled the potatoes, painted the new boards. Every night, they ate at the same table, Beth chattering incessantly, but other than that, when he entered the room, she stood up and quietly left. His mother had ruined everything. With her apathy, her flatness, her ice-boxed affect, she had destroyed the one thing he had treasured.

"War?"

Only once did she react to him. He was seventeen, and had been standing before the sink, running the water until it was cold. She came up behind him, gasped when she saw he was wearing his father's plaid shirt. A torn Feed 'n Seed cap balanced on his hair. He had found the items in a box in the shed. "You can't. No." She grabbed at him, grabbed at his shirt, and he tried to spin away, but she chased him. Chased him around the thick wooden table, down the hallway, out into the yard. When she caught him, she knocked him to the ground, straddled him, slapped the hat from his head. Gripping his hair in both her fists, she shook his head, just barely missing the earth. "Why do you punish me?" she screamed, her face wet and crazy. "All you've ever done is punish me." It was one of the very few times he had seen her cry. The next morning, he received an acceptance letter in the mail. One hundred and thirty-nine days later, he left his childhood home. And never once went back.

"Warren?"

"What was that?"

"I was going to ask you."

"Oh, right, right. I didn't give her attitude." He glanced at Libby, said, "Nope to no attitude," and caught her smile. Nora said something else, but he closed his eyes for a moment, reached up to touch his head. Strange, there were moments when he could still feel his mother's hands on him. Her fingers knotted deep in his messy hair, tugging at his scalp. It had burned, for certain, but he remembered none of the pain. None of the nauseating dizziness as she shook his skull. Instead, he recalled the curious desire for her to continue. To hold him, however forcefully. To not let go.

When he opened his eyes, Libby was still staring at him. She shrugged, as Nora continued to say something about being responsible.

There actually was science homework, a handful of simple Punnett squares. But Warren did not know what was going to happen tomorrow. Who would be teaching his class? Likely the homework he had assigned would be ignored, forgotten. He did not want to mention yet about the school board's decision to put him on leave. What would Nora think? Would she become fearful? He did not want to lose her.

"I wouldn't worry, Nora," he said, feigning calmness. "I'm sure she's old enough to know her schedule, right, Libby?"

Libby continued to glance at him, and he wondered if she was nervous as well. If she was thinking about what had happened in his backyard. If she had questions. If she suspected him of—He swallowed, tried to erase the thought.

"You okay?" he whispered to Libby. "With, you know, everything?"

"Yeah."

"It's a lot. And it's scary."

"Yeah, strange. Just permanent, you know. Someone there one minute, and gone the next."

"Is Evie okay? Her mother made her leave practice."

"I saw. Don't worry, Mr. Botts. I'm sure she's all right. Her mom is just way protective." Then after a moment, she added, "She hasn't really been herself lately."

Warren nodded. "I noticed. Well, I hope she gets better."

"Yeah. I do, too."

"Do you want to play checkers?" Warren could see Libby was upset. He wanted to count something, but there was too much movement in the kitchen, too much chatter, and he could not focus. "Scrabble?" Perhaps she was closer to Amanda Fuller than he knew. Maybe they were good friends. The whole thing was such a shock. While he knew he should try to talk to her further, he did not want to ask. What if he said the wrong thing again? What if he made her cry? What if Nora gripped her daughter by the wrist and walked out the door? "Cards? Rummy, or something? I think we have a bit of time." In a lower tone, "We could do the Punnett squares together. It's super simple. But," he thought of Ms. Fairley, telling him not to come back to the school, "I wouldn't really worry about them."

Libby stopped at the back window, curtain pulled aside. She pointed at the tree. At the streams of tape that lost their glow as the sun descended. "That's where it happened?"

Warren stood beside her. Libby was tall for her age, all skin and bone, and would soon outgrow her mother. "It's best not to look."

"I don't mind. I'm not squeamish."

"Still. It might give you nightmares."

"I rarely dream."

Lucky you.

She folded her arms across her chest. "A lot of kids are talking about it."

"I know, I know." Stephen circled his leg, leaving a line of hair clinging to his trousers. There were almost sixty thousand hairs per square inch on Stephen's back, even more on his stomach. Warren had read that somewhere, though he could not recall. Who had taken the time to make such an estimate? Someone like him, he guessed.

"And the more they talk, the worse it gets. It's almost like a story."

Stephen was a polydactyl cat. Six toes on his front paws.

Warren often thought they looked like opposable thumbs. "Maybe that's what they want. A story. So it's not real."

"Yeah."

"I guess that's the way some people handle things. Cope." He wanted to tell her that if the mind was unable to absorb something, it twisted, coloured, muted it into an absorbable form. That was something he could understand.

"I get it, Mr. Botts."

"It's not bad." He touched the frames of his glasses. "Just the way some minds work."

"Some of them are talking about Adrian. Did you know he had a sister, and they came and took her away?"

"Who did?"

"I don't know. Whoever comes and takes kids."

"That's a shame."

"Not really. She was really messed up. She had this enormous tricycle, and he used to pull her around with a rope. I saw him. He had the rope tied to the handlebars."

"Well, that's nice. Being a good brother."

"Not really, Mr. Botts. One time her hair got caught in the spokes and he didn't stop pulling her until she was tight against the wheel."

"Oh." Fingers to his lips. "Oh."

"And another time, he knocked her over when it rained, and left her there, her face in a puddle."

"Libby!" Nora yanked on oven mitts. "Where did you hear something so vulgar? And to repeat it?"

"I don't know. I hear it around."

"Well, try to unhear it around. I'm sure the girl could've got up and walked away, like any normal person." She shook herself slightly, then clapped her oven mitts together. "Now. Dinner's almost ready. Libby? Get the paper plates from my bag." Then, to Warren, "I brought a package. Just makes life easier."

"Where's your bag?" Flat tone.

"I can help," Warren said. What size package had she brought? Twenty-five? Fifty? He would count them, one by one. "How about I set the table, if you want to feed the fish? The guppies have already eaten, but the lambchops are hungry."

"Lambchops?"

"Rasboras. That's what I call them. See the pattern on their sides?" He pointed at one of the tanks. "Doesn't it look like tiny lambchops?"

"Not really, Mr. Botts." Leaning forward, she squinted. "But I guess some people have a good imagination."

Warren looked out the window. In the slanting light, he could barely make out the yellow scar on the tree where the branch had been severed. A single point in the universe, vanishing. But he could still see Amanda there, hanging by her neck, the navy pompom on her stocking hat rolling back and forth as the wind slid over her shoulder. As he watched her body, her legs began to flick, as though she were running in place, kicking up grass and leaves, and when she opened her dead eyes, waved at him, Warren very nearly lifted a guilty hand to wave back. "Yes," he said. "Imagination. Some people do."

[19]

"EVERYONE IS WEARING WHITE!" I HEARD MY AUNT CHEEP, AS Button and I were coming down the stairs. "Isn't that so classy? A summer send-off party. And if Harv makes a good impression, they might take him on in the business."

"Good impression? Aren't they his family?" My ignorant mother.

"Confusing, right? He did hit some bumpy patches back a ways. Before he got tangled up with me." Pops of laughter. "They need to see he's changed. Reliable. Responsible. That kind of crap. He wants back in the fold." Pumping the air with her fist, "Back in the fold, baby."

"Oh."

"But he can do it. He's real good right now. And Christ, there's a fortune to be made."

129

"Sounds like a lot of pressure on him. Are you sure you want the kids? Button, sometimes, can be, you know. A handful."

"If I didn't want the kids, I wouldn't take them. It's good to show how patient Harvey is now. How much he enjoys regular life."

I walked into the mudroom wearing faded jean shorts, a navy t-shirt. Button wore a polka-dotted bikini underneath a pink sundress, and I had pulled her feather hair into two side ponytails. After looking us over, my aunt frowned, and Button held up one foot, stabbed an enthusiastic finger toward her sneaker. Which was dirty grey, though was once white.

"Jesus." Eye roll. "Do you got anything else? It's a white party, not a polka-dot-navy-crap-t-shirt-shitty-footwear party."

"She hates your sneakers." My breath in Button's ear. "Thinks they're ugly."

"I — I didn't know," my mother stammered. "They can change."

"No time. We're already late. Harvey hates this formal garbage." My aunt touched her hair, glanced at herself in the mirror. Red lips. Even I knew they were too red. And bleeding outside the lines. She placed her hands on her hips, hands off her hips, back on her hips. "No one will be looking at them anyway." She jammed sunscreen into a plastic grocery bag, two threadbare yellow towels, audibly crisp from drying on the line. "Can you buggers move any slower? Your Uncle Harv got the engine running. Wasting gas."

"See soon," Button sang, and hugged our mother.

"Bye, Kiddle," my mother said to me, her fingers grazing my head. "Have a fun time."

To eliminate that vile sensation of her touch, I rotated my shoulder, the fabric of my t-shirt scraping over my ear. When I left the house, I did not look back. I knew she was in the doorway waving at us. Such theatrics upon leaving the house had always annoyed me. It was for the neighbours, of course. Someone was always watching. My mother knew as well as I did that Button and I were going to be puppets for the afternoon. A fill-in family. We were not going to war. We were not going to die. She did not need to wave.

Inside the car, Button pressed in close to me. Her arm against my arm was slippery with sweat, and she pushed her cheek against my shoulder, tiny mouth buckling, my cotton shirt absorbing her drool. I had to keep a grip on her, as she was actually shaking with excitement. While Larva skidded around the corners, she tilted her head, looked up at me. Gently blinking. Giraffe eyelashes, pale glassy eyes telling me she trusted me. I did not know it at the time, but I should have heeded her gaze. Taken it seriously. Taken better care of her.

On our way to Larva's sister's, my aunt twisted in the front seat, faced us. "Best behaviour, right? I don't even got to say it." Her words slid out alongside a thin stream of cigarette smoke. "This is Harv's sister's we're talking about."

"Un-cah Lahvee's?"

"Yes, yes. This is not some trailer park we're going to. These are fancy people. Real fancy! So, watch yourselves." With her knuckles, she struck the air vent, ashes from her cigarette tumbling to the floor of the car. "Gawd, Harvey. This thing's giving off no cool whatsoever. My underwear is right stuck to my ass."

"It's nice to have a second aunt," I added innocently. "The more family the better."

"Aundie Lahvee Sisdah," Button squealed, "Aundie Lahvee Sisdah." I was proud of my protégé, could have patted the little chick on the head.

"Christ, no." Pinched in her fingers, the cigarette circled at high speed. "She is not your aunt. You hear me? Not. Your. Aunt. You will address her with respect. No, scratch that. Don't talk to her at all. Not a peep. Don't even look at her. Don't even look at her feet. If you need anything, and you won't, you talk to me. Or you talk to Harvey. Understood?"

"So bossy," I whispered into Button's ear. "Acts like we're sloppy pigs."

"No, no, dey nice. Dey nice." Button smoothed her hand over mine.

As the drive dragged on, Button pressed her side further into mine, and without looking at her, I could sense that her oversized head was nodding. "How much longer?" I asked, but neither of those losers responded. At some point I heard Button snoring and puffing. I could feel the dampness of her drool on my arm. Outside the window, I noticed the streets were becoming cleaner, trees taller, and larger homes further apart. No garbage or yellow spots on the perfect lawns. No discoloured stain on the cement around the shiny fire hydrant. I wondered if any of the asshole homeowners had animals, and if so, where did they urinate? Just before I could open my mouth to ask this vital question, we pulled into the circular driveway of a two-storey. Yellow siding, black shingles, sweet red door. The trees were trimmed into neat cones and globes, and two potted ferns sat on the front steps. Everything was symmetrical, perfect. I hated the house instantly.

A reedy woman with whip-straight bleached hair swept across the grounds. She wore a long strapless sundress, white, of course, and white square sunglasses. Her chest was an alarming freckled tan. First impression revolved around three words: *chemicals, cancer,* and *cunt.* She reminded me of an expensive mannequin with movable joints. "Ah, brother, dear. You've finally made it." She touched his elbow, angled her chin toward my aunt. "And who did we bring this time?"

Larva cleared his throat, stammered, while my aunt gripped my wrist, painted nails digging in. "This is my family," she said, and she stroked the top of Button's head. Button smiled, cupped and pinched her crotch. I tore my wrist away and gazed at the ropy skin on the woman's neck, her necklace of flat green stones. "Should that not be white?" I asked.

The bonebag ignored me, gestured toward Button. "Does the child need to use the facilities?"

"What?" My aunt.

"The little one. She's—she's—I mean, we won't have that in the pool."

My aunt turned to look, "For goodness sake, Button, sweetheart," then slapped the hand. "Stop it!"

"Yes, well. Come along," the stick said. "Everyone is already here."

My aunt and I followed dutifully behind Larva, while Button skipped, twirled, pranced, tiptoed. Once freed from the cigarette-smoke chamber of the car, she was erupting with energy, ready to moult.

"We've hired a couple of local teens," Scrawny announced. "To monitor the young ones as they swim. We can actually relax. Have a drink. And catch up."

"Yes, a drink. Harvey's been doing a ton of work." My

aunt's voice had crawled up several watery octaves, and I could hear her slurp saliva.

"Is that so?"

"He's got to be the smartest person I know."

"C'mon. Look. Leave it." Larv's articulate response.

Once in the backyard, Button bounced away, and I retreated up the stairs to a raised deck. My stomach was still churning from the car ride, and I took deep breaths so the nausea would pass. Sometimes I despised my body. My own physical shortcomings were pathetic, annoying.

I sat down on the stained wood, and watched. Even though I was right above them all, my presence was disguised by two terracotta planters. The planters were filled with variegated ivy and red geraniums. So traditional, to the point of bordering on banal. I plucked petals and squished them into the lattice, leaving red streaks. Some parts of the deck were peeling, lifting, and with my fingernails, I worked away what I could, let the curls of wood drop through the slats. This exercise was unsatisfying, but it did distract me from my stomach woes.

Spying on the crowd below, I saw several children splashing, screaming, probably pissing in an aqua-coloured pool. Adults clung to a table covered in white cloth, wine bottles, warm fruit, sweating smelly cheese. They were chattering like squirrels, smoking cigarettes, gulping from long-stemmed glasses. And, of course, they were all dressed like moronic angels. The men in white shorts and pressed shirts, the women in flowing white dresses, sheer blouses, basic sandals.

And then, my aunt. The angel whore. Although wearing white, she must have greased her body before she slid into that second, paler skin. It was amusing to see her so out of place, a bloated pear in the apple bowl. Tight jeans, tight shirt with a deep neckline. Hint of yellowing in certain areas, and a classy grey line of sweat on her back. Even from my position, I could hear the exposed nail on the bottom of her cheap white heel scraping the flagstone. Curiously, Larva remained beside her, even occasionally touched her damp spine with his hand. The only reason for this had to be his supreme asininity. Or else he was rendered immobile by a broken flip-flop. His doting behaviour was incomprehensible.

Right beneath the upper porch where I was stationed, the hosts had arranged a children's area. Dishes of dye-riddled candies, disgusting red chips, cheezies, cookies, large bottles of brightly coloured soda. Button had no interest in swimming, and was perched beside the food. Of course. To say she enjoyed junk was an understatement. Her dress had disappeared, and she was wobbling about in a skewed, overstretched bikini. I followed her movements as she skulked around the table, trying to ram as much as possible into her mouth before someone told her to stop. She circled then, like a scolded puppy, only to return moments later, pushing more into her mouth. Revelling in near-limitless access. There was an actual trail of debris marking her path. Then, with unsteady hands, she filled a tall plastic glass with orange liquid. Gulped it down, refilled. Clutching the overflowing glass, she finally left the crap-food table. Her stomach, jutting out over her bikini, appeared inflated. *Way to show some control, Button.*

The speed of what transpired after Button's sugar binge was astounding.

Beverage in hand, she was weaving in and out of the adults, her carbohydrate-induced cackle cutting through the chatter. She was talking non-stop at high speed. While it may have sounded like gibberish to others, I knew she was searching for me. *She was searching for me.* A fact I cannot forget, though I have often tried to erase it from the narrative. I heard her saying my name. Over and over again.

Instead of revealing my location, I pushed in closer to the planter, slid down behind the geraniums. I was not in the mood to be the one to twist the cup from her hand, wash her disgusting face. Force her to sit and breathe while she was wired, frenetic, bursting out of her skin. Music thrumming in the air, she danced among the adults in her undersized bikini, half of her backside and her fatty breasts exposed, distended belly smeared with candy dye.

"Isn't she sweet?"

"Oh, yes, yes, but someone should clean her. Should they not?"

"Can she not clean herself? At that size?"

"Oh, dear."

"Do you remember those troll toys with the big guts and wild hair? I had one as a pencil topper."

"Whoa, whoa. Watch it there, little one."

"Can we get one of the teen helpers over here? Hell-oh?"

"Who *does* she belong to?"

"Jesus, she is so goddamn hyper." I recognized my aunt's voice. "Harv? Harveeee?"

Button continued, fluttering among the recoiling adults. I even heard her belch. Slap her stomach. Laugh maniacally. I had never seen her more *jubilant*, as the doctor would say, than those moments when she twisted and twirled, high on empty carbohydrates and artificial dyes. My sister was happy, full of joy and summer love, until she and her drink-filled hand slammed right into the sinewy body of Aundie Lahvee Sisdah.

SOMETHING SLAMMED AGAINST HIS FRONT DOOR. A THUD THAT made Stephen jump, water from his bowl sloshing onto the floor. Warren knew what it was. The local newspaper, several sheets of articles and advertisements wrapped around three pounds of flyers. Complimentary garbage.

Warren had told the boy, time and time again, he did not want it. Just to skip his house. "Call it in," the boy said. "I did," Warren had replied. "Left a message. No one calls me back." "Not my problem," he said, swinging another deadly bundle through the air.

"It's okay, Stephen." Warren opened the fridge and removed a thin strip of raw meat. He dropped it onto the floor, and rubbing his fingers together, he coaxed the cat out from under the table. "Here," he said. Stephen edged toward the prize and took the meat in his jaws. He chewed until tears dripped from his eyes, moistened his black and white face.

Last night, after Nora and Libby left, Warren had unplugged his phone. Now he noticed the red light on the answering machine was flashing, a repeating pattern. One, two, three messages. Thumb hovering over the button, he flinched, then pushed.

Sarie's voice filling the room. "Warren, Warren? Are you there?" Then a long beep, and her voice again. "Get back to me, darling. Really. Please. I didn't mean to sound harsh on Sunday. You know me. It's important. If you're in touch with your sister, I need to talk to her, too." Warren's mind spat out the exact number of days since he had spoken to Beth.

Another beep. The sound of air sucked through teeth. And then Detective Reed's voice. "Oh, hi, Mr. Botts. Can you come in this morning? We have a—"

He did not need to hear the rest. He felt as though he was being given an opportunity to repair things, and he must hurry down to the station. Obviously people's grief had morphed into anger, and they were misplacing blame. Directing it toward Warren. Which made very little sense — she was his student, yes, and found in his backyard, but beyond that there was no reason anyone should be treating him any differently. After dressing quickly, he filled Stephen's bowl and fed his fish. He would go and talk to Detective Reed. Straighten everything out.

When he stepped out into dull morning, he saw the paper. He crouched, turned it over. There was a small school photo of Amanda on the front page, an elastic band distorting her features, one eye lower than the other. Next to her photo was a picture of him. Plaid shirt, grey tie, solemn expression, taken from a pamphlet the university had produced for his department. He had no idea how anyone would have obtained that photo, but there he was. Side by side with Amanda.

He paused, wiped his hands on his jacket, then kicked the paper to the corner of his porch. It slid underneath a mound of dried leaves. Hidden from view.

"Sorry about the room." Detective Reed leaned across the metal table, took a sip from an oversized mug. "Again. Very sterile, I know."

"It's okay." He could smell coffee on her breath.

"There's just so much commotion outside. Desks are full. Small town, we are, but no shortage of issues."

"I understand. It's okay."

There was a donut on a blue napkin, and one of her fingers rested on top of it. She shook her head slightly, said, "It's a terrible addiction. Me and anything sweet." Two hefty bites, white powder tumbled onto her blouse. "Now, Mr. Botts, we just have a few more things we need some clarity on. Or should I call you Dr. Botts?"

"Please. I prefer Mr." He shifted in his seat.

"Got it. I spoke with Ms. Fairley. Your principal? And she told us about your education. Impressive."

Warren blinked. The room was full of right angles. There was nothing to count. He desperately wanted to tap out a rhythm with his foot.

"Not every day you meet a PhD around here. Can you tell me about it?"

"There's not a whole lot to tell." He had worked in a tiny lab at the university, with a group of developmental biologists. All of whom were better at the game of academia than he was. Massaging their results, minimizing their shortcomings, getting their names on papers, selling their research to those who held the purse. "Some biology stuff."

"Not physics?"

"No."

"I was confused. I thought. Your cat and all."

"My cat?" Warren pressed his glasses against his face, once, twice.

"You know. Stephen Hawking. Your physicist friend in a fur suit?"

"Oh, yes. Stephen. I started out in physics, but I shifted. I became less interested in studying abstractions and models, and more interested in living things. How things grow, change, adapt. I met my first bichir as a graduate student." He would not tell her that he had shifted focus as he needed to escape the constant barrage of numbers. He had no control over his counting then, and it was exhausting. His mind continually considering, calculating, identifying patterns.

"That a monkey?"

"No, no. It's a fish, actually, a small fish."

"You spent years of your life studying a fish?" She glanced down at her chest, brushed the powder from the fabric.

"Well, it's a fish that has lungs. And gills, too. But the lungs are what make it interesting. They can live in water, but can also adapt to living on land. When they're raised on land, the way their skeleton grows changes, their gait adjusts. They—" He noticed her eyes darting back and forth, and he stopped talking.

"I don't understand the point. Why do they need both?"

She began clinking her nails against the metal table, and Warren realized his descriptions were boring. Perhaps he was not explaining it properly.

"Adaptation," he said, slowly and quietly. "If the water's

oxygen-poor, they can breathe through the air. If they need, they can move from one pool to the next." Touching the rim of his glasses. "Kind of scoot over."

"Too bad people can't do that."

"I'm sorry?" He reached up, lifted his glasses.

"Scoot over. If your home is shit. Just scoot over to something better." She grinned, slurped her coffee. "Seriously though, Mr. Botts, how did you go from studying land fish to teaching grade eight science in the middle of nowhere? Substitute teacher seems like a step back, don't you think?"

"It just sort of happened. My adviser is Ms. Fairley's brother. Dr. William Fairley."

"Small world."

"Not really. I met her at his house. She was up visiting for a weekend. She told him about her problems with the school, no teacher. He just up and walked out. And I offered to help."

"That's a mighty big offer. Why would someone do that?"

"I don't know, Detective Reed. I can't say." But he did know. The departmental politics was sludge around his ankles, and he no longer felt as though he were doing something real. Exploring or learning. If only he could be left alone to study his small friends, examine the way they flapped across the sand, lifting their heads, he might have been happier. "I was bored?"

"You make that sound like a question."

He could not tell her there was also something beyond that. The money. Teaching paid better than research assistant. He was saving every penny he could, refilling his envelope for Beth. To help her recover. If she ever wanted that.

"No, no. I just thought to do something different. A change. Thought it would be, well, interesting."

"And is it?"

He pressed his knees together, until his bones ached. "Certainly not this part," he said, volleying a joke toward her. Her face remained flat, not even a hint of a grin. Warren swallowed. "I didn't mean to offend you, Detective Reed. Not that your company is, well, the chairs are—" Stammering. "I mean, it's cold in here."

"No, no. I understand. It's an inconvenience, right?"

"Yes, well." He wanted to tell her the metal rim of the chair was cutting into his thoracic vertebrae. That he had a sharp pain just behind his right temple. That the blandness of the room upset him, made his mind feel distorted, confused. There was nothing he could identify to count. "I mean. It's fine."

Head tilting backward, eyebrows lifting. "A girl is dead, Mr. Botts. We can't forget that, right? And in your backyard. And with some whacked-out science set-up that must be *very* familiar to you. So while it's inconvenient, I hope you understand it's also necessary."

Warren flushed again, the pink of embarrassment, not pride. He tried to ignore the pain in his spine.

"Did you ever notice the pulleys and things attached to the tree, prior to Sunday morning?"

"No."

"Could they have been there for long?"

"I don't know. I mean, I never saw them. Were they rusty? I never spent much time back there. I think I would have seen them."

"We got an expert evaluating everything. Did I mention that? He's going to assess the branch, the equipment, the photos."

Warren leaned forward, brought his pale hands back to the table. "That sounds expensive."

"You said it. But, well. When you're dealing with a child. A young girl. No stone unturned, right?"

"I could. If you wanted me to, of course. You know. Offer my opinion. I can, and I don't mind."

Detective Reed glanced over her shoulder at the mirror on the wall behind her. Then she smiled, thin and practised. "That's kind of you, Mr. Botts. But no—no thank you. I don't think that's, um. No thank you." Audible slurps, close-mouthed belch, and she patted her mouth. "Besides. We won't have to wait long. Someone who knows someone is calling in a favour. I got no idea, but it shouldn't take long."

"Oh."

"But, Mr. Botts? There was something I wanted to talk to you about. With Amanda. We've received some preliminary information. She had something in her mouth. Placed there, we believe."

Warren shook his head, but the image was locked in his mind. *Zooming in.* Her stretched jaw, frozen froth on her lips, a white crumple bunched and pressed into her face. "I didn't see anything."

"Well, it was a test. A science test. Recently completed."

Shaking his head again. He saw the test in her hands as she sat on his front step, crying, then shoving it into her backpack. He felt her arms around his waist, squeezing him. "You're better than him," she had said. "Way better." He had forgotten that. Forgotten that she had rushed toward him, hugged him.

"Odd, that's all." Another peek over her shoulder. "You know, girl hanging from science set-up in backyard of science teacher, I mean science substitute, with science test rammed in her mouth." She bit her cuticle, plucked the piece from her teeth. "Seems odd, doesn't it? I mean, like all of it should mean something, don't you agree?"

He did not know how to respond, other than to nod, say it was odd. Horrible and odd. That he could not fathom what it all meant.

"Mr. Botts, has anyone been in touch with you?" She stared at the sliver of wet skin on her fingertip.

"No. No one." Besides Sarie, and he had still not returned her call. "Who do you mean? Who would be in touch?"

"Channel Four has contacted us. Has done so several times. They haven't contacted you?"

Warren thought of one of the vans outside his house, but shook his head, grimaced as Detective Reed flicked her cuticle.

"People are curious. If they do, you know, reach out to you, do us all a favour, and just don't respond. Do you understand? That's the best advice we can give you. Just don't engage. They may be local, but that doesn't mean they're not hungry."

"Hungry?"

"Wanting a story."

"Oh."

"This is not something that happens around here, Mr. Botts. Maybe you're used to hearing about this sort of perversion in the big city and all, but our lives are more on the quiet spectrum of things."

The quiet spectrum.

"I've never heard that term before."

"Yeah, well. We live simple lives is what I meant. We go to church, Mr. Botts. We leave our doors unlocked. We eat a lot of pork. And ice cream, of course, though not often together." She scraped her chair back, and stood up. "If you think of anything else, you got my number, right, Botts?"

"I do." He was about to stand up when he thought about

his student Adrian Byrd, the healing marks that tracked across his face, his unsettling comments about pain. "Detective Reed?" He considered Libby's story, saw the oversized tricycle, toppled, a girl's face in the water, puffing like a landed fish. Adrian bending, gripping the pedal, cranking his arm as strands of thin hair coiled around the metal. Pulling the girl closer and closer. Her muddy scalp tightening, then a fissure forming, a cracking sound, the peeling of adhesive tape. Adrian looking up at him and smiling.

"Yup."

He lifted his left hand, and knocked his forehead with his knuckles. "No, nothing," he said. It was a story. A story. Passed on from tongue to tongue. A boy was not capable of that cruelty. A child was not to blame for this. "I forget. I forget what I was going to say."

[21]

THE GLASS SLIPPED FROM BUTTON'S TINY GRIP, AND THE ELEC-tric orange soda flew up and out, spattering the woman's face, neck, dress, shoes. Alert, I sat up straight, my cheeks pressed to the wooden bars. The human stick was covered, head to toe, in abstract stains. Pretty stains, yes, unique organic blotches, but she screamed, "Who let this thing back here?" Her clothes were clearly ruined, and I wondered if her bleached hair would suck up the permanent colour. That would be a charm.

My loser aunt moaned and dropped her head back so far, I could see the ridges of her trachea on her throat. "Fuh-uh-uck, Button! Seriously? You are bee-yond fuh-ucking dumb." Then she tried to pat Stick down with napkins, but Stick shoved her hand away, turned, and scuttled into the house. The crowd was silent, and my aunt addressed them,

"I'm so, so sorry. Harvey? Harv? Jesus. I am so, so, so sorry for this. Did anyone else get messed? It was an accident. An accident. We'll pay for dry cleaning, right, Harv? She's got something wrong with her, you know. She's not a normal kid. She's been retarded since she was born. I just try to take her when I can. To help the girl's mother. Me and Harv, helping her. Just a woman overwhelmed. I'm trying to help. Let me know who needs dry cleaning. Harvey? I'm so, so, so sorry."

She reminded me of my mother then, over-talking, over-demonstrating, and as I listened, I ground my teeth. Irritated, yes, but also *so, so, sooo* pleased to see her squirm.

Larva never spoke. He popped the joints in his knuckles, a loud snap in his neck, and floated calmly toward Button. "Come with me," he whispered with a familiar softness, took her wrist in a two-finger pinch. At that moment, I thought of my father. His unreadable expression, fury disguised by a breath of cordiality. As I was witnessing this, seeing both mother and father representations, my head felt somewhat woozy, severed from its core. I should have worn a ball cap. The sun was too strong on my skull.

With his beefy mitt under Button's arm, he lifted her so her toes barely skittered over the cement as they marched toward the treat table. I considered that his bicep must be substantial, as Button was no wilting daisy. "Buddun sahwee," she repeated, as she was trained to do. "Buddun sahwee sahwee." And she smiled at everyone, mouth, lips, and gums practically glowing.

No reaction, as though her words dissolved in the air around him. Unopened bottle of soda in his fist, he directed my sister away from the crowd, brought her closer to the balcony where I was seated. I had an excellent view. Then he twisted the cap off with his teeth, spat it, handed the entire two litres to Button. She gripped it against her stomach, and then he bent toward her, whispered something into her ear. I could hear very clearly what he said. "You want it that bad? Do you? Do you? You fat fucking pest." Button remained cheerful. "Oday, oday. Un-cah Lahvee. Need cup?" I could see she was trying to continue smiling. Still trying to see kindness everywhere. Stupid flowerchild style. Still clinging to her peace and summer love shit.

He whispered something else, ". . . kidding me . . . every last drop . . ." and as he retreated to the adult table, he wiped his hand on his white pants. The hand that had touched Button. My aunt circled around, rubbed the loser's back, and he shrugged like he had taken care of things. It was just another day.

Button remained in that spot and began sipping straight from the bottle. She sipped and sipped, and only stopped to murmur, "Sahwee, sahwee, sahwee, sahwee," at high speeds.

I did not intervene. I watched my sister trying to drink a full bottle of soda, and I deliberately did nothing. I thought the experience would turn her. Once we were home, we would dissect the incident at length, and I would explain that the spilled drink was an honest mistake. No one was actually injured, no animals were harmed in the making of said mess. Someone should have been monitoring her more closely. It was not her fault. Besides, Wafer-Lady surely had a matching dress hanging in her richy-rich closet. People like that do not deserve to live. Who do they think they are? I would say all of those things to Button. Treating her like that. The woman was a cunt, I would tell her, reminding her not to repeat that particular word in front of an adult. A foul yeasty cunt. I knew it when I laid eyes on her. Button would learn this decisive skill. Slits of darkness would penetrate the glitter inside her mind.

As I watched her struggle, I actually felt delighted. This just might be the kick-start we needed. *Thank you, treat table.*

Away from the crowd, Button began to whimper. But she was obedient, and continued drinking. Gulp after gulp, I could see her neck bobbing. She reminded me of a photograph I once saw in a library book. Culinary arts around the world. A *foie gras* duck, pipe shoved down its throat, except Button was being stuffed with dye and water, not grains and fat. I could see her pressing her starfish hand into her stomach.

Glancing around, she tipped the bottle on its side. Slightly, slightly, until a thin stream of soda began to dribble out onto the concrete. Larva was beside her in a flash, righting the bottle, telling her through clenched teeth, "Think I'm stupid? Spill another drop, and you'll get a fucking full bottle." My aunt had slithered over. "Seriously, Button. Show some respect to your Uncle Harv."

I leaned my head against the railing. Yes, after this experience, I would have the material to alter Button. To twist her white-light insides, introduce shadows into her heart. I had been working on her for years, and the thought of progress excited me. What an intense rush that would be when it happened. If it happened. So far, no matter what words I slipped into her ear, no matter how I tainted a memory, she had remained purely good, incapable of anger or malice. Her innocence was confounding, and beginning to grow quite boring, to say the least. The game had gotten old, but here was our dear family handing me an overflowing dish of cruelty. If this did not make Button despise them, there was no hope for her.

I heard her mumbling in a low voice, "Un-cah. Un—" She belched loudly, rubbed her stomach. Button continued sipping, even though she was keening, "Un-cah Lahvee, pleadz. Id hurd hurd, hurd bad. Id hurd me." Bent at the waist, she gripped her middle. Orange snot spilled from her nostrils. She glanced around, discovered me observing from the upper porch. I knew she wanted me to step in, but I did not meet her gaze. I knew she was looking for my permission to walk away, and I would not give it to her.

Even though my sister was in distress, the festivities continued. Surely they were aware of Button, but none of the adults ever glanced in her direction. If a person covers his eyes, a repugnant scene will vanish, will it not? I have always found this toddler mindset bewildering. So many grown-ups were the same as my sister. They could not grasp the notion of object permanence. Never understood that the *button, button* was simply hidden inside of a palm. Instead, they circled back to the wine table, refilled their glasses, created a white noise of voices to drown out Button's distress. One busied himself with a pot-bellied charcoal grill. Skinny Bitch had returned in a fresh (white) outfit, strikingly similar to the first, her damp hair knotted on top of her head.

Button lifted the massive plastic container again. And again. She had almost consumed the entire contents.

Then I saw her stop. She lowered the bottle, and lifted her round filthy face, stared up at me. For a moment, she tilted her head, and smiled. A tiny smile. An innocent, happy, grateful smile. As though I had given her something precious. And she wanted me to know she loved me for it. Loved me best of all.

I closed my eyes. Waited. In that moment, I decided I would stop the game. I would saunter down there and take charge of the situation. Yank the orange soda from her stained fingers, throw the remainder into the pool. See what asshole Larva and my idiot aunt had to say about that. Who the hell did they think they were? Button belonged to me. One hundred percent. They had no right to make her suffer. This pathetic bullshit attempt at displaying authority had gone on long enough.

When I opened my eyes again, Button was no longer looking at me. Her head was drooping, arms limp. She had dropped the bottle, the last of the soda bubbling and tumbling from the narrow opening. Her dimpled knees crumbled, and she flumped onto the concrete deck. For a moment she was still, but then her swollen body began to spasm. I leapt up. This was not what I had expected. Children continued to splash and yelp in the pool. Enjoying themselves. Detached laughter cutting through the chatter as Button convulsed. Her back arching off the cement, neck cricked, eyes rolling backward. I heard choking sounds, like fingers snapping.

I bolted down the stairs. Elbowed through the drunken wave of grown-ups that was moving closer. I knelt down beside my sister. She was stiller than she had ever been, and I knew instantly she was not there. Gone. I pumped her chest until her ribs cracked underneath my fists. Tangerine foam and brilliant strings of saliva rose up through her tiny mouth, bubbled out of her nostrils. Her chest was sticky. She smelled like a candy store. I put my ear to her mouth, heard the delicate crackling of carbonation, but nothing else.

"Button." I spoke directly into her wrinkled ear. Quietly, but with masculine authority. "Don't you do this. Don't. Don't you dare." I brought my fists straight down on her sternum, yelled as loudly as my throat could manage. "I will hate you, Button. Hate you! I swear I will hate your stupid guts if you leave."

"Stoppit!" My aunt behind me. "Stoppit now! Babe? Babe? Do something!"

Larva yanked me up, pinned my arms behind me. I kicked backward, bony heel connecting with his shin. An inch above the band of his fucking white sock. Satisfying pain reverberated through my foot. I flailed and hissed. My aunt's face contorted, black makeup dripping over her cheekbones. She tried to touch me and I bit her hand. Brought my teeth down through the soft pinch of flesh.

She squeezed her hand, yipped, began to cry. "Stoppit! Stoppit, will you? Stoppit." Gentler now.

Someone was on a phone. I heard the words. Heard the intonation. A bald man was hovering over Button. Pushing back her lopsided bangs, pressing on her chest, sweeping the insides of her mouth, trying to find a pulse. "How—how can this?" he stuttered. "A healthy child." The man tried to push air into her mouth. I saw his scalp, freckled and peeling. After forever, he sat back on his heels, swiped his face with his shirttail. Shook his head from side to side.

"She's gone, Kiddle. Oh my, oh, oh. Oh, good—good Jesus. What will we tell your mother? She's gone."

Button. The one who was mine. Inside that sticky barrel chest, her heart was silent. Her floating heart. Her spotless heart. Her perfect wondrous heart.

Something ripped open inside my head, a thousand hands reaching up and yanking. Threads of me were screaming, but I stood, motionless, expressionless, only blinking, blinking, while a putrid cavity formed. I could not see. I could not see. I think I might have been shaking. Revulsion and disgust seeped out into my chest cavity, and I could not take a breath.

"Say something, Kiddle. Say something!"

22

"**J**ESUS, WARSIE. YOU GOT SO MUCH SHIT JAILED IN HERE. IS THIS legal?"

The moment Warren rushed in through his front door, he knew she was there. Her scratchy voice, yes, but before that, her smell. It was the stench of something that lived outside, underneath an old deck or plank of rotting wood. Something decaying had grown legs, found its way in.

"Beth?" Poking his head through the door, he said, "Is that you?" He saw his little sister lying on her side on his kitchen floor, skeleton body facing his fish tanks. His mouth went dry. Had she fallen down? Was she dying right there on the linoleum?

"You need that many, Wars?" she yelled to him, then rolled onto her back, arms out at her sides. "Does it make you feel powerful? To lord over all those fish?"

"Hi." Standing beside her, he did not stop to remove his shoes. "Beth. You okay?"

"What's okay?"

"You?"

Her eyes were sunken, unfocused. She blinked. Hard. "Who knows?"

"Do you—"

"I like your collection. I like your fish. I like the plants, too. The plants are nice. Really nice. All underwater like that. Drifting a bit. They can just relax. Zone out. And just let their leaves float. Man, that sounds beautiful."

"Thank you," he said softly.

"It looks happy in there. Peaceful. In the tanks. Right, Wars? Right? It's happy. And if I cover this eye," grimy hand slapping her face, "I can pretend I'm in there too. And it's somewhere warm. Somewhere on a beach. Feeling—feeling okay. Like I should be okay, right? And I—I. Warsie. Instead? I'm here in this bumfuck town." She lay her arms over her head, arched her tall skinny frame off the floor. "What the fuck is going on?" Her black leather pants were worn, loose, pale grey on the knees, and her t-shirt was sheer, coffee-stained. Perhaps it was pink. Had been pink. If Warren was forced to guess the colour.

"Are you hungry?"

She did not respond, but sprung up off the floor and moved toward him. "What the fuck are you doing here?" The smell was stronger now, like aromatic mould. He imagined her back peppered with greyish patches, spores sprouting and releasing with each shift of her spine. Earthy, natural, but a part of the world he did not want to inhale. "Why are you here, Wars? Not where you're supposed to be. You're not where you were. Not where I looked for you. You ran away from me. Aaaaa-gain!"

"I didn't. I didn't run away. I'm working. I have a job."
Warren counted the windows in the kitchen, the half moon
in the back door, the front window, the vertical windows
alongside his front door. She was there, safe, could not leave
through any piece of glass, could not spirit herself up the
chimney, spool herself down the drain. "Beth. I'm glad to
see you. I am."

"Oh, yeah. Right, Wars. I call bullshit."

"Believe me." He was. He was telling the truth, even
though the sight of her made him nervous.

"I went to that shit apartment, but no no, you weren't
there. Just took the fuck off. Like that." Weak finger snap.
"Why did I have to come all this way to find you? You couldn't
let me know?"

"I didn't know where you were. Or how to reach you."

She dug her finger in his chest, and he could see the corners of her mouth were cracked, festering. Her lips, once
full and constantly pouting, were now chalky grey. "Like
that's any fucking excuse."

Warren glanced into his tanks, did a rapid count of the
fish. "I'm glad you found me, though," he said. Words like
feathers.

"Oh, my brother. I always have to find you."

"How did you get here?"

"I don't know. I don't. I think a bus. A fucking bus. I think
I fell asleep, or something, and then I woke up here. With
your fish. I think they helped me get here. Magnets or some
shit. I don't. Just. It's fucked up." Hands on her forehead, her
fingers were twitching.

"But how did you know where to go?"

With her thumb, she scratched at her crotch, shifted her
pants, winced. "You're listed, Warren. Seriously. You're not

the only one who got brains." She laughed then, and he saw that her teeth and tongue were black. He smelled acid. Vomit. "Though mine are. I don't know. All deteriorated. Bad cheese. But even bad cheese can be good, right? Some people love that shit."

"But how did you get in?"

She started to pace around him. "Oh my fuck, Warren. Do you got a chair and a flashlight. Fucking Spanish inquisition here. Basement. Duh! Window?"

"Oh." He thought of the people outside, the vans, the police cruiser that had taken up its place on the sidewalk this morning and had not left. "Did anyone see you?"

"People outside doing a tour."

"Tour?"

"Yeah. Big crowds. Popular place, Warsie. Did someone die in this house? Get murdered? Or did you discover something big? Some super big shit discovery? I bet you did. They want to see you. Shake your hand."

Shake my hand.

Moving around his kitchen, she tapped everything. Countertops, doorknobs, long metal bar to open his fridge. "You're famous, brother. Famous with a fuck-up sister. Boring story. Predictable."

"Beth. Sit down. Please. You're here now. You're okay. I'm going to get you something to eat." He had bread, butter in the fridge. Maybe a can of tuna or sardines. A piece of onion? "You'll feel better if you eat. And I'll get you a sweater. Your arms look cold."

"You got any smokes?" Her bony hands were shaking.

"I don't smoke."

"I searched your whole fucking house already, and not a single thing. Nothing to take or smoke or drink or snort.

You don't even have aspirin. Jesus, Wars. I really neeeed something."

"You'll be fine, Beth. Just have some food. A bath? That's it. A warm bath."

Fingers gripping her ears, she shook her head, began screaming. "You. Don't. Fucking. Get. It. I won't be fine. I need some shit, or I'm going to slam this head, that's my head, I'm going to slam that fucking head into the fridge door. And I'm going to do it over and over until my cheese brain leaks out." Calmer, "And then I'll feel better, Wars. Then." Rapid breathing.

"God, Beth. God. Do you want me to run out?" Rubbing one hand over the other, he thought of the people outside. Angry people. "I mean."

"Run out? Run out?" She said it as though she did not understand what he was saying. "Run out for what?"

"I don't know. Cigarettes?"

"Cigarettes."

"I mean. I could. But you can't smoke here, Beth. You just can't. The toxins get into the water. And Stephen. You know, Stephen. He starts to sneeze. He's old, you know. Lungs aren't the best."

His sister, six years younger than Warren, stopped and stared at him as though his skull had just spun a full circle. He could not determine if she was about to cry or wail or have a seizure that would squeeze her heart. Fifteen months had passed since he had last seen her. Four hundred and sixty-two days. That last time, she had appeared inside the doors of his apartment building, asleep in the narrow alcove that housed a wall of shiny mailboxes. For three days she slept and ate like an animal. She wore his clothes, cutting the bottoms off his sweatpants, the cuffs off his shirt. Had a shoelace knotted around her waist. Her shoulders were so gaunt, his shirt appeared as though it were on a wire hanger.

On the fourth day, Warren had come home to find the envelope containing his savings was empty. She was there, though, hunched on the couch watching a cartoon. Warren had asked her, gently, if she had seen it, and for hours she scoured the apartment. Continued long after Warren had given up the search. She would not let it go. Adamant she would find it underneath the lid of the toilet, behind the cereal boxes in the bottom cupboard, among the pages of expired magazines, mixed in with the soil of his plants. Searching furiously, her face red and sweating, she squeaked, "Not here either, Wars. Jesus. Shit just don't disappear. It shouldn't, right?"

"Wars?" Three in the morning, and she had shaken him awake, her face pressed into his. "I'm super, super sorry. I couldn't find it." She was sobbing, scratching at her face, her arms. "I just couldn't. But I tried. So hard. I really did. To find it."

"Don't worry," he whispered. "It's okay."

"No, it's not okay. It sucks. Sucks. When something just goes. Just gets gone like that. I mean. How does that happen? It's just not right. It's just."

Each word spoken increasing in speed, force, and Warren had tried to calm her. "Beth. Just sleep, okay? It'll be okay. We can look again in the morning. It'll show up."

Of course, when the sun rose, she was gone. A scribbled note inside an empty bowl on his counter, saying *I took an apple? Love, Beth.*

For weeks, Warren held his breath when he went to check his mail. A small part of him expecting her to be there, hoping she was. He was not upset about the money (he had not been saving the small amount for himself), but upset she had searched so hard. He understood why. Her habits made her steal, but her decency made her search. She wanted to be that person. Wanted Warren to see that good person. Underneath the matted fur jacket, the black fingernails, the scabs and bruises and shorn hair, his little sister glowed. Glowed brightly, and it bruised Warren's heart to witness her destruction. So much of her life had been dedicated to balancing on dangerous chairs, pasting paper in her stained-glass windows, blotting out her colours. Choking her light.

"Stephen?" She coughed.

"Yes, you know. My cat."

"The big fat furball? Shit, Warsie. I'm trying to be serious. To impress upon you the nature of this level of serious seriousness here. Of. This. Situation. Do you get it? I need to get somewhere. I need to get away from. I need to get. Me. Do something. I can't. I mean, I can't just. You know. I. Well." She went to the corner of the room, slid down, wrapped her arms around her legs. "You got to help me. You need to. Do. Do. Do. War. I just. Me."

He shoved his hands into his pockets, rolled back and forth on his heels. "I don't know what to do. I don't know what to do." Squeezing his eyes closed, he felt as though he were a young child, back in that house. He saw his father, standing in a crack of light from the basement window. Then his sister, running through the woods, and tugging spider webbing from her face. Everything was so confusing. He could not think. Could not think.

"Warsie." She fell over, and he heard her bones crack on the floor. "I'm going to die. You don't think so, but I can't. Any air. I can't get air."

He looked át his sister. Her chest, her bare arms were

mottled purple, as though even her blood was dazed. Her body seized, then, and strings of yellow flew from her mouth. She was going to die.

He waited, still rolling back and forth on his heels, counted backward, fifty, forty-nine, forty-eight. When he reached zero, he rushed to the phone. Dialled the only person he knew might be able to help him. "My sister," he said. "She's — she's bad. She needs help to calm down."

23

"FROM OUR UNDERSTANDING, IT'S VERY RARE." I PEERED DOWN at the scene from the top step, and sensed an instant familiarity. The lamplight was dim, but I recognized the female police officer's voice. She was the same person who had come to alert us of my father's death. Seated in the exact same position. My mother and aunt were in chairs opposite, and based on their owl-eyed expressions, they did not recognize her. "Yes, it's very rare indeed. At your daughter's age." "We don't understand," they chimed. Brainlessly.

The woman unwrapped something and pressed it into her mouth. I could hear the hard lozenge clicking against her teeth, saw the tiny lump stored in her cheek when she spoke. "Things do need to be confirmed, but doctors suspect cardiac arrest. Did she have any previous troubles with her heart?"

Her heart was pristine.

"No, no. Nothing like that. I would have followed up."

"Of course." My aunt, perched on the edge of her seat. "We would have followed up." Parroting.

I curled my toes against the dirty carpet. And a sneeze burst from my mouth. The officer twisted her head, looked up at me. Her eyes stayed on me for several seconds, and I lowered my head, lifted my shoulder to block my face.

"We are so sorry for your loss." I heard the candy crunch. "It won't be long before they release her body. And you can put your daughter to rest."

My aunt stood up. "I just can't believe it," she said as she walked the two officers to the door. "One minute running around enjoying the party." Her voice snagged in her throat. "The next minute, she's gone."

I clenched my fist. Rage swelled inside me, and even if I poked holes in my skin, it would not seep out. My aunt had caused this. Her sick need to constantly recreate herself. This time, with me and Button as her family-themed sideshow.

I watched her open the door for the officers and let them out. She looked at herself in the mirror, licked a finger and wiped at the streak beneath her left eye. "I'm leaving," she called to my mother. Sighed. "It's been a day. It's been a real day."

I chewed my fingernails, spit the peeled strips down over the stairs. My aunt was lying. It had not been anything close to a *real day* for her. I doubt she even understand the phrase. How could she, when she was always acting?

That night, I kept waking up. Soreness inside my chest tore me from my sleep. As though foreign fingers had hold of my empty stomach and kept yanking me, stretching my membranes to the point of burning. Time after time, I awoke, already sitting up, mouth screaming, my gut full of sharp pangs. I scratched my cheeks, found them itchy and wet with salty water.

Around 3 a.m., I noticed dark shadows drifting across my wall. I rolled over, peered out the window, and saw a strange sky, clouds skittering over the moon. At once, torrential downpours came, and they gusted in with cooler temperatures, wiping away the heat. It felt as though someone had lifted a blanket up, folded it back over the earth.

I slid out of bed, went downstairs, heard the refrigerator rattle and hum. Two hours earlier, my mother had taken her new usual (one and a half flat pink pills) and gone to sleep. She was upstairs, snoring lightly, but the house seemed empty. Had I ever been aware of the sounds Button made? Not consciously, but perhaps my body heard her. Some part of me that was numb, that was inaccessible, must have heard her. Otherwise I would not have noticed the near silence. Pleasing, almost. To hear my throat swallow, my blood rushing through the cords in my neck. I liked knowing I could do what I wanted, go wherever I pleased, and no one would know. No one would care. If I were gone, not a single person in the world would miss me. There was an ounce of freedom inside that little thought. It helped bring me back to myself after my atypical demonstration of emotions after Button died. For a few wearisome moments, those feely eels had encircled my legs. And pulled. Me. Down.

Outside, in the darkness, everything glistened. The rain had lightened; the air was fresh and cool. In the glow from the street lamp, I could see movement on the pavement. Drowning worms had burrowed though the soil, over the grass, and edged onto the driveway.

Wearing only my father's old t-shirt, I crouched on the asphalt and watched them slither. So methodical in their movements. The army of nightcrawlers. Blind ends twisting, undulating, yet never scrutinizing their direction. Always onward without question. March! Why did they not stay in the safety of soil, soaking in a dirty bath, heads poked above water? What was so bad about a few short moments of discomfort?

Button had been like that, wriggling toward whatever felt good, whatever made her happy. She trusted everyone and everything. A rare human paradigm that led to her dying in a rather grotesque manner. I tried to push the thoughts down. I could feel the eels, cold nubs bumping my calves, my ankles.

At that moment, I can now admit, it was difficult to control my rage.

I stood and moved my toes toward the closest worm. A tap along the swollen length of it, then a light step, and finally my foot settled. The faint sense of pressure, then the gratifying pop. I liked it. I placed my foot upon another worm. A second pop. I took a deep breath, started hopping across the broken pavement, squishing worm after worm underneath my heels. Jumping and dancing, I stomped them into oblivion. There was something soothing about the smears on the pavement, the slippery ooze building on the soles of my feet, the soft smell of digested earth permeating the air. I knew some of them were still alive, worm ends lifting then striking the driveway. Seeking assistance. At some point, would they realize no one cared? No one was coming? They were stuck tight, and when the sun rose tomorrow, they would dry out and slowly die.

I destroyed what I could, and only stopped when a light

in my neighbour's house flicked on. His face was in the window, watching me. I lifted my arm to his image, hoped my waving hand said, *Don't worry, old man, I'm going inside now.* I did not need him trying to connect with me, or worse, speaking to my mother. Telling her about the faceless ghost he saw in the middle of the night, naked but for a now-grey t-shirt, racing around in the rain.

Without wiping my feet on the rug, I walked straight across the kitchen floor, into the hallway, up the stairs. A trail formed behind me. As though my feet were stamps, shreds of flesh, blood, mud, and grit. My organic ink. In the morning, my mother would get down on her knees and, with a rough sponge and soapy water, scrape the worms off the linoleum. She would strip my bed of sheets, stuff them into the washing machine, lean against the wall, and wait for them to tumble clean. She would insist I take a bath, and then she would scour the ring around the tub. This might take her hours, and it would be a relief. Hearing her clean instead of complain.

[24]

FOURTEEN MINUTES LATER, SOMEONE TAPPED ON THE FRONT door. Warren cracked it open and peered out, saw his friend, Gordie Smit, wearing a black bomber jacket with *Andy's Pets* embroidered across the heart. The crowd had not thinned, and the police cruiser remained in place.

"Shit, buddy. You got a major crowd of fans out here. Fucking nosy neighbours." He stepped into the porch, held up an unopened package of cigarettes, and a clear bottle. "You wouldn't believe how much garbage Daylene got in the medicine cabinet." Jingling the bottle. "Where's the patient?"

Warren glanced toward the kitchen, and Gordie moved past him. Within moments, he had knelt down beside Beth, lifted her head. "Wet cloth, Warren. Cold. A glass of water. Now. And a pillow and a blanket."

He helped her to swallow three pills, "Give it a few

minutes, and you'll come right round," and she sat up, shivering, pillow balanced on her bent knees. She tried to stand, but he put up a hand, said, "C'mon, doll. Don't move. Just keep it down."

"What did you give her?"

Gordie stood up, put his palm flat on the countertop. "Sedative. Probably'll take the edge off. Daylene's got them for her nerves. Knocks her fat ass right out. She's going to lose her shit when she sees they're gone."

"I'm sorry, Gordie. I don't want to be trouble."

"Oh c'mon, buddy. Have you ever met me? I spend all day in a pet store, staring at rodents and snakes that nobody wants to buy. This is the biggest thrill I've had in ages. Besides, you got more than enough going on. Your plate is mile high with crap. Looks like the lot out there want your head on a spit."

Warren looked at his feet. He was still wearing his shoes. Twenty eyelets. Ten per shoe. "I don't know why," he said softly, and touched his glasses.

"Why?" Gordie snorted. "Don't be looking for a reason. Human nature don't need no reason."

"Thank you. I appreciate it. I mean. I really do. I just feel bad." Guilty. He felt guilty. For bothering Gordie. For the sight of Beth on his kitchen floor. For the storm of suffering inside her scraggy frame. For running away at eighteen, and never looking back. But he had to leave. When he finished school, he had to walk out those doors. He thought Beth would forget about him. He also thought his father's ghost would stay behind on their small farm. But he was wrong on both accounts. Beth and his father followed him. Followed him every place he went.

"Shit, War. What does she do?"

"I don't know."

"And that's your sister?"

"Yes. It is."

Gordie shook his head. "A librarian, I would have expected. You know? A little matching pair of girly glasses, pencil-in-the-hair type, ready to spew some statistics on book people. But that thing there? Not so much."

Warren said nothing, carefully moved his glasses back into place.

"Geez, buddy. That sounded harsh. Didn't it? Might've been my asshole talking. It's a noisy little fucker."

"It's okay. She is. I don't know. She's in some trouble."

"You don't choose, do you? You don't choose your family."

"No."

"Man, though. You've had some sort of shit week. Haven't you?"

A tiny insect was crawling across the left lens of Warren's glasses, and he took them off, blew. He watched its wings flutter.

"Buddy?"

"I don't know," he mumbled as he slid his glasses back on. He felt confused, only aware of what was right in front of him. "I—" then Beth stumbled to her feet, and reached for the package of cigarettes.

"I'm going for a smoke," she said, and smiled a hazy, suggestive smile at Gordie. An expression that made Warren queasy, and he had to look away.

When the back door closed, Gordie said, "That's my cue. I'm out of here before Daylene knows I'm gone. She'd give me a quiz that you know I'm gonna fail."

"Thank you, Gordie. I don't know what I'd—"

He waved his hand, "Nuff said."

After Gordie left, Warren retuned to the kitchen, paced back and forth across the floor, counting the number of times he swallowed until he heard Beth rattling at the doorknob. When she came in, her arms were full of yellow caution tape. "What's this shit?" she slurred. "It was all over the place. Halloween is done. Over."

Staring at the ribbons of yellow plastic, Warren's mouth opened. How was it possible that he had forgotten all about it? How could that have slipped his mind, even for a second? Since arriving home he had not looked into his backyard a single time. The image of Amanda never once fluttered up behind his lids. *Man, you've had some sort of shit week.* That was what Gordie had said to him, and he could only think of Beth.

"There was — was an accident back there. An accident."

"An accident?" She dumped the tangle of tape on the counter. "And there's three teddy bears underneath a big tree. You getting weird on me, Wars?"

"No, not weird." Teddy bears? Who had put them there? Someone else had come into the backyard, moving about, or hiding. He had spent countless moments peering into the darkness, but had seen no one.

"Then what?"

"Can we talk about it later? I need to put the tape back." That would allow him time to make something up. Beth did not need to know what had happened. It would only upset her.

"Yeah." She yawned, made her way to the couch. He was relieved that the curtains remained closed. "Fuck. I'm wiped. My legs ache. Arms feel like they're falling off. But I feel better."

She sat down, drew her knees to her chin. Warren made her a cup of sugary tea, pulled open the cellophane on some oatmeal cookies, and brought her the package.

Between slurps, she said, "War, why did you leave?"

"You ask me this every time I see you."

"I know."

"I had to go, Beth. Go to school."

"Couldn't you have gone to school closer? Come home on weekends? Come home, ever?"

"I don't know. I thought—"

"You left me alone. I had no one, you know. No one."

"You had friends from school, right? Our mother."

"My friends were shit. And our mother? I don't want to say she was bad. She just wasn't much of anything. I did everything I could to get her to see me. Even a lot of shitty stuff, just wanting her to lay into me. Knock me in the face, even. I think she was afraid of me."

"Why would you say that?"

"She never touched me. Never even brushed against me."

Warren sighed.

"Things might have been better if he were there."

"Who?"

"Your father."

"Your father, too." Warren clasped his fingers together.

"She was just a plain and simple person, Warren. When he died, she died, too. How could she ever trust a single person after that? How could she ever love anyone? Even us? I think about her all the time."

That's not how it happened. He was not to blame.

"Now, Father," she continued. "He was a complicated bastard. Don't think I ever remember him smiling. Not once."

"You were five. You didn't know him."

"Who did? Certainly not you, even though you want to think you did. Want to think he was perfect. A perfect daddy."

"I don't think that and don't want to think that."

"C'mon, Warren. That's the thing with people. They don't see themselves. They don't know themselves. Do you think I can step aside and look at myself? Fuck, no. I'd probably slit my throat if I did. Ear to ear."

"Don't say that." He pushed another cookie into her empty hand.

"It's true. So I fill myself up with shit. It's going to kill me, but it makes me feel glittery. It makes me feel good. Good enough to live. And I can go from there. But I don't dare look underneath it. Scrape it off, and see what I got."

"Beth. You have to. Scrape it off. There's so much good underneath."

"Thank you, brother dear." She yawned, and Warren could see all the way to the back of her throat. "I don't know who your friend was, but this stuff really works."

"Gordie. His family owns the pet store."

"Pet store? Well, thank you, Gordie baby."

"He's a kind person."

"Yeah." She lowered her head, her body onto the couch. "Sorry I'm always showing up, ruining your life."

"You're not ruining my life."

"I am, War. Admit it. Don't keep it in. Say it so I can hear it."

His throat tightened. If he told her the truth, she would never believe him. Having her there, having her safe in his small bungalow, did not ruin his life. It made his life better. It meant there was hope. That there was a possibility things might change.

"I want eggs," she mumbled. "Eggs in the morning. Six of 'em. No, eight. Fried in butter, Wars. Actual butter. None of that spray shit in a can that Mother used."

"Non-stick?"

"Yeah."

"I don't have any. Mist gets in the air. You know, not good for Stephen. I think he might have asthma. And, well, my fish."

Her eyes were closed, but she smiled. "I love you, Warsie. I love —"

And then she slipped under, disappearing from the world. But still there. Right in front of him. Her heart beating steadily, lungs still moving air in and out. Alive. He covered her with a blanket. Ran his hand over the soft stubble on her skull, bent to kiss her crown. She smelled different now. Less like a rodent, and more like something dried and smoked. A strip of brown meat hanging in a darkened room, air full of chemical pollutants.

"I don't know how to help you," he whispered. *The hook. It's stuck tight in your back.*

[25]

FUNERALS BRING OUT THE BULLSHIT IN PEOPLE. I UNDERSTOOD
what to expect, and was not surprised in the least.
Everyone in town was there, shaking their lowered heads
and spewing whispered thoughts about the shock of it all.
Losers. As I waited for the monotonous hour to pass, I heard
none of their drivel, the prayers, or the singing. What I did
hear was a fucking yappy puppy.

Seated at the end of a wooden row, I was near a wide-
open window, and when I stretched my neck, I could see
the piece-of-shit animal tied to a bike stand. Whimpering
and whining. The dog's leash was not long enough for it to
reach the cool grass, and it did not take a genius to know its
paws were burning on the pavement. I stared at its compact
body, its foxlike face, foxlike ears, and then I recognized it.
Noodle. Fucking Noodle. There was no doubt; that was the

dog Button and I had seen after that shitty haircut. Dancing from the heat, she flicked her curly tail back and forth. The tail. Yes. I remembered it all. The same tail Button was not allowed to touch.

The dog yipped.

I made a sincere effort to ignore it. I really did. Tried to face forward and focus on the squat box perched on some wheelie thing with cloth over it. The white box had six closely placed handles on it, which I do not think were necessary. Four handles would have sufficed. Was my mother trying to make a statement regarding Button's mass?

The dog yipped.

The collar on my shirt was chokingly tight, done up to the very top, and I yanked at the cotton. I hated anything touching my neck, pushing against my throat. Hated that my mother insisted I dress up like a stupid puppet. Everything made me sweat. Who cared? "People will be looking at you," she explained as she licked her fingers, patted down the hairs on the back of my head. "God, you should have got your hair cut. So shaggy. In your eyes. Down over your ears like that." I had twisted away from her, disgusted that strands of my *shaggy* hair would smell like her fusty mouth. Besides, where the hell did she find her priorities? In some discount aisle?

The dog yipped.

Back to the box. Stay with the box. It was difficult to avoid. Yes, she was in there. The star of this little show. I closed my eyes and imagined her. Lying down, with the lid on. I hated that the lid was on. Cheap gold-coloured clasps locked. I hated that my mother and aunt had somehow decided that was *The decent thing to do*. To have her sealed in. I was not involved in these choices. When it was me who knew best. Knew *her* best.

Did anyone even wash the fucking orange off her face? The dog was still yipping.

I remained motionless, watching the useless ceiling fans near the front of the church. Circulating stale shitty air caused by funeral breathing. Wailing, weeping generally involved increased respiration. It was vile. The fans did nothing to combat it. Lazy rotations, one moving clockwise, and one counter, cancelling each other out. Sweat trickled down the sides of my spine. My legs were sticking to my pants. I snapped my toes inside my wet socks. The Man of the House was standing on a higher level, speaking in low, even, annoying tones. He probably had better-quality air. The fans turning above him. Maybe the placement was designed for that purpose. The holy man gets the fucking air.

Shit. The dog would not stop yipping. And yipping. And yipping, yipping, yipping.

Sliding forward on the damp wood, I wrenched my body around. Where the hell was the asshole bitch? I scanned the crowd, systematically, and of course, had no trouble locating the negligent piece of shit. The idiot was seated just two rows behind me. Two rows. She wore a prim dark blouse with a prissy cardigan, and was squeezed between dorky mother and fat father, and two barely-clinging-to-life geriatrics. The grandparents, I assumed. The five of them were in the family area, but were not our family. We had next to no family, and my suck-up mother did not want those rows left empty. She had invited them to sit there simply because the loose-skinned grandfather had sent over a few bags of groceries. Not a van full, just a few lousy half-empty paper bags stuffed with nearly expired shit. A way of being supportive to the community, he had said. Not surprisingly, when the local newspaper covered Button's unfortunate demise, they mentioned his generosity in the second-to-last paragraph. They did not mention the green mould creeping across the packaged cheese.

Pinhead Whore caught my angry glare. I expected her to look away, but she glared back. *Un-bloody-believable.* I admit, with some shame, I was caught off guard by her blatant display of hostility. I had expected to have the upper hand, especially while Button was in the box. I narrowed my eyes, once again, willing her to back down. But then, but then, but then, she actually opened her mouth, pushed her index finger slowly over her bottom lip. I could not fucking believe it. The vomit sign. She shook her body as though pretending to convulse. Rolled her eyes back in her head. Like Button.

I stood up, striking my mother's arm (inadvertently). Her prayer book smacked onto the floor, and while she focused on retrieving it, I took a deep step into the aisle. My worn sneakers slipped on the carpet, but I did not fall down. Without making any eye contact, I marched right out of that church. I heard some people murmur, saying it was *too much for me, too much, they were so attached, poor thing.*

Stomping straight across the grass, I stopped at the bike rack. Of course I did. I certainly was not going home. Had no plans to take a thoughtful walk all by myself. I tore some kid's knapsack off the seat of a bicycle, unzipped it, dumped the paper contents onto the grass. Lame pencil drawings, shitty comic book with the cover torn off, chocolate bar that was melted and limp. I leapt onto the bar, and the contents spurted out. I liked the sweet smell. I liked the mess. It spattered onto my pants. Spattered on Noodle.

Distracted by dirty fur, she began cleaning her side. I bent down near adorable Noodle, and called to her calmly, "Come here, my small friend." After unhitching her from the leash, she licked some chocolate from the back of my hand. "Not too much," I said. "Don't you know chocolate is poisonous to your kind?" Gently, I lifted her off the pavement, and slid her into the open knapsack. "Now that feels better on your paws, doesn't it?" She sat there, gazing up at me with glittery eyes, her curled tail twitching. She was bathed in a warm red glow. Sunlight penetrating the fabric.

After zipping the bag, I lifted Noodle onto my back. She barely weighed anything and did not make a sound. We walked four blocks down the street, and turned left into the woods. I could not detect any movement whatsoever in the bag, and when I stopped walking, I assumed the dog was asleep.

I waited for some time before opening the knapsack, but Noodle was fine. Just fine. Appreciative of the cool soil when she emerged from her carrying case. I could tell because she pranced about, twirling, then leaned down, wiggling her back end in the air. We spent time together, Noodle and I, playing catch with tiny sticks. I petted her tail, uncurled it, watched it snap back up again. Like a metal spring. I thought about Button. Thought about her desire to touch the dog. Stroke that very tail.

After some frolicking and a small exercise to make amends, I placed her back in her fabric home and walked up to the road. What would I want with a dog? Especially one so small and repulsive as Noodle? I opened the knapsack just a block from my future home, and my small companion ventured out. Timid at first, but she sniffed the ground and promptly scampered in the correct direction. The lively girl. It was nice to witness that sort of enthusiasm, even though she had been through a bit of an ordeal. Such a relentlessly positive attitude should be a good lesson to her owner.

The pavement was so hot I could smell the melted tar, but after my and Noodle's little adventure, I doubt she even noticed the pain in her paws.

[26]

THE NEXT MORNING, AS HIS SISTER SNORED ON THE COUCH, Warren went into his backyard. When he reached the tree, sure enough, resting against the trunk were three plush teddy bears. The muzzles were covered in a frosty glitter. There was also a pink candle, wick unlit, and a chocolate bar wrapper. Candy eaten. Warren leaned forward and peered at the bark on the tree. Someone had recently carved a diamond into the flesh of the wood, a bar near each sharp point. *A symbol*, Warren thought. His mind immediately filtered through every mathematical figure, but he could not identify it.

He stood up and scratched his head. Then slowly turned around, three hundred and sixty degrees. How could he have lived here for nearly nine months, and never explored his own backyard? He had never noticed the stretch of raspberries, bushes picked empty by chipmunks or squirrels. He had neglected to shape the hedge or trim the shrubs. In all that time, he had never once walked among the tall trees to clear his head.

A quick glance at his house to make sure his sister was not awake and wandering about, and he slipped between a tight row of yews that bordered his property, entered the surrounding woods. As he walked, he made no conscious decision to turn left or right, just stepped where it felt natural, slightly worn. He passed a hilltop that dropped dangerously onto a strip of sandy beach bordering a huge misty pond. A faded wharf jutted out toward the centre. Pausing on a steep incline to watch the steely water, he noticed a line of ice had formed where water met land. Warren sighed, put his palms out, touched the tips of the wild grass, dried and yellow. Two ducks, no, geese, flew above him, squawking, and then they dipped down, skimming over the water. Floated side by side.

Nora. Though they had spoken, he had not seen her since Monday evening. Had not touched her or smelled her, or lain beside her as the tips of his fingers eased over her body. He wanted to see her, but now that his sister was there, he was not sure what to do. What would Nora think of Beth? What might Beth do or say?

Warren continued to walk along the edge of the hill until he came to a chain-link fence, holes torn through the metal mesh, some parts flattened to the ground, gate ripped off the hinges, tossed aside. Without thinking, he stepped over the divider, took a few strides forward, and realized he was standing in a backyard.

A trailer park. A quick scan and he saw twenty-three, though there could have been more hidden by shrubs, trees. Most of them dented, faded, painted white and red, or white and blue. The one nearest him was salmon coloured, hoisted up onto cement blocks. The shutters were askew, striped awning shredded, and beside the door, a black garbage bag rippled as though kittens were pushing out from the inside.

"What the fuck?"

Although it took a moment to recognize him outside of the classroom, Warren saw Adrian Byrd. Appearing there, standing on the sloping deck, lower jaw jutting. He stared at Warren with dark eyes, hands knotted into fists. Even at that distance, Warren saw the stitches on the boy's face. The black threads criss-crossing.

"Hi," Warren said. "I mean. Hi." Adrian had missed Monday. Warren had no idea if he had returned to school yesterday. Was planning to go today. He certainly did not look ready.

Hands gripping the rusting rails. "Why the hell you here?"

Why was he there? Warren looked around, a yard full of dead grass and empty cans. Remains of burned tires. A woman's soggy coat with a fake fur collar. And a dog, on twig legs, rooting through a massive pile of old papers. He wanted to wrap the small animal in his jacket and retreat. "I don't know. I mean. You deliver the papers?"

"Supposed to."

"Oh." He thought of Adrian who biked past his house every Tuesday and Thursday. Doing his job, no matter the weather. "And you leave them?"

"Who the fuck cares?" Adrian's feet were bare, covered in mud.

"Have you been to school?"

"Who's asking?"

Warren walked toward him. Seven steps. "You don't want to fall behind, right?"

"And that's your business?"

"Not really. No." What could he say? That he wanted to help? He searched his mind for positive words. "But. I just. It's important to go."

Adrian Byrd did not soften. He glared at Warren, rocking forward and backward, his expression a tangled mesh of hatred and fear. His throat emitted a low growl, sounding like canine distemper. Warren actually glanced at the dog to see if its teeth were exposed.

"It's been a difficult time," he continued. "For everyone."

"Fuck you."

"I know you're angry, Adrian. Angry at the world." Something his mother's friend, Sarie, had said to Warren when he was a teenager. To make him feel better. But had it made him feel worse? He could not remember, and looked at Adrian.

He grinned, slit his eyes. "The world? You stupid sick fuck. I'm angry at you. You!"

Warren was not certain what happened next, only that he saw Adrian spring over the railing of the deck and bolt toward him. Before he could count a single second, the boy was there, his fist flying upwards, and for reasons Warren could not explain, he did not lean away. Instead he leaned forward. Into the force of the punch. Making it easier for the boy to reach his face. Knuckles striking his cheek, his thin skin splitting under the pressure. Glasses soaring through the air.

"Aide!" A woman rushed from the trailer. "Stop it! Stop it! Adrian!"

The boy ran, then. A startled animal, he darted across the yard, jumped up onto the hood of an abandoned car, and then vaulted over the fence. Escaping into the woods. The dog did not flinch, did not stop its rooting to look up.

A mint green blur rushed toward Warren. He picked up his glasses and pressed them onto his face. They were not broken, but sat askew.

"Oh shit," she said. The woman wore knitted slippers with pompoms on the toes, a long shiny nightgown with a deep slit. Warren could see the sides of her flat breasts, the outline of her bloated stomach. "Shit. Shit. Your face is messed. A real mess."

Daubing his pulsing cheek, he looked at his fingers. Bright thin blood.

"Aide's a good kid. I don't want trouble. He's a good kid. Really."

"I don't doubt that, Mrs. Byrd?"

"Ms." Smoothing her nightgown.

"Ms. Byrd. I'm sure I provoked him. I don't know what I did or what he's going through. But I bothered him. Upset him." Warren retrieved a tissue from his pocket, cleaned the mud from his glasses, slid them back onto his face.

"He's just soft. That's the problem. Born soft in his heart. Trying to roughen himself up now to survive. But it don't work. He still soft. My girl, now, she'll be fine wherever she is. Whoever got her. She'll be good. But Aide. I fought to keep him. They all judge, you know, but I had no choice."

"I'm sorry. I thought I might help. If I just encouraged him. I wondered if he was in school."

"You his teacher?"

"Yes." Warren looked down at his feet. *I was.*

"He's been struggling since that Fuller girl died. Struggling worse. She was here, you know. That night."

"She was?"

"Two of 'em there on the couch. Peas in a pod, now. Like that." Knitted two fingers together and held them up.

"Playing some game with little ships, calling out numbers or letters." She pinched something off her lip, flicked it. "Above my head, that's for damn sure. Couldn't keep up."

"Oh."

"I think he even walked her home."

"He did?"

"I think. All the way home. Like I said, he's a good kid."

"Did you tell the police?"

"Tell who? Tell what?"

"The detective. That's." *Trying to understand?* "She's looking into what happened. The accident. Her last name is Reed."

Ms. Byrd laughed then, bent-at-the-waist type of laughter. Ticking upwards, then a deflated whinny. "I know all kinds about that Deee-tective Reed girl. Used to live here, you know. Three skips away. Too good for us now, though. Driving around, watching us all. Like we're already guilty." She scraped her tongue over her teeth. "Nothing I say'll make no difference."

"But, surely. It might be helpful," Warren offered. *Would be helpful to me.* He bent his neck toward her. "To know she was here."

She straightened her back then, daubed the corners of her eyes. "You are one queer kind of funny. I saw nothing. Aide was home with me. All night. Watching garbage on the television." Her eyes were like her son's now, narrow and dark. "Now why don't you go home, Mister. Not good manners, you know. Traipsing through a woman's backyard. Surprising them. I don't know where you learned that, but we don't act like that around here."

"I didn't mean—" Directly to the left of her head, an iridescent beetle slid through a tear in the screen door. Dropped.

Warren heard the faintest click of shell hitting ground. "I'm sorry, Ms. Byrd."

"Didn't you hear me? Go home out of it. I got to go find Aide."

[27]

EARLY THE NEXT MORNING, I WENT TO THE CEMETERY, VISITED
Button. I had come with a gift, and knelt down beside the
fresh mound, scooped out a hole in the loose dirt. Placing the
item deep inside the hole, I covered it, patted the soil. Button
would appreciate my simple gesture. I knew she would.

After my errand, I returned home, went into Button's
bedroom and sat on her unmade bed. Nothing in her room
had been cleaned. Even though she was now out behind the
church, drying inside her box, her last worn pair of underwear
remained tangled in the corner. A mildewed towel lay beside
it. A butterfly-covered summer dress in a heap beside that.
Everything was coated in a layer of beige dust. My mother
had taken care of nothing, and I was not about to lift a finger.

I reached under her bed, yanked out Button's piggybank.
A pink pottery hippo with faded white polka dots. Holding

it above my head, I closed my eyes, let it drop. I sensed the swoosh of air, heard the splintering smash. I scraped up her coins, stuffed them all into my pockets. Both bulging, hanging down below the raggedy cuffs of my jean shorts, I set off toward Main Street for the pet store.

The store owner was just about to flip over the sign, *Open* to *Closed*, but I slammed my fist on the door, glared at him. He held the door, the bell tinkling above his head, and I brushed past him. The contents in my pocket jangling as I moved.

"Startled me," he said. "Made me jump."

Six foot, easily, and a balding mass I estimated at three hundred and fifty pounds. *I made him jump.* I smirked inside, said, "Sorry, sir."

"A gentle tap would have got my attention."

"I realize that now." I could smell the animals in their cages. A mixture of shit and cedar shavings. Heard them rummaging about, scratching, gnawing, snuffling.

"With that type of determined knock, you know what you want, I figure?"

"Yes, sir," I replied.

"Let me guess. A goldfish." Fingers nipping his chin. "No, no. A hamster. Or a gecko. Yeah, that's it. I've got it. It's a gecko." Firm nod.

"Not even close," I replied, and pointed at the glass-encased bug display on the shelf behind the cash register.

"Well, I'll be damned. I'm never wrong."

I could not tell if he was arrogant or simply attempting humour. No matter, his verbosity was annoying.

"Which one?"

"Third from the left, please, Mister. Upper shelf."

He placed the enormous piece on the counter before me,

and plucking it up, I brought it close to my face and examined it. "Yes, that's the one. That's it." It would make a nice addition.

"It's a beauty, but it's not on discount, you know."

"I know." I did not know.

"Do you have enough?"

Emptying each pocket into my hand, I dropped all the quarters and dimes and nickels and pennies onto the counter.

"Oh. This might take me a while." Meaty hand separating the dimes from the nickels, sliding them off the counter and into the cash register. "You been saving long?"

"No, Mister. Not long at all."

"You must have a good job, then."

"No. It's not my money." He paused his sorting, glanced up, and I, of course, maintained eye contact. Not a comfortable exercise, but I could manage it when needed. "It belongs to my little sister. She wanted me to come and get something."

"Sure, then. You got yourself a nice little sister."

"Yes. She wanted to do something in return. I gave her a gift already."

"One of these?"

"No, no. A tail."

"A tail, you say?"

"Yes, sir."

"Like a squirrel tail, or a raccoon tail? That sort of thing?"

I did not hesitate. "Yes, exactly. That sort of thing."

"Does she like it?"

"Very much, sir. She likes the way it feels. Soft and curly."

"Well, then."

"Knowing her, she'll probably keep it until it disintegrates."

He chuckled gently, and I saw his large molars, metal fillings. "How about we call it even, so I can stop counting the pennies?"

"Good," I said. "That's fair and reasonable."

I turned the Luna moth over in my hands. Pale green wings, four faux eyes, feathered antennae. In a library book, I had read that some cultures believed a Luna moth carried the spirit of a child who died prematurely. A stupidly sentimental notion. Moronic, really. But I admit, I liked the idea of Button sitting on my palms. Trapped inside this large hunk of glass. I would keep her on my night table. She would be the largest insect. The soul of my collection.

[28]

WHEN WARREN RETURNED HOME, HIS SISTER WAS STILL SLEEP-ing on the couch. He examined the mess on the coffee table — three empty cans of soda, a ripped bag of cookies, and the remains of a frozen pizza, barely cooked. Warren nudged her, and she mumbled, "S-s-sorry, Waarhsie," and rolled toward the back of the couch. He was relieved that she was still there. That she was still breathing. He could not alter the fact that he had turned his back on her when she was twelve. Had walked away and never allowed him-self to drift back. For almost a lifetime, he had pretended she never existed. She was a subsection, tucked inside his folder labelled *Mother*.

Touching his face, his skin felt as though it belonged to someone else. He should clean it before Beth woke up. He did not want to give her a reason to be concerned.

A single step toward the bathroom, and he was interrupted by tapping at the front door. Not like the banging from last night. Sharp smacks on the clapboard, the windows, shrill laughter that had torn him from his sleep. This was a gentle, determined tap, and Warren went to the door, peered out through the glass. Ms. Fairley, lips pursed, clutching the bottom half of a cardboard box, three pea plants in terracotta pots.

"Dr. Botts. Thank goodness," she said as he opened the door. She peered over her shoulder at the onlookers. Already gathered. Perhaps they never left at all. "What an absolute frenzy."

"I'm sorry. I'm sorry for this."

She stepped into the porch, laid the plants on the small table. "I thought you would appreciate having them back. They're about to bloom." Warren glanced at them. Eleven buds. Then she handed him a cloth bag. "And these," she said. "I put them away before someone stole them or destroyed them. They're quite beautiful, actually, if you like that sort of thing."

Warren glanced in the bag. Saw the small collection of insects encased in glass, a spider, a stag beetle, a scorpion. "Thank you for taking the time."

He turned then, stepping back into the living room to give Ms. Fairley room. She pulled in a sharp breath, "Dr. Botts? Your face?"

He touched his cheekbone, skin hot and sticky, "I apologize. I just—"

"What happened? What happened to you?"

"Well. I mean. I went for a walk. Behind my house. Just followed a path in the woods."

"A path?"

"Exploring?" He shifted his glasses, tried a faint smile. "Forever the scientist, I guess."

"Are you trying to be funny, Warren?"

"No. Not at all." Coughing. He glanced at her shoes, size seven, he estimated, and he began to skip count by sevens.

She took Warren's wrist, as though he were a child. "Come," she said. "Let me take a look."

In the living room, Ms. Fairley stopped. Beth was snoring. "My sister," Warren said. "She's visiting. And well, she's, I mean, she's sick."

"Nothing serious, I hope."

"Um, an influenza virus, I think. I mean, probably the flu."

"Well, she certainly has her appetite still?" Gesturing toward the coffee table strewn with trash. "I'd take that as a good sign."

"Yes," he replied.

Warren followed Ms. Fairley into the kitchen. Opened the freezer, retrieved an ice tray, and twisted the contents into a clean cup towel. As he sat down, she handed it to him. "Press this against your face. It looks swollen but the split skin is only minor. Better not to bandage it, I think."

Warren sighed. Cold compress. Instant relief.

"You fell? Did you fall?"

"No, I found a home. I went to a home. I was just walking, and it took me to a trailer, a trailer place, I guess. A park? Is that what it's called?"

"Did someone assault you? Honestly." She tapped her foot, one-two-three, one-two-three, folded her arms across her narrow chest. Twenty-four ribs. Twelve pairs. "This community. I've lived here all my life, Warren. It has changed. Significantly. Just completely deteriorated."

"No. I think it was my fault. I didn't know it, but I —

I ended up at Adrian Byrd's home. He lives in a trailer. With his mother."

"Adrian? From your class?"

"Yes, I mean. He was absent on Monday. He and," Warren cleared his throat, "Amanda knew each other. You know. I just saw him. Saw him there, and thought I could talk to him. You know. See if he was okay."

"You went to Adrian Byrd's home?"

"I didn't intend to."

"You can't do that, Dr. Botts. You can't just show up at a student's residence when you feel like it. No more than they should just show up at yours."

He closed his eyes. Saw an image of Amanda sitting on his porch, her head hanging down. Flecks of old blue polish on her chewed-down nails. "I just spoke with him. Wanted to make sure he was managing."

"That may be the case, but to be blunt, no one cares what your motives were. No one cares that you were just wandering through the woods. Having a leisurely stroll. No one cares if you care. There are rules in place to protect everyone."

"That doesn't make sense."

"No, sir. It does not. But if I had a dollar for every thing that didn't make sense with our education system, I wouldn't be here. I'd be sipping a margarita on a beach somewhere." She took the cup towel from his hands, crunched the ice, then handed it back to him. "It's not about caring anymore. It's not about connecting. What we need to do is keep the kids in their seats. Force them through the machine, like some cruel sociological extrusion. They all come in differently, *sui generis*," waving a hand, "but all need to go out the same shape. It's painful and it breaks parts of them and it doesn't work. Sometimes the problems become so overwhelming, you don't see any of the good." She sighed. "Don't get me started!"

"I understand." He stared at the linoleum on the floor. Each square foot had a pattern of overlapping octagons. He tried to calculate the number of octagons in the kitchen. Did the linoleum go beneath the cabinetry? Perhaps the cabinets were a permanent structure, and the installer had to cut the flooring. How much, then, would he have thrown away? He counted quickly.

"Warren? Are you listening?"

He stood up, blinked. The room spun for just a moment, and Ms. Fairley gripped his elbow.

"My head."

"Do you want to sit down again?"

"No. I need to move slowly, is all."

"As I said, my brother is a fine judge of character, Warren. We both stand behind you."

"Dr. Fairley? You spoke with Dr. Fairley?"

"Oh, yes. Several times. He is aghast with the whole situation."

"Oh."

"Are you going to be okay?"

"I am. Yes. Thank you."

She smiled at him, and Warren saw that the coldness she had displayed on Monday had vanished. Something in her gentle expression, the wrinkles around her eyes, reminded him of his mother's friend. Sarie. Warren remembered when he was a small boy, he had stood on a chair beside Sarie and played with her hair. Brownish blond, long, luxurious, and he combed it and braided it. Brought it to his face, his unblemished cheek. So soft and perfect, smelling of vanilla and plastic. He had never seen such beautiful hair on a person. She called him her little hairstylist, said his fingers were relaxing, but when he peered closer at her scalp, he saw a crisscross of threads. Hair woven, sprouting from a strange fabric netting. The sight of it startled him, made him feel queasy and uncertain, and he slid down from his chair, went outside to spin on his tire swing. One hundred and ninety big steps between kitchen chair and tree trunk.

Last night, after Beth fell asleep, he noticed the red light blinking on his machine. Her voice in the room, more irritated this time. "Seriously, Warren. Call me back. It's —" more quietly now, "it's about your mother."

His mother.

His mother.

Warren's skin tightened against his body. He felt as though he were packed in gravel, his arms and legs and chest unable to twitch or shiver. How had everything changed so quickly? One moment he was counting his steps, playing with simple numbers for a simple quiz, enjoying meals with a thoughtful woman. And all at once, the universe sneered, balking in the face of his ease, his contentment. *That will not do*, it said, shaking its starry head. *That will not do.*

Amanda. Beth. Now phone calls from Sarie. Whatever she had to say, it was not going to be positive. Something had happened, was happening. For years, Warren had next-to-no communication with his mother. With some effort, he had pushed her from his thoughts. And now he would have to hear something. Learn something. Possibly even say something.

But how could he? He had made decisions on how to live, and he would stick with them. She was to blame. He had made that decision when he was a boy, and had never once wavered.

When he was ready, he would call Sarie. He would listen to whatever she had to say, and without reply, he would hang up the phone.

"Did you hear me? I should get to the school, Dr. Botts."

Warren looked up. He had forgotten Ms. Fairley was standing in his kitchen. "Thank you for coming by." His voice was barely audible. "And for your kind words."

A strange series of grunts came from the living room, then. Warren and Ms. Fairley both watched Beth rise up from the couch, haul a blanket over her head. A shaking nomad, she stumbled across the floor, dragging her nubby cloak behind her.

"Dead now officially awake," came a grumble from under the blanket. "And going for a piss."

29

MUCH TO MY DISGUST, MY MOTHER STILL ACCEPTED MY AUNT and Larva into our house. These visits were sombre at first, but they soon adopted a surprisingly normal quality. The three of them chronicled Button's death over and over again, and once the truth had been steadily extracted from the story, it developed into an unfortunate, but inevitable fluke. Two months after the event, I even overheard my mother weeping, being bizarrely (and sickeningly) apologetic. "I'm so sorry, sorry, sorry," she repeated. "So sorry." Meaning, I deduced, she was remorseful that my aunt had to have such an experience with Button. That *she* had to be the one to suffer through *that*.

"Don't you even go there!" my aunt said, waving the air, thin minty cigarette in her fingers. "She was not well.

We did our best. All of us. Right, Harvey? She was sickly. That was clear from the start."

"Yes," my mother acknowledged quietly. "She never was a strong child."

"Or a strong baby."

"Sure, even I noticed that." Larva's asswipe contribution. His voice sounded primitive, rounded stones striking each other. "And I spent no to next time with her."

My aunt patted his hand. "Next to no, sweetheart."

"Huh?"

Between these three adults, there was an execrable tone of it-was-bound-to-happen-and-perhaps-it-was-for-the-best. Button seizing, convulsing, body straining on hot cement until her heart fluttered and stopped. It was actually a good thing. Weakness culled. No one blamed the man who forced mouthful after mouthful of liquid down her throat, while she was slick with salt and sweat. Upsetting her electrolytic balance. It only took me ten minutes of research to understand that basic scientific concept. I could not comprehend how no one else came to that conclusion.

The topic of conversation had now shifted to a rise in electrical bills.

"Criminal. The costs."

"Someone is living off our fat." My aunt adopted an appalled air.

Larva next. "They'd have a hard time collecting from you, babes."

I stood up, slid out the back door without making a sound. Leaned against the warm brick of the house. I still did not know how to handle Button's death. How to process it, make it fit neatly inside one of my mental folders. It was not that I was in the throes of grief, but during those months, I experienced near constant irritation. No matter what I was doing, one layer of my mental functioning was dedicated to her, grinding her memory into consumable portions. Who was responsible for stealing something that was mine? Aunt Floozy? Dickface? Lame witch of a mother who so quickly offered total absolution? I did not attempt to distract myself. My brain was masticating, and eventually it would come up with a fitting response.

From that afternoon forward, whenever I was aware of an impending visit, I removed myself from the premises and retreated to the branches of my Mighty Oak. I shimmied up the trunk, digging the toes of my sneakers into the healed scars made by my father's accident. The upper branches were accommodating, providing an exact fit between my scapulae, an appropriate angle for my vertebral column, a flattened area for my sacrum. While sitting in the crook of the tree I was busy solving a problem. I remained disguised for several weeks, and only when the leaves ceased chlorophyll production, and began to drop, did my neighbour discover me hiding there.

The neighbour was an enfeebled baldie, with round glasses and an oh-so-typical brown cardigan. But he was unconventional in other ways. I determined this based on the front bay window of his house. It allowed no sunlight in, as it was full of novels, piled one upon the other, pages facing out. During the fall, he came onto his front step, sat in a chair made of natural wicker, read a paperback. Sometimes he would wave, and being a courteous individual, I would return the gesture. Occasionally, when the weather was decent, he would lumber over to the tree, ask if I knew a good "knock-knock" (No, sir, I'm not big on jokes), or if I wanted kick the ball around on the lawn (I shook my head, thought, *Seriously?*). "My daughter had a swing on that there branch," he said on another attempt. "It's in the garage. I can find it if you like." I glanced over at the open garage door, a floor-to-ceiling wall of boxes and junk blocking the way. "No, no, Mister. That won't be necessary. I don't swing." He had nodded, retreated to his chair.

"Do you want a cookie?" Today, he stood right below me, the tip of his cane lost among the dead leaves. The afternoon was cloudy, cold, and I had begun to grow stiff. This time I nodded, slid down the tree, accepted his offer.

As anticipated, his home smelled of paper, books, magazines, a heap of yellowed newsprint. Not unpleasant in the least. Calming, actually. In his kitchen, all of his food items were neatly out on display.

"My daughter brings me cookies. Every second week she drives for two hours to bring me a houseful of groceries, but she only ever says she's bringing me cookies. She never wants me to think I'm a bother." His hands shook as he struggled with the plastic lid.

"That's kind of her," I said.

"She is kind. She is that." He chuckled.

Careful not to alter my breath or lean forward, I waited patiently until he pushed the container of oversized double chocolates toward me. I took one, two, then he reached over and closed the lid.

"You don't want?"

"No, no, I'm diabetic. I stay away from the sugar."

"Then it's illogical for your daughter to bring you cookies."

"Yes, you're right. She believes I entertain visitors."

"Do you?"

"Well, not really. But, you are here. You are a visitor, and consuming something. So, my response has just turned to 'yes.'" He filled a kettle with water, placed it on the stove, then lifted the lid of the smallest canister, dropped a teabag in a cup.

I finished the cookie, then gestured toward the container. "Might I?"

"Of course. I would offer you a tumbler of milk," tapping his chin, "but I don't have any."

Squinting my eyes slightly, I replied, "And your daughter fails to consider a visitor might like milk?"

"Touché!" Mock surprise. He understood my humour, and sounded delighted with the banter. "You've got her there. I apologize for her obvious lack of foresight."

"Doesn't matter. It makes me sick, and even if it didn't, I'd refuse to drink it. I find the concept quite disgusting. Did you know we are the only animals to consume milk from another species?"

"Yes, I did know that. And I concur. It is vile. Juice, then?"

"Too acidic."

"Soda?"

A flash of Button behind my eyes, orange bubbling from her mouth. "Too many chemicals."

"Water?"

I nodded. "No ice."

"That's perfect. I don't have any."

He handed me a glass, old and etched from years of washing. I avoided the chipped section of the rim. "I see you are quite the bibliophile," I said as I sipped the lukewarm water. "What sort of material do you prefer?"

"Well, let me see. Mysteries. True crime, mostly. Whatever I choose, it must be provocative. Grisly, even. Otherwise I would fall asleep."

"The one you are reading now is not provocative. Obviously."

"How did you guess?"

"I saw you napping on the porch."

"Well, then! Very observant."

I straightened my back. "I wasn't spying."

"I never said you were. I meant that as a compliment, my young friend. Not an admonishment."

There were shelves and bookcases and drawers and countertops laden down with books. Paperbacks, hardcovers, photographic journals. Fiction, non-fiction. The concept of all those stories, all that information so close to me made me salivate. Our local hag librarian had caught me in the adult section many times, and not only was my access restricted, she had taken to following me when I entered the double doors. I believed such surveillance was tantamount to a war crime.

"Yes," he replied. "I had an occupation that required waiting, and I'm not one to be idle."

"What job?"

"Security."

"Where?"

He smiled. "An apartment building. Sometimes in a hospital."

"Oh."

"Nothing terribly exciting, to be honest. People coming and going. Good time to read, though I suppose some people are satisfied with twiddling their thumbs."

"I couldn't be a thumb-twiddler." I tilted my head twenty degrees to the right. The change imperceptible, but an effective method implying sincerity. "May I borrow one?"

Two rapid blinks. "Would your mother permit you to read such material?"

"My mother?"

"Yes. Is she okay with you reading at that level? Some of it is quite grim."

"My mother has never involved herself in my reading selections. I have always followed my interests."

"With her blessing?"

I pressed one sneaker against the other until it squeaked. Why must adults always require reassurance before making a decision? "Yes." A soft smile. "She's very accommodating. My interests tend to be, well, mature."

Nodding. "Well, in that case, you may choose as you see fit. I respect your maturity."

I paused for a moment, not quite used to this refined level of interaction with an adult. Most could not manage it, and I rarely put in the necessary effort. "I appreciate your kindness," I replied. I was quickly developing a mild affection for him.

I ran my fingers over the spines, opened a novel, and touched the pages. As always, I found the sensation of paper on my skin bothersome.

Turning toward my neighbour, I said, "You should use your magnifying glass cautiously. On a sunny day you might just light your book on fire. Or yourself."

He laughed then. He was not laughing at me. I was already aware of that difference.

"That would be a sight to remember," he said. "I'm quite papery myself."

"Not something I care to see, thank you." I smiled at my little lie.

"No, no. Of course not. You've had difficult events recently."

"Yes. Nothing I wish to discuss."

"No one says you must discuss."

"Everyone says I must discuss, Mister. It's terribly annoying."

He placed his palm on the package of cookies, slid the container back and forth on the countertop. "I understand, and I apologize for probing. It's not my place. While talking may help some, for others, a thoughtful silence serves the purpose, don't you think? I believe it should be up to the individual. Do whatever makes you feel better."

Do whatever makes you feel better. I smiled, nodded. My neighbour was right. I needed to do something that would make me feel better. I was not certain of what that was, but I would think about it.

The kettle began whistling, and at the same time I noticed the wind. Something attached to the outside of the house was flapping. The kitchen had grown dark from the rolling black clouds, but my neighbour did not switch on the overhead light. This pleased me. I felt relaxed, enjoying a leisurely conversation in shadow.

Through the kitchen window, I could see my Mighty Oak. Branches unflinching as the wind slid through. I was reminded of my father, then. An imagined flash of his accident. Bursting out of the windshield of his bright red car, my tree bracing for impact. I wish I could have heard the thud when his head snapped. "Does it bother you I have appropriated your goods?"

He did not laugh at my wording, as I had expected. Instead, he went to the kettle, filled his mug before returning my gaze. "Do you require use of my tree at this time?"

"I do," I replied.

"Then it is yours to appropriate. Whatever I have. As you see fit."

"Anything, Mister?"

He showed his false teeth, spread his liver-spotted hands out in a grand gesture. *"Mi casa es su casa*, my small friend."

30

AFTER MS. FAIRLEY LEFT, BETH SHUFFLED INTO THE KITCHEN. SHE tapped her nails against the counter, then began scratching the back of her neck. "Where's those things from your friend?"

"The medicine?"

"Yeah. Pills. The pills."

"In the cupboard. Right in front of you."

She yanked open the door, took the tiny bottle in her white hands, and twisted the lid. When it did not open, she banged the cover on the countertop, tried again. "Piece of shit," she hissed, and she threw it onto the floor.

Warren bent to pick it up, and when he pressed it against his palm, the cover came off easily. "Here," he said, giving her two. "But use water. Just water."

Her hands were shaking and she sat on a chair, bent her

knees up to her chest. Chewed the pills, lay her head on her knees. Audible breathing. "I'm trying, Wars, I'm trying really hard. But it's wicked shit." Warren sat beside her, placed an arm around her shoulders, and watched her silently. After twelve minutes, she lifted her head, blinked. "I'm going to get a shower. Okay?"

"Okay."

"Yup." Back hunched, she stumbled across the living room, knee bumping the coffee table.

After what seemed like hours, he heard the water running, though it did not sound as though water was bouncing off a skull or back. Warren paced the floor. He should knock on the door. See if she was okay. But instead he continued pacing, counted his steps, counted his fish, counted the scattered snowflakes that batted against one square foot of his window. Then the bathroom door opened.

"Wars?"

"I'm here, Beth."

He rushed down the hallway toward the bathroom. She was wrapped in his bathrobe, her shaved head jutting out the top, her tiny feet hidden by the mass of hitched terrycloth. A piece of dried macaroni, smear of yellow cheese sauce, clung to the collar. He should have washed it, but instead, he had hung an unclean robe on the hook behind the door.

"I think I'm going to—" She sat down in the hallway. Then slid forward. "Hot water. Little dizzy. And sleepy, now."

Bending, he lifted her, lighter than he had expected. Even through the thick fabric, he could feel her ribs, the bones in her legs. She smelled clean, and like a male. Mint and spice. He carried her to his bed, and slid her underneath the covers. "This is more comfortable," he said, though she mumbled, "No, no. Warrrrs."

"Stephen and I will take the couch."

She looked at him then, a moment of lucidity. "What happened to your face? Did I do that to you?"

"Soccer ball."

"Ah. That's some kid."

"Yes, with some kick."

He flicked out the lights, and she whispered, "Warsie?"

"Yes."

"I wouldn't play hide and seek with you."

"You can sleep now, Beth. We'll talk tomorrow."

"No. You need to remember." Whining.

"I'm not sure."

"When we were kids." She opened her eyes, struggling to focus on him.

"Yes," he said. "I remember, Beth. I remember." Though he did not. He had very few memories of his sister as a child. Other than a small annoyance that carried around a home-made doctor's kit, and whenever anyone came within arm's reach, she would descend, press her ear to a skull, shine a flashlight down a throat, and write multiple tiny prescriptions for rolls of pastel candy.

"You always forgot to keep looking."

"I what?"

"Forgot to keep looking. For me."

"Oh." He knotted his fingers together.

"Yeah. I waited. And waited." Yawning, and then she brought her chin to her chest. "You forgot you were playing the game. You forgot about me."

Warren sat beside her on the bed, and when Stephen leapt up, he pulled the cat onto his lap. He counted her soft snores. Though he had scoured his mind, he never remembered playing with Beth. He remembered either being with his father, or being alone, and Beth pestering him. He continuously told her to go away, and eventually, she did.

He did grow up with the sense, though, that Beth was the one with potential. She was the smart one, and she had the personality. Warren, as Sarie had said, was just an average brooder. No offence meant, she offered. Though it took him some time to admit it, she was correct.

"I'm sorry," he whispered to Beth. "I'm sorry I forgot about you."

Then he stood up, cradled Stephen in his arms, and left the room.

Just as Warren was shaking dry food into Stephen's bowl, the phone began to ring. It rang seven times, and the answering machine refused to kick in. Warren put down the bag and walked to the phone. The ring was shrill, louder than it had ever been before, and though his hand was unsteady, he plucked it up, brought the receiver to his ear. Said nothing.

"I know you're listening." Anger in her voice. "Honestly, can you just grow up for ten minutes?"

He took a deep breath, prickles of guilt moving up through his abdomen. "Sarie."

"I'm not just calling for a little check-in, Warren. I'm calling about your mother. Which you would know if you'd bothered to listen to my goddamned messages."

Warren's heart began to knock, and he leaned against the wall, slid slowly down until he was seated on the floor, phone cord cutting underneath his arm. Afternoon sunlight angled through the curtains, and he could see dust in the air.

"Sarie? It's not a good time. I can't—"

"Christ, Warren. Do you think the world will wait for

your perfect moment? I won't be calling you back. I've rang you a half-dozen times."

Half-dozen. Equals six. One. Two. Three. Four. Five. Six.

"I'm sorry. I can't talk. There are problems here." .

"You can't talk? Problems? This bullshit has gone on long enough. She told me not to call you. Not to bother. But I'm not meek like her, I say what's on my mind."

Meek?

"And you're being a little shit, you know that? You're her only son, and she is sick. And your sister. Where the hell is she? No one even knows."

"She's with me."

"She is?"

"Yes. She's asleep."

"Well, wonders never cease. You can tell her, then. Maybe she'll want to know. Your mother is dying, Warren. I thought her children deserved that information, but maybe you don't deserve a thing."

"Sarie. I'm—"

"Don't bother, Warren. Just don't. Even a worthless crow flies back to visit. Flies home to see its mom." Sniffing, then quieter, "You're no better than he was."

[31]

THAT NIGHT, MY MOTHER TOOK HER PINK PILL RIGHT AFTER DIN-
ner, and she fell asleep on the couch with the volume on
the television turned down. Lights from the screen flickered
over her face. I perched on the coffee table to stare at her,
saw the skin on her forehead and around her eyes was thin
and wrinkled. I moved closer. Could smell chemicals and
stale black tea on her breath. I touched her dry hair, then
moved the blanket up over her shoulder.

Sometimes I hated being alone, without distraction.
When she fell asleep so early, I often wished she would wake
up and talk to me. Say something. Anything. Ask me if I had
brushed my teeth. If I had considered a new hobby. If I had
taken my vitamins. At that moment, I would even lower
myself to playing a game of checkers with her, because she
could not grasp the strategy associated with chess.

As I watched my mother, I dug my teeth into my knee, pushing through the jean fabric. I despised myself then, my weakness. Pain in my knee did not alleviate my longing, so I straightened my spine, lifted my fist, and punched myself twice just above my ear. Two sharp smacks with my knuckles. Jolts of bright light, my teeth clanking, and the empty throb soon arrived. I appreciated it. It cut through my infantile longing for maternal affection, and revived my objectivity. What relief to be free.

No longer wistful, the sight of my mother in her relaxing slumber now irked me. I flicked off the blanket so a breeze would chill her back. I moved her hair so that it fell over her face, and stuck several strands up her nose. She was too drugged, did not stir. I stood up, went to the kitchen, paused at the sink full of dirty dishes. Traced my finger though the cheese powder on the countertop. Brown curling pasta stuck to the burner.

In the darkened window, I caught my reflection. My face was narrow, hard, and if I squinted my eyes, turned my head quickly, my peripheral vision saw not me, but my father. I found it abhorrent that elements of his face were creeping out through my own. We had the same eyebrows and nose. The same dip in our top lip. Maybe that was the reason my mother never looked me in the eye. Avoided me at every turn. I reminded her of a person who had tried to destroy her.

Feet stuffed into sneakers, I closed the door quietly behind me, and wandered the sidewalks of my neighbourhood. The night was cold and blustery, and I crossed paths with no one. Not even a stray cat or dog. Dead leaves scraped over the roads, and in the faint glow of street lights, those leaves appeared alive. Large brown insects scuttling toward me. In pursuit. I pretended I was being chased, and I darted behind bushes, jumped low white fences. One portion of a fence had been knocked down, waiting replacement. I plucked up several long rusty nails, dropped them into the pocket of my jeans.

I turned left, then right, and right again. When I walked at night, I never really knew where I was going, but it did not matter. The homes were cookie cutouts of each other. Small identical bungalows, wide lots, front doors painted garish colours. Many were already decorated for the holiday, strings of festive lights on shrubs and roofs. I stopped in front of a family home, red and green Christmas bulbs hanging from thread along the porch, front lawn a display of inflated ornaments, lit up from the inside. The wind moved through them, made the display shudder. The grinning Santa had one finger lifted, in a you'd-better-be-good gesture, and when I darted toward it, walloped it in the stomach, the finger shook back and forth. Telling me I was naughty. Not nice.

Santa was such a fat ugly bastard.

The family was home, and yellow light glowed from the front window. Tiptoeing over, I peered in at them. I enjoyed doing that. Spying on families. Slipping through the darkness, no more detectable than a fragrance in a snow-storm. I liked it best when I discovered them fighting. A father yelling at his wide-eyed children, or grabbing the upper arm of his mousy wife. A casual slap across a timid face. Lifting a toddler up by his wrist, and once, his ear. Those moments always made my mouth water. Made me feel strong. Balanced. Even good (*suck that, Santa!*). When I witnessed their coarse behaviour, I made a connection. I understood. They presented a clean cover to the world, but lift the skirt, and under the bed were dust balls and stray hair and crumpled garbage.

Noises in the kitchen, and I stretched upwards to see into their home. I had never spied here before. Everything was bright and warm. Perfect father, bearded face, navy pullover, was opening mail with a silver letter opener. In a yellow apron, the mother buzzed about the kitchen, buttering toast, pouring milk into double-handled mugs. Seated on matching stools at the counter, two young twin boys wiggled and waited, their washed hair slicked, striped pajamas on. Enormous Sasquatch slippers swinging. Perfect Mother slid their bedtime snacks toward them, and Perfect Boys bent their heads, ate and poked each other with greasy fingers. Perfect Father glanced up from his mail, mouthed something. I imagined his words inside my head, *Now, now, fellas. Easy does it. Almost time for bedsy.* I watched them giggle, swing those furry slippers.

My knees bent, and I turned, slid down the siding, leaned against the house. *Bedsy. Almost time for bedsy.* A tide of disgust washed over me, nearly made me vomit. Why had I thought that? Why had his words been kind? Watching them, I began to shake, and I could feel the ache in my temple. I hated Perfect Family.

Do whatever makes you feel better.

Without making a sound, I crawled toward the blown-up Santa. I held the massive piece of crap in my arms, and for an instant, closed my eyes and hugged his softness. He was cold and hard and overinflated. Unwilling to hug me back. That did not surprise me.

I retrieved two rusty nails from my pocket, made a fist. Gripped those nails so the sharp ends were sticking out between my fingers. I punctured Santa's beard first, and then his body, poking holes in the vinyl, dragging a nail across his bloated neck. Tainted air began to seep out, his jolly face sinking, ever so slowly. I stabbed the reindeer next. Hit them in their chests, their abdomens, their groins. Then I slashed the blown-up sleigh.

A line of Christmas elves watched from the steps of the family home. So jolly, their chubby faces tilting to the left or to the right. One at a time, I picked them up, used the nails to gouge out their eyes. The bright layer of enamel was hard, but underneath, the plaster was soft and forgiving. I had thought to score the faces, but I liked the empty look they offered when their cheerful blue irises were removed, revealing dull white underneath.

Surveying my accomplishment, I felt calmer. Excited, even. My only regret was that I would not hear their reaction. I could envision it, though. Come morning, they would skip from their home in their matching ironed school clothes, and they would find heaps of deflated vinyl. Spinning around for answers, they would discover twelve blind elves standing around in wonder. The boys would sense an invisible threat and realize they were unprotected by their parents. The illusion dissolved, they would whimper. Though Perfect Mom and Perfect Dad might embrace them, cover their faces, that damp awareness would never leave them.

[32]

WARREN PACED FROM THE KITCHEN TO HALLWAY TO LIVING room to porch and back to kitchen. He did not know what to do. His mind was overflowing with nervous thoughts, and he sensed something else was going to happen. Trapped inside his house, he could only wait. He pushed everything out, erased the tangle inside his brain. Instead, he counted the ticking of the ceramic clock on the mantel. Counted his footsteps. Counted the number of times Beth's breath hitched in her throat, the number of times she gasped. Warren looked out the window at the tree with the missing branch. It was completely bare now, all the leaves were gone. Once the snow had melted, investigators had come to take photos of the ground. He had cracked open a window, eavesdropped on their conversations. The yellow tape had done nothing to prevent people from sneaking into

Warren's backyard, and the earth was trampled with prints. Boots and sneakers and animal paws. "If there was anything here, it's surely gone now."

He tried to read, tried to listen to a discussion on the radio, but he could not focus. Kneeling down in front of his tanks, he saw a faint build-up of algae on the glass. A water change was overdue, and this would pass the time. Underneath the kitchen sink, he retrieved plastic tubing, a bucket, his bottle of water conditioner, the glass scraper. Lifting the lid on the first tank, he set to work, checking parameters, establishing a siphon. His breathing calmed with the monotony of the cleaning, calculating the ratios of tank size to conditioner, gently scouring the glass, counting the numbers of swipes it took to remove the stubborn growth. He spoke quietly to the fish, explaining each procedure, the chemicals he was using, his future plans for each tank, and he wondered if they could hear his voice. If they recognized his face as he peered in at them. He wondered what it was like to exist in a school, surrounded by six or eight identical fish. Never to be alone.

Sleeves rolled up over his elbows, Warren moved slowly from tank to tank. He could hear the clean water moving over the plastic lip near the filter, tumbling onto the surface. A simple, natural, distracting sound. The tinkling was random, and he was grateful his mind could work endlessly trying to distinguish a pattern between the notes.

Piercing screams came from the front of his house. Warren's head jerked up, and he looked into the living room. His first thought was Beth, but he could still hear her snoring from the bedroom. He jumped up, blood rushing from his skull, and the bruise on his face throbbing. Gripping the edge of the counter, he waited for his spotty vision to return to normal. The screaming continued, and he stepped softly away from his tanks, moved toward the front curtains. Pulled back the corner and peeked out.

A woman was standing in the middle of his lawn. Wearing a skirt and short-sleeved blouse. No coat, no hat, no scarf. She was jabbing her finger toward his house, belting out garbled words that Warren could not identify. People surrounded her, a man tried to place his coat across her shoulders, several others joined her in her shouting. Light flashed from a camera, illuminating her face. Warren saw her clearly now, and even though he had never met her, some part of his clanging heart knew who she was.

Amanda Fuller's mother.

He froze, floral curtain still gripped in his fist. What if she came to the door? Wanted to yell at him? He could think of nothing to say to her, nothing that might bring comfort or understanding. Facing her, he would stutter and press his glasses into his face. He would repeat a string of numbers in his mind so that her voice would recede into the background.

Another flash of light burst through the fabric of the curtains, this time a swirl of red and blue moving over his walls, over his hand. A loud whoop of a siren. The police had arrived. He did not dare look out, but he heard doors slamming, a voice that sounded very much like Detective Reed's.

Without thinking, he walked away from his front window, went into his kitchen. As soon as he turned the corner, he could smell garbage rising up from the plastic bin. His hands automatically reached for the black bag, gripped and rolled the edges, knotted them. The siren outside had stopped. Everything was quieter, and Warren took a deep breath, stepped out his back door, and walked toward the metal garbage bin near the side of his house. Through cracks in his fence, he could see Detective Reed talking to Mrs. Fuller. Their heads were close together, and Detective Reed placed her hand on Mrs. Fuller's shoulder.

Warren grabbed the cold metal handle and lifted the lid. He was about to push the plastic bag into the dark hole, when he noticed several crumpled papers sitting on top of the garbage. He had not placed those papers there. Every item he dropped in the can was double-bagged in order to prevent leaks. He never just tossed random junk inside. Behind him, he knew the tree was there, a circle of trash around its trunk. Had someone used his garbage can? Had Beth thrown something away?

Even as he was picking them up, his mind told him to ignore them. Not to touch them. Not to pluck the sheets of loose leaf out of the can, smooth them on his leg, and angle them toward a window so that he could see more clearly.

Pages illuminated, his hand stopped. In the dim light, he could see the drawings. Scratched in dark red ink on white paper. As though a person had answered the question on his science quiz, but the parameters had changed. The branch, the pulleys, a thin rope. The weight replaced by a stick figure, lines to indicate moving legs, head angled forward, two xs for the eyes. The only item of detail was a striped stocking hat drawn on the simple circular head.

Warren peered through the fence again. Mrs. Fuller was gone, and Detective Reed was edging up the driveway toward his house. Her whistling slid through the air, filling Warren's ears. Glow from a flashlight then, scanning the fence, flickering over Warren's torso. His fingers locked around the drawings, pressed them to his chest.

He rushed into his house. Standing inside his bright kitchen, his eyes watered, and for a moment he imagined Sarie there. Leaning against the countertop, arms folded, disappointed clicking coming from her throat. If she could see him now, shivering, a mob of angry people outside his house, strung-out sister sedated in his bedroom, police lights invading every window, she might have understood his avoidance. But there was no excuse. Warren could not think about it, danced around the edges of it, glancing at a cold image through slit fingers. His mother was — *No, it is not real.* If he allowed that information to snake into his mind, it might choke him with regret.

Three loud thumps on the front door. So forceful, he heard the windowpanes rattle. Three more thumps. From the bedroom, Beth slurred, "Whooooo?" and then, "Wahhrsie. You got compaa —" A breeze curled over his face. His front door had been opened. He heard the shuffle of feet, a sharp crack of chewing gum, and Warren looked down at the drawings in his shaking fist. "You here, Botts?" Detective Reed was in his porch.

33

"WE'RE PREGNANT!"

Seeing my mother's reaction, so soon after losing Button, affected me in a willowy way. I felt long and asymmetrical and unable to stay still. As though I were an inflated ribbon on the sidewalk outside a car wash, and the generator was coughing. Swaying, my feet were not quite rooted to the carpet. For a moment, I closed my eyes, strained against my senses, but still, I could not identify what was happening inside my mind. And that murkiness irritated me. My aunt's *good news* and my mother's expression were making me itch. I wanted to leave, but instead I folded my arms, scratched until I developed two raw spots near my ribs.

"What do you mean?" my mother asked, sounding stupid. She sat down. Her shoulders rolled inward over her heart.

"We just don't know how it happened, do we, Harvey?

I mean we've been so careful and all. Taking precautions. But I guess it's just meant to be!"

A grunt erupted from his mouth. *Is this thug incapable of conversing?* He snapped open a beer, placed the can on his crotch.

"Well," my mother managed. "That is some big news. Unexpected. Congratulations?"

"We are beyond excited. Bee-yond! So, so looking forward to raising our little one. Aren't we, babes?"

"Uh-huh." Gulp.

"I've always been the aunt," she warbled, practically flapping her wings. "Now I get to be the mom."

"It's a lot of work."

"Now, Harv and me don't mind work. Raising kids is the most honest work around. You'd say that yourself, sure. And Harv's family is all about the young ones. Babies. Cousins. Harvey's sister'll just love it. It'll bring everyone closer together."

"Yes. Yes." My mother twisted her head toward me. Her neck looked stiff, full of taut cords. "What do you say, Kiddle?"

Under her strange watery glare, that willowy sensation evaporated. Oily contempt bubbled up through the carpet, and I was standing in a puddle of it. Did the silly housewife expect me to squeal and offer congratulations to my whore-aunt? They had barely cared for Button. Not much more than frying an egg or swiping peanut butter across a slice of stale bread. I did everything important. I washed her hair and folded her clothes and took her to the doctor to get shot up with dead viruses. I read her entertaining material, and picked candy out of her teeth and snot out of her nose. I scrubbed her skin with baby oil after she stuck her hands in warm tar. I took it upon myself to teach her about the badness in the world. About shitty people. To open her eyes.

Not that I was very successful.

My aunt ignored my weighted silence, continued, "Oh my God. I'm so hoping it's a girl."

These words pricked me. "You want a girl? A girl?" My voice was even, flat.

"Oh, yeah. Not that there's anything wrong with boys, of course. A boy would be just fine, too, right Harv? But you should see the cute stuff they got in the stores. Ahh-dorbable! You could look after her. Protector, and all."

Protector. And all. I took a deep breath. "Like I was with Button?"

My aunt froze, then. Her lip mid-flap. I could have sworn she was about to say, *Who*?

"Well, Kiddle," she stammered. "I — we — you see . . ."

I allowed the dead air to curdle for a count of one, two, three, before saying, "You clearly don't realize I'm joking." Then I turned, walked out of the house. Heard my mother's habitual sigh, offering, "Upset, that's all. It's to be expected. After, well, you know."

My mother was so wretched, she could not even say Button's name. Six weeks after my sister had dropped dead, my mother decided to clear out the room. Gave away all of Button's possessions. Never invested any energy into Button when she was breathing, but here that woman was, garbage bags full of stuffed animals, pink sheets, unwashed clothes, tossed on the front step. Bed dismantled, dragged out the door. She scoured crayon artwork off the white night table, put it on the curb. I watched that night table, like an angry hawk, until a man drove by, stopped, tossed it into the back of his pickup. For some asinine reason, I had thought my mother might clean Button's room, and keep it as it was. But instead she made Button disappear. Furniture dents in the carpet were the only evidence my sister had been there at all.

I went to my tree, crawled up the trunk, sat in the crook. As the days were shortening, I sensed even my tree was growing distant. The energy inside the outer rings slipping inwards, the branches drifting, dozing. I never resented this winter sleep, but I wished it were otherwise. Wished I were lying on something fully alive. Can I admit my spirits markedly improved when my neighbour emerged from his home holding two mugs? The sight of his desiccated face was strangely welcome. I slithered down the cold bark, made my way toward his front porch.

"Hello, Mister."

"Rough day, my friend?" He made eye contact which I could not sustain.

Wiping my wet cheeks in my sleeves, I replied, "No. Nothing. Just the wind."

"Wind?"

"There's more wind up in the tree. At that altitude. More wind. Makes my eyes water."

"Yes, yes, I understand," he said, holding up the steaming mugs. "Well, the key to wind resistance is hot chocolate. It's instant. Not instant resistance, I mean, just instant hot chocolate."

"I get it, Mister." I was cold. Even though those early December days were mild, it was hard to stay warm while remaining stationary in the crook of a sleeping tree.

"I used water, but there's still a bit of real milk in the powder. I think it's real. Is that all right?"

"Yeah. Sure."

"I know you don't drink milk."

I took the mug in my hands, smelled the sweet steam

rising up from the thin liquid. "Only an ignorant person is rigid in their beliefs," I replied.

"Right. Of course." A gentle chuckle. "But your intestinal tract might disagree with your apparent flexibility. I wouldn't want you going home in any pain. Getting me in trouble with your mother."

Getting in trouble with your mother. The stupidity of that comment made me gulp the hot chocolate, burning my tongue and throat. I choked slightly.

"Watch it, watch it," he said, and when his fingers grazed my shoulder, patted me very gently, my eyes started leaking once again. My tear ducts were irritated by the steam, or the burn in my throat, or something.

He brought his hand back to his chest. "You okay, friend?"

"Don't worry about my mother," I said, blinking. "She's preoccupied."

"I understand. It's not natural to lose a child. It will take a long time."

"Button was mine. Not hers." An unintentional blurt. Rare for me.

"I'm sure she was. You loved her."

I peered into my mug. There was a layer floating on top of the hot chocolate, and when I blew, it crinkled like skin. I hated that word. *Love.* People tossed it around so easily, as though it was the epitome of existence. Common stupidity. I hated that my connection with Button was reduced to such a meaningless emotion.

But I smiled at my neighbour, said, "Thank you for noticing."

"You must miss her."

I nodded, lowered my eyelids. *I do.* I could not deny it. *I miss her. Every. Single. Day.*

"Do you want to come inside and warm up? Or are you needed at home?"

Needed at home. Seriously! "No, Mister. I can come in."

"I've got new cookies. Something with nuts, I think."

"I'm not hungry."

"I understand. I'm not hungry most days either. Once you've tasted everything as often as I have, the thrill is gone."

Nodding, "I know what you mean."

Once inside, we sat in silence. A comfortable silence, which I enjoyed. I ate one of his peanut butter cookies, and he was right, there was no thrill.

"How's your stomach?" he asked when I had taken several sips.

"Not a problem. Yours?"

"All good. Besides, I take something every day. Knocks what belongs out out, keeps what belongs in in."

I stopped mid-slurp, licked my lips. "An odd phrase."

My dear neighbour appeared a little sheepish. "Sorry. Too much information to share. That's what happens when you're alone most of the time. Your sense of sociability flies out the window."

"No, Mister. I was, I was just thinking it was a convoluted sentence. Definitely some type of grammatical error in there."

I repeated his words in my head.

And then, click, I sensed something was growing in my mind. The seed of an idea.

"Never did do good in grammar. The only term I remember is a *dangling participle*. And only reason I remember that is because I thought it was something inappropriate. Funny how a young man's mind clamps on to that sort of thing!"

"Sipping hot chocolate, the wind started to howl outside."

He cocked his head to the side, tugged his long lobe. "Hey, what's that? The wind is coming up? I don't hear it."

"I was dangling a participle, Mister. As an example. To demonstrate the error for you."

Again, with the easy laughter. "There you go. Put it right in front of me, and I still didn't see it."

No different than most people.

"The wind was not drinking hot chocolate."

"Yes, yes, I get it now."

Another slurp.

Click, click. The idea had a shape. Hard and smooth like a worn stone.

Opening my eyes, I angled my head into its innocent position. After a thoughtful sip from my mug, I asked, "Do you take a lot of medication, Mister?"

"Not really, no. Mostly natural stuff. Though that doesn't stop the doctors from trying to push tons of prescriptions on me. I can't be bothered with most of it, but my daughter takes every one to the pharmacy and gets it filled."

"Hard to keep track, I would guess. What you have and what you don't."

"No doubt about that. These days, it's hard to keep track of which foot is left, and which foot is right."

"I understand." I finished the remainder of my drink, patted my stomach. "Might I use your washroom, Mister?"

I am abashed to admit I actually grinned when I entered that cramped space. Grinned like some sort of asinine fairy-tale cat. As in the kitchen, his cabinets were empty and all his personal items were organized on a narrow shelf. I scanned the products, glue for his dentures, a bottle of shaving lotion, hair paste (irony, here?), and among it all, nearly two dozen orange bottles of pills with peeling labels.

Yes, I had definitely developed a certain affection for my neighbour. *Mi casa es su casa*, right? Even though he was old and obviously decrepit, he was becoming a useful friend. The very best kind of all.

34

WARREN DROPPED THE SKETCHES. WITH THE TOE OF HIS SLIP-per, he kicked the papers into the corner beside the stove. Everything felt surreal. Detective Reed's voice was distorted, as though it was pulled through a watery membrane. *Inhale, exhale, inhale, exhale.* He heard a stomach growling. Stephen was purring. Wind circled down the chimney, a thin stream of displeasure.

"Botts?"

"I'm here," he said, as he hurried into the living room. "I'm here."

"Sorry to barge in on you. That a problem?" Detective Reed stood in the porch, a uniformed policeman hovering behind her.

"No," he pressed his glasses up his nose. "I didn't know the door was unlocked. But it's okay."

She nodded toward the blankets and food on the coffee table. "You got a visitor?"

"My sister," he said. "She has the flu."

"That's a drag." Detective Reed glanced at the police officer behind her. "What happened to your face, Botts?"

Warren touched his cheek. "Slipped. In the shower. I used a different kind of cleaner this week and I guess I didn't realize it was so slippery. I didn't rinse enough." He was talking too much. Obviously lying.

Inhale, exhale.

"Well, I've got a couple things to clarify. And seeing as I'm here, you know. Trying to manage the skirmish outside." She took a step into the room, pulled out her notebook. "Okay if I come in?"

"Ah. Yes. Sure. Of course."

"Lot of people pissed off out there."

Warren nodded. Blinked hard several times. Pressed his glasses up his nose again. He had to stop touching his face, and he slid his hands into his pockets.

"There are things bothering me, Botts."

"Bothering?"

"Your neighbour. Directly across from you. Mr. Wilkes."

Warren closed his eyes, pictured it. The fabric and springs stretched so that the man's body was only inches from the cement floor. He thought about the force needed to extend those springs on Wilkes's lawn chair. Force was proportional to the distance.

"You listening, Botts? Says he seen Amanda Fuller at your home. More than once. Sitting on your step last Friday afternoon, in fact."

"Oh." Warren felt his throat tighten. His glasses were sliding, bit by bit, down his nose. He resisted the urge.

"Is that an accurate statement? Was she at your house?"

Leaning against a chair, he jiggled his left leg. Detective Reed was not looking at him, but examining everything in the room.

"Seems you're slow to answer, Botts. Do you know Wilkes was my next-door neighbour as a kid? He's come up in the world now, since those days, but damn, he used to rat me out to my mother time after time. Eyes like a hawk, that guy. Reliable, too. He says he saw you two having a heated conversation. Then he witnessed an embrace."

"Yes," he mumbled. "She was here."

"Well. That's interesting news. And you chose not to share that?"

He shook his head slowly, knowingly.

"Why was she here, Botts? Why would a grade eight student be making teacher house calls?"

"I don't know. I don't know why. She just was."

Detective Reed smiled, mouth open, teeth showing. "In this circumstance, 'I don't know' is not an acceptable response. Try harder."

"She was—she was—" He pressed a hangnail against his lower lip, the sharp point stinging him. "She was here three times. Maybe four. I came home from work and she was sitting on the step. Once she was inside my house. Right there," he pointed to the couch, "petting Stephen. I sometimes forget to lock the door. She came in. I talked to Ms. Fairley about it. You can ask her. When I came home, she only stayed for three minutes. I told her not to come back. I tried not to hurt her feelings. I tried to be kind."

She wrote something on her notepad, then took another step into the room, stared at him, held his gaze. "Exactly how'd you try to be kind, Botts?"

He felt his cheeks begin to pulse. He hated how she kept repeating his surname so forcefully. A suggestion in her tone. He coughed, straightened his back. Stopped his leg from jiggling. "I listened. I just listened to her."

"What'd she say?"

"I told you already."

"Refresh my memory, Botts."

"She was worried about her grades. Angry about her father. He's on a beach somewhere, she said, selling coconut monkeys. Angry about having to change homes. She had a nice house before, one of those historic homes near Main Street. She didn't like her new one. Lots of things."

Detective Reed unwrapped a candy, spit the gum from her mouth into the cellophane, flicked the ball onto the messy coffee table. Then she pushed the candy into her mouth. "Shifting gears for a moment," candy clinking against her teeth, "I heard the call you made. After you saw Amanda hanging from that tree."

"I." Hand to his nose. He could smell artificial cherry.

"How about we give it a listen?" She pulled a small recorder from an inside pocket, pressed a button with her thumb. Warren's voice filled the room. High-pitched and anxious.

"I'm so sorry." Heavy breathing. "I didn't mean it."

She snapped another button, and his voice stopped. The police officer behind her scowled, shook his head. "Sounds like you dropped your Adam's apple there, Botts." Loud crunch, candy smashed. "That's quite a confusing statement to make, isn't it? You're sorry. You didn't mean it. Can you clarify that?"

He looked down, could resist no longer. He adjusted his glasses, lifted them twice. "There's nothing to clarify."

"Nothing?"

"I was overwhelmed."

"Really?"

"Yes. Overwhelmed." For a moment, he closed his eyes, imagined the cube-shaped room flipping outward, and instead of being on the inside of the die, he was standing on one of the faces. All he had to do was shuffle backward, and he would tip over an edge. Detective Reed would stay on the six, and he would slip ninety degrees onto the four. No longer facing each other, a right angle between them.

"Botts?" She continued to crunch, pulverizing the sugar in her mouth. "You got my attention."

He could not share that he had seen her, ignored her, even though her presence so early on a Sunday morning was strange, unexplainable. He could not admit he was annoyed rather than concerned. Irritated that his quiet morning was disrupted. His toast was burnt. Greasy butter on the toe of his slipper. He could not share that when he discovered she was hanging, he rushed toward her, but stopped. Was unable to approach her. He was a coward. He was a small useless boy, trapped inside a man's body. He wanted to cover his eyes, his ears, and tried to believe that if he could not see her, she was not there.

"You in there, Botts?" Detective Reed shook her head. "Come out, come out wherever you are." Singing.

"I'm sorry."

"There will come a time when you need to be straight with me."

She moved the tip of her shoe back and forth over the floor in front of him, as though she were erasing a drawing in the sand. Warren watched the muscles in her lower jaw, flexing, relaxing, flexing. One thousand, eight hundred, and eleven seconds had passed since she entered his home, but he recognized there was a large margin of error in that number. Counting large digits one by one took longer than a single second. "I'm trying."

"I'm sure you are. Mind if I take a look around?"

Warren's heart crept up into his throat, but he nodded. "But don't disturb my sister, okay? She's got the flu. A virus."

"Yeah, yeah. You said."

Warren watched Detective Reed stepping around his house. Peering here and there in the living room, wandering through the kitchen, pulling open cupboards, rifling through old newspapers, shoes scuffing over the linoleum at a predictable rate. Then there was silence. He knew Detective Reed had stopped moving. His heart rate increased, thump, thump, thump, and saliva pooled in his mouth as he was unable to swallow. He heard her whistle, then, "Well, lookie here," and he knew exactly what she had found.

Moments later, she re-emerged, a satisfied expression lighting up her face. Her hand was inside a thin yellowish glove, and she was holding the pile of drawings, nipped near the edges.

"Found these in plain sight, Botts. Just lying there. I'd guessed you'd be a better housekeeper than that."

"Th-th-th-they're not mine." He pushed his glasses up, the skin on his cheek was pulsing.

"Warren Richard Botts, I'm placing you under arrest on suspicion of the murder of—"

Warren heard nothing else. Detective Reed's words were trapped in individual bubbles, and they did not burst near his ears. White noise flooded his mind, and he tilted his head. He was only dreaming. The feeling of metal on his wrists, the tightening clicks were imaginary. No one was gripping his upper arm, escorting him from his house without jacket or shoes.

How did he end up in front of his house? Cameras flashing, people yelling. Detective Reed, eyes bright and wide, opened the car door, and as he eased into the back seat of the cruiser, she placed a confident hand on his scalp, pushed him down ever so slightly.

Another whoop of the sirens, and the car pulled around. Warren stared out at the crowd in front of his home. Wilkes was in front, jeering at him, waving goodbye with one hand. Fat fingers rippling as though he were playing a piano. Then, behind Wilkes, he saw another familiar face. Evie. The brightest girl in his class. In the glow of the street lamp, her face appeared puffed and shiny. As though she had been crying.

35

I WAS IN A FESTIVE MOOD.

I wore navy pants and a pale blue dress shirt, and even buttoned it up to the collar. Not once did I complain about the tightness around my throat. While I waited, I watered the tree and organized the few gifts. I squirted icing onto the faces of gingerbread men, giving each of them a surprised *o* for a mouth. I strung stale popcorn on a thread. I even cleaned the toilet. When I could think of nothing else, I watched out the window. My behaviour reminded me of Button, except that I was calm. Perfectly calm. My heartbeat, my breathing, my steady hands. When the doorbell *finally* rang, I swung open the door, and offered a warm holiday greeting to my blossoming aunt and her charming fiancé.

Okay. Just joking about that last part. But I did open the door.

My aunt stomped onto the rug, shook snow from her shoulders, her hair. "Jesus it's coming down, isn't it? Roads are freaking treacherous."

"I like it," I said.

"Yeah, that's cause you're a kid and don't got to go nowhere."

"No, I like it because the snow makes everything look clean. All the dirt is disguised."

My aunt sighed, dropped two boxes, silver wrapping, onto the bench. "Do you want to argue with me, Kiddle, or do you want to be useful?"

Argue, of course. "Useful, of course. You may give me your coats?"

"Hear that, Harv? Oh, so formal! We got ourselves our very own mini-butler."

Grunt.

The odour of cigarettes and perfume billowed in my face as she squirmed out of her nubby winter outerwear and dropped it in my arms. Larva gave me his, too. Heavy black leather that smelled like fecal matter. I could not decide which scent was worse.

As I slung them over hooks, I heard her say, "Harv, darling? My shoes? I—I can't even lean over, my skirt is so damn tight." Then I turned to see Larva on bended knee, unzipping her leather boot, sliding it from her heel. How gallant!

"Thank you, dearest. You are theee best." She was practically chirping, and the sound of her voice made vomit pop up in my throat.

"Come on in." I could faux-chirp with the best of them. "I've got a fire going."

Hand on her pregnant hip. "*You* got a fire going? Now, how's that happen?"

"I don't know. I just did it."

"Well, your mother shouldn't be letting you handle fire at your age, now, should she?" *Newfound Parenting Expertise? Check!* "Harv-sweets? Can you go take a look? Make sure the house isn't about to burn down?"

"On it."

"I have some skills," I said, obviously annoyed.

"Skills don't matter." Then she said to me with practised words, "Your Uncle Harvey is exhausted, Kiddle. I don't want you being no trouble. I know Christmas is all about the young'uns, and that bullshit, but keep your noise down, no crawling over the furniture, making a racket with your toys, bugging Harv to play with you. You know the drill."

A racket with my toys? Bugging that loser to play with me? The drill? She had me confused with Button? Who, I imagined, would already be sitting on the asshole's foot, arms and legs velcroed around his leg.

"I think," I offered in my gentlest, most accommodating tone, "I can manage that."

"Good." She brushed past me, and even though she was barely pregnant, she already kept her right palm against her lower spine, adopted the slightest waddle into her step.

I followed her, waited until she was seated on the couch next to her beloved.

"How are you feeling?" I inquired, my head tilted, hands cupped.

"You know what, Kiddle? Just perfect. Top of my game. Top of my game. Right, Harv?"

"Would you like an extra cushion for your back?"

Snuggling into Larva, she said, "Nope. I got all the cushion I need."

"Cushion's getting fatter with all the Christmas parties." The loser yawned, scratched his stubble.

"Oh wow, Harv. Your eyes are so bloodshot." Then, to me, "Plows couldn't keep up with the snow last night. He was out until dawn."

"Impressive work ethic," I said. "Would anyone like a beverage?"

She leaned forward. "What has gotten into you? One minute a butler, and now you're a waiter. All you need is the fucking bow tie."

I smiled, lifted my eyebrows, sang, "It's just such a happy day, isn't it? Christmas together with family."

"I bet Kiddle's excited for the baby," she said to Larva.

"Doubt it." He yawned again, hands making no move to cover his mouth.

Though I wanted to place a toothpick vertically in his gaping gob, I ignored his boorish behaviour. "Did anyone decide on a beverage?"

"A beer," Larva burped. "Cold."

"A juice for me," my aunt twittered. "Well, maybe with just a splash of something. Just a hint of a splash. Do you think, Harvey? Is that okay?"

"Makes never mind to me."

"*No* never mind."

"Huh?"

"Nothing. Kiddle? Just a splash, okay? A generous splash."

"You got it."

Then, as I was walking away, "And tell your mother to get her ass out of the kitchen and come say hello to her glowing sister."

"She'll be right there."

When I returned to the family room, drinks on an enamel tray, my mother was perched on the edge of the coffee table, discussing the winter storm, the size of the turkey, then complimenting my aunt on her complexion.

As a good server should, I waited for an appropriate break in the conversation, then handed out the beverages.

"Thanks, Kiddle," my aunt said as she gripped the over-sized glass full of sugary fruit cocktail. "I am constantly thirsty growing this little thing." Fingers drifting across her abdomen. "Drinking for two!"

I watched as she lifted the glass. "Merry Christmas, everyone," and she brought it to her bright red lips.

"Yes," I breathed.

She took a sip. A second sip. She smiled at me. I smiled back. Even crinkled my nose.

There. I had dropped the figurative stone into the figurative bucket. Parts of my contraption were starting to move, shift, marbles rolling, elastic bands snapping, yardsticks lowering. I could feel momentum building. This time, though, the outcome was unpredictable. Uncertainty was part of the fun.

36

WARREN OPENED HIS EYES. HE WAS ALONE INSIDE A DAMP cage. A fluorescent light flickered above him, and everything was cast in grey: the walls, the ceiling, the ledge of a narrow window. The room reeked of sweat and urine, and when he lifted his head, he saw he had fallen asleep on a striped mattress without a sheet. Sandpaper blanket still underneath his hip. He had not wanted to touch the blanket, as his fingertips were stained with ink.

Last night he had spoken to a lawyer. Someone young and hyper in a cheap suit, dry white lips, dilated pupils. Warren had tried to explain the errors, the misconceptions, that he was with Nora that evening. No, he could not recall the movie they were watching. No, he was not certain what time she left. The lawyer's mouth was open while Warren spoke, as though his response was already prepared.

Nothing Warren was communicating would change that. He had spoken rapidly, then, about a forthcoming bail hearing, no criminal record, that Warren was a professional.

Warren sat up, leaned against the cement wall. His throat was sore, and he pushed his glasses up with the back of his wrist. He counted the seventeen bars in front of him, and then started identifying as many prime numbers as he could remember. It did not help. He was worried about Beth. She had certainly woken up, and he pictured her wandering around his house, calling his name. He would have to talk to her about the phone call from Sarie. But not yet. He was unable to absorb the thought himself.

Warren closed his eyes again. A faint hum of a motor started outside, and though he knew it was too close to winter, the sound reminded him of a lawnmower. He remembered a time when he was a boy, he came to a slope near the back of his house, and he had to mow a hill. Instead of pulling the machine, he pushed. That morning it had rained, and when he slipped on the damp grass, the running machine rolled back over his sneakers, his legs. He felt shock, spikey tingles in his feet and hands, and then the mower choked, went silent.

Warren had lain still, sipped shallow breaths. He was afraid to move, afraid to shift the machine, and though he felt no pain, he was afraid to see the condition of his feet, his limbs. Could the motor start up again by itself?

Only a moment or two had passed, before nine-year-old Beth bounded up over the horizon with her small bag of "equipment" in her fist. She crouched beside him, tugged the drawstring on her bag, and reached in. Pushed a sugar cube into his mouth. "Eat that," she said. "You're suffering from *dismay*." Then she gripped the side of the mower and flipped it. "Watch out, Warsie." A piece of elastic from the cuff of his gym pants snapped off the blades and flew outwards.

"You are lucky today," she said. "That thing could have chewed you up."

"How did you know I was here?"

"I was watching you."

"You were?"

"I'm always watching."

"Oh." He lifted his legs.

"Don't budge," she yelled, then punched him in the stomach. "I need to examine you."

"Get away from me. I don't need to be examined."

Tugging at the leg of his pants, she touched a cut, raised her fingers to show him the blood. "You got a serious wound there. Can I use a tourniquet?"

Warren leaned forward and looked at the scrape. "I don't need a tourniquet."

"You could bleed to death."

"It barely broke the skin."

"Oh, c'mon, Wars. I've never done one before. I want to practise."

"Like that's a life skill you need." He stood up, then, turning the mower back over, yanked the cord.

"Please?"

"Leave me alone." It coughed back to life, and he shoved it back and forth, tried not to look at the cuts in the rubber soles of his sneakers, the shredded leg of his pants.

"You're so dull," she had hollered over the motor. "Just dull. You need to talk to someone, you know. My chair is open! I'm cheap!"

Warren touched his glasses, pressed them back into place. Why had he not thought more about Beth when he left home? Why had he not realized she needed him? Wanted a brother, a friend. He could not understand how, in the years since he left, she went from child charlatan to what she was now. Had his absence contributed? He could have offered for her to come live with him. Gone to his school, studied something. She was more than capable. Instead he took off, and never looked back. Held so tightly to the barb of hatred he had for his mother. As though that emotion were the elastic keeping his blades from spinning.

He stared up at the ceiling of the jail cell. He tried picturing his mother's face. Her shy smile. He had been so certain of that small, single fact. His mother was to blame. And now, nearly two decades later, when he turned the whole thing over in his mind, he could not identify one logical reason to support it.

"And can someone get the man a pair of shoes?"

Wood smacking against wood.

A slender man with a gun on his waist was removing the cuffs around Warren's wrists. The judge had spoken for several minutes, but Warren drifted away. In the courtroom, everything was made of darkly stained wood panels, and he tried to determine how many individual pieces were needed to build the entire room.

"Dr. Botts? Do you understand?"

"I'm sorry?"

"Judge says there's not enough to hold you." His lawyer did not blink. "Seems the detective's actions were a bit premature."

"I can go?"

"Yes. Absolutely you can go. But you need to stay close to home for now. I'll check in with you, though."

Warren rubbed his wrists, shuffled through a low swinging door, moved between the benches. Detective Reed's eyes focused on his face, did not waver, and Warren looked down at his socks. Felt them catch and hitch on the rough wood. He did not have to go with her or talk to her. He would take a taxi home.

As Warren left the station, a woman approached him. She wore black pants, a jean jacket, and a looping orange scarf. The heels of her boots dug into the grass, but she did not move to the cobblestone sidewalk.

"Sir? Excuse me, sir?"

Warren blinked, touched the arm of his glasses, traced the plastic line back to his ear. He did not recognize her, but believed he should. "I'm sorry?"

"Do you have a minute?"

Tiny stones were digging into his feet, and icy cold moved up through the soles.

"I would really appreciate it."

Her gentle insistence made him pause. Perhaps she was a marketer. Warren always pitied those people who came knocking door to door, or strolled up to him in a supermarket, clipboard in hand. Selling subscriptions to magazines or pushing credit card applications or lawn-care services. What terrible employment, he always thought, and did his best to listen attentively before explaining that he was in no position to purchase their services. He was always apologetic.

Even now, looking at the woman's hopeful face, he felt a soggy guilt.

"We'd like your side, Mr. Botts. It's your time to talk. Tell us what really happened?" A fat microphone appeared out of nowhere. "What really happened?" Another step toward him, her hand moving closer to his face. "Give us your truth. We can set the record straight."

Warren felt dizzy, exhausted. "I can't. I can't talk to you." How could he have thought she was a marketer?

"What did you see—hear? That night. Take me through it. Every detail. I can give you a platform, Mr. Botts. Tell us your side."

Warren shook his head.

"Tell us how Amanda died."

Hands up, "Leave me alone. Just leave me alone."

Then a man rushed closer, stout, bearded, black plastic in his hand. Swift movements, jostling Warren, and lightning flashed in his face. One, two, three pops. "Got a good one," the man yelled.

Warren, tripping in front of the courthouse, in a sweatshirt and dirty socks, glasses askew, smudges of navy ink beneath his eyes.

37

MY AUNT LIFTED HER FEET ONTO THE COFFEE TABLE, FLICKED her toes inside her pantyhose.

"Like a picture, isn't it?"

When I turned my head toward the window, the street light burst to life, as if on cue, and the thick snowflakes were visible.

"Isn't it, though? Here we are. A perfect holiday scene." Cheerful Mother.

Perfection, indeed. How to describe it? The fire was crackling and the Christmas tree twinkling. Smells of turkey and spice hung in the air. Someone on the radio was singing carols with a soulful voice. My mother was humming, and my aunt (bless her and her unborn child) was nestled into the shoulder of her sleeping amour. We were like a holiday card of joyfulness. And to steal my sister's special word, we were jubilance personified. A pretty, pretty picture.

Button, are you watching this bullshit?

My aunt emptied her glass. Again. And I was up on my feet before she could say *Kris Kringle*, wrinkled cup towel over my forearm.

"Another?" I said.

"What's gotten into you, Kiddle?"

"I don't know." Sweet grin. "Holiday spirit?"

"Well, I like it. But I shouldn't. Really. Should I?"

"It is Christmas."

"Harv?"

"He's passed out."

"Okay, Kiddle. Seeing as you look so sharp in that shirt. Don't want to disappoint the butler."

I plucked the glass from her hand. "Another of the same?"

"Sure, Kiddle. But don't tell Harv."

"Not a chance." I winked, went to the kitchen. Dumped gin in her glass, each drink progressively stronger. I could hear my aunt and mother cheeping around the corner, Larva's snores whenever they paused for breath. Two loser hens. One fat rooster.

"Yes, oh, yes." Slightest slur. "The doctor said a splash here and there was perfectly acceptable. Harmless."

"Of course it is."

"Women have been growing babies, sure, for thousands of years."

What did they do before that? Pluck them from a tree?

"Yes. People always going on about this and that, but I doubt we got much control over what happens in there. Why stop living your life?"

That was my mother, announcing her support of fetal drunkenness. Severe underage drinking was totally acceptable. Why not have a chug or two at twelve weeks in utero? Not like the thing can get into much trouble. Get all rowdy and punch up those uterine walls. Jab to the placenta. Pass out in its amniotic fluid.

I dribbled in a little more, then returned, pleasant faced, with the refreshments.

"Isn't it quiet this year?" My aunt, again.

My mother knotted her fingers together in her lap.

"It's so much more peaceful this Christmas, and I, for one, appreciate the calm. In my state, it's a welcome relief. I'm sure I won't have it for much longer!"

My aunt took a long sip, and I watched my mother's chest rise and fall. She said nothing in response. We all knew the house was peaceful because of my sister's absence. Why did my mother not react?

"Mother?" A distraction to control my anger.

She straightened her back, frowned at me. I loved how she always appeared nervous when I directed my attention toward her.

"What."

"I think it's time."

"Time?"

"I would like you to open my gift."

"Oh—oh. Your gift." Relief in her settling eyebrows. "Yes, I can do that. It's okay, right? Nobody minds?"

"Who would mind?" I glanced at my aunt, who had her chin pressed into her chest, and appeared to be admiring her swollen breasts. "Besides, it's nothing much. Not worth getting excited over."

"Now, now. I appreciate it, whatever it is."

Liar.

I handed her the box. "Okay. I'm excited," she trilled.

Liar, again.

One of the many things that annoyed me: watching a hesitant person opening a gift. My mother picked at each individual piece of tape with her chewed fingernails. Next, she unfolded the paper and laid the box aside. And then she folded the used sheet of wrapping into a neat square. One side over another side, smoothing, creasing. I wanted to get very close to her greasy face and yell at her, *Time is passing! Time is passing!* But I counted my teeth with my tongue. I counted my mandibular cusps. I thought about that little flap of skin that connects the upper lip to the gum. Did that membrane have a name? *Time is passing.* Finally, she brought the box to her lap and opened it up.

"I thought you'd never get around to it," my aunt said.

Rare words of truth from that filthy mouth.

Inside: two bottles of salon-quality styling products, a boar-bristle brush, and a nail care kit.

"Where did you get this?"

I widened my eyes, blinked. "At the hairdresser's."

Unzipping the nail kit, she opened it up to find shiny metal tools laid out on a velvet interior. "It looks so — so expensive."

"I did chores for, you know. Our neighbour." She glanced at me. "I know, I know. You think it's weird that he's always on his front porch. My estimation, though, is that he's quite average."

"You're right. Of course, you're right. He just keeps to himself. Who am I to judge?"

It was exceedingly easy to alter my mother's opinion. Just a few words, and she had morphed from neighbour-phobic to neighbour-receptive.

She stood up, held my shoulders. "Thank you, Kiddle.

That was very kind of you to spend your hard-earned money on me. I appreciate it."

Then. She. Hugged. Me.

Actually placed her arms around me and squeezed.

Of course, I flinched. My waiter towel fell to the floor. I was not startled, but I despised the tactility. Pressed out against it, in fact, the way I imagined a moth might press against a cocoon. "Yup, yup. That's enough. That's good enough." My words were muffled in the shoulder of her fuzzy sweater.

In that moment, I abhorred my mother. Found her repugnant. Loathsome. No better than trash. It was not simply a hug, but an over-hug. Her gesture had nothing to do with the junk I had stolen months ago, wrapped in already-used Christmas paper. No. It was a second-rate attempt at connecting, designed not to show affection, but to alleviate her guilt. Her vulgar display had nothing to do with me.

"Stop it. You're choking me." I broke free from her grasp, stepped back, scowled at her. Her lips were parted, and she was breathing through her mouth. I watched her eyes glaze over again.

"I—I don't remember you being so hard." Stuttering. "Your bones all sticking out like that."

"I'm not har—"

"Well," singsong voice again, "I should check on the turkey. Get this dinner underway."

Then she left the room. Left me alone with my aunt and sleeping Larva. My aunt moaned. "I've been glued here too long. Can you help me up? I'm bursting to piss."

I picked up the towel, wrapped it around my forearm, and let her touch me there. Away from my skin. With further moaning, she hoisted herself up, "The springs on that couch are abominable," then wavered down the hall to the bathroom, stopping to touch the walls, putting her palm to her cheek, pausing with her hand on the doorknob, finally disappearing, closing the door.

I followed. Of course I did. My aunt was looking decidedly unwell.

After several minutes, I gently tapped on the door. "Are you okay?"

"Oh, Kiddle? You there?" Bathroom door cracked open, my aunt was leaning on the toilet, peering out. "Can you go get your mom?"

"Oh, geez. She's just lifting the turkey out of the oven." I leaned my head to the side. "Do you need extra toilet paper?"

"No, no. Not that." Coughing. "I'm just feeling a little light-headed. Not myself."

"Oh, dear. Should I wake up Uncle Lar—um, Harvey?"

"I think I'm fine. I'm just. I don't know. Maybe a drink of water?"

I nodded, mock concern. "You want a drink of water while you're sitting on the toilet? No offence, but isn't that kind of nasty?"

"Of course I don't. Of course not." She slammed the door.

Sliding down against the wall, I began counting backward from one hundred. There was no way I was leaving the hallway. I wanted to witness everything. I had only reached sixty-three when I heard the familiar creak of the door. In the narrow opening, I saw her bloodshot eye, a bunch of fabric, a flash of her bare leg.

"Kiddle?"

"Yes?"

"You still here?"

"Apparently so."

"Is your mom still at the turkey?"

"Yep, again."

"Can you get her?"

"If you really need her. But you know how she is about the turkey. Is something wrong?"

"Well. I don't know. I can't be. I mean. I'm having a bit of. Well."

"You don't feel good?"

"I don't. No. I don't feel right."

"Stomach pain?"

"Yes, yes. And a bit of. Well. Something not normal."

"Normal?"

"I don't know."

"You know, you did have a few glasses of, well—"

"Splashes, Kiddle. Not glasses. Mmm."

"That could make you feel off. Especially in your condition. Did you know your blood volume increases during the early stages? Plasma is increased at a greater rate than red blood cells, so that's probably why you're feeling a little off. It's called hemodilution."

"Thank you, Kiddle. That's, um, reassuring."

Gentlest expression. "I thought it would be." Then, "Why don't you just put some water on your face? A cold cloth?"

"I—I'm afraid to get up."

"It can't be that bad."

With both hands, she gripped the inner portion of the doorknob. "Someone turned on the tap."

"You want me to turn on the tap?"

"No. The tap. Like. Inside me."

She was bleeding.

Shivering, she closed the door again, and I continued my backward count. After I reached zero, I counted all the way down to absolute zero (Kelvin, of course), and then stood up, pushed open the door, peered in at my aunt. She was bent over on the latrine, one hand gripping the countertop, the other reaching outwards, grasping handfuls of air. Her skin was pale, appeared damp. Likely sticky, but I was not going to reach out and examine it. Obviously. I could see blotches of red on her legs, on the side of her thigh, on the toilet, her fingers, the shower curtain. To be honest, the entire scene was rather grotesque, and I was not quite sure how to absorb it. Everything appeared slightly, well, distorted. I had planned for stomach upset, a ruined meal, maybe she might crap her pants in front of Uncle Larv, but not quite this.

Cause and effect. I had not fully defined the parameters in my contraption, and suddenly the effects were out of my control.

"Button?" she whispered. "Is that yooou? Buh-uht-ton!"

Button?

Elastic band snapping. Why was she asking for Button? My Button. Was she delirious? I stared at her, hating her. Hating her. Hating her. I remembered watching Button convulse on the cement, orange soda trickling from her nostrils. I remembered the sounds in her throat, the candy smell on her skin. I remember my aunt telling her to "Show some respect to your Uncle Harv."

I hated that whore pig. Hated her guts. Hated the cells that lined her guts. Hated the molecules that made up those cells.

She reached out, dirty filthy hand trembling, her eyes squeezed shut. Her feet were spread on the linoleum, but connected by a ridiculous stretch of pantyhose. She was trapped, and the sight of her suffering did not frighten me. If anything, it made me feel warm. Full of a curious satisfaction, as though I had eaten a nutritious meal, high in protein.

"Button's not here," I hissed.

Then, in between (rather unflattering) groans, "Need help. Call help." She twisted her head, and our eyes locked, in a genuine, touching moment of personal connection. "Oh god oh god oh god. Please, please."

Between retches, I heard a punchy cry erupt from her mouth. "Hurry."

"It's okay, it's okay. Don't worry, I'll go wake your boyfriend. Post-haste." And I turned the knob, ever so quietly closed the door. So as not to wake anyone.

38

"**H**EY, HEY, HEY," GORDIE SMIT CLAPPED WARREN ON THE BACK as he came into the kitchen. He dropped a paper bag on the table. "Saw this on your front step." Newspaper folded underneath his arm. "Not your best look, buddy."

"No," Warren said, as he took the paper. He saw his face. A tall man with slit eyes, scowling, body leaning to the left. A man that looked as though he had something to hide. Warren angled the paper, read the headline just below the fold. *Student hangs from teacher's tree*. Then, in smaller text: *Gifted student dies, teacher expresses remorse*. He folded it again, placed it in the corner near the fridge.

"I don't even get it. It's not like they get paid more to write trash. The newspaper's fucking free."

Warren adjusted his glasses. "But people read it."

"Listen, buddy. Don't let it bring you down. You should

see my mugshot. Stole my grandmother's car when I was eighteen, and she called the bloody thing in. Wouldn't let it go, either. What a piece of work she was." He tore open the bag, and spicy steam rose up. "Come on. I'm starved. Could eat a whole cow, hooves and all."

"Thank you." Warren's voice cracked slightly. "I appreciate this."

Gordie sat down, pulled a barbecue wing from the pile, and pushed the whole piece into his mouth. "Okay," Gordie said, talking around the small bones. "I can't avoid it anymore. I got to ask. About the girl."

A scoop moved through Warren's stomach, hollowing his gut. He could not talk any more about Amanda Fuller. He wanted to forget. Pretend none of that had happened. Was happening.

"I mean, how is she? Your sister."

A moment of relief, and then a second scoop, duller, wider, scraping at him. His sister. His mother. When he returned from his night away, he found her crouched in a chair, watching television, hood up over her skull, chewing on her nails. He still had not told her anything. The moment had not been right.

Warren shrugged at Gordie, used a fork to lift two wings onto his plate. Tongs to serve French fries. "Good. Better, I think. It's hard to determine with any accuracy. She's sleeping now. Took some of the medication you brought."

"She's—" Gordie twisted a tall can of beer from its plastic holder, snapped open the lid. Three long gulps, followed by a pop of gas. "Your sister. She's, um." He wiped his mouth.

"I'm sorry?" Warren shifted in his seat, pressed his spine against the back.

"Okay, War. I can't sugarcoat it for you, buddy. Your sister looked like shit."

"I don't know what to do with her."

"Fuck. Superglue her to your wall until she quits whatever it is she's sticking in her body."

"I don't know how to do that. I would try, if I could."

"Yeah. Shit. I got no sister, buddy, but I'd say that sucks."

Warren nodded, with knife and fork pulled chicken from the bones. Chewed gingerly, sniffed.

"Extra spicy, hey?" Gordie said, and winked. "Don't like them no other way." Spitting bones onto a cardboard lid. He leaned toward Warren, said, "Did I tell you Daylene's on about having another one?"

Eyebrows raised, "Another one?"

"Kid."

"That's nice. Isn't it?"

Gordie shook his head. "You got to be kidding me. I already got three, and I'd give two and a half of them away. If I could."

"Did you tell her?"

"Yes, and she's right on my back. Says even numbers are better. Even makes more sense. Two boys, and two girls. She needs another girl. How the fuck do you make life decisions based on even and odd? It's not a goldfish she's talking about."

Warren glanced at his fish tanks. He understood numbers. He understood goldfish. He tried to keep his focus on Gordie, remain attentive. It was good to have a conversation about something normal.

"I mean, it's a whole creature," hand pulling another wing from the pile. "And they don't stay little, buddy. They might be cute when they tadpole-sized, but I got a nine-year-old. He melts down, and fuck me if I'm not afraid of the little bastard."

"It can't be that bad." He thought of Nora. The pain in her expression when she mentioned her desire to have a dozen children. But with her husband's constant back and forth between home and hospital, Libby had remained an only child.

Gordie shuddered, gnawed bones, then rubbed his greasy fingers on the paper serviette, bright orange stains. "You got no idea, my friend. No idea."

They were silent for a moment. Warren stabbed a fry, brought it to his mouth.

"The police thing going to stop now? They stop bugging you?"

Warren frowned. "I don't know. Detective Reed, she thinks—"

"Detective Reed? Jennifer Reed?"

Warren could not remember her first name. Or if he had ever learned it.

"Jesus, Warren. Watch your back with her. She's as squirrely as it gets."

"You know her?"

"Everyone knows her." Grinding a handful of French fries between his teeth, he snorted. "She was the go-to in high school."

"Go-to?"

"C'mon. You know what I mean. She banged every single dude who was ready and willing, and believe me, there was a lineup. Around the corner and across the parking lot. Then she went away for a couple years, and came back with a gun on her hip. And now she's giving *us* the shaft. Fucking us sideways. Every chance she gets." Waving a wing in the air. "Three tickets last year. One for jay-fucking-walking. Not a car in sight."

"Oh. I didn't know."

"Trust me, buddy. She's squirrely and she's a man-hater. Chip on her shoulder the size of a boulder. But she's hot though, isn't she?"

"Hot?"

"I know you're with Nora and all, but don't tell me you haven't noticed. Why else do you think she's the one chasing you? To put you at ease as she slides her hand up your ass, tickles your kidneys."

"She's not, um, putting her—"

"I wouldn't talk to her no more, my friend. Wouldn't touch her. Wouldn't even look the bitch in the eye. I'm sure your lawyer said the same shit. She gets an idea in her head, and she won't let it go."

"He said I don't have to talk to her. I'm not supposed to. It doesn't matter if I've done nothing."

Gordie continued ripping meat from tiny bones, but Warren drifted out of focus. He saw the sticky wings, smelled the spice and vinegar, the grease on the fries, on Gordie's cheeks and lips. Warren had eaten only three wings, while he estimated the remains on the cardboard lid to be closer to thirty. If there were four consumable portions per chicken, Gordie had now consumed the wings of seven or eight birds. And he was still going. Warren wondered about those maimed birds. He wondered if he should save some for Beth. He wondered about Gordie. All that he did and said. His comfortable banter. Was it only a costume? Did he worry about anything real? Was he the same as most other men? Needing to distract himself from the simple fact that he existed?

"Yeah, everyone's gunning for your head on a platter." Gordie smacked the table and Warren clicked back into the conversation. "Daylene didn't even want me coming over here. I told her to lick me, of course. Food and beer with a buddy. Who's going to pass that up?"

Warren placed his fork on the serviette, knew the tines would stick to the paper.

"I mean, I tell them they're stupid. I got a nose for shit, and you're as straight-laced as they come. That the girl was some messed-up teen acting stupid. Probably some prank gone wrong."

Warren's stomach twisted. Scoop moving through again. "Oh."

"The lot of them. Like to talk, talk, talk. Hens in action. Few roosters, too. I seen Wilkes out front. Nosy bastard."

Warren gazed out the back window. Even though his view was blocked by his own reflection, he knew the tree was there. Branch missing, cut weeping. A growing mass of toys and notes and unlit candles piled around the base of the trunk.

Gordie stood up and dragged the garbage can closer to his seat, scraped bones into the black bag. An empty tomato juice can had fallen out, lay on its side in a puddle of rusty red. Beth must have drunk it, missed the can when she threw it out. Warren blinked, heard the first wave of Gordie's words, tried to continue listening, but they began to morph into the background.

An involuntary snapshot of his mother jumped into his head. Sleeping in the days after his father had left. Her head on a pillow, but he could not see the usual white of the pillowcase. When he crept toward her, he realized she had stuffed the pillow inside of his father's favourite sweater. She pressed her face into the mound of worn knitting, and Warren could hear her slowly inhaling and exhaling. Her fingers picked out little bits of bark and seed husks, then tucked them back in among the woolly strands. When he tiptoed backward, he heard her say, "Come back. Please. Please come back." But he did not move closer. He left her lying there, unable to determine if she were speaking to him, or speaking to his dead father.

"Hey, buddy. You in there? Warren? You didn't eat much."

"I'm sorry?" Mouth open, Warren glanced around. They were in the porch of Warren's house. Through the glass he could see the people, shuffling their feet, talking amongst themselves. Warren looked up, focused on the moon, low and bright orange in the black sky. Stars flickering.

"I hope your sister's up and around soon." There was a shimmer on Gordie's face. "Thanks for hanging, buddy," he said. His open hands held his waist. "If someone poked me with a pin, I'd bloody burst."

Warren nodded, smiled, but he did not know how he got there.

As Warren closed the door, he could hear Beth vomiting in the bathroom. Retching, retching, then gasping and moaning. Without calling out, he walked into the kitchen, turned off the offensive overhead light, began to tidy up the beer cans and remains of the food. He decided against saving the sticky leftovers for Beth. Even a healthy stomach could barely manage the spice and the grease.

While he waited for her to emerge from the bathroom, he sat on the floor and watched his fish, different species clustering together, moving in unison. Small teams. His lone Betta wriggled through the fernlike plants toward him, and Warren lifted the black lid, pressed a pellet of food to his fingertip, and let it hover over the water. The fish leapt up, biting his skin, pellet consumed.

There was silence for a moment, then the gagging continued. Warren imagined his sister was a child with a stomach virus. No older than six or seven, cheeks flushed, nest of uncombed hair sticking out of her head. He would make her a tea, spearmint with honey. She had liked that as a child. He remembered her slurping it from a doll's spoon. Maybe while she sipped the tea, they could talk. About the mess his life was in. About their mother.

As he was about to fill the kettle, he saw movement in his backyard. Near the tree. Without the glare of the kitchen light, he could see things clearly. In the bright moonlight, a person, a boy, walked out of the woods, and stood there. Light-coloured sweater, ball cap. This was the first time he had caught someone trespassing, and anger shot through his limbs.

Warren rushed out the back door, across the wooden deck, but not onto the frozen grass. "Hey!" he yelled. "Just what do you think—"

He stopped when he saw the boy's face.

It was Adrian Byrd.

The boy did not skitter away, as Warren expected, but held his ground, facing the house, hands thrust deep into his jean pockets. He wanted Warren to recognize him, to know that he moved at his leisure. Ten, eleven seconds passed between them, and then the boy turned, took several delib- erate strides, and dissolved into darkness.

"Adrian?" Warren tiptoed toward the tree.

A dog remained. Warren guessed it was the same dog he had seen in Adrian's backyard. Emaciated and indif- ferent. Head bent, it chewed a discarded wrapper from a chocolate bar, then rooted through the pile of stuffed animals. A small bear caught in its muzzle, the dog shook its head left to right.

He heard the animal's teeth crunch down through a plastic eye.

39

AFTER A FEW MOMENTS OF WAITING, I WAS UNCERTAIN EXACTLY what I should do. Uncle Larva was in a deep slumber, and my mother was completely distressed by pasty lumps in her gravy. I drifted around the house. I did not want to think about my aunt and the mess she was making in our bathroom. In my head, I kept hearing her call Button's name. The repetition, her needy nasally voice, made me furious. I had to find a way to dampen my anger.

Eventually, I found a nature book, and began to read about a fascinating type of salamander scientists called a "walking fish." They do not grow lungs and crawl on land. Instead, they prefer their gills, and stay in water. I like that they had a choice. The one in the accompanying photo was pleasant looking. Had a very congenial expression. Happy and smiling. I focused all my attention on the feathery frills near its head, the small hands that could scoop water, its baby grin. It looked almost fetal.

Distraction failed.

"Where's your aunt?" My mother was right in front of me. I did not see her coming.

Looking up from my book, I shrugged. "Bathroom, I think."

"Bathroom? All this time?"

"Yep."

"Well, dinner is ready. Can you let her know?" Then, an afterthought, "I'll wake Harvey."

When I tapped on the door, she did not answer. I did not want to open that door. I pressed my ear against the wood, heard nothing. I did not want to open that door. I tapped again and said her name. I did not want to open that door.

I called my mother. I called out to Larva. Something was not right. I sensed my contraption had collapsed under the weight of itself. Cracked and fallen, bits and pieces of plastic and wood scattered all over the basement floor.

Lights whirring, but siren silenced, the ambulance arrived through the clog of snow. Things were grim, my mother had explained. The baby was surely lost, but my aunt might be okay. Might. She had lost a lot of blood. They gave her a shot in her thigh with a thick needle, then loaded her onto a gurney, pushed her out into the snowy evening. My mother climbed into the back of the vehicle with her and they slammed the double doors, backed out of the driveway. Larva skidded down the road behind them. The house was silent. Someone had turned off the radio; two strings of Christmas lights had failed, leaving half the tree in flickering darkness.

I was alone. Of course I was. No one had asked if I might like to come along.

I sat down on the hearth, poked the fire with a sooty stick. Expulsion of the jelly ball had not been my intent. But I told myself I had saved the bastard from its own misery, so to speak. I knew what type of existence it would have had under the care of my sleazy aunt, and I was really doing it a service. Was I not? Returning it to the black abyss. *Better luck next go round, little person.*

Stabbing the log in the waning fire, I saw a brilliant array of sparks flying up the chimney. I peeled off my socks, and using an enormous set of tongs, I laid a red ember on my foot. Pain shot up to my brain, and the stench of burnt skin immediately hooked my nose. But I breathed slowly, willed myself not to move. Not to remove it. I needed to remain in control. Prove to myself that I was in control. I burnt the tops of both feet, and gently rolled the socks over the injuries. The sensation was a relief.

Then, the phone. A foreign noise cutting through the air. It never rang in our house.

"Your aunt." A breath. "Didn't, didn't make it. Too much blood too fast, they said. Couldn't stop it. I don't know what to say. I can't believe it."

"Mom?"

"Complicated by her drinking. The drinks. The doctors wanted to know. Not that that has anything to do with anyone else. She wanted what she wanted. She's the adult."

"Mom?"

"All a fluke. She should never have been drinking. Why didn't she call out to me? In this day and age. To have this happen. Surrounded by all this medical stuff, and still. They couldn't manage. To save her. Can you? Oh, I can't believe it."

"Mom."

"Oh, I'm beside myself here. Just beside myself. The turkey must be ice cold. Gravy like goo. Ruined. Why am I thinking about a turkey? Who cares about a turkey?"

"Mom!"

"Oh, I got to go. Hello? I got to. Sign some papers. I can't believe it. I just can't believe this. I see Harvey. Oh, he's white as a sheet. White as a bloody sheet."

A bloody sheet. What a stupid thing to say.

She hung up the phone, and I stared at the receiver. After a moment, it occurred to me she had not called to talk to me about my aunt. She called only to talk. Only to dislodge that tangle of thoughts inside of her. It could have been anyone on the other end of the phone. It did not matter that I was me. I could have been dial tone.

I walked upstairs, and sat down on my bed, waiting for something to happen. Should I be shaking? Was I in a state of disbelief? I anticipated some sort of tingle would soon arrive inside the joints of my wrists or ankles, the tips of my fingers. Shock or regret, or guilt, or fear, or dread, or nervousness. At least a hint of dizziness. A *splash*. Nothing arrived. Nothing at all. I simply felt sleepy. Hungry, also, for a turkey leg. If any emotion was there at all, it was a vague disappointment. But even that was a puff of smoke in the wind, quickly dissipating.

Afterwards, I attempted to assess. I had set into motion certain circumstances that contributed to the death of another human being. A never-coming-back type of death. It was a strange and heady concept. I would never hear my aunt's nails-on-chalkboard-voice again, be assaulted by her cheap perfume, or see her snake-mouthed laughter. Would the world miss someone as lame as her? Should I be concerned over my casual detachment? Would others assume I was traumatized? The simple fact was, I could not care less. I understood then, I could do whatever I wanted, with no repercussions. As long as I did not get caught.

Button was gone. My aunt was gone. I had accomplished what was necessary. A fair exchange of energies. I am certain most people would agree, if only they had not been swallowed by a culture as soft-bellied as ours.

Eventually, I went to my window and tugged it open, saw the escaping heat from the house wavering through the icy night air. With my mother's tweezers, I held the empty bottle of medication just outside my window, pulled a lighter from my pocket. The plastic began to shrink and bubble and blacken, and then the flame consumed the label. Destroying my neighbour's personal details, address, the phone number of the pharmacy. And the word *warfarin*. I chose that bottle from his bathroom because of the interesting name. Only that evening, skimming the details in a pharmaceuticals book, did I discover it was a blood thinner, though first used as a rodenticide. Rat-killer. This is what I served to my shrew bitch aunt. Disguised by a *splash* of alcohol. That was what had killed her. When the bottle curled in on itself, I opened the tweezers, let the remains fall downwards. Into the snow-laden branches of the chokecherry bush below.

Later that evening, I opened my gifts. Books from my mother, and an edgeless puzzle. Then, from my aunt, a scorpion encased in its glass prism, of course, with its tail up, ready to strike. An interesting and thoughtful choice, and after the evening's events, the irony of her selection was not lost on me.

40

THE NEXT MORNING, WARREN WENT OUT TO THE BACK DECK WITH a cup of tea. The wood and grass and trees were covered in icy glitter. If Warren had the mindset to appreciate it, he knew the beauty would have moved him, but he felt nothing stir inside his chest. As he sipped his tea, he thought about Adrian Byrd. How long had the boy been standing in his backyard last night, gliding through the darkness without fear, without trepidation? In Warren's imagination, he did not hesitate on the deck when he rushed out, but instead ran toward the boy, demanding an explanation. Pointed at the tree with the missing branch, told Adrian to stay away. *You are trespassing. You've got no right.*

But even inside his mind, Warren could not make Adrian back down, could not make him bend. The boy sneered, spat on the ground, called Warren a coward, a fake. And Warren accepted the insults, did not argue, as he knew what was inside the boy's head. Adrian was nothing more than an angry child, grieving the death of his friend. Grieving how his life had suddenly changed in an irreversible way.

That was one thing he had in common with Adrian. How do you ever sew up the hole?

That evening, when Warren emerged from a long shower, the air was heavy with the smell of food. A savoury scent, strong and familiar, but Warren did not find it comforting. It reminded him of the kitchen where his mother made meals. Where, likely, his mother now sat in a worn wingback chair, staring out the window behind the table, coughing and waiting for darkness to arrive.

Sometimes you got to put the weight down. Were those his mother's words? Warren put the back of his hand against his mouth, squeezed his eyes closed, but before he had a moment to catch his breath, Nora appeared in the hallway. "Finally," she said, reaching for him. "I thought you'd never come out."

"No, no." He blinked, adjusted his glasses. "I was. Was I that long?" Once again, he had lost track of time. "How did you get—"

"Your sister, War," grinning, "she let us in. We've had a lovely conversation. Just getting to know each other. Why didn't you tell me you had a visitor?" She locked her arm through his, nudged him forward. "You are a man with secrets!"

Inside the kitchen, it was too bright and too warm. He wanted to open a window, let the November wind cut through the dusty screen, clean out the heaviness.

"You must be starving," Nora said.

Beth was seated at the table, her knees bent underneath her body, sleeves of his oversized hoodie pulled down over her hands, fabric drawn inside her fists. Libby was seated next to her, and their heads were together, whispering. "No, I'm not kidding," Libby said. "Right outside there. In the backyard."

"Holy fuck, Warsie." Beth glared at him. "How come you never told me?"

"Beth." Warren angled his chin toward Libby. "You can't talk like that."

She clapped a hand over her face. "Sorry. Bad mouth, bad mouth. But c'mon. Why didn't you tell me?"

"I—I didn't want to worry you."

"I could have listened." She chewed on a loose thread. Then said softly, "I would have tried to listen."

"Totally sucks what they're doing to you, Mr. Botts. It's not fair."

"It'll be okay, Libby." Water from his wet hair trickled down the back of his neck.

"Libby?" Nora swatted her gently with an oven mitt. "There's a basket of warm biscuits there. Can you put them out? And the spoons. I forgot to put out spoons."

Libby stood up, and reached for the basket. "No more time to talk," she said to Beth. Then, flatly, "Busy, busy bee, here."

"I never knew these existed," Beth said, bumping a paper bowl on the tabletop. "I've seen plates, but never bowls."

"Clever, right?" Nora replied. "Sometimes life is so hectic, you just need to go for convenience." Lifting a huge pot toward the middle of the table, she continued, "Now, War, sit. Just some beef stew and biscuits. I stole the recipe from a magazine in the dentist's office last week."

"My mother." Libby groaned. "The *thief*."

They sat side by side, a mismatched family, chatting as though nothing in the world were wrong. Nora talking about the strange fall weather, rain then snow then rain again. Beth said it was the sort of weather that would make a person sick, especially if they lived outside. Slept on a steaming grate. Nora nodded, and replied, "No matter, it gets us all. Like you, Beth. You probably caught whatever you got from the wacky weather."

"Um, there might be other factors." Warren coughed, touched the bridge of his glasses. "When, you know, a person gets sick."

"Like?" Nora lifted her eyebrows.

"Like a virus," he said. "Or bacteria."

"Leave it to you, War, darling, to make everything all science-y."

He swallowed a mouthful of stew. Soft vegetables, perfect cubes of stringy meat, dark rich gravy.

"Lots of other shit can make a person sick too." Beth dropped a biscuit in her bowl, liquid spattering. "Not just crap weather and viruses. What about drinking a whole bottle of gin? Or smoking some chemicals your friend, Bob, just gave you? Or sucking—"

"Beth!" Warren shook his head quickly, motioned toward Libby again. "Please," he said. "Not now."

"It's okay, Mr. Botts. I won't repeat it."

"Well, then." Nora tilted her chin downwards, pulled her lips in.

They ate in silence for several moments, and then Warren asked, "How's Evie doing?"

"She's good, I think." Libby said.

"She seemed upset."

"I'm sure she'll be all right, Mr. Botts. Pretty much everyone is freaked out. I mean, it's a crazy thing to happen, right?"

"Just awful." Nora chimed in. "What kind of mind would think that up?"

Warren looked at the window. The glass was covered in condensation, and the four of them were slightly distorted in their reflections. "Are you doing okay, Libby?"

"I guess so. I just wish things would get back to normal."

"Everyone wishes that," he replied, as he stirred his stew. "It'll take some time."

"I'm going for a smoke. Appreciate the home cooking, though." Beth smiled, stood up, sleeves of the hoodie hanging mid-thigh. "It must've taken you all afternoon to make it. What a spread!"

"Oh, well. I mean. I hope you had enough."

Beth never responded, quietly closed the door to the backyard. Warren could not see her through the hazy window, but he knew her grey shadow was moving toward the tree. No doubt she was leaning against it, probably punting the stuffed bears with her foot.

"Well." Nora, clapping her hands together. "I guess that's that. I'll clean up. War, can you take a look at Libby's homework? She's struggling. Ms. Fairley's doing her best, I'm sure, but she doesn't have your knack for teaching."

"I'm not struggling."

As Nora piled bowls into the garbage, Warren and Libby moved to the couch. Unopened knapsack between them, Warren said, "Should we take a look?"

"No."

"Pretend to take a look?"

"Sure." She pulled a paper out, smoothed it on her lap. "I like your sister, Mr. Botts."

"Me too. I like her, too."

"Her hair is cool."

"Or lack thereof."

"Yeah. She doesn't care what anyone else thinks."

"Don't be inspired, though. Your mother would kill me if you shaved your head."

"Your sister seems kind of mad though."

"Mad?"

"Not crazy-mad, just pissed off. With the world, kind of thing. You know."

"She's not well. She just needs to get better."

"She's going to be A-OK, Mr. Botts. I can tell you're all worried, but she'll be fine."

Warren's throat hitched. Libby had a sense of empathy that he rarely witnessed in his life. Especially in someone her age. "I appreciate you saying that." *This time, she will be fine.*

"That's a weird painting, don't you think?" She pointed to the canvas hanging above the fireplace. The woman's head. Eyes replaced by ears.

"I thought it was unique."

"I'd say more weird. But I like it, actually. A lot."

Warren smiled. "We have something in common, because I like it too." He shifted in his seat. "I wonder what it means."

"How so?"

"I don't know." Stephen sauntered across the carpet, lay on Warren's feet. He leaned forward, placed his palm on the cat's warm back. "I just wonder what it all means."

"So. Bro. So. I fucking hate her."

"What?" Warren was confused. Hated who?

"Kid's got her shit together, I really liked her, but that other one." Beth tossed two pills into her mouth, tilted her head underneath the faucet, and gulped. "I can't stand her. Her face reminds me of a shrew. You know those furry shits that lived in our walls?"

"I know what a shrew is, Beth."

"You can see it, then? And those teeth! And the way she moved around like she owned your place." Lifting her arms, two wooden rulers inside fleecy fabric. "And that smug little smirk on her ugly face."

She was talking about Nora. She hated Nora.

Warren nipped the inside of his cheek between his teeth, then spoke. "I like her face. Her face is perfectly fine."

"That's because you go all whacked for animals. You don't see what's there. I mean, Warren, Stephen is your best friend. A cat. You got fifteen thousand fucking fish."

"Oh." Warren glanced at the glasses that Nora had washed, still wet and glistening on an opened cup towel. "She's a good person. She is. She just cooked us dinner. Brought it here."

"Dinner? You've got to be kidding me." Beth's hands were shaking, and she wiped black liner from underneath her eyes. "She's so fucking fake. I can't believe you'd fall for all that crap. Jesus, Wars. Her little homemade stew? Totally fake. Did you not notice the carrots were all cut perfectly? That's cause a machine did it. It's from a can, War. How many fucking cans did she have to open to fill that huge pot. It's gross."

"What?"

"And those biscuits she made? From a tube. Supermarket cooler. I stole enough of that shit to recognize them a mile away. She popped open a paper tube and brought them on a sheet. Like she'd made them. Stole the recipe from a dentist office, my bony ass. That woman never made a real meal her whole fucking life. Mark my words."

Warren removed his glasses, cleaned them in the tail of his shirt. He could feel his pulse in his face. The place where Adrian had punched him. He looked at his sister, wanted her to be out of focus. "I—I don't care."

"You don't care? What does that mean?"

"It means, I like her. I really like her, and I like Libby. If the carrots are from a can, what difference does it make?"

"You can't be serious."

"I am." He cleaned the lenses of his glasses, then slid them back onto his face. "And she cares about me, too."

"She doesn't even know you. I don't know what she wants, but it's got nothing to do with you."

"That makes no sense. Why else would she be here?"

Beth threw her arms in the air. "You think that's what you deserve. I got no idea why. Why? Why are you like that? You should have so much better."

"It's just carrots. Just stew."

"Not just the carrots. If she lies about that, what else is she lying about?"

"Nora doesn't lie." As he spoke, a tickly sensation of uncertainty arrived in the pit of his stomach. He clenched his jaw, tamped that feeling down.

"For someone so smart, you know, you're really, really stupid."

She yawned, as though the sudden flashes of movement had exhausted her. Her eyes were hollow, cheeks sunken and blemished. Warren stood up, went to the window. Stared out at the place where the tree stood. He could no longer see it in the darkness, and he wondered if it was even there. Perhaps he had imagined it all.

With his back to Beth, he spoke as gently as possible. "You're hurting me by living the way you do. Hurting yourself."

"What did you say?" Her words sounding like a truck moving over crushed stone.

He turned. "Please listen, Beth. I have almost enough money saved to help you. Not yet. I—I lost the money I had before. But when I do, I want you to accept my help. Okay? To get better." He thought about the envelope in the sleeve of his coat, and it was getting fatter. Again. In another year, maybe even six months, he might have enough money saved. Then he would find her and send her to a place where experts could help her.

"Jesus fucking Christ, Warren." Her words had taken on a medicated slur. "You sound like a poster boy for fucking baby cereal."

"It's a repulsive way to live."

"Repulsive? *Repulsive?* You're saying I'm repulsive? At least I'm living my repulsive life, and not wearing a massive set of blinders. Running away. Hiding from reality. Ignorant to everything."

"I'm sorry you think that."

"You're sorry? Why the fuck don't you ever get angry?"

He lifted his head. "Because I'm not angry."

"Why are you looking at me like that?"

"I'm not."

"You are. I can see it in your eyes. You think I'm a screw up."

"I don't. I mean. I'm not looking at you."

"You think I'm a fucking drugged-out loser whore who knows nothing about life. That's it, isn't it?"

"Beth. I just want to help you."

"You just twist all this shit around. *I* was trying to help *you*. To get you to open your beady little eyes and see what's right in front of you. But you twist it up and make it about me."

"Beth, I—"

"Don't say you care about me. Just fucking stop. It only makes my life hurt worse."

"I'm sorry."

"Just shut up, Warren. I'll be out of your hair in the morning. If it don't cramp your style to stay another night."

"I didn't. I just—" He lifted both hands, adjusted his glasses. "Beth. I still haven't told you—"

She rushed down the hallway and slammed the bathroom door.

About Mom.

Beth remained in the bathroom for a long time, then slipped into his bedroom, clicked the lock. Lying on the couch, Warren tried to stay awake. Listening to the quiet gurgling of his tanks, the sound of Stephen's claws on the arm of a chair, the occasional squirt of water moving through the toilet. He did not hear the floor creak a single time.

In the morning, she was gone. He felt her absence when he placed his feet on the cold floor.

"Beth?"

No answer.

"Beth? Are you here?"

The bathroom was empty. His bedroom was empty, bed a jumble of sheets and blankets. He knew he would not hear her voice. Answering him.

How had this happened? He closed his eyes. Images

flashed inside his head, snapshot after horrible snapshot. Amanda Fuller hanging from a tree, Beth pale and shivering. Then his mother's face, flushed with illness. He saw Ms. Fairley with her hands clasped. And Nora's eyes. Detective Reed, finger pointing, accusing him with the twist of her lips. He saw the scratches on his car. Heard those palms banging on the windows of his house. The crowd outside, a constant hum with occasional shouts. Adrian Byrd's fist mid-swing. The missing handles on the inside door of the police car. The back of his lawyer's head. Too many pictures inside his brain. Too much pressure. His skull wanting to explode.

When he was a boy, he would have described them all to his father. Image by image, he would tell his father what troubled him. What was building inside his mind. It was so easy then, flicking them away, cards from a scary deck. His father always took them, and said, "Just count something, War. Just count." Warren had felt soothed, but that sensation of comfort, of security, did not last. His father was unable to hold those cards, to keep them pressed to his chest, and in the end, he gave every single one back.

Another image shot through his mind. Nail-bitten fingers, sneakily reaching down between layers of dark fabric. Warren's stomach squeezed and bristled, and he went to his closet, gripped the sleeve of his woollen winter coat. Checked the lining. The sleeve was empty. The envelope of money he had been saving for Beth was gone.

41

"**O**H."
             I had not expected someone else to respond to my knocking. A girl, skinny, wiry brown hair pulled into a ponytail, was smiling at me. Glancing over my shoulder, I saw my neighbour's ratty chair, covered in snow, and the bare oak tree standing in the front yard. For a moment I thought I had lost track of myself, had knocked at the wrong house.

"Sorry," I said.

"For what? Why would you possibly feel sorry?"

She stood a little too close to me. I could smell peanut butter on her breath. "I don't know." Of course, I did not actually feel sorry. I had no idea why I said that. I had only wanted a hot drink, to spend some time with my elderly neighbour and have a little respectful banter. It had been six weeks since my aunt was wheeled out, and I found it exhausting to continually wear a weighted mask of grief. My neighbour forced no such condition upon me. During my first visit he asked if I was managing, I said I was, and we moved on from there. A finger's snap, and no more fuss than that.

"Are you looking for my granddad? I'm the granddaughter, as you might have guessed. My mother is his daughter. She's inside. We're just visiting. Leaving soon. I think. Sometimes my mother is unpredictable."

I blinked, pushed my hands into the pockets of my jacket. "I was just—just—"

"Lost? Confused? Tired? Bored? In a dreary state of ennui?" Rapid-fire assault.

"Um, No. I mean, I don't think so."

"Well, I am. The two of them have been in the kitchen talking for over an hour, talking about *finances*." Quotation marks in the air with four fingers. "Totally boring. Snore! They think I have no idea what's going on. I hear it all. Every single word. When I shut up long enough to listen, that is!" She giggled.

"Oh."

"My mom might lose her job. If that happens, our *finances*," more finger quotes, "will suck. And then life will suck. Majorly. No one is going to give me a job, I'm too young. She says we can't live on dirt. We can't eat dirt. That's what people think we can do, she says. But I don't think people think anything. Do you?"

I frowned, shook my head.

"He wants us to come live here, but she won't. Won't even talk about it. Why not? I don't know. It's a pretty cool spot, right?"

"Um. Not really."

"And of course I have no say in the matter. I mean, like, zero. Why would someone my age possibly get a say?" Hand fluttering, eyes rolling. "Because what matters to me, doesn't really matter. But it should matter, shouldn't it? I should matter." Hands in fists. "Why don't I matter?"

Feeling dizzy, I took a step back. This rarely happened. This humming, buzzing, droning girl was overwhelming me. Sensory overload. It seemed as though I was hearing through gauze. Seeing through gauze. "You're, um, letting in a lot of cold. I'll go. Come back later."

"No, don't go. I'm bored out of my tree here. There's no one to talk to. Let's do something fun. Come on! Want to knock icicles?"

"What?"

"Icicles. Off the roof." She leaned out of the door, pointed at the side of the house. "See? Those silvery spikey things are formed by the continuous freezing of dripping water. They're called icicles."

"I know what they are."

"Well, I hope so! I was only joking! Did you know if they are made from salt water, they're called brinicles?"

"I did."

"Puh. Do stalagmites come from the ground or the ceiling?"

"Ceiling," I replied, even though I knew the opposite was true.

"Gotcha! It's the ground." She wiggled then.

"Stupid me."

"Don't say that! Lots of people get confused. It doesn't matter. Let's crack off some icicles. It'll be fun. As long as one doesn't drop down, spear you through the top of your head. Spissshhhhh. Make a braincicle."

Her fingers agitated the air, and I closed my eyes. An image of my aunt appeared on my inner eyelids, an icicle piercing her hair, the weapon melting, bloody wound sealing. But that was not how she died. Natural causes, the doctors had called it.

I took another step back.

"Well, hello there, friend." My old neighbour was behind the girl now, put his hands on her shoulders, and then he smiled at me. "I thought I heard your voice. Just what is my granddaughter saying?"

I opened my mouth to speak, but before I had drawn a breath, she had already launched. "Nothing, Granddaddy! We're just talking. Testing our knowledge. I think I'm smarter. Do you mind if we establish the strength of your gutters?"

"Establish away."

She ducked, ran around him, and I heard her shuffling with boots, snow gear.

"I'm sorry," he said to me. "She speaks without thought."

"I don't mind." Though I had not yet decided whether I minded or not.

A blur of pink and brown rushed past me. I smelled damp wool.

"And there she goes," my neighbour said. "Better run. If you want to, that is. Don't feel obliged."

I was grateful he had no expectations, but my curiosity made me follow her footsteps through the snow. When I found her around the corner of the house, she had a long broom in her hands, and was smacking silvery spikes. "Do you think I can't reach you? That you're impressive? Get down here! Boom! Gotcha!" Yes, she was actually talking to them. With each swing, a shower descended, and she would jump back and squeal.

"That's dangerous, you know."

"What are you? Some sort of dorky wimp? You just need to move, that's all." She tossed me the broom and picked up a plastic shovel. "If you get hit, you deserve to get hit. Because you're slow and lazy. And a total idiot."

"Hmm," I said, and I lifted the broom, knocked a cluster of ice near a downspout. I failed to see the amusement, failed to understand the game. "This sort of ice build-up can be linked to heat loss, you know."

"You're kidding, right? Have you been in his house? It's like the inside of an oven. Cooked a whole ham dinner for us right out on the countertop."

"Really?" I did not really mean *really*.

"No, I'm just joking."

That was not very funny.

"Don't you ever laugh?"

I shrugged.

"Don't those ones look kinda like teeth? All neat in a row?"

"Not like my teeth."

"Not like mine, either." She grinned, and I noticed a wide space between her two front teeth. Enough for three pennies.

"You have quite the diastema."

"Yes! That's me. Miss Diastema. Are you trying to impress me with the proper term?"

I shrugged again. *Is she impressed?*

"Did you know French people call them *des dents du bonheur*?"

"Happy teeth."

"My mother says it means lucky teeth."

"Oh."

"I'm a walking four-leaf clover. Or a horseshoe. Or a number seven. Or a rabbit's foot."

"Oh." I envisioned the rabbit, stiff in the snare, eyes without fear, a blade slicing through its joint.

"Scratch that. Who wants to be a rabbit's foot? That's kinda disgusting, isn't it? I'd be covered in dirty fur and the top of my head would be all gunky where someone cut me off." She swung the shovel at the teeth, and a spray of icicles flew down, stuck straight into the snow. "Hoo-hoooo! Good one." She leaned on the shovel, looked at me. "I think my mother says they're lucky cause we got no money to fix them."

"Why would you want to fix them?"

"So girls don't call me a gap-tooth hick. They can still call me a hick, but they will have to drop the gap-tooth. A step in the right direction, don't you think?"

"I don't know. I don't think anyone should care about someone else's teeth. How someone else looks."

"Are you kidding me? That's all people care about. What type of clothes you wear or if your watch is real or if your car is falling apart, which ours just happens to be."

"That's stupid."

"Stupid? Are you strange or something?"

"I don't know."

"I think you might be strange. Just totally weirdo."

"Um, okay." I did not want to argue with her. Not that she would have allowed me a moment to formulate an argument.

"I like strange, though. It's good."

Um, okay.

She jumped, cracked off two low-hanging shards of ice, and handed me one.

"What do you want me to do with this?"

"Eat it."

"Eat an icicle?"

"Sure. Don't tell me you've never eaten an icicle?"

"No."

Spearing the air. "You have not lived!"

"Do you know how many birds sit up on that roof?"

"Just what are you trying to say? So what? It's full of gross stuff. Toxins and stuff, but are you a fattie?"

"I don't think so."

"Well, toxins stick in your fat. And if you got none, you'll be fine. Eat it."

"My brain has fat."

"Oh yeah. Well, warning! Warning! Eating an icicle might damage your brain." She crunched down on the ice stick, then grabbed her head, dropped into a mound of snow, cried, "My brain, my brain. My brain is shrivelling." Then she abruptly sat up. "Does that mean if you're on a diet, your brain loses weight? You can get a skinny brain? That's terrible."

I sat down beside her, tentatively licked the shard of ice. It tasted like the smell of car exhaust. Not too bad. "No."

"How come?"

"Your brain has a certain type of cell called oligodendrocytes. They wrap around axons, which are part of the nerve cell. It's like insulation. Those special cells are mostly made up of lipids, which is technically fat, of course, but it's not like fat cells. The cells are structural, part of the nerve. They aren't affected by weight loss."

She gaped at me, silent for just a moment. "Well, now, aren't you a smartie pants. Super-strange smartie pants."

Was she mocking me? "Well, you asked."

"I wasn't making fun. I wasn't. It's good to know. It really is. Could you imagine if your brain shrunk? You'd have suction inside your skull. What would happen then, I wonder?

Probably a terrible headache. Can you imagine if your ears got pulled in, sucked right inside your head, your whole ear? Just to alleviate the pressure. Sssslup!" She slapped the sides of her head. "Ears gone! We'd all know who was on a diet cause their ears would have disappeared. Just holes would be there. It'd be horrible. Fat women with ears would give themselves away. Their husbands would know they were sneaking cheezies. They'd be slicing off their ears to show they were trying. Making an effort. Trying to hide that they were diet cheaters. Oh God. It would be such a horrible reality. Really terrible." Lying back in the snow. "I'm so glad the brain doesn't lose weight. My mother's ears would be totally gone. She's always on a diet. Then if you gain weight, and your ears pop out again, they would probably stink, crammed up like that for months. It's totally vile, and I can't stop thinking about it! Argh! It won't leave my fatty brain!"

Though my face remained still, something inside me smiled. She was overwhelming, yes, but in an emptying sort of way. When she rambled, so close to me, everything else vanished. I had not a single moment to think of anything else. Lying in the snow, staring up at the pinkish sky, tiny snowflakes drifting down, I was pleasantly vacant. In that moment, I remembered an experience I had shared with Button. When we were together, lying inside the abandoned tent, her pudgy body pressed against mine, surrounded by the insanity of the flies. This girl was like that. A million buzzing insects all tucked inside a single body.

The front door creaked, and a woman was on the front porch, bags in her hand. "Hey, you!" she called. "Butt. In. Gear. Time to hit the road."

"Coming," she screeched, and she gnawed down her icicle like a dog with some kind of bone. Then she shot a hunk of ice straight out of her mouth, and the wet chunk hit me in the face, just below my left eye. "Just so you remember me," she said, grinning again.

I sat up and just stared at her. For once in my life, I did not know how to respond.

She popped over to her mother, and then ran toward the car, arms straight as though she expected the wind to lift her. Even seated in the front seat, she continued to bounce. As they were backing out of the driveway, she furiously rolled down her window, screamed out into the bitter air, "See you later, alligator!"

I tossed my icicle, walked over to my neighbour, who was standing on his front step in burgundy slippers. As I approached, he said, "You're supposed to say, *in a while crocodile.*"

"What?"

"That's what you say after."

"Why would someone say that?"

"It's a silly thing kids do."

I raised my eyebrows, looked at him. "Mister. I acknowledge I've not reached my full stature, but I've never been a kid."

He laughed. "Yes, yes. I forgot myself for a moment. Hot chocolate?"

"That would be appreciated."

Inside his kitchen, we sat opposite each other, and sipped in comfortable silence. Then he said, "Thank you for being nice to my granddaughter."

"You don't need to thank me." I found her unusual, yet could not decide whether I would rather have her roaming in a cage or trapped in glass. "I wasn't being nice. I wasn't being anything."

"Well, you weren't being mean."

"No, Mister. I was not."

"She's had her share of challenges. Her mother tells me. Between you and I, of course," I nodded here, "other kids don't seem to take to her. She's had problems."

"There's nothing wrong with her."

"Some people are taken aback by her, well, verbal exuberance. I don't think she can stop moving. Or talking. She even mumbles in her sleep. When she manages to sleep."

"Maybe she's surrounded by too much smallness."

"What do you mean?"

"I don't know. Too many walls around her."

"Perhaps."

"Or maybe she's just happy?"

"You could be right. It's ironic, isn't it? The sight of happiness makes a lot of people uncomfortable. Angry, even."

A kettlebell dropped into my guts, and I pushed my nose into the mug. Inhaled the sweet scent of chocolate, miniature vanilla marshmallows. *Button.* I saw her playing hopscotch, blowing dandelion seeds into the air, running in tight circles as though she were chasing her invisible tail. She was happy. Through and through and through. Her happiness made her special, but it also made her vulnerable.

"Yes. It does. But then again, a lot of people are assholes."

I decided then that I liked her. I liked my neighbour's granddaughter a lot.

42

TEN-YEAR-OLD WARREN HAD BEEN CUTTING THROUGH THE neighbour's wheat field, his backpack slung over his scrawny shoulders, when he saw his father off in the distance. It was the middle of the afternoon. A Wednesday in September. Hump Day, the teacher called it, and then one of the boys transformed the noun into a verb. Humping Day. They snickered, though Warren did not understand the humour. When he offered up Humpback Whale Day, everyone just stared at him. Humpty Dumpty Day? They shook their heads.

His father was rushing toward him, moving quickly, the distance between them closing. Warren felt his heart flutter with excitement. He had news to share with his father. Wonderful news. Only moments earlier, he had gotten his math test back, and he had earned not 90 percent, not 100 percent, but a whole 106 percent. Not only did he get every question correct, the bonus question had hiked his grade past perfection. A band of pride encircled his chest, and when he saw his father ripping his way through the wheat, Warren started to run, screaming, "Hey, Dad! Guess what? Guess what?"

As he came closer, he saw that his father was not rushing, but stumbling. His tall frame like a quivering stalk, plaid shirt open, face whitish grey. He wore no shoes, only a pair of knitted socks on his feet. The Feed 'n Seed ball cap that normally covered his head was missing, and the hair on his head was thin, scalp glistening in the sunlight.

"Dad?"

Knees buckled, and his father fell to the ground. "War? Is that you?"

"Of course it's me." The band of pride burst, and his lungs filled with salty fear.

Reaching upwards, his father whispered, "Take my fingers. Can you feel my hand? Can you? Can you?"

Warren gripped the bones. "Yes, dad. Yes. I've got it. It's in mine. I got your hand."

"But can you feel it? Son? Can you feel me?"

"I'm squeezing it now, Dad. Squeezing it hard. Super-duper hard."

His father arched his neck backward, face contorted like an animal in a snare, and all at once his expression looked rife with fury, sadness, desperation. Warren could not tell, but the sight of his father made him feel like his body was being pulled, sucked toward something dangerous, as though he were too close to the tracks, train barrelling past.

Warren suddenly wanted to sit on a toilet.

"What's wrong? Dad. What's wrong?" Relaxed his grip.

"Did I hurt you? Is it your fingers? Dad? Did I break your fingers?"

"I couldn't," he said, his mouth near the dirt. Eyelashes covered in dust. "I couldn't do it." Then he pulled his hand away, and he rolled, tucked his arms and legs inward, chin to his chest, fingers knotted over the base of his skull. Inside that mound, Warren could hear moaning, crying. He noticed his father's heel, a stretched hole in the sock, edges curling and ragged.

"No, Dad, no, no, you can." Fingers formed into fists. "You can. You listen to me, Mister. You can do anything you want. Like you always say to me. Whatever you dream, Dad. You can do it."

"I don't dream," he cried. "I am lost. I am lost. I am lost." Even though his words faded, Warren could hear his father continue to repeat them over and over again.

Warren threw his backpack down, thoughts of his math grade disintegrated, and he climbed onto the back of the sinewy turtle with the soft plaid shirt. With his full weight, he tried to push his father's frame into the earth. Like a seed pressed into the safety and warmth of soil. But no matter how widely he stretched his legs and arms and fingers and neck, he was not big enough to cover him. To even make a single dent.

"Mom." He waited. She was seated on the bench beside the table, facing the tiny box on the countertop. "Mom! Dad is. Something ha—"

"Not now, Warren. Can't you see I'm busy? My show is on."

[43]

IN THE SPRING OF THAT YEAR, SHORTLY AFTER THE SNOW MELTED and the ground thawed, there was a great lightning storm. Streaks of brilliant yellow tore through the darkness, illuminated the sky. Thunder boomed, rattling the house. From the small window of my bedroom, I watched the show.

Life was quieter now, even though it took a while. Two months after my aunt was out of the picture, Larva started coming around again, fixing this or that. Tightening a doorknob. Replacing a flapper in the toilet. Plastering a hairline crack in the drywall. I had not expected it, did not understand it, and chided myself for not anticipating his presence. Or my mother's reaction. The warbling sound of her appreciation annoyed me. I despised it, in fact. Her feminine neediness. "Oh, thank you so, so much, Harvey." I hated how she took her pink pills, sometimes two of them, and slept, only rising when Larva was due to arrive. And Larva, cracking his knuckles, popping the bones in his neck, acting like he was a holy man with a cheap hammer.

Did he think he could just move on to my mother? Did she think she could just move on to him? Humming around each other like a pair of slutty wasps.

Just what were those idiots planning?

That little interaction became number one on my list of "Things to Quash." Of course, I had many creative ideas, but as I have previously explained, sometimes a simple approach is the best. As soon as the loser was through the door, I started speaking in raised tones about my benevolent aunt, the tragedy of their joint loss. I reminded both Larva and my mother over and over again what might have been. Truly heartfelt reminders. "She would have been how pregnant now?" "How big would the baby have been at this point?" "Did you ever find out if it was a girl?" I would tilt my head, blink, whisper, "She was so very special, my aunt." *Vomit.* "I bet they miss you, Uncle Lar—um, you know. Mother. Wherever they are." I identified the pain in their twisting faces, and tried my best to conjure a tear. "At least they're together, right?" Palms clasped. "I hope they are at peace."

A basic experiment in Guilt 101.

"It won't take long," I heard her whine on the phone shortly after the dishwasher started leaking again. "I can't fix it myself. I just can't." A pause. "It's too expensive to call someone out here for every little thing, you know that, Harv." Then a disgusting purr, "You did such an amazing job last time. Besides, I thought you liked helping out." Finally, "Everything is so overwhelming. I have no one. Absolutely no one."

You have me.

That night, after my mother had fallen asleep, I repaired the dishwasher. The electrical panel was unlabelled, so I cut the power to the entire house. With a flashlight, I removed the screws fixing the dishwasher to the countertop, and slid it out. The issue was obvious—the drain hose had come loose. Again. I dried it, stuck it on as far as I could, and re-clamped it. Then pushed the appliance back in place, replaced the screws. Two minutes of effort, when it would have taken Larva all afternoon, several beers, lots of grunts, wipes of his sweaty forehead. His hand shoved into the pocket of his trackpants, scratching his crotch. The asshole.

In the morning, my mother was amazed that the machine had fixed itself. "Magic. Like elves came in the night. Too bad they didn't clean the kitchen while they were at it."

After that last embarrassing conversation with my mother, dear Larva never came back. And then it was just my mother and me, two distinct wheels on the same rusty bicycle. Quiet, and to be honest, a little boring. We developed a routine. We spoke only when necessary, which was fine by me. I went to school and she watched the television. We ate at the same table, mostly sandwiches and instant soups and milky tea. On weekends, she scrubbed the bathroom and I did the laundry. She vacuumed, as I could not tolerate the sound of the machine. When snow fell, we shovelled the driveway side by side. When spring arrived, she planted pansies and I edged the yard. I would not say those times were nice. But they were decent enough.

At that moment, there was a loud, wet crack outside. I sat up in bed, looked out my window just as the street lights were shutting down. All the houses went dark, and the blackness swallowed everything. A second flash, and the tree in my neighbour's yard was illuminated, every branching finger white against the sky. For several minutes, I saw sparks in the street. Deep inside my neighbour's home, a light flicked on (the momentary glow of a flashlight?), then dimmed again. Everything was dark.

I did not want to think about my tree. What if lightning had struck it? Surely with spring arriving, it was just waking up. Stretching. Yawning. Wiping rheum from its eyes. Not a pleasant welcome back into the world. Maybe only the very tips of it were singed. Like a haircut. A branch-cut. I fell asleep full of an odd and uncomfortable tension in my chest.

Early the following morning, I awoke to a terrible noise. A disgusting revving sound that made me feel sick. Metal eating away at wood. When I peered out my window, I saw a row of pickup trucks, men in orange suits and helmets, chainsaws raised and coming down. They had crawled up into my Mighty Oak and with each bite of metal, branches crashed to the ground. Like carpenter ants, those men were dismantling my tree, dragging it away, loading parts into trucks, shoving smaller branches through a mulching feeder. Others were working on a downed power line. Wires snapped. No longer sparking.

I witnessed the entire death. Bit by bit, my tree came down. Down to its stump, a weeping yellow round on the ground.

I pushed my face into my pillowcase, and cried.

HEART POUNDING, HIS EYES POPPED OPEN. HE WAS ALONE, IN his living room, lying on the couch in near darkness. The cushion underneath his cheek was wet, and he could feel the moistness all the way up to his ear. There was a weight on his chest, and he lifted his head, saw the curl of Stephen's back, a single paw lifted and bent in the air.

Warren sat up on the couch, and Stephen slid off his lap, then jumped onto the carpet. Even without the cat, the weight inside his chest remained. He had not meant to fall asleep, but he was exhausted. There was no one to talk to. No one who might listen. Beth was long gone, and he knew she was likely crouched in an alleyway somewhere, jittery and high. Nora was working an evening shift at the deli counter until closing, then taking part in some sort of inventory. Even though he had offered to help with the counting, she shook her head, "We are fine, we are perfectly fine." They had more than enough staff to look after it. Though he wondered if she did not want him there.

For a second, he thought about calling Sarie. Asking her what he should do. How does a person change the choices he made, even though they seemed so compelling at the time? He had gripped those thoughts so tightly, and now how could he turn stone back into sand? Should he ask for more details about his mother? Knowing was better than not knowing, was it not? Warren was confused, but before he could talk himself out of it, he got up, went to the phone. Dialled her number. All the digits adding up to sixty-one.

"Hello—"

"Hi, Sarie. It's me, W—"

"—you have reached—"

The answering machine's tone sounded, and he slipped the phone into its cradle.

As he walked toward the bathroom, he glanced out a crack between the front curtains, noticed the blanket of darkness. There was something odd about it, as though it were too intense for a neighbourhood. The lamp at the end of his driveway was not working. He leaned forward, lifted the curtain, saw the street light was also out. All of the homes were darkened. Against the night sky, he could barely make out their edges.

Then he saw the tiniest flicker, like a spark, in the middle of the pavement. He opened his mouth, blinked. Within seconds, one flicker turned into two, and two into four. Four into eight, and eight into sixteen. His mind continued counting, exponential growth. The dabbles of light slowly spread over the street, onto the sidewalk, up onto his lawn. Candles. Held in gloved hands. Inside the dim light, he saw dozens of people materializing in front of his home, side by side, humming or singing, he could not tell which one. They moved about, surrounding his little brick bungalow, the shape of the lights shifting and swaying, and he was unable to accurately count how many people were there, how many candles.

Warren did not turn on a lamp, but moved from window to window, watching the crowd, the flickering lights floating toward his house. Voices growing louder. A rivulet of light crept around the side, and he heard the clasp on the gate shaking, straining. A man shouted, "Fuck that!" Metal clanged, wood smacking against wood. He tiptoed into the kitchen, and Warren saw the brightness seeping into the blackness of his backyard. Neighbours moving onto the deck, across the lawn, circling the tree.

A vigil. They were holding a vigil for Amanda.

Candle held to the glass, a face appeared in the window just behind his table, and Warren lowered his skinny frame into the corner beside the fridge.

A fist knocking at the back door. A second candle in the window. Another face. Hand to the forehead, peering in.

More knocking. Pounding. Door shaking. Voice pushed into the doorframe. "Come out, Botts," it hissed. "Come out here."

Heart throbbing in his throat, Warren opened the cupboard to his left, groped behind the toaster with a shaking hand. It was still there. A surprise, considering how Beth had scoured the entire house. Tugging out the label-less bottle, he unscrewed the cheap plastic cap. The smell was sharp, pure, like a chemical he might have used to clean his lab.

Even before the colourless liquid touched his lips, he winced, ready for the pain. It burned his tongue, his throat, his esophagus. He could count on one hand the number of times he had done this, and as he did so, finger by finger, he swallowed, and swallowed, and swallowed.

When he opened the back door and stepped out, Warren could not see the men's eyes. The children and women, yes, but the men wore ball caps pulled down over their foreheads. In the wavering candlelight, he saw chins and thick necks and flannel collars. He saw glowing open mouths. Wilkes was there, his fat fingers pressing deeply into Warren's chest. Pushing him. Words hovering around him, currents underwater. "Not so big now, are you, Botts?" "No," he mumbled. "I'm not so big."

He sensed a dream was continuing. He was not a man in a backyard full of angry strangers, but a child. A boy. Eleven years old. Moving among the cluster of unfamiliar mourners after his father's funeral, black pants and shirts, the air stale, drained of life. Several were singing a hymn about going home. A woman was crying. Children were squealing. Some of them clutched stuffed animals in mittened fists. He could not hear or see Beth. She had run out the back door of their farmhouse, across the field. No one had bothered to chase her. In the darkness, Warren saw the owner of Feed 'n Seed. A handful of men who worked the fields surrounding the home where he had grown up. His math teacher, clapping him on the back. The janitor. The overweight gym teacher who always frowned at Warren, a gangly failure who tripped over his own feet. "What the fuck is wrong with you, Botts?"

A child yelped, "Ow, watch it," and Warren detected the sharp scent of singed hair.

He pressed his glasses into his face, and with socked feet,

walked across the crowded deck of his rental home. Took several steps, and moved onto the grass. Icy water instantly absorbed through the cotton, soaked his soles. People everywhere. Dark coats, odour of fried dinner, of cigarette smoke, icy breath, wax burning, paper cups burning, wool burning. Someone sniffed. Wept. On his cheek, he felt the spray from a watery sneeze.

Was he walking? Or floating above, moving through. All he had to do was relax the muscles and breathe. These were mourners. Weren't they his father's mourners?

And yes, he was a boy, his heart overflowing with guilt.

"We know," someone yelled at him. "We know what you did."

And Warren nodded. "I'm sorry," he said. He wanted to curl into a ball and cry. He wanted to see Beth, so she might give him a tiny peppermint candy from her doctor's bag. Scribble him a prescription for numbness. A second candy to dissolve reality. As he walked toward the tree, every distorted face stared at him. The responsibility on his shoulders was overwhelming. So much he had to try and do. At only eleven years old. Now he had to be a man. Look after a house and a garden. Attend school. Find ways to make money and pay for things. Cans of soup and light bulbs and rubber boots for Beth. She needed them.

Once he reached the tree, he ran his hands over the bark, traced the carved diamond with his finger. A girl moved toward him, and he squinted at her. "Hello, Mr. Botts." It was Evie. "Go inside. You shouldn't be out here." There was too much movement, the ground buckling. "I don't know," he mumbled, hugging the tree. "There's nothing inside." "There's nothing out here, either, Mr. Botts." His backyard was full of stars, and some were swirling, some were hovering. Their movements were not logical, and he could not predict their orbits.

"Look at him."

"Wasted."

"We don't need the disturbance."

An elbow struck Warren in the stomach. Shock of pain registering inside his head, a shot of white light. Another star. Relief, it was. He understood the neural pathway, messages firing back and forth between his abdominal wall and his brain. Something tangible, workable. Something healable. A smack on his shoulder, and his arm flew forward, making him twist. Wilkes, his neighbour, pressed his face into Warren's, smell of yeast on his breath. Then a crack to his shin, and his leg bent, knee dropped down onto soggy grass. The side of his face slid against the trunk of the tree.

Looking up, he saw Detective Reed, and he wondered how she could be there. So out of place. Shakily, he pointed toward the house. There were sandwiches in there, he wanted to say. On plates. And jelly casseroles. And cookies. Someone is making tea right now. In a tarnished silver thing that has a levered spout at the bottom.

"Go ahead," he said, and knelt down. "Get something."

Somewhere inside his gauzy thoughts was his last conversation with Detective Reed. A phone call that morning. She should not have tried to contact him. He should not have answered.

"Your father died when you were a boy."

Warren held the receiver away from his ear. Her voice a scratch on metal.

"By hanging."

"He—"

"He hanged himself in the basement of your home. Is that accurate?"

"No," he replied, staring at a mug balanced on the edge of the sink. "That is not accurate. He did not die in the basement of our home."

"So, my information is incorrect?"

Warren stepped toward the sink, tapped the mug. It clattered onto the other dishes. There was no way he could explain. His father was a hollow man, an empty form, and he had died years before his son even knew him, for reasons his son would never know. Whatever it was that kept him alive, whatever strength Warren had given him, it eventually faded into nothing. "You are the only reason I stay," his father had said nearly every single day. At some point, Warren was no longer enough. It was his fault. Not his mother's. Warren had been unable to admit it, but he had stopped doing whatever it was he was supposed to do. Being whatever he needed to be.

Another flash of light. Hard pain in the back of his head.

"That's enough, that's enough." Two wide hands digging into his armpits. "Come on, Botts. You don't belong here."

"My house," he slurred.

"We're going to take a little drive."

"Uhhh."

"Hell to pay, Botts, if you puke on my mats."

[45]

SOMETHING STRANGE HAPPENED TO MY MOTHER.
I cannot quite pinpoint the date, but it was sometime during mid-spring. More and more often she was awake in the evenings. The water glass she kept in her bathroom was brought to the kitchen sink; the bottle of pink pills placed in a drawer. She cut her hair, and took on a part-time job. She even went to a cosmetics party, whatever that might be, and returned home doused in cheap perfumes, painted like a whore, but happy nevertheless.

"What's wrong with you?" I asked, as I stood in the doorway of her bedroom, watching her pull on a pair of pale blue terrycloth gym pants.

"Nothing's wrong with me. I'm just—"

"Just acting freaky."

"Freaky?" She turned toward me, and tried to look me in

the eye. I stared at the gaudy colour of her pants. "Just what do you prefer?"

"I don't know."

"Should I mope for the rest of my life?"

"Hardly. You've moped enough for the whole neighbour-hood."

"That's exactly right. And it's high time I stopped. People can change."

"And what might be the cause behind this fresh new you?"

"No cause."

Of course she was lying. Her response was illogical, defied the rules. Such an effect had to be preceded by a defined cause. Things did not function any other way.

"Oh."

"It was time for me to wake up, is all. Hear the birds, smell the flowers. I've been down for so long."

Maybe she had joined a therapy club, or some such garbage.

She pulled on a matching sweatshirt, her head popping out of the hood. "I don't know the reason, Kiddle. Does it matter?"

No, it doesn't. Your life is not that interesting.

"As long as you're happy," I said, and I tilted my head, smiled.

"Not that my heart isn't still broken." An addendum for my benefit? "It is. I miss your sister. Miss your aunt."

I took a step back. The line of conversation was straying into uneasy territory. My hands and feet were going numb, starting to feel cold. The eels were still there, disguised by darkness.

"Is that so?"

"Like someone yanked out my insides. You know?

Stomped on them." Pulling a brush through her hair, she gazed at her reflection in the mirror.

I stared at her. Again, I questioned how I could have existed inside of her for nine full months, then emerged from that gap between her legs. It was illogical. Foreign. The notion made me feel ill. "I don't want to talk about it."

"I know. I know you don't. And I agree, Kiddle, I think that's best. Let's not talk about them anymore. Okay? Let's just not. We can keep what we have, our memories, inside of ourselves. Like a secret." Touching her chest. "Otherwise we'll just always feel sad."

I could feel rage seeping into my stomach. *Our memories? Our fucking memories?* I reached up, touched the base of my skull, stuck my fingernails into my scalp. Closing my eyes, I imagined my hand reaching out, gripping that vase on her night table, full of shitty pink carnations, and smashing it into her face.

"Kiddle? You okay?"

I opened my eyes. The vase was still there. Carnations untouched.

"Do you agree? Do we have a deal?"

I swallowed, burped, waited a moment for my stomach to settle. "Sure. Yep."

"Good. I think it's best. I really do. Let's look to the future!" She opened a box on her bed. "See? I bought new sneakers."

"Oh."

"Listen. I just had a thought. Why don't you invite some kids over from school? Invite them over to the house? You can boil some hot dogs. Play some games. We've got a game or two poked away somewhere. Don't we? What do you say?"

"Nah."

"But why not?"

"Because they're all idiots."

"C'mon, Kiddle. They can't all be idiots."

"Can't they be? Have you met them?"

"There's got to be one decent kid. Surely if you try. You just need to make the effort."

"I hate them all," I said.

"Hard to make friends with that attitude."

"It's not attitude. It's the truth."

"Well, I see you're in an arguing mood. I, for one, won't be drawn in by it."

Annoyed, I said nothing else, left her bedroom, walked quietly into my own. Took a box of matches hidden underneath my mattress, and the glass prism that contained the Luna moth, off the shelf above my bed. Then I went down to the kitchen, into the porch. Opening the second door, I descended the narrow stairs to the basement. In the stairwell, I passed a straw broom dangling from a hook, three blackened pots hung on nails. When I reached the basement area, I swiped my hand through the blackness and found the string, yanked, and a dim light illuminated the space. Though there was a bolted door to the outside, there were no windows, no sunlight. I liked that. Liked that it was always midnight in the basement of our house.

Three walls were concrete, and for unknown reasons, someone had framed the fourth wall, tacked up drywall. My mother, in a strange burst of housewifery, had glued wallpaper to the drywall. An entire expanse of thin brown stripes, clumps of faded marigolds. Not only was it pointless, it was ugly, damp, and curling near the edges. I could see black mildew or mould blooming near the bottom. It should be peeled off, thrown away, so that the spores did not damage the lungs. But no one ever came down here. No one but me.

Then, shoes on the linoleum above me. Rubber squeaking from new sneakers. My mother's shrill voice descending through the floorboards. "I'm leaving! Not sure when I'll be home."

I held my breath, quietly laid the glass prism on the ground, waited.

"Try to get outside," she continued. "You're like a ghost, for God's sakes. Get some fresh air!"

A door clicked. The house was silent. I was alone.

I exhaled, looked around the basement space. My last contraption remained in the corner, very close to a wall. I had built it last fall, sometime in November, but had completely forgotten about it. It was a simple construction: metal bearings, narrow plastic pipes, string, rubber bands, and a wooden salad fork I had stolen from the kitchen. The eventual effect involved a basketball dropping, a string tightening, and a soup spoon snapping forward. Very simple, but affixed to that spoon was a sharpened nail.

Once the machine was functioning, I needed a target. Something just right.

Enter: the doll.

I had taken one of Button's old dolls, the kind that was a perversion of the female form with unnatural distensions and an impossible waist. I hated that doll. Told Button it was not allowed to play with her other dolls. (No surprise that it was a gift from our aunt. She had been another perversion of the female form, had she not?) I found it after Button died, lost in the back of her closet, and for some reason, I kept it. A few days after Halloween, I brought it down to the basement, removed its clothes, and with a permanent marker, I blackened its bright blue eyes. Then I cropped all the blonde hair, except two stupid strands. With those strands held tight at either side, I fixed that doll to the wall with grey tape. Taped her feet so that she was immobile. Could not kick. *Heh. Heh.*

To be honest, it was not exciting. For many afternoons, I reset and reactivated my simple system, making tiny adjustments here and there. The fork poked the basketball, it dropped, the string tightened, the nail flew forward and struck the doll's smirking face over and over again. Sadly, it did very little damage. There was not enough force. I could barely identify a scratch in her perfectly painted lips. It was disappointing, and eventually I gave up, left the doll hanging there, a piece of tape jammed over her pointed face.

The sight of it now made me angry. I tore the doll off the wall, taking strips of wallpaper with it. Threw it across the room. Then I kicked the contraption until it was a disassembled mess on the floor. I stared at the pieces. The whole thing destroyed. I hated that I had constructed something that was unique, even though ineffective, and no one was there to witness it. Button was not there to clap her hands and squeal. Button was not there. Button was not.

I dug out the box of matches in my pocket and, crouching down, tried to light the edges of the wallpaper. It would not catch. I wasted six matches, and nothing happened. Flame held against it, the paper scorched, smoked slightly, made me cough, but eventually extinguished. Pointless. I smelled the chemicals on my fingers and tried not to think about my mother. I was not sure which was worse, when she was drugged and depressed, or now this disgustingly cheerful optimist.

I decided to think about Button instead. Not that last time, when I had failed her, but other times. Better times. I remembered when she was given two sheets of velvety ant stickers and I allowed her to place them all over my face. She gave me a moustache, a thick beard, enormous eyebrows, sideburns. All made with tiny black ants. I did her face next, gave her the same, and she pushed her cheek next to mine. "We bwuh-thas," she said. "We haiya-wee bwuh-thas." I was happy to be Button's hirsute sibling. My mother even did something she rarely does. She took a photograph.

Reaching up, I yanked the string again, and the light vanished. I lay down on the damp cement in the pitch darkness, and felt around for the insect in glass. I moved it so that it was directly in front of my face. Positioning my hands behind it, I struck a match, let it flame and die, and then struck another. As each flame burst into life, all I could see were the feathered antennae, spots like eyes on the delicate green wings of the Luna moth. A reminder of my sister. The light shining through.

46

KEY IN A LOCK, METAL SLIDING OVER METAL. A CLANG.

"Up," someone said. A boy's voice.

Placing his feet on the floor, Warren leaned forward, brought his hands down to stabilize himself. A rough mattress, the smell of urine and damp cement. He knew instantly where he was.

"Up," the boy said again.

"I'm sorry?" he whispered.

"Don't be sorry. Just get the hell out. We're not running a hotel here."

A hand came at him though the darkness, a clamp under his arm. A familiar sensation, as though someone else had recently touched him that way. Warren stumbled to his feet. His head throbbed so fiercely his whole body shook from the pain. Even his teeth had a silvery heartbeat. Gripping his upper arm, a young police officer led Warren down a narrow hallway, walls grimy mint and covered in black streaks. The officer opened a door to a waiting area, a row of scratched orange chairs, fluorescent lighting, Gordie Smit standing by a counter.

Warren lifted his fingers toward his friend. His shoulder ached.

"Buddy. You look like absolute shit." Gordie's white t-shirt strained against his stomach. "Let's get you home, man."

As they drove, Warren lay his swollen face against the cool glass of the passenger-side window.

"Daylene heard what happened. Her sister-in-law's sister's friend was there last night. Right in your backyard. Saw a few of them having a go at you." Gordie shook his head. "Had to check up. Make sure you were okay."

"Uh," he replied. His brain was still hammering so sharply, he could not form a thought. Could not concentrate enough to count.

They pulled into the driveway, and Gordie rushed around, opened Warren's door. It was just before sunrise, and there was no one standing outside his home. Everything was strangely quiet. "We got to get you inside, buddy. Watch your step. There's a thin layer of ice."

"Uh." As he shuffled up the driveway, Warren peered at the side of the house. The gate was destroyed, torn from the hinges. A portion of the fence had been trampled, posts snapped at the base.

Gordie followed him into the house, through the living room, and into the kitchen. He pulled out a chair, and Warren eased his body into it. The knees of his trousers were stained green and brown. His fingernails were ragged. There were several burn holes in the fabric of his shirt.

Dazed, Warren looked around his home, looked out into the backyard. Early orange light was seeping through the gaps in the trees, casting long shadows over the frosty grass. His lawn was littered with abandoned taper candles and cardboard disks. Areas were trampled, and some patches nothing more than muck. A forgotten jacket was hung over the railing of the deck. A lone mitten next to it, pulled onto a post.

"Look at you, buddy. Someone popped you a few good ones." Gordie went to the cabinet, shook pain relievers from the white container.

"Seems so."

"You don't deserve this."

Warren sipped water, swallowed the pills. "Maybe I do."

"What are you talking about?"

He shrugged. "I made a mistake," Warren whispered.

"What sort of mistake, buddy? What are you talking about?"

"I ran away."

"From Amanda Fuller? Are you undone about that girl? Stupid teenagers, that's what I got to say. Sure, I was one myself at some point. Not a girl, obviously, but dumb as all fuck."

Warren lifted his head, then. Gordie's face was only a few inches from him. "Beth. My sister." *And.* He swallowed the sour mass rising up in his throat. *My father. My mother.*

"Shit, buddy. You had me worried there for a second." He gripped Warren's chin, lifted a section of his hair, blew air out through tightened lips. "Beth'll be fine. She'll find her way."

And my father?

Gordie went to the sink, lifted out a blue dishcloth. Water

running, he rinsed and squeezed it, brought it to Warren. One warm hand holding the left side of his skull, he pressed the cloth to the right side of his skull. Warren felt wet crumbs drop onto his neck, tumble down the inside of his shirt.

"You're gonna be fine, old buddy. All superficial." Lifting the cloth, then patting. "You'll get 'em next time, right?"

Nodding.

"You want more water? Something stronger? Hair of the dog, and all that."

Shaking his head.

"Get up, let's get you to the couch. Time to rest. Enough crap for a full day already."

A rapid sip of air, and Warren stared at Gordie's mouth. "Why did you say that?"

"I don't know. Just popped in my head."

Those were his father's words. Not exactly, but the same sentiment. He had heard something similar slide out from Nora's mouth, and now Gordie's. Warren had an awareness that his father was all around him, trying to tell him something. Trying to make him understand. Warren brought his head to the cold kitchen table. Maybe his father never meant for him to reach for all the negative things that had happened. Polishing them up, standing them side by side, an impenetrable wall that obscured everything else. Maybe what he actually meant was that Warren should grasp what was beyond. The warmth and sunshine on the other side.

Tears sprang to Warren's eyes, and the salt burned his skin.

"Jesus, buddy." Gordie patted the back of his neck. "Whatever darkness you got inside of you, you got to let it go. You understand?"

"I do." A croak. "I think I do."

47

ON A SUNDAY AFTERNOON IN EARLY MAY, I FOUND MY NEIGHBOUR stark naked on his bathroom floor. I had gone to return a book, and as he had told me never to knock, I marched straight up the front steps and into his house. The house was silent except for a soft whimper. Not an embarrassing or dramatic whimper, just an indicator of severe discomfort.

I followed the sound, and found him splayed on the linoleum beside his bathtub, his lower region covered with a stained bath mat. His face crinkled with pain, but he laughed when he saw me, said he was all out of cookies. Then he asked me "to fetch" an ambulance, and I asked if I was expected to use my paws and teeth, and he laughed again. I went to make the necessary call.

When I returned to the bathroom, I questioned him, even though the events that had transpired were obvious. I thought it best to engage him in a level of conversation, to assess his cognitive functioning.

"Got a little dizzy. Slipped."

"Bad?"

"Bad enough."

His skin was pale, except for a blue circle around his mouth.

"Have you broken anything?"

"Something, yes. I'm struggling to get up. I'm a bit brittle." Faint snicker. "As you might suppose."

Tapping my foot. "Not to be insulting, Mister, but that's very unimaginative. Falling out of your bathtub when you're a hundred and fifty years old? Couldn't you have had a more creative accident?"

He laughed again, then moaned as his body moved. "Leave it to you to say such things. But, yes, I do apologize for being mundane."

I covered him with his terrycloth bathrobe, placed a rolled towel under his head. I knew he was conducting heat into the floor, but I was uncertain how to prevent that.

"Good thing you're not a horse."

He raised his eyebrows.

"If you can't walk properly, you'd get laminitis. They'd have to put you down. Humanely, of course. I would see to that."

"Well, good thing I have you on my side." He hiccupped then. Pain shot through his face, and he panted, "Oh God, oh God."

"Are you okay, Mister?"

"No, no."

"I—I could help. If you want to end your misery. You are old. Really, really old."

Lifting his hand, "You have to stop making me laugh, my friend." Deep breaths. "Thank you, though. It's nice to have the choice."

"Okay. But I would, you know. I would." And I would.

"I have a daughter."

"I know. The one who brings you cookies you can't eat? Wins the thoughtful award." Sarcasm. Of course.

"Yes, her. And my granddaughter. They're going through a difficult time. My girl lost her job."

"Oh."

"I wouldn't want to add to her stress by dying. Planning a funeral is a bother. Most people don't realize."

"I understand." After a moment, I added, "That's kind of you to think of them."

"I hope so. I hope I'm not being selfish." A thin smirk. "Maybe I should consider your offer."

"They'd probably miss you."

"I think they would, too. Everyone should feel that. That someone might miss them."

For the first time that day, I thought of Button. I saw her pink face, staring up at me as I watched her from that upper porch. Her cheeks stained with orange. Pleading with me. I could not face her, even inside my imagination, I had to look away.

"Do you want me to keep an eye on your place while you're at the hospital?"

"You can," he said, then he edged forward, grunted in pain. "But if my hip is fractured, I won't be coming back."

"Never?"

"Don't know. But I will tolerate my treatment. I promise you. I'm no horse. Won't thrash in my stall."

"Do you think it's broken?"

"I do."

"Oh."

"I don't know for certain though, my friend. Don't worry, okay?"

"Will you live with her?"

"My daughter? No, no. Never. I don't want to interrupt her life."

"Smart," I said.

He tucked his head into his chest, sighed. "The tree first, and now me. Fallen."

"Yeah." I brought my hand to my mouth, chewed the curling skin beside my thumbnail.

"I was sorry to see that happen, you know. It hurt."

"Yep."

"It mostly belonged to you, didn't it? If we're honest here, and this is a good time for that. A bit of honesty. Even though it rented a space on my lawn. That tree. You've loved it ever since you were a tiny child. If trees could walk, I'd have evicted that thing, told it to uproot its barky duff and go over to your front yard. Settle in to watch you grow up."

"Really?"

"Without a scrap of indecision."

My throat tightened. A strange and unpleasant sensation. "Thank you, Mister."

He reached his bluish fingers out, and I touched his hand. His warm skin did not feel disgusting.

"They'll be here soon," I told him.

With his eyes closed, he said, "I know."

"I should open the front door."

"Yes."

I stood up. Then my neighbour said something that made me feel slightly disturbed.

"You've got a good heart, you know."

I stopped moving. So many colourful images flickering inside my mind. Things I had done. Things I wanted to do. "No, Mister, no."

"I may be a decrepit old fossil, but I'm wise," he said. "Don't argue with me."

And the doorbell rang.

The paramedics were the same who had taken away my aunt, but they did not recognize me. Instead, they thanked me for my competency, hoisted my neighbour onto a padded gurney, packed blankets and pillows around his body to keep him stable. They wheeled him out the door. His eyes remained closed, skinny fingers wiggling in my direction. *Goodbye*, those birch twigs were saying, *goodbye*. And I knew I would never see him again.

Though I maintained his grass and shrubbery, his house remained locked up. Even with my vigilance, some bastard stole the wicker chair from his front step. Then one day, a sunny day, I noticed a car parked in the driveway. Without my tree trunk in the way, I had a clear view from my bedroom window. I saw the old man's daughter emerge from the driver's side, her daughter explode out of the passenger side. They rummaged in the trunk, hauled out overstuffed suitcases, lugged them up to the house, and unlocked the door. Those suitcases did not look like a visit. Those suitcases looked like a here-to-stay.

Within forty-five minutes, there was someone at the side door of my house, tapping on the metal. I went there, stared at her through the screen. She wore a pale yellow sundress with thick straps tied over her bony shoulders. There were tiny buds on her chest, hiding just underneath the fabric. I could see them, but I did not stare. Her face was tanned, nose and cheeks covered in precise black freckles. Threads of her hair, which was full of static, glinted in the air like spider-webbing.

"Do you remember me?" Her words were little bells.

I shrugged.

"My mom changed her mind. We're going to live here now. My granddad is in a home. For old people. Really old people. He's okay, though. He likes it there. Lots of books, he said. He says hi, okay? And then my mom, well, she lost her job. Ugh. Remember I told you about that? We knew it was going to happen, so it's not unexpected. No surprises. But it'll be okay. She says that a thousand times a day, which is kinda annoying. Kinda makes me wonder. If it's okay or not." She clicked the heels of her shoes together. "Do you — do you want to go and do something?"

"Like?"

"I don't know. Anything. We could do anything. Besides icicles." She grinned, and I saw the wide gap in her teeth. Her diastema.

I held up a finger, then turned and rushed upstairs to my mother's room. She was getting ready for an afternoon doing — I did not know.

"There's someone there," I said. "At the door."

"For me?" I detected anxiety in her tone.

"No. Me."

"Oh?"

"A girl. Wants to do something."

"A girl? For you? Well, well. Someone from school?"

"No. Someone else. I don't know. What do I say?"

"Just go out," she replied, as she daubed lipstick on her upper lip. "Pal around."

"But I don't know how." *To pal around.*

"Try. It's not that hard." Glancing at me over the upper rim of her glasses. "I bet you can figure it out."

And it was as simple as that. On a sunny afternoon in June, a very nice thing happened to me. I made a friend. That is not a word I have often used before or often used since. As can be inferred, I take my friendships very, very seriously.

48

GORDIE WAS GONE WHEN HE WOKE UP FROM A DEEP SLEEP. AS he sat up, every joint ached, and he felt as though his bones had been squeezed through a machine. Dry and deflated. At least his headache had subsided.

Warren went to the kitchen and opened the fridge. There were new containers of milk and orange juice on the middle shelf, a hunk of yellow cheese, a plastic bag filled with bread, and a can of meat. Four green apples and an enormous underripe tomato. His first thought was of Nora, but then he realized she was working all weekend. Doing inventory. Gordie must have slipped out and returned with groceries as he slept.

Then Warren saw a note. *Fish and the Steve-man are fed. Look after yourself.* Warren shook his head. Gently. Did not understand the source of this kindness. He lifted the bottle of orange juice, drank straight from the bottle. Then he boiled his electric kettle and poured water over two scoops of instant coffee.

Seated at the kitchen table, he slurped the acrid liquid, and opened a folder containing notes for his science lessons. While preparing for his substitute role, he had created such careful lessons. He should have passed the folder along to Ms. Fairley. Or the next teacher. Warren was aware it was unlikely he would ever return to the school.

After reading the same line several times, the words blurring together, he decided he needed to move. To do something. He stared into his backyard. Garbage still blowing about, though the jacket and mitten he had seen earlier had disappeared. He could hear a piece of wood banging against the side of the house. He would need a black garbage bag for the trash. A screwdriver and some screws for the fence. He would not be able to repair it, but he could make sure it did not get worse.

As he stood, a jackhammer sounded inside his home. Warren grabbed both sides of his head, startled. His glasses fell to the floor. It took him a moment to realize it was only the phone. Someone was trying to reach him. Hesitantly, he picked it up, brought the receiver close to his ear, but not touching.

"It's me," her voice said. "I—I thought I would try again."

"Sarie."

"I was harsh when we spoke last time. When I shared the news about your mother. It was not the right way to do it."

Warren's throat closed.

"None of this is easy, War."

He bent, picked his glasses up, held them hard against his face.

"I just wanted to try again," she continued. "Hoping to see if you'd come."

"I don't know." He had been so full of anger, of bitterness, but as he lowered his head, he recognized those feelings were no longer pressing out from the inside. Stretching his skin. "I don't know anymore."

"Did you talk to Beth?"

"She's gone."

"Should I bother asking where?"

"No point."

Warren heard Sarie sigh. Then he heard the squeak of springs, as though she had just sat down.

"You know," she said, "when I was young, before I had my own kids, I used to think it was all about how you raised them. What sort of experiences they had, how much they were loved, whether they got enough fresh air and exercise. But as I got older, I think that's all garbage. Right at the moment those little things are made, the instructions are written down. You can do what you want, and some people will just glide through life, happy as a pig rolling in its own crap. Others, though. They seek out the misery. Only feel at home, only feel comfortable when surrounded by hardship. Struggling against something. And if they can't find it on the outside, they'll turn against themselves. Fight with their own hearts." Her voice cracked. "It kills me," she said. "Kills me that people can't really see each other. Because all that pain, it's stamped on their set of instructions."

Warren pressed his forehead against the wall.

"She's a wonderful friend, she truly is, but I know she wasn't the best mother. I understand that, Warren, and I'm not trying to suggest anything otherwise. She just didn't know how to reach out. How to be soft. How to offer comfort. She just couldn't do it. Lots of kids grow up with that, and are just fine, but others, like you. Like Beth. You need that. Crave that. It's what you are."

"Sarie. I—"

"You know, I don't know why your father chose your mother. I never understood it. He should have married someone dim and silly and always ready with a joke. Instead he sought out a woman with a metal soul. Though I love her as my best friend, she can be hard and cold and heavy. Neither one had the strength to lift the other up, balance the other out. Too busy torturing themselves, if you ask me." She paused, then sniffed. "They could have had a nice life. But they had terrible instructions. Look, War. I'm sorry to be calling and saying all these things. But you know me. I don't let stuff fester. That's not my way."

"What should I do, Sarie? I don't know what to do anymore." He had spent so many years being angry, he could identify no clear path to anything else.

"I'm sure you've made a good life for yourself. Teaching and all that. I'm sure you're okay, whatever you're doing. Wherever you are. But can you just think about your mother? I'm sure she rarely crosses your mind, but I'm just asking you to think. Think about setting aside the blame. Releasing it. Forgive her. Forgive yourself, too."

Warren paced back and forth, the cord keeping him connected to the wall. "I haven't done anything wrong," he said, though his words came out broken, stilted.

"Exactly my point. A person who's done nothing wrong shouldn't hurt all the time. That doesn't make sense."

He stretched the cord until he reached the countertop beside the sink. Opening a yellow box, he tugged out a folded garbage bag. "I have to go. There's a lot going on here."

"So you said."

Bag in hand, he hung up the phone, and left his kitchen. The crisp air would help. Wandering around his backyard, he plucked up every piece of candle and cardboard, every candy wrapper and beer bottle, every fabric flower and broken balloon. Mushy bits of papers with Amanda Fuller's image, some dates, and verses from a hymn. He did not look at any of it, just moved robotically, picking and shoving, and when it dropped inside the trash bag, out of sight, it no longer existed.

He knotted the bag, brought it to the deck, sat down. The icy air felt pure in his lungs, and clean on his face, his neck. Skin chilled, he could no longer feel his bruises. When he moved his mouth, grimaced, the pain was bearable. His shoulders and back still felt sore, but it was a better sore. Working its way out, rather than settling in.

Spindly shadows crept across the backyard, and a directionless wind scattered soggy leaves, made the cold plastic of the bag crinkle and snap. In the gusts, he could smell a faint mix of vanilla and pig farm. Nose running, eyes watering, Warren wiped his face on the sleeve of his coat. He balanced his elbows on his knees, then cupped his cheeks in his hands.

Though he shivered with the cold, he remained there, his eyes closed. He was aware the sun was dropping, the light shifting and hiding. He could not estimate how long he stayed there. His mind was not thinking, not counting. Ears cupped inside the swirling wind, he heard nothing, felt nothing.

Until something kicked at his shoe.

Warren opened his eyes. Adrian Byrd was standing right in front of him. Hands shoved deep into his pockets. Rims of his eyes pink and swollen.

"I got to talk to you," he said. "Mr. Botts, I got to talk about something important, and you got to listen. It's my fault," he said. "What happened to Amanda. It's all my fault."

"Adrian. I really think you should—"

The boy started pacing in a tight line, hands curled into fists. "I'm 'bout to explode, Mr. Botts. I really think I'm 'bout to explode."

Warren touched his glasses, leaned away from the boy. He tried to maintain an even tone in his words. "I think, you know. I think, you shouldn't be here."

"I got nowhere else to go."

"I don't want to fight with you, Adrian." In the cold, Warren could see a jagged line where Adrian's face had been injured. The stitches were gone. A purple scar snaked across his forehead.

"If I don't talk to someone, I don't know what I'll do."

"Maybe I'm not the right person? Maybe your mom?"

"You got to be kidding me. She's so strung out all the time. Last night she kept talking about my friend. 'What's his name,' she kept saying. 'Why don't he say nothing.' She was gawking at the spot next to me. Smirking and shit. And then I realized she was seeing two of me. So high she thought I had a fucking twin."

"I'm sorry, Adrian. That sounds really terrible."

"But it was better, you know. When I had her to talk to. She'd come by, and then it was better."

Amanda Fuller. Warren nodded, glanced at the tree.

"She didn't care about anything. Didn't care that I live in a shithole or that my mother's cross-eyed. She didn't care." He threw his hands in the air. "She started hanging around me just to piss her mother off. You know. I was the asshole. The problem. But then she started to think I was okay. I was cool. I could tell. She laughed a lot. I would've done whatever she said."

"Adrian, I hardly—"

"It's true, Mr. Botts. She told me everything."

"I'm sorry. I didn't know her well."

"She used to talk to you, she said. She used to come here and talk to you."

"Only a couple times. Three, maybe." Warren's hands had turned blue, and he rubbed them together. "And then I told her she couldn't come back."

He stopped his jerky movements, and turned to face Warren. "Why did you tell her that?"

Swallowing. "Because I'm her teacher. I'm not her friend. I don't know." *Because Ms. Fairley insisted? Because those were the rules? Because I couldn't be bothered?*

He wondered why he had forced her to leave. To stop talking to him. She really was doing no harm, and perhaps all she wanted was someone to listen to her. To hear her. And Warren understood those were two separate actions.

Adrian knelt on the lawn, yanked up handfuls of dead grass. "She talked about it, you know."

"Talked about what?"

"About what she wanted to do. How she would make her father regret leaving. Make him miserable for the rest of his life."

"I don't understand."

Rocking back and forth, he said, "You know, do something big. Something no one would ever forget. I knew what she meant, but I never thought she'd do nothing. I said, that'd be crazy. I actually said that, Mr. Botts. And that he'd hate himself. Her father deserved to hate himself. For running away. I told her not to give a shit, but she said

I didn't understand. It's way worse when your father runs away after he knows you, not when you're just a stupid baby."

Warren edged forward. He could still sense the ache inside his skull. Not the throbbing pain, but the absence of it. As though the drumming had tapped out a hollow. An echoing dome.

"I never thought she'd do nothing. I never thought. We were having fun. She left late. Said she was fine to cut through the woods. I thought she wanted her mother to get mad. And I never walked her. I was going to. I was. But I never walked her home."

"It's not your fault, Adrian."

."It is. It is. I done lots of shitty stuff, Mr. Botts. Lots. But this is the worst. I told her offing herself would be cool. I actually said that. I was just acting big. I never thought about it. Never thought about what I was saying. And now I just got to keep it all inside. Stuffed inside. Forever."

The boy stood up, then flounced down on the step, and Warren held his breath, faced forward. Small flecks of ice shot out of the sky, pinging off the deck, the grass, the barbecue, their heads. The slishing sound of the ice was loud, but it did not drown out the boy's crying. Out of the corner of his eye, Warren could see him, a thin sweater, head lowered, a clump of uncombed hair covering his eyes.

"I'm sorry I punched you in the face," he mumbled. "I should've punched myself."

Waiting, Warren stared at the tree. He considered the mark someone had cut into the trunk, and then it struck him. A diamond, with a line close to each point. It was not a mathematical symbol, as he had assumed, but two capital As. Joined at the stems. Adrian. And Amanda. The boy had done that.

Warren's leg twitched up and down, and he started to skip-count by nines. Then he stopped himself, lifted his arm, and clamped a hand on Adrian's bony shoulder. Squeezed until the boy's shaking subsided.

49

THAT SUMMER, SHE CAME TO MY HOUSE ALMOST EVERY DAY. One morning, when she had stepped into the porch, she pointed at the second door and asked where it went. I was about to say, *Bathroom*, but then decided if she needed one, she would discover my lie. A pointless lie. I had nothing to hide down there. "Basement," I said. "Just a dirty basement."

Of course, she did not wait for an invitation. She yanked open the door, patted along the wall, and descended even when she had not located a light switch.

I liked the fact she appeared to have no fears.

"Wow, it's dark down here."

I was beside her. Could smell the fragrance that was caught in her hair, some type of flower, the faintest odour of sour milk and oats on her breath. I knew she had showered, then eaten cereal for breakfast.

"Where are you?" she said. "I can't see a freaking thing."

"I'm here. Behind you."

A light breeze on my cheeks as she turned.

"Um, lights?"

Quick yank, and the light flickered, then glowed.

"Well, that doesn't help much."

"Give it a minute. Your eyes will adjust. There's not much to see anyway."

She was turning, blinking. "You're right. Not much to see."

"We can go up."

"In a minute. It's cooler down here. And it smells like my grandfather."

"Bad?"

"No, just old. I like it."

I appreciated the fact that she no longer spoke in paragraphs full of run-on sentences.

Turning around again, she said, "And holy wallpaper. Someone got real creative."

"Yeah, my mother. I think."

"Why?"

"I don't know." *Maybe it felt like an accomplishment? Maybe it was one place in the house that looked clean?*

"Cozies the place right up."

"Do you think?"

"Of course not." Tinkling laughter.

I tried to laugh along, though as usual, I did not understand the humour.

She walked to the corner with the pile of pieces from my contraption. I had not bothered to clean it up. Unfortunately. Now she was going to ask me about it. How would I explain my stupid pastime?

"What's all this?"

See? I knew it.

"Just something I built."

"For?"

"I don't know. One thing connected to the next. Cause and effect."

"What's the purpose? What did it do?"

I inadvertently glanced behind me, saw the discarded doll in a darkened corner. Tape smothering its face. I hoped she would not notice it. That would be impossible to explain. I made a mental note, put that doll on my list of "Things to Hide."

"No purpose."

She knelt down, picked up a piece of pipe, rolled a ball around on her palm, picked up the spoon. I was grateful the nail had come unglued, was nowhere in sight.

"I think in French they call these things *usine à gaz*."

I laughed. A joke. Maybe?

"I'm serious! They call it *gasworks*. You know, a place with all the pipes sticking out of the roof, steam and smoke going everywhere? Can you just imagine it? Any minute the whole place might explode."

"How do you know that?"

"You didn't?"

"No." For once.

"Point for me! I read it. I read a lot, you know, when I can manage to shut myself up." Clicking two pipes together, she said, "Now, let's fix this thing up. This is going to be super cool."

I was surprised and delighted at her unexpected enthusiasm. As a team, we spent the next three hours rebuilding the *usine à gaz*. It was almost the same configuration, only we shortened two of the elastic bands, and I had to saw one of the pipes in half otherwise the ball travelling through (she pointed out) lost too much momentum. The alterations were successful. The spoon snapped forward with greater force, but it was much further from the wall.

"What should we do with it?" She tapped her foot, paced in circles. "Hmmm." Then, "I got it! I got it! Don't move. I'll be back in a second," and she stomped up the stairs. The screen door slammed.

I waited, in the dim light. Two minutes later she was back, dropped a box full of small paint tubes on the concrete, then started fixing two large pieces of paper onto the wall, masking tape ripped with her teeth. Once the paper was in place, she reset the machine, squirted paint on the spoon, and then triggered the system. It went through the motions, then snap, the spoon flew forward, stopped suddenly, and the paint, adhering to the law of inertia, continued in motion toward the paper. A splatter in crimson red. It made a beautiful pattern. A beautiful sound.

Another reset, another colour.

"Don't stand there with your mouth open. C'mon. Choose a colour. Let's shift this thing to a different angle."

"It would be easier to move the paper."

"Good point."

We untaped and taped.

When the tubes were empty, we leaned against the opposite wall, stared at the wet artwork, a mess of blobs and drips. And the stains on the wallpaper.

"Will your mom be pissed?"

"At what?"

"We ruined her wall."

"She won't care. She never comes down here."

"Good. Cause look what we made! It looks ahhh-mazing!"

"Not bad," I said.

"Not bad? Seriously. It's modern art. Fine art. We could sell it for big bucks, you know."

"Do you think?"

"Of course not. I'm kidding."

"Yeah. I knew that." *I did not know that.*

She turned to me, "Why do you build them?"

"I don't know. I started building them for my sister. For her amusement. She liked to watch me make them and watch them go. I always let her start them." *I thought it would make her feel powerful.*

"You got a sister? No way! Lucky you!"

"Had."

"What does that mean? Had."

"She's gone."

"As in, um, lives somewhere else?"

"No."

"With a rich old uncle in Switzerland or something? Looking after goats?"

"No."

"Some other totally sucky family because you're not part of it?"

I shook my head. I had never spoken to anyone about Button. It was difficult to squeeze out the words. They stuck in my throat like a dried burr. "As in. I don't know. I don't know. She's just gone. You know. Gone forever."

For once, my friend said nothing. Was actually silent. Like, really silent. She came over to me and put her two skinny arms around my chest and squeezed. I just stood there, spine straight, body rigid, but she did not let go of me. It was a long minute, maybe more. It seemed like it was more. I could smell her hair, her skin, her clothes. Sweetness.

Orange blossom, I determined. I could identify the warmth in her core. I had never experienced this before. It made me feel the same way as when I saw those kindergartners singing at the Christmas concert when I was a child. That moment when I was holding newborn Button in my arms. Their untainted voices echoing off the metal roof. A moving uneasiness, like bands around my pulse points.

How to explain this? In her arms, I was a hollow channel, water pulled in on the top, but flowing straight through.

I wanted to cap the bottom. Cap the bottom and tape the whole thing up. But I did not know how.

Then as quickly as she gripped me, she let me go. When her body moved away from mine, my skin erupted in goosebumps.

"I just had to do that," she said, shaking her head. "I'm sorry if you didn't like it, but I just had to."

"Um, okay."

"And now!" She stuck her index finger in the air. "I have to go."

"For lunch?"

"No, for a secret mission. I have a plan. It just came to me as I was compressing the marrow in your bones. There's something I really need to do."

"What?"

"Secret missions are secret, idiot!" And she bolted up the stairs. "See you later, alligator."

The screen door slammed. Again.

Two full days went by. I was beginning to feel irritated. I did not like jokes. Or games. I peeled her artwork off the basement wall, rolled it up, and decided to deliver it. If she did not want to be my friend, that was her problem. She answered the door on the second knock.

"Perfect timing!" she said. "Come, come with me. Now. I need to show you what I made." Squealing, hands flapping. "It is so beyond cool. So much beyond cool, it's cooltastic. Super coolistic. I'm really excited. I've definitely got some major skills. Major! Hurry up. C'mon, c'mon. Leave your sneakers on. Who cares."

I went down into her basement. My old neighbour's basement. I had never been there before, and it was much brighter and cleaner than I had imagined. There were windows, walls, beige carpeting, several wooden shelves full of novels. In the corner was a yellow sheet, covering something that was unusually lumpy.

She gently removed the sheet and, balling it in her arms, she bowed slightly, cried, *Voilà! Mon usine à gaz!*

Similar to mine, but with gears and weights. Very clever. "You built that?"

"Yep. All by my lonesome. My mom bought me a couple things, but the rest of it I found in the shed out there. You wouldn't believe what he's got poked away. A fortune's worth of stuff."

"Really?"

"No, I'm kidding. C'mon! Just junk."

Ugh.

"I smell something minty. Spearmint?"

"Dental floss. I ran out of string."

"Innovative."

"That's me. Now shut up with the questions, and stand there." She pointed to a gap in the machine. On either side of the gap she had positioned back-scratchers. Cylindrical lengths of painted wood, a plastic hand poked on the end of each.

"Now watch."

She lifted a small weight off a ledge and let it dangle. It descended slowly, making a gear wind, which tightened an elastic, which moved a pencil, and so on. Eventually, the final gear turned, pulling a thread, and the two back-scratchers closed together. I remained between them, and the wood and plastic hands grazed my front and back, applied the slightest bit of pressure.

I stepped back. Put my fingers on the places where the back-scratchers had touched me. "You made this? By yourself?"

"For you!"

"I don't get it. Why?"

"What? You can't be serious. Were you not here? Did you not see what happened?"

I blinked. I thought I had missed another joke.

"Because you are my first and only friend. Because I like you very, very much. And because more than anyone else I've ever known, you need hugs, silly," she said, and started to reset her machine. "And here you have an unlimited number of great big giant hugs!"

50

DETECTIVE REED STOOD IN HIS LIVING ROOM. SHE WAS NO longer smirking. Instead, her forehead was wrinkled with lines, mouth turned into a sneer.

"You're not supposed to be talking to me," Warren said. Stephen sat next to his leg, banging his heavy tail on the floor. Sixteen, seventeen, eight—

"Where do you think this is? The big city?" She glanced over her shoulder at the police officer near the front door.

"I don't want to talk anymore."

"Do you know people are getting ready for the holidays? Little lights around their windows, wreaths stuck up on their doors. It looks real nice. Real normal."

Warren coughed, touched his glasses.

"I know you're a liar, Botts. I know you told me a bunch of bullshit, and I smiled the whole time. You painted a pretty picture of yourself. A real pretty picture. Friendly teacher. Trying to do your best. Upstanding member of our little town here."

"I try to," he said. He began to sweat, and when he shifted, he could smell his wet skin. Something made of iron. Rusting.

"You know what? I know you got crazy shit going on up there inside your skinny head. I tried to dig it out, and even though I've been told to stop, I'm not done." She turned to her partner. "Are we done?"

"No, not done."

"I've done nothing wrong."

"So they say."

"Who? Who said?"

"You got questions, too, hey?"

"I do," he admitted.

Detective Reed pushed her hands into her pockets.

"Preliminary report is in, Botts. Some hotshot forensic physicist who's obviously a blowhard. Can you even believe there's such a job? An idiot, though. Lots of technical bullshit about height of the branch and shape of the bruising around Amanda Fuller's neck, and how the rope was evidently tied around the tree first. The neck was broken, which is rare, apparently. We don't got much experience with that sort of thing."

"Oh."

"Means a lot of force was involved. Means she dropped from at least six feet."

"Yes." He considered the downward pull of gravity. The upward force from the rope. The vertebrae in her slender neck. It made sense.

"Report says she jumped." Detective Reed cracked her gum.

"Oh." He closed his eyes. Stephen had stopped slapping his tail, the counting interrupted.

"That's what the picture tells us. But it leaves me wondering. Who rammed a science test into her mouth? What type of dumbass would forget about that little detail? Did she eat that herself? Shove it down her throat before she climbed the tree and leapt off? Did she?"

Warren opened his mouth to speak, but nothing emerged.

"And did she just make all those drawings herself? Stash them in your house? Smells like bullshit to me."

"I don't know what to say," he managed.

"Well, you know what I say?" She looked him in the eyes. Warren had to look away, but he still heard her words. "I say, like fuck, Botts. Like. Fuck."

Light poured out of the window, and Warren stood in Nora's driveway, watching her through the glass. She was seated on a wine-coloured couch, a small television set balanced on the coffee table in front of her. Leaning forward, she was twisting a knob, then raised a fist, smacked the side of the set. Libby was there, did something on the back of the television, and Nora clapped her hands, settled back, folded her arms across her chest.

Warren hesitated, then walked up the peeling wooden steps. Flecks of snow were falling, and he pressed the doorbell. He had nowhere else to go, and he knew Nora would be happy to see him, to hear what he had to say.

"What!" she said when she yanked open the door. Then, seeing Warren, her tone softened, "Oh. I wasn't expecting you." She touched her hair.

"I should have called. But I was just. Wandering."

"No. No. I'm delighted to see you. Of course I am. Come in. Come in from the cold." She moved out of the way, and he stepped into the porch. "I'll make you a tea. Or coffee. Do you want a cream soda? I might have that."

Though they had been spending time together for months, Warren realized he had not been to her house. He had never asked, and she had never offered. Often she would mention she was painting a room, shampooing a rug, or clearing out closets. His home was so much more convenient, she repeated. A quick detour on her drive from the store.

"It's nice," he said.

"Well." She patted her hair again. "It's a work in progress."

"Like most things in life, I suppose." He inhaled. Could not detect paint, or cleaner, and no closets were open, contents spilling out. But he understood. Her home was full of private happy memories, her husband, her life with Libby, and perhaps she was not ready to incorporate Warren into them.

Every overhead light and lamp was on and, coming in from the darkness, his eyes narrowed, began to water. The room smelled like cardboard. But it was full of her things. And Libby's. Their coats on hooks, Nora's purse on the floor, a book Libby had mentioned dropped beside it.

"Hey, Mr. Botts."

"Hey, Libby. Everything okay?"

"Getting better every day."

She disappeared upstairs, and Warren followed Nora into the kitchen. It was larger than he had expected, but only had a bar-sized table, two stools. The sink was full of dishes, red sauce smeared on white plates. Warren resisted counting them.

Her face flushed when she glanced at Warren. "Sorry for

the mess," she said. "I just got home from work. Libby made dinner. I asked her to clean up, but something happens to their listening abilities once they hit thirteen."

"I can hear you!" An eagle screech from upstairs.

Then Nora whispered, "It becomes very selective."

Warren smiled, nodded.

"Your face is healing. Getting better. Swelling's gone down." She touched his shoulder. "Honestly. I don't know why you didn't file a report. What kind of people would do such a thing? Sometimes I think the whole community is crawling with animals." Moving around her kitchen, she opened and closed cupboards, yanked open the fridge door, then closed it. "It'll have to be water, War, darling. Seems the girl drank all the cream soda."

Another screech. "I can still hear you!"

"Um. Are you sure I'm not interrupting?"

"No, no. Don't be silly."

"Water is nice." He sat on a stool, his legs lifted, heels of his shoes hooked into the metal bar. "I. Well. I have some news."

"News? Good, I hope."

"I don't know if *good* is the correct word. But." Back hunched, he tried to rest his elbows on the table, but the distance was too far. He let his arms dangle, and he felt the stiffness in his muscles. "There's news about Amanda."

"The Fuller girl?"

He cleared his throat, touched his glasses. "They think she did it herself."

"Oh, yes. I heard already." She laid the glass of water in front of him, then tapped her head with her knuckles. "Late nights at the store. My mind is gone."

"An accident, they're saying. I guess they had an expert

evaluate everything, and they say it might have been an accident. Or. You know. She was by herself."

"Jesus, War. No matter how you paint it, it's a terrible thing."

"Yes."

"What goes through their minds? The poor girl really needed some help, and no one stepped up. Sometimes they go a little crazy when they're teenagers."

He shook his head, slurped water. Warm and tasted of chlorine.

"They don't have any more questions for me right now. My lawyer said I will need to check in. Make my whereabouts known. That sort of thing. Things could change. The report is only preliminary. It's not final."

She took his hand in hers, brought it to her cheek. "It'll be fine." Smiling at him, that same lopsided smile. "I doubt you've ever done a thing wrong in your life."

Warren slipped his hand out from hers, and brought his glass to the sink. As he poured the water down around the clutter of dishes, he saw the avocado plant he had given Nora on the window ledge. So many months ago. It was pushed behind the bleached fabric of the curtain. Curling his finger over the edge of the pot, he eased it out. The slender stalk had grown, but as he shifted it, the leaves tumbled off, drifted into the sink. He could see the scars where each leaf had been attached. The soil was so dry, it had pulled away from the ceramic pot.

His mind flashed an image of Nora's stew, then. Perfectly cubed carrots rising to the surface, then disappearing. The feeling of uncertainty was there again. In the pit of his stomach.

Warren coughed. Looking down the hallway from the

kitchen, he could see the stairs. Near the top, he saw a pair of feet, black-and-white striped socks, wiggling on the carpet. Libby was seated there. Listening.

He turned to face Nora. Said in a whisper, "Why didn't you have any questions?"

"Questions? About what?"

"About me. You never asked a single thing."

"Oh, War." Leaning her head back, her eyes widened, eyelashes fluttering. "I know you. From the first moment I saw you at the store, I knew you were good."

"How?"

"I don't know how to put it. You're not like the rest of the world. You're an open hand. Nothing hidden inside."

THIS MIGHT SOUND UNIMAGINATIVE, BUT WHENEVER I WAS WITH my friend, my interaction with the world became more acute. Yes, I felt the line-dried cotton on my skin, smelled sun-warmed dirt, heard bees buzzing from one chamomile flower to the next. Inane, I know, but I wondered how had I not noticed how alive the world was? So many things that existed in the background had now jumped to the fore-ground. The sensations were almost overwhelming in their sharpness. She was the cause of this shift in consciousness. She had woken me up.

We spent our waking hours together, often doing noth-ing more than absorbing vitamins from sunlight. But my mind was quiet, contented. How can an existence be totally aimless but full of direction at the same time?

Many afternoons, we made the long walk through the

woods, and swam in the lake (of course I never mentioned the eels by the rock). Whenever the sun was hot, the water felt even colder. *Refreshing*, she called it, and when I complained about the cruel temperature, she laughed, said, "You're just a wimp."

The bottom of the lake was slick. Everything was covered with a fine layer of green and gold algae. When I peered through the murky water, I saw rusting cans and broken bottles, and I plucked them up, tossed them further out so she would not cut her feet. After all my efforts to create a safe area, she splashed me and tried to push my head beneath the surface. My instinct was to lash back, but I soon grew used to her game. I even began to enjoy it, especially when she attacked from behind, gliding through the water like a skinny brown shark. I wondered if it was difficult for her to stop talking upon approach.

When we were both freezing, we climbed out of the water and dried off on the beach. I watched her as she sat up, sand stuck to her shoulder blades. Full of lake water, her hair lifted up into a massive chestnut frizz.

"What? You forgot how to blink? Forgot what I look like?"

"What?"

"You're staring at me."

"Am not."

"Are too."

I did not reply. There was no point arguing against the truth.

We spent hours in the shadowy woods that stretched behind our houses. I had already scoured that area a million times, had it mapped in my mind, so I let her lead and discover. She tripped over the gnarled roots and found dips hidden by shrubs. She located the squirrel homes and bird nests.

She coughed after darting through a cloud of tiny flies, and screamed when she jumped onto the red-ant mound. I had to warn her of the low-hanging papery nest that was full of hornets. Otherwise, that would have been depraved. Right?

Occasionally she reached behind her, and would catch up my hand as it swung forward. She wove her fingers through mine, and hand in hand, we would meander. An unusual word choice, but that was what we did. *Meander.* Like old people. Like happy people.

One time, as we were exploring, she found a large puddle of stagnant water near a grove of trees, and she lay on the ground, peered into the dark glass.

"Look how still it is," she said. "I can see myself perfectly. You do it."

I lay down beside her, the hair on our arms lifting, barely touching.

"We're perfect," she whispered. "You and me. How we appear."

I stared into my face. Leaning over like that, my mouth was downturned, and my eyes looked worried, a little scared. That was certainly not an accurate reflection, as I worried about nothing. I was afraid of nothing. I turned my head, could not take the whole thing seriously.

When I shifted, dirt from the edge of the ring tumbled into the water, distorting our faces.

"Hey, you broke the mirror. That's bad luck."

"Yeah. I'm so worried." I nudged her, then threw a handful of dirt and leaves into the water. "Let's go. We can't swim in this. It's probably a cesspool."

"I doubt it. It's probably perfectly clean."

• • •

My friend did not have a bicycle, but after digging through her grandfather's shed, we found one. The paint was bubbled and chipped, seat torn, and both wheels needed patches, but she was excited about it. We made the necessary repairs and that afternoon, we took our bikes into the woods. I made sure to stick to the best paths, the safest paths, as there were so many hills that just dropped off into nothing. We had planned to go swimming in the lake, but when we came out on the other side near the water, a boy was there. He was lying on his stomach on a bleached wooden wharf, his skinny arm reaching, hand moving up and down over the water.

We stopped our bikes, and she said, "Who's that?"

Of course I had instantly known who it was. "A moron," I said. "I hate him." He lived in a trailer, propped up on cement blocks, no curtains, overgrown weeds for grass. A mangy dog that always circled in his yard. I saw him chase his sister and kiss her on the lips. It was disgusting. I was not surprised to see him there, pulling scrawny fish out of a freshwater lake.

"Why?"

"He's stupid. He's an asshole. He stinks. And did I say he's stupid? Need any more reasons?"

She jumped off her bike, and when I was within reach, she punched me in the arm. Not enough to hurt, though.

"C'mon," she said. "Let's go see what Stupid Moron is doing!"

Before I could stop her, she laid her bike on its side, and was skidding down over the hill toward the wharf.

"Hey you! Hey! You catching dinner? What can you catch in this sort of lake? Does it taste any good? I guess you'd have to do something with it, right? Season it up? Clean it first, of course, before you do anything else." Giggling.

"Can't just cook it." Her babbling was the worst when she met someone new.

He lifted his head, twisted his turkey neck. Sunlight struck his bony face, and he squinted a single eye. I hated that someone like that was looking at someone like her. "Hardly." Then he saw me. "Hey, loser," he said.

"Asshole."

"What dragged you out of your basement?"

"Nothing."

"Girlie, here? You got yourself a little follower, loser?"

"Go to hell."

She seemed to ignore our arguing. "What're you doing then? If you're not catching fish? I see a line in your hand. Are you hooking up garbage? Cleaning the bottom of the lake? It's filthy, you know. We were swimming, and there's tons of dangerous stuff down there."

"Yeah, yeah, I'm hooking up garbage."

"Oh, good for you! That's such a considerate thing to do. Very community minded! Don't you think?" She was look-ing at me, here, palms facing outwards, eyebrows in a *see-he's-not-an-asshole* position.

I did not know what the creep was doing, but I knew he was not hooking up garbage, trying to clean the lake. "C'mon," I said. "Let's find somewhere else to swim." She ignored me, lay down beside him, and peered into the murky water. I leaned to the left, and even without getting closer, I could see what he was doing. On the bottom of the lake, they were moving around, walking with their seesaw gait.

"What are those?"

Even I was surprised by her question.

"You never seen crabs before? Where you from?"

"Oh. Yes, yes, I know. I always get crabs and lobsters

mixed up. Don't ask me why! They are completely different, aren't they? Well, not completely. You know what I mean! We didn't see many crabs where I'm from. Too many apartment buildings and not enough lakes. Sometimes you couldn't even see the sun, the buildings were so high. It wasn't very nice. I like it here much better. Where you can get out, you know. See real stuff. Not bubblegum stuck to a sidewalk."

He looked at me. "Does your girlfriend ever shut up?"

"Why? Do you think the crabs can hear me? Am I bothering them? Are they getting in the way of the garbage? I can scream if you want, see if they'll move."

"Ffffuck," he whispered, and he glanced at me again, jaw open.

When he lifted his line, there was a large crab on the end. A metal hook caught under its arm. The moron dropped it on the wharf, keeping a hand on its shell. I knelt down on the warm boards, and stared into its glistening face. Saw its irritated expression. On thin stalks, its black eyes reached, scanned its waterless world. Confused. Angry. I could relate.

"You caught a crab? Are you keeping it? To eat? Poor thing."

"Fuck, no. This water is full of shit. Didn't you just say so yourself? Would you eat shit?"

She laughed. I think she was slightly nervous. "No," she replied. "No shit for me!"

"Then why'd you expect me to eat shit?"

"I didn't know. I—I don't think shit is very healthy. To be honest."

The loser's facial expression did not alter, and she peered at me. I assumed she wanted to see if I understood her attempt to educate him, but then she said, "That was a joke. Seriously, you guys!" Then she reached out and slid one finger between the crab's wet eyes. "You don't want to be someone's lunch, do you? You're so cute. Isn't he cute?"

"Yeah. Fucking adorable."

"But it probably doesn't like being away from home. You should throw it back, now."

"I should, should I?"

"You pulled it out by mistake. It's not garbage. Garbage doesn't breathe."

"Says who? Lots of garbage breathes."

"Well, I guess it doesn't hurt to stare at it for a bit. Isn't its shell beautiful? Have you ever wished you had a shell? Wouldn't that be nice? People would probably ruin their shells, paint them up and stuff. Make them look all gaudy. But a simple shell would be so pretty to have. Good protection, too."

"Watch this, asswipes," he said, and retrieved a magnifying glass from the back pocket of his torn jean shorts. He angled the lens, concentrated the rays of the sun. Smoke rose up from the wharf where the sunlight burned a black line across the grey wood. Then he shifted the lens, and with his other hand he shifted the crab, and the rays focused on the crab's black eyes. "This really fucks them up."

I heard the sizzle. Faint smell, like burning vegetation. He destroyed the first eye, then turned the crab, altered the beam of light, and obliterated the second eye. Pinned to the wharf, the mottled brown shell never moved, but it lifted its legs and dropped them, scraping the wood. I think the creature was experiencing pain.

"Now watch this shit," he said, and lifted his hand. The blinded crab began to move, slowly at first, edging left, then to the side, then turning in a circle. Drunken directions, claws clicking against the wood. "Look at it, it's totally fucked up. Totally. Got no idea where to go." His laughter

escalating then descending, a rapid scale. I did not understand what he found so amusing. Finally the crab tumbled
over the edge of the wharf, a flash of white as it flipped on
its descent to the bottom. "I've caught eight so far."

"What a waste of time," I said, and I stood up, started to
walk away. "C'mon. Let's go swim somewhere else."

As I spoke, I caught sight of her. I was not expecting to
see her face like that. Hands pushed into her cheeks, skin
around her eyes contorted. Water pooled on her lower lids,
and when she blinked, it shot out onto the wood. I could see
the dark flecks on the wharf. Marks from her tears. "Let's
go," I repeated. "C'mon."

She was silent as she stood. When she lowered her hands,
her face was red and splotchy, as though she had broken out
in hives. She opened her mouth, but no words emerged. No
words emerged! Then she bolted up the hill, hauled her bike
from the ground, and tore off through the woods. I yelled,
"Wait!" But she did not wait.

"Seems your little friend got no guts," the moron said.
"Prisses don't survive round here long."

"Watch it." I took a step closer to him. Blocked his sunlight. "Watch your mouth."

"Hard to do, isn't it? Watch my mouth. When I don't got
crab eyes." And he laughed. As though he had made an
acceptable joke.

"I saw what you did."

"And that matters how?"

"It will matter, asshole. You'll see."

"Fuck you. I'm sure you don't give two shits about a crab."

"What was that?"

"Fuck you, loser."

"Your vocabulary is extensive, as always."

He lay down on his stomach again, carefully lowered the hook into the water. "Get the fuck out of here, shithead. I got work to do. An even dozen before I leave."

My flash of anger had dissipated, replaced by calculated thought. I looked at his rusted bike, saw the narrow path he had taken to get to the wharf. And then I told him, "It's good to have goals, jerk."

"You said it, fucktard."

When I arrived home, I found her sitting on the front porch. Slowly I walked over to her and sat down. My shoulder brushed hers, and she did not slide over. In her hand, she held a glass full of ice cubes, and she fished one out, crunched it.

"You want one?"

Her voice was scratchy and her eyes were swollen, pink.

"No," I said. "No thanks." Then, "Do you know people who crave ice sometimes have iron-deficiency anemia?"

She shoved another piece in her mouth and drove her teeth through it. "You my doctor now?"

"No. I don't want to be your doctor."

"Just for your information, I'm pretending each one of these is that boy's head."

"Oh," I replied. *That's something.*

"It makes me feel better."

"I understand." Though, to be honest, I did not fully understand her distress. His activity was boring, meaningless. Crabs were nothing more than copper-coloured robots, crawling around on the filthy bottom of a lake.

"It was the cruellest thing I have ever seen. Don't you think? It was so cruel. So horrible. It was terrible. I feel so disgusted and helpless. Those poor creatures." Her voice hitched again. "What gives him the right to blind something else? Take away its ability to see! They weren't doing him any harm."

"No, they weren't." Now I understood. He had no reasons. Reasons were important. For a moment, I was reminded of the tent Button and I had visited several summers ago. The thick coating of black flies. How I had instructed her to be careful as she crawled out through the canvas doors. Those flies did not deserve to be injured.

I was softer then, though. Believed in different things.

She placed her head on my shoulder and sighed. "I'm just so upset, is all. I feel completely empty."

I paused for a moment. Straightened my back. "Empty?"

"Yes. Like there's not enough good in the world anymore."

I took a breath.

"Don't you?" She looked me in the eyes. "Don't you ever feel that way sometimes?"

"Empty?"

"Yeah."

I shrugged, turned away. I did not know what to say. Though I wanted to explain it to her, I could not. I had always been empty. Would always be empty. My heart was smooth and slick. A fist-sized rock covered in algae. Ugly and slippery and hollow and lonely. If anyone ever dared pick it up, surely it would slide from those hands.

I leaned against her. "I told you he was an asshole."

The following day I returned to the wharf. Alone. The loser was not there, but I waited. It took many afternoons, but as I have mentioned before, I am a very patient person. On the fifth day, an opportunity presented itself. He came cycling by, the wheels of his bicycle dangerously close to the edge, on an embankment. He did not see me, of course, as I was no different from a thin tree or a flickering shadow. And people rarely see what is right in front of their stupid faces.

Only a moment before he passed in front of me, I picked up a hefty stick and threw it, javelin-style. My brain did a rapid calculation of velocity and direction, and I aimed several feet beyond where he was.

Snap. *Ah!* Perfection.

The stick caught in his front wheel, locked it, back wheel coming up and over, his body moving through the air, and then, bloop, disappearing. I heard a weak girlish scream, then branches cracking, leaves ripping. There was silence then, other than the intermittent chitter of cicadas. I maintained my position and watched — of course I did. After about fifteen minutes, I detected moaning, then gravel crunching, a stream of cuss words. The loser crawled up over the side. His blue t-shirt was torn, face and chest swollen and bloodied from split skin. His left arm hung limp. Like a scene from a gory movie. Perhaps he had a broken collarbone. He would definitely need stitches. His wounds would heal and leave bright purple scars on his face. I doubt his mother would have the means to pay for pain relievers.

How unfortunate.

Obviously I could not tell my friend of my success, but she would see him when school started. She would see him, and she would imagine that some sort of balance had been achieved. Some sort of cosmic restitution.

Imagining this made me feel a flapping joy. I wondered how my expression appeared at that moment. If I were to encounter our doctor, would he use Button's term, *jubilant*? I believed he would.

I was jubilant. I would do anything for her.

I never wanted her to experience emptiness again.

52

AFTER WARREN LEFT NORA'S, HE GOT INTO HIS CAR AND DROVE until he found a field. It was about a mile south of the pig factory, and he pulled onto the soft shoulder, got out. A barbed wire fence surrounded the property, and a small glowing house sat back from the road. Light snow covered an old truck, and smoke twirled from the chimney. Warren spread the wire, slipped between, and walked across the barren field. In the wintry twilight, he wanted to remember. He wanted to remember every detail of his father's death.

In the middle of the field, an enormous tree had been left to grow. Someone had tied a tire swing to a sturdy branch, and it took sixty-four long strides to reach it. Then he eased his lanky frame in through the hole. Gradually he settled his weight, adjusted his position so the edges of the tire did not cut into his skin. When he was confident the rope would hold, he lifted his two feet from the earth. Warren gripped the frozen rope, let his head hang back, and with barely any force, he began to turn. A cool breeze kissed his cheek.

As a boy, he had often worked side by side with his father on their expanse of land, a family garden, carrots, red potatoes, fleshy tomatoes tied onto stakes with strips torn from an old t-shirt. After breakfast, Warren always plucked weeds, watered, but on that particular morning his father had asked him to help with mulching. They used a mix of grass clippings and hay, and it smelled sweet and slightly rotten at the same time. Warren shovelled it into a plastic bucket, and when full, he carried it to his father.

They were working on a row of Brussels sprouts, when his father looked at him and said, "The mulch. It keeps their feet cool."

"And they like that?" Warren had replied.

"Of course. Who doesn't like cool feet in the summer?" Then he said, "War, my love? When the sprouts form, can you remember to snap off the leaves underneath each sprout? That way the energy goes to the sprout, and not to the leaf. Do you understand?"

"I do."

"So you'll remember?"

"Yes, Dad, I will."

And his father grinned at him, his face and eyes bright. Warren thought his father looked happier than he had in a very long time. Jubilant, almost.

"I know it, son," he said. "You'll do just fine."

Task complete, and Warren wandered over to the tree in their front yard, hopped into the tire swing and kicked back off the trunk. Each time his sneakers struck the bark, his stomach lurched. He began to wonder about his insides. How his muscles and bones, connected to one another, stopped from the force of the jolt, but his insides continued to move. *An object in motion wants to stay in motion.* He had learned about inertia from his father's old science book. When his rubber soles collided with the tree, his guts wanted to stay in motion. They continued downwards, until they were contained inside the cradle of his pelvic bones. He glanced up at the sky. Were his guts somehow glued to his body cavity? Or were they simply piled on top of one another, a bit of tissue holding the mass together. He would have to ask his father. A man who was always patient, excited even, to share his seemingly endless knowledge. Warren kicked off from the trunk, closed his eyes.

Body swinging, and he felt a cool hand brush his cheek. Rough fingers moving like threads of wind through his overgrown hair. A gentle tug near the nape of his neck. "You!" he squealed, and turned, expecting to see his father. Smiling over his successful creeping, catching Warren off guard. But there was no one there. The entire backyard was empty. Not even Beth lurking around. He climbed down from the swing, pushed the rubber tire so it thumped against the tree. Ran his fingers on the back of his neck to smooth the alerted hair.

His legs felt weak, stomach queasy, throat tight and dry. He wondered how long he had been in the tire swing. Crossing the backyard, he went to the door to the kitchen. Stopped to admire a Luna moth clinging to the screen door. Bright green wings, span wider than Warren's whole hand. Four vacant eyes. His father had told him the Luna moth does not even have a mouth.

"It can't eat or talk?" Warren had asked. "What's the point? No one will hear it if it's in trouble."

"Good point, it needs someone to watch over it. Protect it. But that said, it can fly," he replied. "I suspect soaring above everything is a beautiful experience."

Warren entered the kitchen, took a glass from the cupboard, and filled it with water from the tap. Gulping. He wiped his wet mouth in the crook of his arm, could smell sunshine on his skin. How had he absorbed it? All those rays of light penetrating him, making him smell like summer. Making him smell sweet.

After his eyes had adjusted, Warren looked around the kitchen. His father's lunch was still on the table. The same as it was every single day, a large lemonade, a sandwich made on thick white bread. Warren touched the glass, still slick with condensation. No one had tasted the sandwich, but someone had lifted one half, laid it down on the plate again so that Warren could see the line of meat and mustard, thick layer of butter. For a moment, Warren paused and stared at the glass. An expanding puddle of water surrounding it. And then he stared at the sandwich. He was confused why it still sat on the plate.

He turned around.

"Dad?"

The house was still, but through the open window, Warren could hear the distant yelling of farmhands working the neighbour's field. An engine stuttering, then dying. The slish of a breeze through drying corn stalks.

"Dad? Da-aad?" His father's muddy boots were placed neatly on the rug by the back door. "Where is everyone? Geez, it's so quiet around here." He did not yell this out, but continued talking, his voice cluttering the silence.

The door to the basement was ajar. Warren nudged it with his foot, and it swung open. Cool damp air rose up out of the darkness. When he flicked the light switch, nothing happened. "Dad?" He knew his father spent considerable time in the cellar, tinkering with anything tinkerable. Sanding rust off of old saws. Sewing up worn corners of seed bags with a sturdy black thread and massive blunt needle. He ventured down into the darkness, each step squeaking.

Three steps along the cement floor, hands outward, and he felt his father's soft plaid shirt. "There you are, Dad." Words a melt of relief, though his heart refused to slow. "Why're you standing here with no light? Did it just blow out?" Warren pushed his face into his father's back, hugged him. "Your lunch is ready. Probably drying up. Fly food."

The first thing Warren noticed was that his father's belt was a little higher. The second was the sharp odour, the stench of a dirty chicken pen. The third, and most disturbing, was that with the gentle pressure of Warren's hug, his father's body swayed slightly, edged away from him, and smoothly returned. Warren squeezed, but the affection was not returned. "Dad? You okay?" Silence, except for a rhythmic creak. Like rope from his tire swing burning the branch.

Something gripped Warren then. Panic. As real as a thousand hands squeezing his skin. He dropped to the ground, felt his father's swaying legs. Moving his hands down over damp pants, he reached his father's grey socks. A hole in the heel. Area of muck on the floor, and for a moment, Warren thought his father was dripping, like the condensation coming off the glass in kitchen. He nearly giggled, was about to tell his father about this curious occurrence, but then, sliding his fingers further, Warren touched air. Air where it did not belong. The space not more than the width of his hand. Between his father's feet. And the damp clay floor.

Warren remained in the kitchen while two neighbours arrived, cut his father down. His mother told him and Beth to wait. Not to budge. He obeyed, sat at the table. Beth swung her legs, backs of her buckled shoes hitting a metal bar beneath her. A steady clack. Clack. Clack. Warren counted each clack, then lifted his arm slightly, and she abandoned her drumming, slid underneath his elbow, pushed her ribcage against his. "Warsie?" "It's okay, Beth. Don't look. Just don't look." When they removed the sheeted body, Warren pressed his hand over Beth's eyes, could feel her lashes tickling against his palm. "Eyes closed, Beth," he said, though he knew she was straining to see through the gaps in his fingers.

He stared at his father's last meal. Uneaten. A black fly buzzed through the open window, landed on the edge of the plate, rubbed its greedy legs together. He shooed the fly away, but it kept coming back.

"Did anything happen today?" The neighbour asked his mother.

"No, no, nothing." Unnatural pitch. "He got up and had toast and an orange and put on his boots and went out the door. He did the same thing. The same thing he did every day. I heard him singing. He left the peels right there beside the sink."

Then to Warren, "And with you? Anything?"

He shook his head. "We cooled the feet on the Brussels sprouts."

"What?"

"We mulched."

"And that's it?"

"He told me to snap off the leaves. When they start to grow. I promised I would." Looked down at the grit underneath his nails. "I won't forget."

Warren blamed his mother for the death. She had made that lunch and left it there. A dull lunch that his father touched, but when he saw the contents of the sandwich, he could not bear to consume it. Did it strike him as boring? Did the monotony of a cold meal every day destroy him? Could his mother not have managed a scrambled egg, a melted cheese? Was the plain meat and mustard and way too much butter a sure sign that his mother no longer loved his father? Was the sandwich just one in a stream of a thousand slights?

Warren did his best to pinch the thoughts. They were stupid. Childish. No one destroys a life over a sandwich.

Even so, as a boy, he could not shake it. The notion that his mother was at fault. Wispy at first, but it morphed into something concrete. Something certain.

"Hey! Just what the hell do you think you're at?"

A shadow had emerged from the house, was marching across the expansive field toward him. Warren could not see his face, but he noticed the shape of something long and skinny resting on the man's shoulder.

Sliding out of the tire swing, Warren started backing up, palms showing. "Nothing, nothing. I was turned around. In the dark. I needed to remember. I'm sorry."

"Sick fuck in my kid's tree?" Then the sound of metal sliding, definitive click. "Last time you'll be remembering."

The man raised the gun, pointed it at Warren's head, and without thinking, Warren turned and ran. His feet skimming the top of each furrow. Ignoring the tenderness in his limbs, his ribs, his skull, he rolled underneath the fence, tearing the fabric of his jacket. Then he scrambled over the ditch and fumbled with the car door. High above his own panting, he heard the man's voice behind him. Splinters of good-time laughter. Flying toward Warren, and sticking in his back.

The next morning, Warren awoke to the local paper slamming against his front door. Warren inched open the screen, reached for it. The headline read: *Science run amok*, and beneath that, the words: *Gifted student dies trying to solve deadly question*. He sighed. Everything would be okay, now. Everything would go back to normal. People's suspicions would dissolve.

53

ON THE FIRST DAY OF SCHOOL, MY BEST FRIEND BURST THROUGH those doors like she owned the place. She was wearing a lemon yellow dress, and her frizzy hair had been tamed, pulled into a tight ponytail, her bangs pushed back with a silver headband. Her white patent leather shoes shone, and inside them she wore neon green socks. They crinkled around her ankles, making her calves appear more fragile than they were.

"Take it easy," I whispered. Her arms were down, bent slightly at the elbow, wrists out at ninety degrees. "Can you just walk, you know, normally? In a straight line?"

My words were illogical. I admit that. Even if she were not skipping awkwardly, she was still an explosion of colour and energy, hurtling down the hallway, yelling, "Hello!" to everyone. "Hello, new friends. Hello, everybody!"

She paused her twirling happy dance when she noticed a student slamming a smaller kid into a locker. Elbow pressed underneath the kid's chin, the punk was spitting, "Bucktooth, give it here."

"Hey, hey," she breathed, touching the aggressor lightly on the shoulder. "C'mon, now. There's nothing wrong with his teeth. They are perfect and functional and spaces are good. I mean, didn't your dentist ever tell you that? You should be nice to him."

The loser appeared surprised at her boldness, then just gaped at her, mouth twisted in disgust. Freed from the chokehold, the small boy slid sideways, eased out, and darted down the hallway.

"It doesn't hurt to be friendly," she said, smiling. A beaming sort of smile. "It's easy!"

I breathed through my mouth. Once again, she reminded me of Button. Those wide eyes, that positive grin. An unshakable belief that everyone was capable of holding hands and humming kumbaya. The entire scene made my muscles tighten. In my neck, my jaw, my upper back. A nerve compressed inside my stomach. It was like something out of a 1960s television show. She was practically singing "Good Morning Starshine." But unlike with Button, I did not want to change her. I wanted her to stay exactly the same.

"Hey," I said, and she slowed down. I went up behind her and fixed the zipper on the back of her dress. With her flurry of movement, it was creeping downwards.

In class, our teacher asked the three new students to introduce themselves. She snapped up from her desk, jack-in-the-box-style, and squealed, "I am totally excited to be here. Do you know how bad my old school was? How horrible all the kids were? Nobody liked me. Nobody at all. And here I am! In a new place. With tons of new friends. There is nothing! Absolutely nothing! Better than a fresh start!"

I heard several snickers. Someone mumbled, "What the fu-uck is wrong with her?"

"Thank you," the teacher said. "Thank you, and welcome everyone. It's going to be a great year. I know a lot of people your age are afraid of science. I'm hoping you will see it's not something to fear, but something to embrace. Science is everywhere! In our bodies, our cars, our homes, our backyards."

"Our bodies?" That crab-blinding asshole was in our class. He slapped his desk three times. "What parts, hey? What parts got the science? And what do they do with that science?"

I stared at his face, lines of stitches where it had been torn and repaired. I was disappointed not to see a cast or a brace or anything indicating serious injury. Then I noticed our teacher blushing, and at once my friend's arm was waving in the air. Frantically. As though she were drowning, had gone underneath the surface, and had just re-emerged, desperate for oxygen.

Popping up again. "We are full of molecules and energy, and did you know that every part of us is actually billions of years old? Sounds crazy, but it's true. And we've got lots of iron inside of us. Just like the iron in cooking pots. Weird, hey? And if you count the number of human cells in my body and the number of bacteria in there, there's *waaay* more bacteria cells. So we're mostly bacteria, and we're totally all science. Every part of us." She shrugged, smoothed her dress. "So that's totally cool. Does that help?"

The teacher nodded, said, "Well done," while the crab-killer stared at his fingernails, then clipped some dead skin with his teeth.

I put my head down on my desk, and closed my eyes. The cool of the dirty veneer moved through my cheek. This was day one, and my friend was already sticking out, a glow of blue fire inside the dimness of a foggy classroom.

When I opened my eyes again, and scanned the room, I caught the biggest bitch in the entire world staring at my friend. Noodle's owner. The whore that lived in my future home, and had treated Button like shit. She was gawking. That same snotty expression that was engraved in my mind. As though a photograph was hanging there, interrogation light shining straight on it. Her lips were parted, lower jaw jutting out beyond her upper teeth. She was not blinking. Her face was dripping with disgust.

At that point, I took a deep breath and closed my eyes again. I felt agitated, slightly vertiginous, and I did not want to reveal this to anyone. As the teacher droned on about the thrill of being a scientist, my hazy mind drifted out of the classroom and into a dream. About Button. She was taller and had borrowed my friend's yellow dress, and every time she swirled, the hem of the fabric hitched on a hidden nail. I ran my fingers along the walls, reaching upwards, crouching down, touching baseboards and trim, but I could not find the offending piece of metal. The dress was being destroyed. Snarl by snarl. I was seething, though as Button spun around and around, she did not seem to notice, did not seem to care.

From the first day of school, my one and only friend had a target on her back. Circles of red and white, a bull's eye in the middle. At first, she skillfully ignored the multitude of tiny arrows pinging off the target. Then, gradually, as September came to an end, those slender arrows began to wheedle their way in. Cutting through the fabric of her clothes, through her skin. Pricking her soft heart.

I took notes inside my mind. Though many taunted her, that biggest bitch had the largest quiver, her arm always drawn back, ready to fire.

"I don't understand." We walked through the drifts of dead leaves on our way home. "What I've done."

"Ignore that idiot," I told her. "Ignore them all."

"I can do that." She sniffed, swallowed. "I've got practice."

"Good. Because being nice won't change anything."

She kicked the leaves, a burst of orange and red and brown flying through the air in front of us.

"It's the same, isn't it? Same here as it was there. No matter where I go in the world. Everything will always be the same. I'll always be a weirdo. I'll always be an ugly freak who can't shut up."

I wormed my fingers in through hers. Squeezed her tiny hand. *The world is a shitty place*, I wanted to tell her. *It is so mired in its own filth, it's unable to see something that is beautiful.*

As each day passed, I did my best to shield her, but I could not watch her every moment. Besides, she insisted, time and time again, not to bother about it. She was fine.

"Just leave it alone. It's no big deal. I'm used to it. I'm good. I really am."

Okay. Okay.

And she seemed good. At first. Then gradually, my friend grew more and more silent. Her words, her verbal outbursts, diminishing day by day. She started shrugging and shaking her head. Saying nothing. I soon realized her happiness and her intelligence were a threat to those around her. Especially that one particular girl. She mocked my friend, prodded her, tripped her in the hallway. Wrote lies about her in permanent marker inside bathroom stalls. Pedestrian teenager bully shit. She was attempting to destroy the one person she feared.

Her name was Amanda Fuller. The stupid slut did not realize I was in the shadows, witnessing each transgression with growing understanding.

As always, I was patient, cautious, but something happened to push my hand. Near the end of October, I came around the corner and my friend was there. She was wearing her yellow dress again with the long zipper down the back, even though it was too cold for summer clothes. Her brown shoulders were bare and smooth. I imagined she was cold, but I also knew she had very few clothes hanging in her closet. I saw that loser from the wharf was talking to her, with his scarred-up shit face, and my friend was actually smiling. Laughing. I did not trust the congenial appearance of the interaction, and I stopped, hyper-focused.

"Can you help me?" I heard him say. My ears perked up, as his tone was warm, friendly. "I'm sorry about back awhile. You know, in the summer?"

"Are you?"

The blinded crabs.

"Yeah. It was dumb."

"We all make mistakes. It's just good to learn from them, right?"

"Yeah. That's for sure." Frowning.

"What do you need help with?"

"I don't know. Stuff."

"Oh. Okay. Um. Well." She swung her body from side to side, pulled a strand of hair into her mouth.

I leaned against the locker and continued my observations. That jerk kept looking behind my friend, as though he were watching something else. I squinted my eyes. I suspected the asshole was up to something, but he was too stupid to do anything on his own. Someone jostled me then, and I twisted my head. A giant girl, her hat pulled down over her eyebrows, was hovering above me. "That's my locker, dork. Move it." She was easily six inches taller than me, and I could not see through her.

"Yeah," I said, annoyed, but I shifted my body left. Refocused.

"Okay," I heard my friend chirp. "I'm happy to help. Thank you for asking me."

And then, everything happened in a single moment. An event I had not predicted. Amanda Fucking Fuller was behind her, slamming her in the spine, knocking her forward. I witnessed Amanda's hands jumping, up, down, up again. Metal teeth ripping open. A sudden flash of fabric, and my best friend's bright summer dress was crumpled around her feet.

She stood there. Not moving. A crowd of bubbly scum circling around her. People pointing and gasping and whooping and laughing. For a moment I wondered if she realized she was naked. So much skin, a concave stomach, her white bunched underwear with worn elastic, toothpick legs holding her up. Each rib was visible, as though slender fingers were reaching around, gripping her torso. I saw her chest. An unnatural plumpness there, pale pink nipples. I admit I stared at her. I could not help myself.

She did not lift her arms to cover her body. Did not grab her dress from the floor. She simply continued to stand there.

Then I caught her eyes. She looked at me, without a single sound. Her expression just like my sister's, that afternoon by the pool, as she sought my permission to run away. There was no anger or fear or embarrassment. The only thing I could identify was disappointment. A penetrating disappointment.

"Hey, squirrel face, you forget your clothes?"

Finally she gathered the ball of fabric, and rushed out through an emergency door, the alarm whooping. I followed, and found her tucked in between two cars, hauling on her dress. Arms cricking, fixing the zipper behind her. When she was covered, she bolted out into the parking lot, running toward home. I did not know what to say, and I called out the first thing that came to my mind, "In a while, alligator?" but she did not turn. Did not yell out some idiotic phrase about a crocodile. She did not even slow down.

After school, I knocked on her door. She would not see me. Her mother said she was sick, in bed. "Could be contagious. You don't want to catch anything." Days went by, and when I went to her door again, her mother asked me, "Has something happened? Did something happen to her at school?"

I shook my head. "Nothing. No."

I could not stop thinking about her expression when she stared at me. I played it over and over again in my mind. Was she disappointed in the shittiness of the world? Or was she disappointed in me? That I had not stepped forward? I had not protected her?

I decided then that I would act. Sooner than anticipated. I would not stay seated on the deck above, waiting behind dying geraniums, picking splinters from the wood. I would not take small steps. There were no lessons my friend would learn from suffering. I realized that now. And before anything worse happened, I would rush down. Rush down from up above, and control the ending to our story.

54

HE STEPPED ONTO THE WHARF, AND WHEN THE WOODEN PLANKS creaked, the girl looked up. "Libby?"

"Oh hi, Mr. Botts."

"I'm surprised to see you here."

"Well." Shrugging. "I'm here."

"I mean I didn't expect to see anyone. It's cold."

"Yeah. I come here sometimes. Take the trails through the woods." She was seated on the edge of the grey wooden planks, her legs dangling over, swinging. "It's a good place to stop and think."

"Am I interrupting you?"

"No. I can think somewhere else."

Warren put up his hands. "No, no. I'll leave. You stay."

"I meant in my head, Mr. Botts. I can talk to you and still think. Just need to shift things around a bit."

"Interesting." He walked to the end of the wharf, sat down beside her. The wood was damp, and a chill moved up through his spine. "I can do that, too. Different things happening on different shelves. But sometimes I give the thinking a rest, and I count instead."

"Count? Like what?"

"I don't know. Raindrops. Buttons. Snowflakes. The number of steps I take. Stairs. Cupboards. Cracks in the sidewalk."

"Like a blind person. Keeping track?"

"Sort of. But I guess a blind person has a purpose."

"Your counting has a purpose, too, Mr. Botts. A blind person might count to understand the world, but you count to distract yourself from it."

Warren laughed lightly. "Very smart response. You're probably right."

"Anyway, it gets kind of boring," she continued. "Thinking all the time. So many ideas no one else would understand."

As she spoke, Warren could sense a weight in her tone. A hard sort of sadness. Shifting toward her, he said, "Do you ever think about getting a job? That's a wonderful distraction, too."

"Too young. No one would hire me."

"Babysitting?"

She put her hand over her mouth.

"Well, you could start your own business."

"Seriously, Mr. Botts. I know you're my mother's person, and all that, but sometimes your thoughts are a bit off."

"Not really," he said. "I managed it. Just find a job no one else wants, and do that."

"Like what."

"My first job was Nest Destroyer." He stuck his index finger in the air. "Hornets, wasps, that sort of thing. I wasn't afraid and I wasn't allergic. I didn't care if I got stung."

"Me neither."

"I stuck a little filing card up in the supermarket, and these women would drive right up to my house looking for me."

"Popular guy."

"Yes." He smiled. "I remember one of the first calls I had. A woman noticed hornets flying in and out of a hole near the roof of her house. She was one of our neighbours, and she said her son was afraid of them, wouldn't go up and look. Sure enough, I climbed the ladder into her attic, and found an enormous paper nest. It's kind of a beautiful thing, you know, in its ugliness."

"I get you." Nodding. "That must've been a surprise."

"No, the surprise was the doorknobs. Dozens and dozens of doorknobs in a pile. Brass, silver, dull metal, gold coloured. New ones and antique ones. Some shiny. Some rusty. Every kind you can imagine."

She frowned, tilted her chin. "Doorknobs."

"She was embarrassed when I mentioned them. Her son, she said, steals. Can't help himself, he's been taken with doorknobs since he was a small boy. She didn't know he kept them up there."

"Strange."

"Yes, but I guess he had his rationale." An icy breeze ruffled Warren's hair, and he lifted his hand to smooth it. "Maybe he liked them because they opened doors?"

"Or locked them up."

"Good point, Libby. I like the way you think."

She nudged him with her elbow. "I was just joking. We are projecting too much intention into his mind. He probably just enjoyed stealing."

"Most likely."

"Did you manage to get rid of the nest?"

"Actually, no. She decided to leave it, leave the hornets. They weren't bothering her, said they were probably doing something good for someone somewhere."

"Doubtful."

"She told me not to tell on her son, and I never did."

"Until now."

Nodding. "Yes, until now. But I suspect you are a trustworthy person."

"Ha! That's a weird story, Mr. Botts. Weird kind of funny."

"But that's what makes life interesting, isn't it? Everyone is different. Experiencing the world in different ways."

"I guess so." She sighed, knocked her sneakers against the swollen wood beneath her feet.

"Everything okay, Lib?"

He waited, counted to forty-one before she spoke.

"I don't know," she said. "Sometimes things never turn out the way you imagine they might."

"Are you arguing with your mom?"

"Always. But it's not that."

He spoke gently. "What, then?"

"Sometimes I feel alone. That sounds lame to say, I know."

"No, not lame at all."

"I'm just getting tired of it, Mr. Botts."

"I understand. It's not easy being your age. I remember it. And then you lost your friend this year."

"My friend?"

"Amanda. It takes time. To process."

"Yeah," she said. "Yeah. You're right. I lost my friend."

The cold burned his ears, his eyes. Warren blinked, said, "My father died, too."

"He did?"

"Not like yours, you know, after an illness like that, but he still died."

She bit her lip, lowered her head. "Mmm."

"I don't want to upset you by talking about it. Your mom told me. About the complications with lupus. You were young. I know."

"Yeah. Yeah. Though I don't think it matters how, does it?"

"No. You're probably right. In the long run, an end is still an end. Though it mattered to me at the time."

"How did he die? Your dad."

"At home." Warren coughed. "He. He hanged himself." Warren had never said those words before, and his throat was suddenly powdery dry.

"Wow, Mr. Botts. I never knew."

"How could you know? I was a little younger than you are now. I will never forget how lonely I was."

"And then with Amanda. You know. Hanging herself like that. No wonder you're acting a bit buggy."

He pressed his glasses onto his face. Felt cold plastic against the bridge of his nose. "Have I been acting *buggy*?"

"I don't know. *Buggy-er* might be a better word. You were a bit buggy to begin with."

He laughed again. "Libby?"

"Yes, Mr. Botts?"

"I think I might be leaving."

"What do you mean, leaving?"

"I mean going back to my old job. At the university. Continuing my research."

"Oh."

"I'm not sure. I haven't decided. I need to talk to your mother about it. But if I do, I'll come back. I will. She means a lot to me."

"She does?"

"Yeah."

Libby frowned. "Why?"

Warren looked out over the lake. Even with the breeze, the water was mostly still, except for the occasional bubble that emerged from the depths, burped through the surface. They were pleasingly random, impossible to time.

He did not know how to respond. He did not even know if his statement was entirely accurate. A woman named Nora did mean a lot to him, but he had a developing suspicion the Nora he adored only existed inside his mind.

"It's okay, Mr. Botts. Sometimes it's hard to put things into words. And it's what you do that matters. Not what you say." She tucked her hands into her armpits, shivered. "Words are easy to fake."

"Do you want these?" He said, wriggling his fingers.

She nodded, and he slid his hands out of the wool gloves, handed them to her.

"You can keep them. I have another pair."

"Thanks, Mr. Botts."

"It's okay if you call me Warren."

"That's all right. I'm already used to calling you Mr. Botts."

"That's good too."

She stood up, shook her arms. "I got to go. Homework."

Warren smiled. "I understand."

Then, rolling her eyes, "Yeah, you've met my mother."

"Can you not tell her I'm leaving? I should tell her myself."

"It's for certain, then?"

"I think so."

Warren watched as Libby stood up, walked off the wharf, up over the embankment. She paused there in the tall yellow grass, but did not turn to look at him. She just stood there with her head lowered. Perhaps it was the bend in her narrow shoulders that reminded him of himself when he was a boy. He remembered standing in the neighbour's field hours after his father died. The dried wheat, like skinny fingers, scratching the bare skin on his legs. Everything seemed so small, the house, the car. In miniature. And he had the sensation that he could scoop everything up in his palm, his entire life, and if he closed his fingers around it, it would disappear inside his fist.

Though, when he reflected on that moment, it was not the distorted appearance of his surroundings that he remembered most. It was a soreness tucked in behind his ribs. That warm, dry afternoon, as unseen cicadas called for their mates, he had the acute sense he was unloved. Or perhaps unlovable. Which was even worse.

When he returned home, the air smelled like a beach. Salty water, seaweed washed ashore, bloated fish. When he opened the front door to his house, he felt cold air moving through, as though the back wall had vanished. He paused, heard the sound of filters straining to function without water. Warren's heart began to strike, and he rushed toward the kitchen, slipped on the skin of water pressing against the door jamb. Pain shot through his hip, and his left leg kicked outwards, leather shoe sliding through the debris. Shards of glass, sand, neon gravel, slimy clumps of green, a ceramic pirate's ship broken into pieces. And dozens and dozens of tiny fish. Lying on their sides. Still and silent.

Warren reached out and touched one closest to him. He picked it up. A small black molly. The upper side of its body was dry, its short fins were curling inwards, gills pressed down. Others were scattered across the linoleum. A pair of tetras was underneath the table. Someone had entered his home. Smashed each one of his tanks.

Mouth open, a shallow cough emerged. Another. And another. He bent his knees underneath his body, took his glasses off, bent the arms toward the lenses, and held them. Then he lowered his head. Sobbed. Loud choking sounds. Like an eleven-year-old boy who had lost everything. Like a fully grown man who had nothing.

Then he remembered Stephen. The back door was wide open, and Warren stood, tiptoed through the glass and debris, stepped out onto the deck. His cat was there, hunched into a corner, tail wrapped around his body, fur puffed. When he picked it up, Stephen's body was cold and stiff. Warren tucked the old cat inside his jacket, and felt instant relief as a raspy purr made his ribs vibrate. Stephen stretched inside the fabric, pushed a six-toed paw upwards, placed the frozen pink pads against Warren's neck.

"It's okay, my friend," he said. "It's okay, now. It's okay."

With Stephen cradled in his arms, he walked back into his kitchen. Then he noticed dust on his kitchen table. A powdery ring of white. As though a person had dropped something there for a moment, and had picked it up again. Warren ran his finger through the fine powder, smelled it, brought it to his lips. He knew it would taste sugary sweet even before it touched his tongue.

55

LIVID IS A WORD I APPRECIATE. IT CAN MEAN BOTH FULL OF ANGER or fury, but also mean grey, bluish, a purple hue. A man could be livid, wrapping his hands around his wife's skinny neck, leaving distinctive marks that might also be described as livid. With the slightest wordplay, one form of *livid* is funnelled neatly into the second form. Both categories fascinating and enticing. Unique.

Is it unusual to find something pleasing about that? How a single word demonstrates the cycling, but consistent, nature of rage. It moves outward, is transferred and visible, witnessed by others, and also moves inward, is steady and silent, concealed behind a charming grin.

Livid.

My muscles were cold and beginning to ache. Crouched in that tree for far too long, I was beginning to accept I would have to descend from my hiding spot, return another evening. I decided to give it a few more minutes, and in that time, I thought about Button. How I had tucked myself behind those geraniums, monstrous terracotta pots, and watched her agony. I had my reasons, but they were feeble reasons. Then again, how could I have predicted how things would unfold? As well read as I am, when Button died, I was unfamiliar with water intoxication.

Then I thought about my only friend. Though fanciful, I liked to imagine that somehow Button had orchestrated our introduction. It was her way of letting me know she had forgiven me. That I deserved to experience some element of joy in my existence. A shred of jubilance. But there was caution tape around the edges of our relationship. I recognized the level of responsibility, and would never again hesitate. As I had hesitated before.

A light flickered on inside the bungalow. With curtains wide open, I could see my teacher wandering around his kitchen, lifting his enormous cat off the stove, placing it on the floor. I watched him get a drink of water, and then he came to the window, stared out into his backyard. I checked my watch, pushed the button on the side, and the screen glowed bright yellow, read 1:46. I looked up again, and if I did not know better, I would have guessed he was staring straight at me, straight at the light from my watch. But I knew he was staring at nothing, nothing that anyone else could see. I was invisible, and I liked it that way.

I saw his back next, and he was leaving the room. Lights out.

I edged closer to the trunk, was ready to abandon my effort, but then I heard footsteps. Girly footsteps, tiptoeing through the woods. The sound of her voice, humming an idiotic pop song. She was coming from the loser's slum house, and I knew she had plans to sneak across the back-yards, creep into her home undetected. She had announced as much in school on Friday, thought she could do whatever she liked. Never have to face a consequence. Why do lame teenagers have such a struggle with forethought?

I got into position, and when she was directly beneath me, I leaned forward and slipped from the branch. I liked the concept, swooping down through the trees, arms outstretched, air whirring past my cheeks. But that sort of description would be embellishment. It was more of a slight drop. A heavy plunk. Eight feet, not much more, before I landed on her soft body.

Parts of me were entirely visible when I was seated on the branch. If only she had of taken her head out of her ass, for just a moment, she would have seen my legs, seen my white sneakers in the moonlight. But almost everyone is stupid. Oblivious to their environments. People rarely see what is right in front of their faces. Until it is too late.

Perhaps it was fear in her eyes, or perhaps she was impressed with my skill. When her head knocked backward, I was certain she was smiling. Or grimacing. Sometimes human expressions are so difficult to pin down. To be honest, it did not matter if she was scared or excited. Either one made me feel that saccharine warmth of satisfaction.

Her eyes were wide, mouth open, and she breathed, "Seriously?" just before I rammed the rope over her head. *Yes, seriously.* She thought it was a shitty joke. I scrambled to my feet then, took a deep step backward. Grabbed the end around my stomach, slipknot released. She was wearing a thick turtleneck, and for a moment I thought that might protect her. But no, the rope tightened, and crawled upwards, neatly gripping her just under her jaw, pressing around the flesh of her neck. My sturdy pulleys played their part, the rope moved, wheels turned, the branch held, and my system cut the force. Though I never completed the bonus question, I instantly knew the answer. Amanda Fuller, complete bitch, was the load, and I would have to lift a fraction of her mass. I pulled her to her feet. Watched her kick and struggle.

With the rope braced around my back, I edged backward. She was on her toes now, and then, and then, and then, aloft. I lifted her as high as I could, and let her drop. Did it again. Legs thrashing in the darkness, the seams of her black jeans rubbed against one another. I could hear it, and contemplated the force of friction, opposite motions of the fabric. While it certainly generated heat on that icy night, it did not affect my calculations in any way.

I was sweating slightly, and was grateful for her skinny frame, for the winter gloves protecting my palms. One of the pulleys, I understood, offered no mechanical advantage. I had planned to toy with her for longer, letting her toes touch down, then hauling her up over and over again, but I had clearly overestimated my own musculature. Or how heavy she would feel. (Sometimes a physics question does not reflect the reality of a situation.) Instead of following my plan, I held her in place for several minutes, twitching in the air, and then eased myself twice around the tree trunk, letting out small increments of rope. Using a cow hitch knot, I secured her position. It was a basic knot, yes, uncreative, but effective.

Once everything was quiet, I looked around. The scene was not quite as jarring as I had expected. A bit clichéd, to state the obvious. Dead-girl-hanging-near-edge-of-woods sort of thing. And now, the rope had slipped, branch sagging, and her frame had lowered several inches. In fact her toes were grazing the ground. Annoying, the entire thing, but considering I had no opportunity to test my system, it was a respectable effort. I noticed she had kicked up dirt and dead leaves, but she was still now. The rope making the faintest creak. The friction forces were gone, tension and gravitational remaining.

Overall, it was an interesting study. Real-life application of the concepts. *A-*. Maybe. Or *B+*.

Walking around her, I noted her limp head, grey face, tongue jutting between parted lips. That tongue appeared foreign, out of place. It just did not look right, and I found the sight of it troubling. Her knapsack was on the ground, and I bent, unzipped it. Retrieved the first paper I found. Her physics test. Covered in ink circles, red, I guessed, from the teacher. The exact quiz on forces where I had gleaned my inspiration. The moron had failed with 38 percent. Oh, the irony. Inside my head, I laughed and laughed, and crumbled the test into a ball, rammed it into her mouth. A paper apple for the paper pig.

I heard clicks then, high up in the sky. The radio had predicted another heavy rainfall, and it had commenced. Striking the dead leaves, pulling the last of them from the trees. I turned and began walking home, knowing the sheets of icy water would obliterate my footsteps. The expected change to snow in the middle of the night would blanket the scene, but not diminish the intensity of it. The beauty of it. The magic.

In the nights after, as questions and accusations swirled, I frequently dreamed about death. The same dream over and over again. Amanda Fuller was not walking through the woods, or hanging from the tree, instead, I was on top of her, straddling her in a dirty field. Remains of a harvest dried and bent toward the depleted soil. Nighttime sky, though I could see everything with help from an orange harvest moon.

There was no rope. I gripped a flat stone in my hands. Amanda's sneering head shook from side to side, but her face soon morphed into my father's, then my aunt's, then to Larva's, and sometimes even his Stick Bitch sister's. Inevitably, though, the transformation stopped when the face became my mother's. Her waxy skin, droopy eyes, I knew my negligent mother was drugged and sleepy. I could see dust from her pink pills clumping in the corners of her wrinkled lips. On her face, there was a smear of blood coming from somewhere. Her mouth? Her nose? Her ear? "Don't touch me," she mumbled. "Don't touch me."

I lifted the stone, and at the same moment, I heard a soft crinkling behind me. Thin layers of chitin moving over one another. Button was standing there, her moth wings folded down, feathered antennae curled. I did not think she should witness this, and I whispered to her, "Close your eyes, Button. All of them. And keep them closed." Then the stone came down.

The stone came down.

56

AS HE WAS DOING A FINAL PASS THROUGH THE RENTAL HOME, he paused for a moment in front of the framed print above the fireplace. The stylized face of an unknown woman, her eyes replaced by two oversized ears. It was ugly, but for some reason, Warren liked it. A reminder to him to listen more. Not only to trust what he saw. He went toward it, gripped it with both hands. It was hanging on a single nail, and Warren lifted it, brought it out to his car. He had never stolen anything in his life, but he slid the print into his open trunk, and slammed the lid.

"Hey, buddy. You clearing out?"

Warren turned, saw Gordie standing in the driveway, hands stuffed into the pockets of his puffy jacket.

"I was going to stop in to the store. On my way. To say goodbye."

"Saved you the trip, then." Gordie was chewing on a toothpick, and the wood flicked up and down between his lips. "You all set?"

"It's just best. You know? Better to leave. I have to check in with the police when I get there. My lawyer said I needed to confirm my address. But there's nothing stopping me."

"I get you."

"You've been a good friend. I don't know what to say."

"Ah. Kindness don't cost a person nothing, do it?"

Warren shook his head, dipped his hands into his pockets.

"Wanted to tell you something before you left."

"Tell me something?"

"I wasn't sure what to do, buddy. Just trying to do every-thing right, and bound to piss someone off."

Shaking his head. "I don't know what you mean."

"Your sister."

Warren glanced at the road, the place where Gordie had parked. For an instant he expected to see Beth there, her healthy face behind the passenger's-side window. Smiling.

"She stopped by the store. Morning after she left here. I— I thought I could help her, you know? Let her stay above the shop for a few days. Cool off. Get her head in order."

Warren opened his mouth, waiting.

"I tried, buddy. But she split. Lasted two days."

"Oh." Warren blinked, pressed his glasses into his face. "Did she take anything?"

"Nah. Just a shitload of my frozen pizzas. But she didn't take nothing."

"I can pay you back. For the pizza. And the mess."

"C'mon, buddy. That's not why I'm here." Gordie rubbed a thick hand over his face. "I just wanted to help. Couldn't have you leave without knowing. I messed up."

Warren shuffled his feet; the brown grass was frozen, and crunched underneath his boots. "No. You didn't mess up." *How can you mess up when you're trying to fix things?* It was the first time Warren had had such a thought, and it made him pause. He was aware of a lump in his throat. But it was not rolling and growing. It was dissolving.

"Ah. Shit."

"You're a good friend, Gord."

Gordie rushed toward him, wrapped his arms around Warren, and squeezed. Clapped him on the back three times. Hard. Warren coughed. "I should get going."

Gordie leaned back, wiped his nose on the back of his hand. "Going to miss you, buddy."

"Me, too," Warren whispered. "Me, too."

Nora slammed a door well inside the house, but Libby remained on the porch. "I knew you'd leave," she said to Warren. "I just knew."

"I'm hoping to come back and visit, Libby. I just need to talk to my mother. Check my lab. Think a bit. And see what I'm going to do."

"Okay, Mr. Botts. Go." She looked down at her hands, then shook her head. "But don't turn. It's better not to turn."

Warren glanced at the stairs that led up to Nora's bedroom. He had never seen it. "Do you mean, don't turn back?"

"She'll be fine, Mr. Botts." Smiling. "I'll make sure of it."

"Yes." He handed her a plastic bag. Something clinked inside. "These are yours. I wrapped them in paper towel, so they wouldn't chip."

"Oh, yeah."

"Thanks for lending them to me. They really added to the classroom. When I was there."

"No problem, Mr. Botts. It wasn't a big deal."

He began to count the repeating bouquets in the wallpaper border, but stopped himself. "You know, Libby. I think you and me are a lot alike. I know that sounds weird."

She laughed at him, shrugged. "Not really."

"You're going to do something important someday. I just have that feeling."

She shrugged again. "I'll try my best, Mr. Botts. I'll try."

Warren sunk into his seat, pressed gently on the gas, felt the car roll forward over the smooth road. Small streets soon gave way to an openness, both sides of the road lined with barren fields stripped from the harvest. Stephen was in a crate on the passenger seat, his wide paw sticking out through the crisscross of metal, hitching the fabric of the seat.

He drove past the ice cream factory, and the pig farm. Someone had strings of tiny white lights trimming the roof of a mint green shed. He drove past the field where he had used a stranger's tire swing. And past the place where he had imagined his father leaning against a signpost in the rain. His foot hovered over the brake, but he never slowed down. Though he had expected it, he did not feel anxious. His stomach was settled. The hitch in his throat was gone.

Warren thought of Beth. Next time he saw her, he would once again try to help her. But no matter how hard he willed her to get better, nothing would change unless she wanted it to change. He understood that now. While he could stand beside her, she had to take those steps by herself. He thought of his mother next. She and Beth had the same lilt in their voices, the same curve in their backs. He wondered what he would say to his mother. What she might say to him. "Most good things start slow," his father had told him when he saw Warren watching newly planted soil. "You can't force it, my darling. They'll push through in their own time."

Snow began to fall. A scattered flake, an eyelash against his windshield. There was calmness in the landscape. A curious and welcome calmness inside the car. He moved past telephone pole after telephone pole, but Warren had no desire to count them. He focused on the road. There was no rush. No one was chasing him. The ground was colder now, and the snow would stay.

57

MY MOTHER PEELED OFF HER FAKE PINK NAILS, TOSSED THEM in the garbage beside her night table. Then she yanked the sneakers from her feet, dropped them onto the carpet. Kicked them.

"We were supposed to go for a walk. And," she snapped her fingers, "he just ups and leaves. Can you believe that?"

I could. Of course I could.

"Not even a warning." She shook her head. "What the hell is wrong with me?"

"Does it matter?" I asked.

"All I wanted was someone to care about me. Just a bloody little bit. God. I know how to pick 'em, don't I?"

At that moment, my mother's curdled face looked too much like my aunt's. Desperate and overdone, and acting as though she had been wronged. The sight of her annoyed me, and I closed my eyes to obliterate her from my vision.

"There was nothing wrong with Mr. Botts," I said. "Maybe you should take a look at yourself."

I stood up, walked away. In my room, I unwrapped the insects I had lent him in September. I thought having such a display on his desk would make him appear more like a science teacher. Instead of a lost little boy. I knew from the first day in class, with his flushed cheeks and jittery hands, he was a person who needed all the help he could get.

I placed the glass prisms back on the shelf, next to Button's Luna moth. Light shone through them, and I could identify not a single scratch. Not even a greasy fingerprint. He had taken care of them. Which, of course, was what I had expected.

I will admit I had not considered Mr. Botts when I chose to appropriate his backyard. I did not consider the implications in using his bonus question. Or tossing my scribbled drawings into his garbage can. His yard was convenient, and the question just happened to inspire me. I did not mean to hurt him. When I saw his anguish because of my choices, I had searched my mind for a filament of remorse. And I found it there. Spindly, unstable, like a structure made of damp matches. I determined that was regret. Present, but hollow, and easily trampled. Mr. Botts did not deserve the pain, but I simply did what I had to do.

"Kiddle?" My mother was yelling down the hallway. "I've lost something. Can you come here?"

I ignored her.

"Kiddle?"

As he was leaving, Mr. Botts had waved and smiled at me. Young wrinkles around his grey eyes. His fatherly gaze was soft and willing. Even now, after everything he had experienced, he was still the same. There was no anger or animosity inside of him. I understood his personality was an aberration, that gripping innocence, that perpetual openness. Even when the world slammed its fist in his face, he still smiled.

Some people are like that. I remember a book I once took from my elderly neighbour's window. It was full of weird cases where people lived totally shitty lives. And did shitty things to each other. One was about a little girl whose parents kept her in a small crate. When cops found her, pulled open her metal door, she emerged from squalor, and back hunched, she grinned for the cameras. That kid was happy. She was laughing. She was jubilant.

I found it difficult to wrap my head around that mindset. I recognized it was a form of illness that afflicted Mr. Botts. Definitely afflicted Evie, too. And in its purest form, it had afflicted my little sister, Button. I found the idea of it weak, detestable, but also beautiful. More beautiful than anything else in existence. It needed to be protected, insulated from the world. I had not understood the value of it when Button was with me. These rare individuals had something broken inside of them. Their hearts were blinded. And even though there were moments of doubt, they believed through and through that the world was a compassionate place. A loving place. That good would inevitably flutter up and shadow everything else.

I glanced out my window toward the direction of her house. Evie and I had slid through the densely packed cedars so many times, we had created a teardrop hole in the hedge. I could see her just now, on the other side of the gap, peering up at me. She was wearing the red and white striped hat I had stolen for her. The matching gloves.

I touched the glass, and she motioned for me to lift my window.

"Hey," I called out. "What's up?"

"Ice cream. That's what's up."

"You want to go and get ice cream? It's freezing out."

"What? You can only eat ice cream in a t-shirt? That's totally weird. And lame, Libby! Put on a sweater. A scarf. And get your butt out here. Ice cream is the best thing three hundred and sixty-five days a year. I'm going. Like, in literally ten seconds. Don't ask me to bring you anything back. Not like it would melt or anything." She shrugged forcefully, laughed. The sun caught the metal crisscrossing her teeth, braces realigning her *dents du bonheur*.

"Okay, okay." Her rambling always made me feel slightly dizzy. As though someone had smacked me in the side of the head. But in a good way. "Give me a minute."

I pushed the window closed with my fingertips. With Evie, things were starting to shift back toward normal. It was taking a lot longer than I had thought it would. There were moments when I wondered if she would ever be the same, but she was gradually returning to her usual self. Which meant bouncing constantly, and talking a mile a minute. Seeing her waiting there, I was aware of those sneaky eels sliding around my rib cage. Squeezing firmly. Letting me know that feelings were present, and if they chose to do so, they could pull me down. Crush the air from my lungs.

Maybe I did love Evie. In the same way I had loved Button. But also, in a different way. One was not a substitute for the other. My love for Evie was arresting and wistful and furious and benevolent. A swirling storm that had claimed me. There was nothing I would not do to protect her. Protect her blinded heart. From that moment when she had looked at me, practically naked in the school hallway, I had decided she would be safe. I would never leave her. And she would never leave me.

My mother was stomping around the kitchen, slamming cupboard doors. "Where the hell is everything gone?" she yelled. "Kiddle? Have you seen my pills? Those pink ones? Did you take them?" Another door slammed. "Jesus."

I pulled a thick sweater over my head, and looked in the mirror. My hair was full of static, and ragged bangs covered my eyes. For the first time in my life, I was trying to grow it out. Though I had never bothered with my appearance in the past, for once, I wanted to look different. I would admit it. I wanted to look pretty.

"Kiiiidddd-ulllll!"

"I haven't seen your stupid pills," I yelled back, as I dug through the clump of clothes on my closet floor. There was a crocheted scarf hidden in there somewhere. "Leave me alone, will you?"

"Kiddle. I was calling out to you. You didn't hear me?"

Looking up, I saw my doughy mother blocking my door-way. Her voice was calmed, and I assumed she had found her medication. Had the promise of numbness already swallowed, dissolving inside her acidic stomach.

"I heard you. You just didn't hear me."

"Come on, Kiddle. Why are you giving me such a hard time?"

"Don't call me that again. You know my name."

"Sorry, sorry. Libby." She held out her sneakers. "Do you, ah, think I could take these back? I cleaned the bottoms. Rubbed a tiny bit of corn oil into the black to shine it. They look completely unworn to me." Turning them to show me the soles. "What do you think? At least a store credit?"

"Do what you want." I saw the fringe of the scarf and tugged it out from the pile, knotted it around my neck. Loosely. "Some salespeople are dumb enough."

"Doesn't hurt to try, I guess."

"Whatever. I don't care."

She sighed. Frowned a thin frown. "We got to get along, you know. It's just you and me, Lib. Like it's always been."

Like it's always been.

The words volleyed back and forth inside my skull. Testing the strength of my bones.

"Close my door." I tilted my head, raised my eyebrows ever so slightly. "Would you, please, Mother?"

I could feel the blood moving through my veins. Feeding every part of me with oxygen and nutrients. Allowing me to think. Imagine. And, thanks to the influence of Mr. Botts, I had started counting.

How could we be so different? My mother and I?

I did not know if I ever resisted myself. Pushed back against who I was. But my mother! She had reinvented herself. Slid parts of her past out of her story, inserted others. Within the snarl of her lies, her scum husband had adopted a softer personality, a pitiable illness. She told gullible Mr. Botts he had died of complications related to lupus. An infection. Kidney failure. Something like that. No mention he was a drunken wife-beater who nearly smashed her skull. And she omitted the part that he had damaged my favourite tree when his forehead burst through a windshield and struck it. I did not mind those lies, to be honest. In fact, I thought her story was creative and, in a way, I respected her ingenuity. But then. But then my mother took it too far.

She erased Button. Never so much as mentioned her to Mr. Botts. Her stunted life. Her perfect heart. Her sticky,

gaggy death. She had pretended none of it had ever happened. How could she do that? Act as though Button were
nothing more than a piece of plastic in a kid's party game.
Tucked inside some loser's clammy fist. As though out of
sight were really out of mind.

Was that necessary? To edit Button from our shared narrative? The first person in the world who actually loved me?

It needled me. Like a twist of black hair caught in the
throat. I could not swallow it. I could not cough it out.

I would communicate that to her. Let her know of my
disappointment. Maybe, at some point in the future, I would
build a machine to fully express myself. Me and Button.
Sisters, side by side. I would show my mother everything
that she had missed. All the wonder that was tucked inside
my sister's tiny body. Then my mother would realize her
mistakes. And she would experience humiliation.

When the time was right, I would uncurl my fingers,
open my palm. Show her what was hiding there.

The End

ACKNOWLEDGEMENTS

I would like to thank my wonderful agent, Hilary McMahon, of Westwood Creative Artists. She is unfailingly enthusiastic and supportive, and her words of encouragement keep me moving forward. Thank you to my first reader, Aniko Biber, for her genuine insight and never-ending kindness. On this novel, I was blessed to have two extraordinary editors: Adrienne Kerr and Douglas Richmond. Their astute observations transformed this book. Thank you to everyone at House of Anansi; I am grateful to be in such fantastic hands. And finally, much love and thanks to my children, Sophia, Isabella, and Robert, three beautiful lights that guide and inspire me every single day.

NICOLE LUNDRIGAN is the author of five critically acclaimed novels, including *Glass Boys* and *The Widow Tree*. Her work has appeared on best of the year selections of the *Globe and Mail* and *NOW Magazine* and she has been longlisted for the ReLit Award. Born in Ontario and raised in Newfoundland, she now lives in Toronto.